THE CROWN OF THE DARK PRINCE

A House of Hyrax Novel

Arcadia Rayne

THE CROWN OF THE DARK PRINCE

A House of Hyrax Novel

Arcadia Rayne

PRONUNCIATION GUIDE

Characters

- Theadora – (THAY-uh-dor-ah)

- Clayton – (CLAY-tun)

- Iris – (EYE-ris)

- Rankor – (RANGK-or)

- Camilla – (kuh-Meel-ah)

- Kent – (kent)

- Nessira – (nes-EEr-uh

- Samsa – (SAM-suh)

- Caldrius – (KAL-dree-us)

- Veric – (VAIR-ick)

Gods

- Ciclopia, Goddess of Beasts – (Sih-kloh-pee-uh)

- Hyrax, God of the Dead – (HIGH-racks)

- Zion, King of the Gods – (ZYE-uhn)

- Herea, Goddess of Women – (HER-ay-uh)

- Palaemon, God of the Water & Oceans – (puh-LAY-mon)

- Delia, Goddess of Pregnancy & Childbirth – (DEE-lee-uh)

- Hypatia, Goddess of the Earth – (hi-PAY-shuh)

- Harmonia, Goddess of Peace – (har-MOH-nee-uh)

- Arto, God of Violence – (AHR-toh)

- Athene, Goddess of Wisdom – (uh-TEE-nee)

- Pasnia, Goddess of Madness – (PAHZ-nee-uh)

- Asclepian, God of Medicine – (as-KLEE-pee-an)

- Angerelia, Goddess of Love – (an-jer-EE-leee-uh)

Places

- Athenia – (ah-THEE-nee-uh)

- Republic of Inanis – (in-AN-is)

- Promissa – (PRUH-miss-uh)

- Tenebris (TEN-eh-bris)

- Gelumont – (GEL-uh-mont)

DESCENDANT LINES
OF THE HIGH GODS

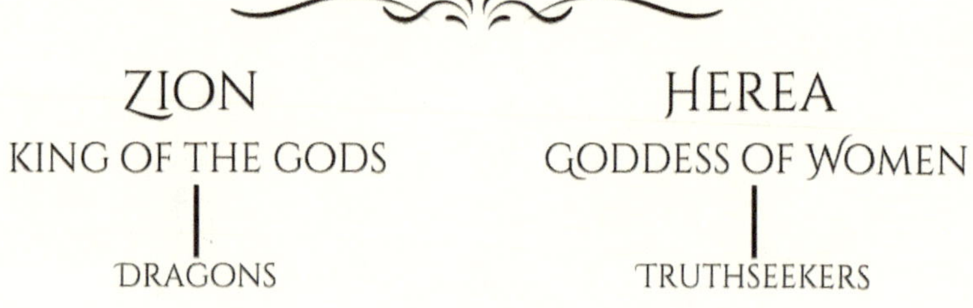

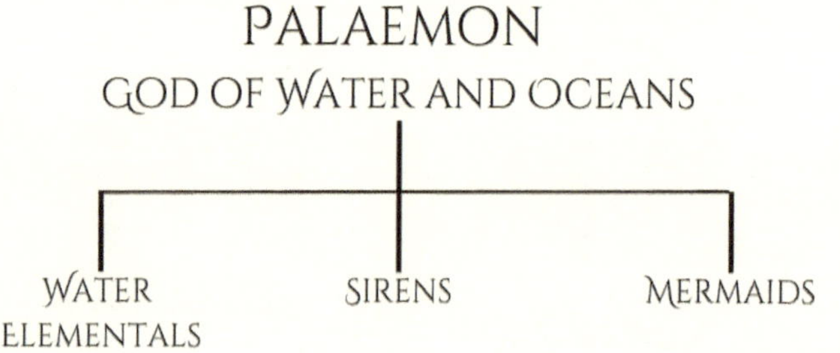

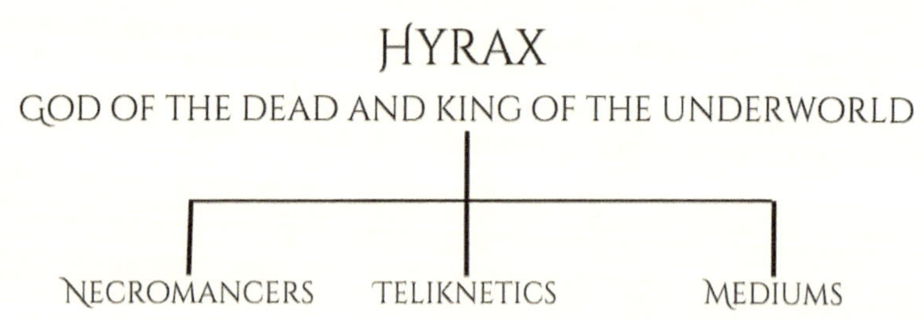

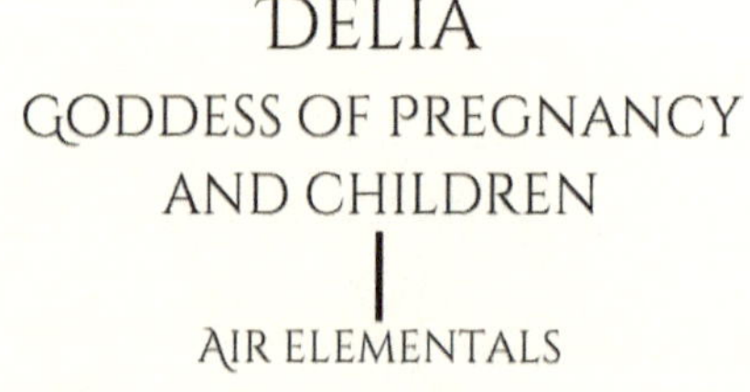

ADDITIONAL DESCENDANT LINES

GELUMONT
Sea of Palaemon
Copun
CLANIS PROVINCE
Great Lake of Atheria
EAGIRTON PROVINCE
Eiylen
MELLYUN PROVINCE
JEZUMI PROVINCE
ATHENIA
ALEPOLIS
Charlington
TIKON PROVINCE
BEYOU PROVINCE
Anstopia
Tenifro
Lake Treyon
CITY OF THE SUN
TENEBRIS
Sea of Delia

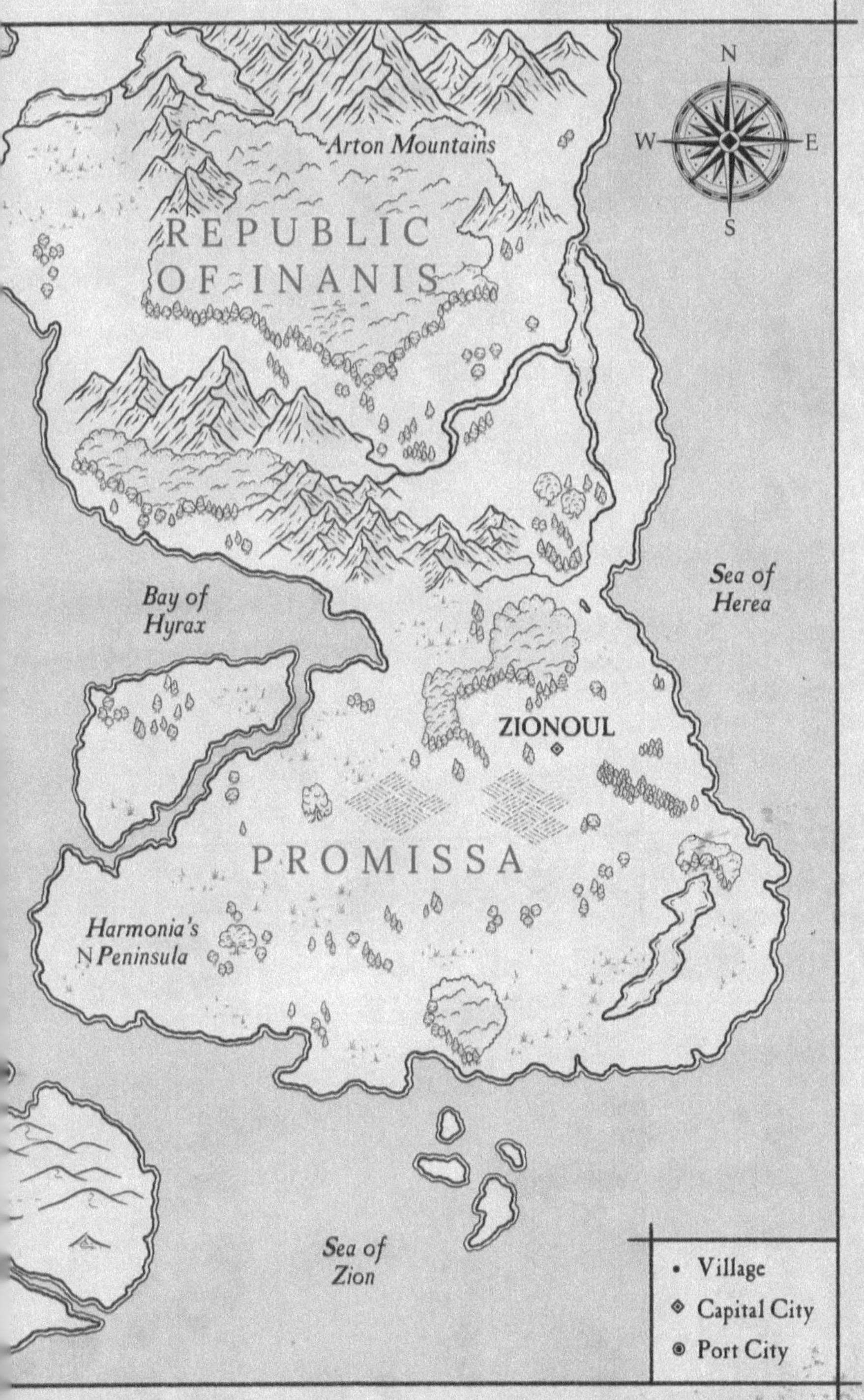

N
W E
S
Arton Mountains
REPUBLIC OF INANIS
Sea of Herea
Bay of Hyrax
ZIONOUL
PROMISSA
Harmonia's Peninsula
Sea of Zion
Village
Capital City
Port City

PREVIOUSLY IN THE HOUSE OF HYRAX SERIES

Hello there!

Welcome back to the *House of Hyrax* series! I'm so happy you've decided to return to Athenia.

The Crown of the Dark Prince is the second book in the *House of Hyrax* series. By now, you've probably read *The Rose in the Shadows* and the prequel novella, *To the Edge of Athenia*. If you need a refresher, I've put together a quick recap of what's happened so far.

Fair warning—this section contains spoilers for *The Rose in the Shadows* and *To the Edge of Athenia*.

If, however, you're all set and ready to dive right in, no worries—just flip ahead and get started. Either way, we'll chat again in the author's note at the end of the book!

THE ROSE IN THE SHADOWS

BOOK ONE IN THE HOUSE OF HYRAX SERIES

Theadora Moore wakes in the infirmary of the Athenian castle with no memories, only a Bident tattoo—the Mark of House Hyrax, an extinct High House essential to the Athenian Royal Council. Crown Prince Clayton Vail, a dragon-shifter descended from Zion, King of the Gods, quickly interrogates her, suspicious of her motives. His cousin, Iris, suddenly recognizes the significance of her Mark, and Thea is instantly thrust into the treacherous world of Athenian court politics.

As Thea is forced to begin training for the trials that she will now need to pass in order to ascend to the Council, she struggles to summon her powers. Her frustration grows, especially as recurring dreams pull her into haunting visions of a stranger warning her not to trust her new friendships with Clay, Iris, Lorelai, Rankor, Kent and Camilla. When a witches hex bag is found in her room, and nearly kills her, its clear that someone wants to extinguish the Hyraxian bloodline. Clay becomes her reluctant ally, saving her and vowing to find her attacker. After learning that her marriage will be arranged to ensure the possibility of heirs, Thea panics, shaking the trees around the castle and it is Clay who calms her and finally teaches her to control her powers.

Desperate to understand how she arrived at the castle, Thea sneaks into the city with Iris only to leave with more questions than answers. She continues training for her trials until a second attack - a massive explosion - destroys an entire wing of the castle. Clay walks through the fire to carry her out and the tension between them grows too strong to resist. When they finally give in to that attraction, Thea forces herself to pull away, reminding them both that whatever exists between them is dangerous—and impossible.

Thea is left devastated, but is forced to attend Clay's birthnight celebration. Just when she can't take it anymore and attempts to leave the party an ambush erupts. She watches as her friend Lorelai is killed, triggering a surge of power from deep within her, unleashing abilities no Descendant has displayed before. As the truth unravels, it becomes clear that Camilla, the trusted witch in their circle, is behind it all.

Just as the warnings from the stranger in her dreams grow more urgent, Camilla strikes again, drugging and power-stripping Thea. All seems lost—until, against all odds, Thea's magic resurfaces. She fights back, turning Camilla's own dark power against her and proving that she is stronger than anyone imagined.

In the aftermath, Thea stays by Clay's side as he recovers from battle wounds, unable to deny her feelings any longer. But before she can act on them, the Dragon delivers his cruelest threat yet: if she does not stay away from Clay, he will exile her forever. As Thea processes her fate, she visits Camilla in her cell, where a final, chilling revelation unfolds. Camilla's betrayal wasn't just personal - it was driven by an ancient prophecy foretelling that the daughter of Hyrax would shake the Veil and unleash the God of the Dead into the Mortal Realm.

Shocked, Thea rushes to Hyrax Manor, tearing apart the library until she can find a depiction of Hyrax and finally recognizes him as the stranger from her dreams.

The realizations don't end though, and Camilla is the one to learn that her grandmother is not who she seems. Pasnia, the Goddess of Madness, has been orchestrating everything from the shadows, manipulating events to obtain Thea's blood.

TO THE EDGE OF ATHENIA

PREQUEL NOVELLA IN THE HOUSE OF HYRAX SERIES

Rankor, Kent, Lorelai, Iris, and Camilla are more like family than just friends, but in the months before Thea's arrival at the castle, they each find themselves facing their own individual struggles.

After his mother's death, Rankor interrupts his tour of the country to escort his younger brother, Elaijah, to a new caretaker. The two, having grown up apart, struggle to find common ground. Rankor, already bonded with his fellow soldiers, sees no need for another connection. But when a beast from Ciclopia attacks, the brothers are forced to fight side by side. In the aftermath, they realize the importance of their bond, finding camaraderie before parting ways.

Lorelai is returning to the castle when her carriage is attacked by bandits. She escapes into the woods and meets Helena, a wild and unruly woman who offers to help her get home. Helena takes Lorelai to Charlington, a crime-ridden port city where rules mean little. Though initially out of place, Lorelai lets her guard down for one night, drinking at a tavern and, for the first time, truly enjoying life.

Kent returns home for the wedding of his childhood love, Seralyn. Though he swears to his family that he has moved on, he can't help but use his power to sense Seralyn's emotions. When he realizes she still loves him, he rushes to stop the wedding—only to discover that Seralyn is pregnant, and her fiancé, Jaxon, is the only way to secure her future. Heartbroken and mistrustful of his abilities, Kent leaves, questioning everything.

Iris has just become an official member of The Order, an elite group of spies and assassins. Her first mission is to kill the infamous criminal known as the Serpent. Disguising herself as the Serpent's daughter, Joliette, she infiltrates Eagirton but falls into the hands of Nikolai Legum, a rival criminal. Trapped in his home, she struggles to gather useful information while fighting her growing attraction to him. When Joliette is attacked, Nikolai saves her, and Iris knows her feelings have become too dangerous. During a brutal confrontation, Iris realizes the true mastermind behind the Serpent's empire isn't him—it's Joliette herself. When the Duke of Eagirton betrays his kingdom, revealing that Clayton Vail is planning a coup, Iris kills both the Serpent and the Duke to protect her cousin. Nikolai discovers her true identity, and while they vow to keep each other's secrets for now, they know their next meeting will be far from peaceful.

Camilla's grandmother is determined to see her married to Clay. But when the Crown Prince ends their relationship, Camilla is sent home, where she is treated little better than a servant. She begins hearing voices and seeing things that aren't real, her grip on reality slipping as the days pass. The hallucinations grow worse, leaving her unable to tell what is real and what is an illusion. Then she stumbles upon a box of ancient prophecies and is drawn to one in particular: *The daughter of Hyrax will shake the Veil.* When her grandmother finds her reading it, they make a vow—to ensure that the prophecy never comes true.

CONTENT WARNING

Please note this is an Adult/New Adult fantasy novel written for a mature reader.

This story includes scenes of sexual content, violence, experiences of depression and grief, suggestions of self-harm and suicide, suggestions of abuse (off-page) and portrayals of insanity. Please read at your own discretion.

Your mental health matters.

To the women who sat on the floor thinking they weren't pretty enough,
loving enough, worthy enough.
Let me be very clear, you were and will always be enough.
Sometimes beautiful things come out of darkness.

CHAPTER ONE

The Dragon must have finally decided he wanted to kill me.

That was the only explanation for why my combat trial involved a gladiator-style ring, where I had to fight members of the Athenian royal guard in front of a packed stadium. Surely, he intended for me to die on this battlefield.

A blade slashed toward me—I barely dodged in time, my breath sharp as I twisted away. My heart pounded, but my mind stayed detached, calculating. It had been two months since the last time I fought for my life—since the night I stood across from a friend-turned-traitor and watched her summon an army of shadows against me.

But there was no time to dwell on the past. Not when the present demanded so much.

It had been a surprise when I even took down the first guard, a blade pressed to his carotid artery, but my victory had been short-lived. Before the crowd even stopped cheering, a door had opened on the other side of the arena, and another guard strode forward.

He ran at a furious pace, intent on tackling me. I moved to my left and watched as he spun on his heels to face me. By the gods, he was fast, wasting no time recovering and launching a quick jab toward me. In my haze to deflect it, I didn't even notice his arm reaching for my wrist until it was too late. He pressed down on the tendons there, and I unwillingly released the blade, grunting as it fell to the sand at our feet.

I heard Rankor's voice in my head as I watched it fall. *He's bigger than you. You have to be faster.*

My friend and trainer had given me that advice so many times in our preparations for this trial that I swore I heard him reciting it while I brushed my teeth in the morning.

As the guard released my wrist, I went for speed… and surprise.

I ducked to the ground, crawling between his widespread legs.

The crowd gasped at the childish maneuver, and even the guard himself seemed surprised. That moment of hesitation was all I needed, though. I threw my leg back into his rear end, sending him stumbling forward. Rolling, I launched myself back to my feet and set my sights on him once more.

This would be so much easier with my magic.

As a Descendant of Hyrax, I had the unique ability of telepathy. To our knowledge, I was the only person to have that ability… ever. I desperately wanted to use my telepathy to blast the guard across the arena, but the rules strictly prohibited using magic during the hand-to-hand combat trial. They had even dosed me with Mortal blood to prevent me from accessing my powers. Little did anyone know that the Mortal blood had no effect on me or my powers, and it was only my sheer will that stopped me from tapping into them.

It was just another thing that made me different.

Like the fact that I was a Descendant who had lived through a power-stripping and still had my magic.

Or that I was a Descendant who didn't bear the Mark of her ancestor like a permanent tattoo across the skin.

These days, it seemed like there was more and more that set me apart from those around me.

A crushing punch to my stomach broke me free of my thoughts and had me gasping for air. I stumbled away from the guard, desperate to catch my breath. I could almost feel Rankor's eyes on me from the audience, criticizing me for not staying focused.

As the guard unsheathed the sword across his back, I reached for the dagger I'd strapped to my thigh. They'd given me the option between a sword or knives, and while I didn't hate using swords, the weight of knives was easier to manage, and I could maneuver them more quickly. And as Rankor liked to remind me, most people were bigger than me, so I needed to be faster.

The guard stalked toward me, and I again opted for surprise. Might as well give the citizens in the stands a show. Turning on my heels, I sprinted. To the audience, it might look like I was fleeing from him as I launched myself at full speed toward the opposite end of the arena. I heard him following, his heavy steps picking up speed behind me. I just needed to make it a little farther.

I threw myself toward the wall, kicking off it and spinning, throwing the blade as I hovered momentarily in the air. It was a bit of a shot in the dark, not allowing me time to aim, but Rankor had made me practice this move a million times. We'd done it over and over until he was confident that I could use the sound of footsteps behind me as a judge of distance. And the practice paid off. The blade bounced off the center of his forehead.

I was glad they gave us toy weapons for this. I would have chosen not to carry anything into battle if they had insisted I use real steel.

I landed in a heavy crouch that sent pain radiating up my arms and legs, but I had successfully bested him. The roar of the crowd was deafening as the guard bowed and exited the arena... only for yet another one to take his place.

How many are they going to make me fight? I wondered as I pulled the next blade out of the sheath on my wrist and launched myself toward my new target.

I fought as hard as I could, ignoring both the protest in my fatiguing muscles and the noise from the crowd that threatened to distract me. Truthfully, the crowd had been another surprising aspect of this trial. The Royal Council hadn't given me much information regarding what to expect, but my first trial had been so private that I had expected this one to be the same.

I beat the third guard with a blade pressed against his kidney and the fourth by unarming him and using his own sword against him. Exhaustion and rage filled me by the time the fifth guard entered the arena.

The Dragon, our king, had once told me these trials would be more of a formality than anything else in my case—since I was the only person who could serve as the Hyraxian Council member. The Dragon didn't much like me, but he wanted a complete Council more than anything—a governing body filled with representatives from the Houses descended from the High Gods.

Even so, this felt like more than a formality. This felt like the Dragon wanted to see me bleed.

By the end of my fight with the fifth guard, I was in fact bleeding from a broken nose, but I had won with a blade pressed directly above his heart.

There was a pause.

No more doors opened.

Turning on my heels, I looked up to the crowd, and the perched box where the Dragon and the other members of the Council sat watching the show. Carefully, I avoided the gaze of Clayton Vail, our Crown Prince.

The Dragon met my gaze without flinching. With careful slowness, he raised a bushy eyebrow at me and smiled. And that's when I knew this wasn't over.

Both doors on either side of the arena opened. From the left came a guard I hadn't met before. From the right came Dimitri, the head of my personal guard team.

Oh, come on now.

I glared at the Dragon while I pulled a second blade from my left thigh.

"I am sorry for this, my lady," Dimitri said as he approached.

Groaning, I wiped away the blood from my broken nose with my forearm and took my fighting stance.

"Let's just get this over with."

The last fight was a blur of flying arms and weapons. My muscles screamed in protest and my head swam as the exhaustion threatened to take me under. Still, I carried on. Dimitri grabbed my wrist and twisted, pulling the muscles there so tightly that I couldn't help but scream out. He flinched as I did, but still I carried on. I couldn't care about pulled muscles or broken bones right now. The palace healers would take care of all of that once this was over. I just needed to finish it.

I defeated the sixth guard with a blade across the throat and took down Dimitri with a blade to the back. Dirty fighting for sure, but successful.

Music filled my ears as the band began playing the Athenian anthem and the crowd erupted around me, chanting my name. Slowly, the Dragon raised his hands and clapped. I had done it. I had passed the combat trial. I was officially two-thirds of the way to taking my place on the Council.

"You fucking did it!" Rankor cried, sweeping me into a bear hug that lifted me from the ground and knocked the breath from my lungs.

"Did you doubt me?"

I struggled to laugh while he squeezed. Rankor was a brawn from House Arto, making his strength magically fueled. He suddenly seemed to remember this, and that he could literally kill me from hugging me too tightly, and sat me on my feet in a rush.

"No!" he replied in a rush, before sighing when I raised my brows at him in disbelief. "I believe in you, of course. I've always known that when you're at your best, you can handle anything that's thrown at you."

"But?"

"But you haven't been at your best."

His hand cupped my face affectionately, his thumb stroking the skin under my eyes that was hollow and dark from lack of sleep. "You've been so exhausted. I've been worried."

Yes, well, I *had* felt exhausted lately. Exhaustion was the unhappy consequence of refusing to sleep. For weeks, I'd barely been sleeping. Ever since I'd discovered that I'd somehow been communicating with my ancestor, Hyrax, in my dreams, I'd been terrified to return to that place - the Underworld. Hyrax had lied to me. He hadn't pretended to be someone else, but he also hadn't openly admitted who he was. For months, he had taught me how to use my magic and counseled me on how to navigate politics and relationships in the Mortal Realm, all while hiding his true identity. And a lie by omission was still a lie.

And if the God of the Dead was lying to me, then I had to question why.

What did he want from me?

"You care to tell me what's been going on with you?" Rankor pressed, pulling my focus once more.

I sighed dramatically. "Oh, I don't know, Rankor. It could have something to do with the fact that someone in my inner circle tried to kill me for months and only ended up killing one of my best friends instead."

We rarely spoke about Camilla, or how she had fooled us all into thinking she was our friend, while she secretly got addicted to forbidden magic in her attempt to kill me. In her addiction-fueled rage, she had planned an attack during a palace party. The attack had been the first time I'd had to battle during a real-life threat, and I hadn't been good enough. I wasn't fast enough to stop an assassin from killing Lorelai, the fiery-haired Truthseeker who had been one of the first to befriend me. Camilla's betrayal had shocked everyone in the kingdom. No one else had deciphered why she had lost herself in blood magic.

But I knew.

In the immediate days after her capture, I had visited her in the palace dungeons and she had told me of a prophecy she had once found. A prophecy seemingly written about me: *The daughter of Hyrax will shake the veil, and the King of Damnation will rise once more to rule over the children of the Gods. She will create a new death in the Mortal Realm and will stand at his side as his armies usher in the new age. Prepare for the Final War of the Gods.*

That prophecy was yet *another* secret I was keeping because the last thing I needed was people in this palace thinking I would destroy the world. Not that it mattered anyway. Regardless of what some stupid prophecy from hundreds of years ago said, I would not shake the Veil between worlds. I *couldn't* shake the Veil, not even the Gods themselves could move it. So, giving voice to the delusional concerns of a dark Witch was entirely unnecessary.

"Go bathe," Rankor commanded, flopping onto the settee in the parlor of my apartment suites and reaching for my bar cart. "The party in your honour begins in about an hour, which doesn't give us much time to get fashionably drunk beforehand."

I rolled my eyes, but did as I was told, eager to wash the sweat and blood off me. After the trial, nurses immediately pulled me into the infirmary to set my broken nose and heal all other injuries until all that remained were bruises and small red welts. From there, I'd found Emeryn, my new chief-of-staff, waiting in the hall. As my ascension to the Council became more imminent, the Council decided I would need someone on my staff to help manage my schedule, engagements, and public image. The role seemed ridiculous to me, but Emeryn had been my constant shadow since we were first introduced. She was a stern woman, always dressed in simple black gowns with her hair pulled back into a tight knot. And she took her job very seriously. When my hour break was up, she would knock on the door to take me to my celebration dinner.

Nessira, my lady-in-waiting, had prepared a steaming bath with lavender oils and left several bottles of soap and fresh towels for me, one of the many reasons she was one of my favorite people.

"We should discuss the young women who have applied for the opening within your staff, my lady," she said, as she began twisting my long blonde hair into an elaborate knot at the back of my neck.

I didn't miss the way Rankor flinched at the mention that I needed a new lady-in-waiting. The second spot had recently become vacant after my initial lady, a cheery young girl named Geia, betrayed me and helped Camilla kidnap me away from the palace. I took the glass of wine he offered me and downed it in a single sitting.

"Perhaps I do not need a replacement," I said. "You manage just fine."

Nessira raised a brow at me disapprovingly. "Surely I do not deserve more work because you are hesitant to admit that the girl was never the friend you wanted her to be."

I bit down on my lip.

"Bit harsh, Nessira," Rankor chastised.

Nessira shrugged. "My lady used to like when we spoke honestly to her."

She was right. I had always encouraged her to speak to me as an equal. I had embraced the advice and companionship of my ladies-in-waiting. Look where that had gotten me.

Still, Nessira didn't deserve more work because I was too afraid to move on with my life. So I nodded my agreement and promised to glance over the recommendations that she had left for me in the morning. She dressed me in a floor-length gown the color of blood. Its boned bodice hugged my torso, emphasizing the curve of my breasts and the swell of my hips before falling effortlessly to my feet. Two long capes of tulle hung over my back, secured by the sparkling golden applique that hung over my chest and shoulders. She painted my lips dark and lined my eyes in kohl.

"You look magnificent," Rankor complimented.

"I look like the daughter of Hyrax," I mumbled, staring at myself in the mirror as Nessira tucked a matching golden crown into my hair.

Rankor chuckled. "You are a daughter of Hyrax."

Didn't mean I had to be happy about it.

"There is one last thing, my lady." Nessira sighed and approached me with the black ink.

I desperately wanted to protest as she set about painting on the Mark of Hyrax on my chest, but I ground my teeth until I was sure they would crack and allowed it. The Dragon had decided it would be better for the public to not know about my missing Mark. He believed it raised too many questions that could make my standing in society too precarious. In other words, he needed me to be unquestionably a Descendant of Hyrax and that came with a descendants Mark.

But I liked the appearance of my bare skin without that Bident on my chest. I liked not having a reminder of Hyrax, his lies, or the prophecy so blatantly in my face.

"Come on," Rankor drawled, linking my arm through his. "Your adoring fans are waiting."

I excused Nessira and ushered Rankor to the door, asking for a minute to relieve myself in the restroom. Rankor only smiled and nodded, heading to the parlor and allowing me the briefest moment of privacy. For a second, I stood frozen, victim to the dread that had taken root in my gut.

"You coming?" Rankor called from the door.

"Be right there!" I cried, rushing to my closet in a frantic haze.

With a quick glance over my shoulder, I went to the trunk hidden in the back corner under my cloaks. I opened it gingerly, careful not to let it make a sound as I lifted the lid and began filtering through the weapons. I looked until I found the small dagger and thigh sheath I'd grown accustomed to sneaking onto my person. As I clicked it into place, I reveled in the warmth of comfort that filled me when I tucked it under my dress. When Camilla sliced me open and drained my magic, I had been totally defenseless.

Powerless.

When I fought my way through that battle, I vowed to myself that I would never allow myself to feel that way again.

"Ready!" I announced, joining Rankor in the parlor. Emeryn was waiting outside for us, hand poised to knock on the door just as we stepped out. She looked over at me appraisingly and nodded, as if to say this look would work. She dipped her head respectfully and motioned for us to follow her.

"We expect full attendance for this evening's festivities, my lady." She wasted no time in getting to business. "The Dragon will announce you and give the celebratory toast to begin the evening. Dinner will take place at seven sharp and you will sit at the head table with members of the Council and their families. Dignitaries vising from Tennebris and the Republic of Innais are also in attendance this evening and will be eager for an audience with you."

"Are you sure we have to go to this?" I whispered to Rankor under my breath while she continued detailing the night's itinerary.

"Yes," Emeryn barked, not even bothering to glance back at us. "Now that we've caught Camilla, it's time for you to focus on your ascension to the Council and your overall role in society. This is your duty, my lady. You cannot delay it any longer."

The truth of those words settled into every fiber of my being.

CHAPTER TWO

I had seen the palace ballroom decorated for parties and celebrations before, but the sheer magnificence of its splendor never ceased to amaze me. And tonight was certainly no different, especially when I stepped over the threshold into the room and suddenly realized the theme of tonight's decor.

Me.

"Well." Rankor whistled. "This is really something."

The limited candlelight bounced off the crystal chandeliers, sending tiny rainbows dancing across the room. Sparkling black and golden tapestries hung from the ceilings and the walls. Scarlet place mats and golden dishes sat atop black dinintroug tables. The Council all already sat at the table in the room's front, under a scarlet banner portraying the Bident of Hyrax.

I shivered, feeling a growing itch everywhere my dress pressed upon my skin. The similarity between my gown and the decor was no coincidence. The Dragon wanted me to look every single bit like Hyrax's chosen successor. And I didn't quite know how I felt about that.

No, that wasn't true. I knew how I felt about it.

"It's a bit much for my taste."

Rankor snorted. "That's because if it were up to you, we'd be drinking in a tavern while you hand me my ass in cards and then demand to arm wrestle every man in the joint."

I jammed my elbow into his ribs, but laughed.

"Ah, ladies and gentleman," a booming male voice silenced the chatter of the room around us. "It seems our guest of honor has arrived."

The Dragon beckoned for me to join him at the front of the ballroom and, with an encouraging squeeze from Rankor, I did so, curtsying low as I approached the king. He wore his finest attire, a golden jacket with diamond clasps in the shape of miniature dragons. His thick hair was well-combed but grayer than when I had first met him a year ago. As I met his dark eyes, he passed me a crystal glass of red wine.

"My darling," he purred, a slimy smile spread wide across his face. "You do look lovely in red."

I shivered involuntarily, and the Dragon chuckled. By the Gods, I swore making me uncomfortable was the man's favorite pastime. He snaked an arm around my waist and pulled me to him, unbothered that his young wife sat only a few feet away from him, as he raised his glass of whiskey and began his toast.

"We have gathered here tonight to celebrate Lady Theodora Moore's successful completion of the combat trial," he announced, his voice smooth and commanding. "Already, we have seen that Lady Moore is a fine young scholar on her written trial, but today she has shown that she can be a fierce warrior as well."

A polite murmur of approval rippled through the crowd, though some guests exchanged knowing glances over their goblets. I clenched my fingers around the stem of my wineglass, holding my expression neutral.

"This is, of course, no surprise to many of us," the Dragon continued, his gaze sweeping the hall as if daring anyone to contradict him. "Lady Moore has already proven her courage, intelligence, and dedication to the Athenian people in battle on more than one occasion in the past year. These are times I do not look back on fondly, as no ruler can be proud of times when his own people turn on each other, but I am grateful that, by the grace of the Gods, justice has prevailed and our Lady Moore is more prepared than ever to step into her birth-given role in our government."

I kept my posture still and poised, even as I fought the magic that roared wildly inside me.

The Dragon lifted his glass higher. "So please, raise your glasses in a toast of congratulations to Lady Moore and join me in wishing her luck in the trials that will come next: the final Council trial and her greatest trial yet—creating an advantageous marriage."

The hall erupted with cheers and gossip. My name swirled through the air in hushed whispers, speculation weaving between the clinking of glasses. It was nothing new. The court had been whispering about me since the day I had arrived in Athenia a year ago, battered and confused, with no memory of the life I'd led before. But lately, their talk had shifted—from questioning my motives to predicting the details of my future wedding.

As if my life was nothing more than entertainment to them.

I took a careful sip of my wine, ignoring the flutter of uneasy butter-flies in my stomach. All Council members had arranged marriages. Our partners were chosen based on their ability to uphold the purity of noble bloodlines. My marriage would be no exception. While the thought left me cold, the rest of the kingdom reveled in the promise of a royal wedding, their excitement palpable.

Slowly, I stepped away from the Dragon, putting distance between us as I let the wine coat my tongue. My retreat did not go unnoticed. His smirk curled at the edges, almost playful, but I caught the flicker of gold in his dark eyes.

"Sit," he commanded, his voice like silk over steel. His hand flicked toward the empty chair beside him. His eyes lingered on my crown before dipping over my breasts. I cleared my throat aggressively, which earned me another mischievous grin. I fought the urge to vomit.

"You did well today," he complimented, as the palace staff began bringing out the evening's meal.

I couldn't help but glance quickly around the table. The Dragon's queen sat to his right, dressed in a shimmering golden gown with long sleeves. The dragon shaped bangles on both of her hands that marked her as his wife shimmered under the candlelight. Next to her, Gregory Handel, the Council member from House Herea, sat with his wife. Though he was far more engaged in the conversation that he maintained with his lover, Davide Moroe of House Angerelia. Athenia had no prejudice against their love, but the Council forbade their marriage because of the men's inability to produce heirs. Still, they'd been happily and publicly engaged in their affair for decades. Next to Davide sat Rosalia Blackmore of House Delia and her husband, who chatted happily with the widowed Clara Reid of House Palaemon. There was one notably empty chair at the table.

Clay wasn't here.

"It was quite the show," the Dragon continued, cutting into his veal.

"Perhaps more of a show than necessary," I remarked pointedly.

He grinned. "Perhaps. But that was, of course, up to my discretion."

There was never any doubt of that. I should have known the Dragon wouldn't want anything about this process to be easy for me. Still, his words sat on my stomach uneasily. After all, this process wasn't done. There was still one more trial to pass, and I shivered to think about what he still had planned for me.

"I see you've been following my guidance."

I flinched, remembering his *guidance*. Clay suffered an injury after Camilla's ultimate attack. While he was in the infirmary, I'd spent every moment I could with him. I'd needed to know he was okay. The nights I'd slept in Clay's room hadn't escaped the Dragons' notice, though. None of my relationship with Clay had escaped the Dragon's notice, and he had cornered me, threatening to force me out of the kingdom if I didn't cut things off.

"As I have already assured you, your majesty, my intention is to fulfill my responsibilities to this kingdom. I'm well-aware that responsibility comes with stipulations about who I can and cannot be with."

"Yes, well, that is a matter we will need to discuss soon. I've narrowed your list of prospects down to a few I'd like you to look over."

I finished my glass of wine quickly. "Does it matter? I will marry who is best for my House and my realm. I believe it was you who said love was a useless notion for people like us."

The Dragon's arm snaked behind the back of my seat and his fingers grazed against the skin on the back of my neck. I scooted my chair away from him quickly, earning another laugh.

"Oh my dear, you're much more enjoyable when you're *agreeable.* I'm so looking forward to all the time we'll have to spend together when you've ascended to the Council."

I ate in silence, ignoring the Dragons innuendo's as best I could and answering politely when anyone deemed to talk to me directly. As the guests began finishing their dinner and the music started, I knew it was only a matter of time before Emeryn dragged me to my feet and started pointing out the people I needed to socialize with, but I stayed for as long as I could. I stayed, and I watched the doors of the ballroom waiting for the prince to arrive.

He didn't.

Where in all of creation was he?

It seemed unlike him to miss an important castle event like this.

It seemed unlike him to miss a party meant for me.

Eventually, Emeryn called for me. Under her watchful eye, I danced with the visiting dignitaries. I held babies and played games with children. I smiled at the women and flirted with the men. I did everything an eligible young princess should do. And when the evening finally started winding down, I spotted Rankor chatting with our friend Kent and, as discreetly as possible, made my way over to them.

"You finally escaped." Kent wrapped me in a hug and quickly congratulated me on my successful trial.

"You really have to get better at hiding your emotions," Rankor remarked with a grin. "You've been so obviously miserable all night."

He said it like a joke, but he didn't know how serious his comment was. Playing this role was my job, and if I wasn't convincing enough, the Dragon had been clear that others would suffer for my failure. Sneaking a glance at his throne and noticing his eyes on mine, I let loose a dazzling smile, intent on improving my performance.

"I don't know what you mean," I said sweetly.

Kent rolled his eyes. "Liar."

"So what's the plan for the after party?" Rankor asked. "Because there's a stunning little fire elemental across the room that I'm dying to continue this evening with."

I followed his gaze across the room to a young woman with short brown hair in a black gown with a slit that left very little to the imagination. She grinned at him from across the hall and wet her lips. The weight of jealousy landed heavily in my stomach. Not that I didn't feel happy for my friend, but it had been a while since someone had looked at me like that. With *desire.*

The last person to do that had been Clay, when I'd had my legs locked around him and his lips pressed to the curve of my throat in the archives at Hyrax Estate. But then I'd pushed him away, and he'd hated me for it.

And after that I'd called to him in a battle. I'd slept by his side in the infirmary. I'd told him that when I thought I was dying, all I could think about was kissing him again.

Then I started avoiding him for weeks on end.

No one gave mixed signals quite as well as I did.

"I'd say our princess here probably needs to go to bed and skip the after party," Kent noted, and I turned my face away from them to hide the dark circles under my eyes from their view. It didn't matter how much product Nessira caked on my face, they simply refused to go away.

"Thea."

I froze.

I would recognize that small bell-like voice anywhere. Even now, after it had been *weeks* since I'd heard her.

Without hesitation, I spun on my heels to meet the gaze of my best friend. Iris had lost weight, looking more like skin and bones than she ever had before. She'd been the first person to befriend me here and had quickly become more like a sister than a friend. Iris was famous for wearing her hair in bright, elaborate colors and for donning the most extravagant fashions, but today her dark hair was in curls around her tawny skin. She wore a simple black gown, still mourning the loss of our friend Lorelai.

Lorelai and Iris had been particularly close. In fact, with more time, they might have even become lovers.

They'd never gotten that chance, though.

She blamed me for Lorelai's death, and I didn't hold that against her. If I'd been faster, if I'd done more, maybe Lorelai would still be here, standing right next to us with those bright eyes and sweet smile.

"You're here," I blurted, shocked at seeing her.

It had been weeks since Iris and I had even been in the same room. Rankor and Kent had assured me she just needed some time, but it had hurt to know she had gone to them while avoiding me. I understood her pain, of course, but I wanted to be there for her, regardless. I wanted to be the one to help her.

I missed her friendship desperately.

"Yeah," she mumbled. "I'm sorry I'm late. I wasn't much in the mood for a party."

"That's okay."

"I just wanted to say congratulations. I know you've been working hard."

Her hands twitched uncomfortably at her side, as if she didn't quite know what to do with them, and I folded mine in front of me. When did it get like this? Things had never been so *awkward* between us before.

So much had changed.

"Thank you," I whispered quietly. "It means a lot to me you're here."

Her eyes clouded as she dipped her head. For a moment, we both stood there like that - frozen in silence, both unsure how to proceed with the other. Rankor reached up and squeezed my shoulder supportively.

"How are you?" I asked.

She smiled grimly. "I'm doing my best."

Her words cut through me viscerally, leaving me speechless once more. Four words with such weight. My beautiful, spritely friend, who danced at *every* party, who always was ready to joke and tease, who had once been the very embodiment of life, now had to work so hard just to get through her days. What could I say to her? I'd spent weeks wanting to be with her, wanting to comfort her, and now, when she had finally given me the opportunity, I was hopelessly unaware of how to best proceed.

And *that* was the moment that the Crown Prince entered the room.

The room seemed to dim, the silence heavy and thick, as if mirroring the aching void within me that his presence only emphasized. His blonde hair was longer than he normally wore it, curling slightly around his ears and hanging close to his grey eyes. Now that the weather was cooling, and the days were shorter, it had darkened ever so slightly. His jacket was dark grey, nearly black, with golden embroidery on the lapels. I watched as he searched the room for us, eyes landing first on Rankor, then me, then Iris.

His sharp jaw tensed as he assessed the situation and I could just make out the flash of worry on his face before his expression smoothed and he gave a bright smile.

Not everyone could identify the difference between Clay the man and Clay the prince, but I'd always been able to see when he donned that mask.

"You look awful," he said to Iris, ruffling her hair as he came to stand by her side.

"Gee thanks." She gave her cousin a soft smile as he pulled her for a quick hug.

"You're late," Rankor told Clay, with an edge to his voice that I hadn't heard him use before with Clay.

Clay, Rankor, Kent, and Iris had grown up together. Despite their longstanding friendship, though, Clay was still their prince and the others never dared to speak against him.

Until tonight, apparently.

"I had some business to attend to," Clay replied, words clipped and short.

Curiosity flared within me, more intrigued by his irritation than by the words themselves. What business was there to attend to when the entire court was here in this room, celebrating? And yet, the question died on my tongue as Kent began passing around drinks to us all, commenting on how happy he was that we were all back together again.

"We're not," I exclaimed, which earned me four sets of wide, confused eyes. "We're not *all* back together again."

Iris met my gaze, and for a moment time stopped, until finally she nodded her agreement. "No, we're not. But us five are all we have left, and Lorelai would want us to be here for each other."

Wordlessly, I reached over, took her hand in mine and squeezed. When she applied gentle pressure back, my heartbeat fluttered.

It had been weeks without a nightmare about Hyrax.

Clay and I were back in the same room together as friends, nothing more or less.

And Iris was here, squeezing my hand.

For the first time in a long time, I felt like things might be okay.

Once Emeryn realized the Prince had finally joined the party, she fluttered to my side again, declaring that several wealthy merchants were eager to meet the young prince and future Council member. Something about us being the 'future of Athenia.'

The way she linked Clay and me together in that phrase made my skin crawl slightly, but I knew better than to challenge her. So, after inviting Iris to join me for breakfast in the morning, I let Emeryn lead us around the room and began mingling and networking as she instructed.

Throughout it all, Clay was the perfect prince—friendly and gracious. He took charge of most conversations, which suited me just fine. As the night wore on, though, I couldn't ignore how sparse our exchanges were with each other. We moved from merchant to diplomat to courts person, and all the while, he barely acknowledged me, not even on the occasions when I did make small comments to contribute to the conversation.

Until, all too suddenly, he decided he wanted to speak to me.

All night, he must have been waiting for a chance to get me alone, and when the merchant we were talking to excused himself and Emeryn was briefly pulled away, he had it.

The next thing I knew, Clay's hand gripped mine, and he began tugging me out of the ballroom. I gasped as he pulled me along, his speed not leaving me any chance to protest.

"Come," he commanded, with a finality that had me tripping over my skirts as he hauled me into a dim, private office and shut the door.

The space was nearly bare—a large oak desk with dragon carvings along the legs, stacks of paper on one side, books, a quill, and a wax seal on the other. A settee beneath the window held a discarded cotton shirt and leather trousers. I didn't need to look around to know it was Clay's office.

The scent of cinnamon and ash was a dead giveaway.

"You shouldn't have done that," I muttered, smoothing my wrinkled skirts before folding my arms across my chest as he quickly rummaged through a drawer.

He didn't answer immediately. Instead, he pulled out a decanter of whiskey and drank deeply. His silence stretched, heavy with tension. I could feel the weight of his stare as he studied me, waiting for me to crack. When I didn't, he exhaled sharply and set the decanter down with a dull *thud*.

"I want to know what's wrong with you."

"Excuse me?"

"Don't play games with me."

"I'm not the one who dragged you away from a party to ask vague questions!"

He raised an eyebrow, giving me that familiar, irritating look that always lit my blood on fire with both fury and something else I'd rather leave unnamed. "Dimitri tells me you've been spending more nights at Hyrax Estate than in your suite at the palace."

Of course I had. I was studying Hyrax and my family's history. I was avoiding sleep by doing anything I could to identify what Hyrax wanted from me. I couldn't very well say any of that to Clay, though. So, I just shrugged. "Didn't know there was a problem with me staying in my own home."

He had been the first one to show me Hyrax Estate, the sprawling gothic mansion south of the palace. As the last descendant of Hyrax, the property was mine, along with the archives inside it, a collection of family heirlooms, and Hyrax's Bident—a weapon made from the bones of some ancient beast.

"And Rankor tells me you haven't been sleeping," he continued.

I was going to have to speak to him and Dimitri both about keeping their observations to themselves. "I don't see how that's anyone's business but my own."

Clay's expression softened, his voice dropping. "I'm serious, Thea."

His eyes held that rare look of concern—the one that wasn't from the prince, but the man behind him. The man who cared about me, perhaps too much.

I knew I should pull away, to harden myself against him, but part of me didn't want to.

"As am I," I replied, my voice sharp.

Clay sighed and stepped forward, close enough that I felt the heat of his anger mixed with something more. I could feel my pulse quicken, half of me wanting to retreat, the other half desperately wanting to close the space between us.

"Do you think I'm not acutely aware of you?" he murmured, his voice low. "What you pulled in the arena today was reckless, lazy even. I've seen you fight in far worse conditions, and you were brilliant then. Natural. But today? Crawling on the ground, running from attackers? You're avoiding the castle, avoiding Iris, avoiding me. You're not sleeping and you're not talking. I want to know why. I want to know what you've been keeping from me."

A shiver passed through me, betraying the effect he had on me. But I couldn't afford to let my walls crumble. If Clay knew the truth, it wouldn't be long before his father knew. And if the Dragon knew, I'd be as good as dead.

I forced a steadying breath, preparing to say what I knew would end this conversation before it went any further. "Your concern is touching, Your Grace."

His frown deepened. "Excuse me?"

"I just hadn't expected you to be so concerned with Council affairs," I replied, coldly polite. "I assure you, I'll take better care of my health. And please, pass along my regards to the other Council members when you have this same talk with them."

His eyes flared a dangerous gold, a shade that rarely showed, but practically blazed in that moment. "Thea."

"Clay. I just assumed this conversation was because of my role on the Council. Otherwise, we have no reason to discuss my well-being alone in a locked room." I dropped my voice with a hint of warning. "You are the Crown Prince, and I am a future Council member. We are nothing more than that to each other. We cannot be anything more than that."

He knew as well as I did that our relationship went beyond what society would allow. We were walking a fine line, and if things went any further, the Dragon would marry me off to some noble with a title—and I'd be dead the second I'd produced an heir.

"And here I thought we were friends," Clay said, drawing out the words, an eyebrow raised in mockery.

"Did you now?"

"No." His voice dropped to a growl as he stepped closer, his eyes glinting. He lifted a hand, his fingers grazing from the base of my throat down to where the Mark of Hades lay painted on my skin. "I rarely think about fucking my friends as often as I imagine laying with you."

"You should watch what you say, Your Grace," I warned, though it came out in a breathless whisper.

He smirked, noticing the way my breath caught. "I thought you weren't playing games, Miss Moore? Are you really going to pretend you don't want me to lay you across this desk?"

He was taunting me, trying to draw me out, to break through the defenses I'd put up against everyone. And the worst part? It was working. I knew what he was doing, and yet the low, sensual edge in his voice, the way his gaze swept over me, possessive and unrestrained, made my resolve tremble.

We stood there, locked in place, pressed together, breathing each other's air. It would only take a tilt of my head, and his lips would be on mine. The longer he stood there, the more I felt his desire pressing against me, the more my defenses faded.

"Well." I cleared my throat, breaking the spell. "I suppose I should get to my suite since you're so concerned about my rest."

His eyes lingered on my lips, then traveled slowly down my body. He exhaled sharply, as if forcing himself to let go. *Like he wanted to close the distance between us just as badly as I did.* But instead, he stepped back, turning to face his desk. Without him, the space was colder, emptier, and I released an audible sigh.

"Very well," he replied gruffly, refusing to look at me as I practically fled from the room.

CHAPTER THREE

As much as I hated to admit it, I couldn't avoid this any longer. I needed sleep. My body was like lead, every limb weighted down by exhaustion. A dull, insistent ache throbbed in my head, never fading, and my eyes burned from countless sleepless nights spent tossing and turning in fear of my dreams. Weeks had passed without a full night of peaceful, uninterrupted rest and I couldn't spend the rest of my life surviving on limited hours of sleep. If Clay's visit had proven anything, it was that I couldn't keep going like this. It was only a matter of time before everyone else noticed how much I was crumbling apart.

I needed to rest—even if it meant seeing him. Hyrax.

With a resigned sigh, I pulled back the duvet on the plush mattress in my bedchamber. Nessira had brought in heavier bedding to ward off the encroaching chill of winter, and the weight of it was almost intoxicating as I settled beneath it. The familiar scent of lavender clung to the fabric, a quiet reminder of home, and it was enough to coax me into loosening the tension in my shoulders.

I sank into the pillows, my head falling back as if the mattress itself were cradling me. Above me, the shadows of the candlelight flickered and danced along the ceiling, a silent performance that demanded no audience. I watched them until, eventually, the flame guttered out.

Darkness enveloped the room, and the silence pressed close around me.

Finally, I closed my eyes, and it took only a moment before sleep found me.

Even though it had been weeks since I'd last stepped foot in the winding, maze-like caverns of the Underworld, I found my way effortlessly. My memory held the paths as if I had walked them every day of my life.

Honestly, I should have realized the truth about this place sooner. I had no one but myself to be angry at.

Well, myself—and Hyrax.

I was furious with Hyrax.

And now that I'd finally allowed myself to return, I would not be leaving without some answers from the God of the Dead. After all this time, and after all the lies, he at least owed me that much.

I stormed through the caverns, ignoring the ever-present chill in the air until I reached the massive steel doors that led to his throne room. With a sudden strength that surprised even me, I ripped them open and stepped inside.

Hyrax's throne room had always been where we met during my visits, though he rarely occupied his throne of skulls. More often, I'd find him lounging at the dining table, sipping wine and listening to melancholic music while the black onyx fireplace burned warmly. Today, though, was different.

Today, he sat atop the dais on his throne, draped in black robes, radiating authority. Beside him stood a tall, broad-shouldered man with sharp features, his long dark hair falling in waves to his shoulders. He gestured to a stack of papers, drawing Hyrax's attention as the God of the Dead scanned them diligently.

The moment I threw open the doors, the stranger's dark eyes locked onto mine—steady, unflinching. The air between us crackled, and my magic coiled beneath my skin, reacting to him before I even knew who he was.

"Theadora," Hyrax's deep voice carried across the room, tinged with surprise. "I wasn't expecting you."

I scoffed, my tone sharp. "Am I only permitted here when you allow it?"

A grin spread across Hyrax's face as he waved the man aside, gesturing for him to leave the papers on the table. The man stepped back, but his gaze didn't waver, still assessing me with an intensity that sent a slow, involuntary shiver down my spine.

Hyrax stood, descending from the platform with a lazy stretch of his neck. "Of course not, my dear. It has been some time since you've visited, though. I had hoped to hear what became of you after our last meeting, but you never returned."

His words hit a nerve. The last time I'd been here was during the height of Camilla's attack. I had traveled between the battlefield and the Underworld as my consciousness wavered, hovering dangerously close to death. Camilla had flushed Mortal blood through my veins to strip me of my powers, and it had been Hyrax who had helped me reconnect with my magic, guiding me back to life. Hyrax had saved me.

And yet...

"You lied to me," I spat without hesitation, the accusation venomous.

His eyes narrowed, and from the corner of my vision, I saw the man at the dining table turn away slightly to hide his soft chuckle.

"I did no such thing," Hyrax replied coolly, his voice betraying the slightest flicker of irritation. "I never pretended to be anything other than what I am. And what I am has always been rather obvious, Theadora. You've explored *my realm, sat at my table, drank at my side. If you refused to see the truth, that willful blindness is not my fault."*

My stomach twisted, his words sinking in like barbs. He was right. It had been so painfully obvious, the truth of it laid out on a platter for me. He could have been more upfront with me, yes, but he was also right. I should have known better.

"You could have told me," I insisted, my voice cracking slightly.

He scoffed. "And would you have wanted to hear it? Look at you now—disapproval etched across your face."

"Of course I'm disapproving! You were banished for a reason, Hyrax!"

The man beside the dining table stepped forward, his movements slow, deliberate—like a predator deciding whether I was worth his time. His gaze flicked over me, assessing, calculating, lingering just a beat too long before he spoke.

His voice, when he finally did, was low and controlled, yet it carried an undeniable weight. "You are speaking to a High God, Theadora. I would caution you to mind your tone."

Magic rippled through me, rattling the ground beneath our feet. This was a private conversation between my ancestor and me. I didn't need input from a stranger I had never even seen before.

"And you are?" I said, hostility rolling off of me. Hyrax chuckled, summoning a chalice of wine with a flick of his hand and taking a leisurely sip as he approached the man. He clapped him on the back with a somewhat surprising air of paternal pride.

"Forgive me, my dear," Hyrax drawled. "Allow me to introduce my right hand. This is Caldrius Dagon, Supreme Lieutenant of the Underworld."

The name struck me like a blow, fragments of memory surfacing. The name sent me back to Hyrax Estate, to the Archives where Clay had recounted the tale of Caldrius stealing Hyrax's Bident. Zion had allowed him to keep it, but the Bident's magic had poisoned Caldrius, leaving him as nothing more *than a murderous shadow of himself. It was Caldrius' younger brother, En-noss, who had taken the Bident from Caldrius, fled, and founded Athenia.*

"Caldrius," I echoed, my voice tinged with disbelief. "As in the Descendant—"

"Of Zion?" Caldrius finished for me, his lips curving into a knowing smile. "Perhaps, in life. In death, I am loyal to his highness." He inclined his head respectfully toward Hyrax.

"Most loyal," Hyrax confirmed, that same odd pride gleaming in his eyes.

"But why?" I pressed, my mind reeling. "Why would you serve Hyrax if you're descended from Zion?"

Weren't the two brothers known to be at odds with each other?

Caldrius laughed, a rich sound that echoed through the room. His eyes gleamed in the flickering firelight, alight with dark amusement. "And why would you shun Hyrax when you're descended from him?"

Hyrax clapped his hands together, a delighted grin spreading across his face. "I can already tell the two of you will get along famously."

I frowned, the weight of his assumption settling uncomfortably on my chest. "You think I'll be returning here?"

Hyrax and Caldrius exchanged a look, their expressions identical in their smug certainty.

Caldrius tilted his head slightly, studying me as if I were some riddle he'd already solved. "You will," he said—not a question, but a promise.

I didn't answer.

I woke feeling uneasy. My trip to the Underworld was supposed to bring clarity, to explain why I could do the impossible and what Hyrax truly wanted with me. Instead, I left with even more questions.

In all my prior visits to the Underworld, I'd only ever seen Hyrax. I had assumed—obviously—that his realm held other souls, but actually seeing one was... shocking. And that someone being Caldrius made it worse.

Caldrius' life was legend. During my written trial, I had to memorize the tale of how he stole Hyrax's Bident, a relic of immeasurable power. He had been one of the first Descendants of Zion, chosen by the King of the Gods to aid in banishing Hyrax to the Underworld during the Second War of the Gods. Of all the souls to stand as Hyrax's right hand, Caldrius was the last reasonable choice.

So how had he found himself in such a position?

Then again, Caldrius' greed for power had driven him to madness when he tried to wield the Bident's magic. Perhaps that madness had forged a bond with Hyrax—an understanding deeper than lineage.

A knock at my door pulled me from my spiraling thoughts. Rising from the bed, I wrapped my robe tightly around my shoulders and padded through my suite to pull open the tall wooden door.

"My Lady," Emeryn greeted me, dipping her head respectfully. "You look well-rested."

I doubted that. The shadows under my eyes and the unease in my chest begged to differ. I may have slept, but it certainly hadn't left me feeling any better.

"I wasn't aware of any engagements this morning."

"You have none," she confirmed, her tone brisk. "However, the Royal Council is meeting this afternoon. They have requested your presence."

"For what purpose?"

"Council matters are confidential, my lady. I am not told such details."

Right. Of course.

"Very well," I said, suppressing a sigh. "I intend to have breakfast with Iris this morning. Ensure the Council knows I will attend promptly."

Emeryn nodded in approval but paused, her mouth opening as if to say something and then shutting as she decided against it. I watched it all with raised brows. Finally, she turned, ready to leave, and a wave of guilt washed over me.

"Emeryn!" I called after her. She turned, her eyes narrowing with suspicion.

"Please instruct Nessira to evaluate the potential Ladies-in-Waiting and employ whomever she sees fit."

Her brows lifted slightly in surprise, but she recovered quickly, dipping her head once more. "At once, my Lady."

I watched her retreat, her footsteps fading into the quiet corridors. Nessira would be happy to receive that message, happy that I was returning to my senses. It's not that I felt particularly confident about my next steps in this castle, but even I could recognize that I needed to stop avoiding reality. Ignoring the court, refusing sleep, and avoiding the sting of Geia's betrayal wasn't sustainable. It was over now. Camilla was locked up, Geia was gone from my life and Lorelai wasn't coming back.

I needed to accept those things and start moving forward with my life.

CHAPTER FOUR

B reakfast with Iris had been... awkward. We were both clearly interested in attempting to reconnect, but the heartbreak and trauma between us made that process anything but easy. Most of our meal passed in uncomfortable silence, broken only by the occasional attempt at small talk.

When she'd first arrived in my parlour, we'd greeted each other with a stiff, formal hug. Nessira brought out food on a tiny cart and we'd both taken our time carefully picking which pastries to settle onto our plates, both commenting on how beautiful the spread was. From there, our conversation had lingered on the weather: it's really getting colder, and the food: the pastries are very sweet. Nothing either of us said seemed to distract from the tension that lingered between us. The uneasiness of the entire encounter ruined my appetite, but I'd found myself eating just for something to do to pass the time.

Finally, when it became all too unbearable, Iris rose abruptly, tucking her hands behind her back. Her movements were sharp, deliberate.

"I should get going," she said.

I scrambled to my feet after her. "Of course. I... I have to prepare for the Council meeting soon, anyway."

Her lips curved into a tight, polite smile that didn't quite reach her eyes. "Good luck with the meeting."

"Thank you." I walked her to the door, the distance between us feeling larger than ever. "Thank you for joining me."

She hesitated, looking as if she might say something more, but only offered a small nod and stepped through the threshold. I closed the door after her and sagged against it, letting out the heavy breath I'd held since she arrived.

A few months ago, I would have never imagined a conversation with Iris to be so forced and dull.

I missed her desperately. I missed my lively friend who snuck out of the castle with me and always obsessed over gowns and fashion. I missed the surprise of opening my door and seeing what color her hair would be.

Even though she had been here with me, I felt her absence like a missing limb.

Still, she was trying. I was trying.

For now, that had to be enough.

The heavy door loomed before me, it's golden handles gleaming in the dim corridor light. My stomach churned, bile rising in my throat. The last time I'd walked through this threshold, I'd been taken to the Dragon's private office, shackles had bitten into my wrists, my cheek had pressed hard into his wooden desk, and the skin of my back had split open after he whipped me. My chest was tight, panic suddenly freezing me in place.

When a servant opened the door suddenly, my breath hitched and I braced myself to return to that office, but she led me instead to a large meeting chamber. Relief flooded over me as I glanced around the space. The room had no windows so the candles hung in sconces along the wall provided the only light. The Council sat in rigid silence at a long oval table made of fine cherry wood, their eyes snapping to me as I stepped into the room.

In the corner, Clay sat apart from the official members, an unoccupied chair beside him. I assumed they left it for me.

"We're here to listen," he explained as I sank into the velveteen seat next to him and crossed one ankle in front of the other. "Only speak if addressed directly. Since we're not officially on the Council, these meetings are more about preparation than participation."

I nodded, trying to push away my lingering nerves. "Understood."

His gaze lingered on my face, searching. "Did you sleep?"

I hesitated. "You could say that."

One brow arched, a silent invitation to elaborate but before I could summon a lie, the Dragon began speaking, his commanding voice cutting through the room like a blade.

I never thought I would be grateful for the Dragon interrupting me.

"What news is there?" the Dragon questioned, rifling through a stack of parchment.

Rosalia cleared her throat. "There have been reports, Your Majesty, of three House Archives being raided. Two in the city of Alegra and one in the city of Mansala."

Tension settled over the room like a storm cloud and my attention flicked to Clay, hoping for some additional insight, but his furrowed brow told me he was just as confused.

Who would break into Archives, and why?

"What Houses?" Clara asked sharply.

"Two Herea Archives. The other was an Archive maintained in honor of Harmonia."

The Dragon's bushy eyebrows rose sharply, and he exchanged a pointed look with his son. Clay only tilted his head in a slight shake. He knew nothing about this, either.

"What was taken?" the Dragon pressed.

"Nothing, Your Majesty," Rosalia assured him. "As of now, we have no reason to think that this is anything more than the work of rebellious teenagers."

The glare he sent her could have made flowers wilt.

"I won't tolerate it. Send a team of guards to find these criminals and publicly discipline them."

Rosalia's hesitation was subtle, but I caught it - the faint tightening of her lips, the clench of her fist beneath the table. It was the first crack I'd seen in the Council's deferential show of obedience.

"And what updates do we have on the Tenebris situation?" the Dragon asked, pivoting topics sharply.

Gregory scratched his beard. "We believe Fort Charu is now at full occupancy."

The Dragon's golden eyes flared. Fort Charu was a base in Tenebris, a country we were supposedly allied with, but if our suspicions were correct and they were housing Promissan soldiers in a fort that close to Athenia...

"Your recommendation?" the Dragon asked.

Gregory hesitated, considering. "A scouting mission, perhaps?"

"Nonsense," Rosalia sharply stated. "We have no evidence that Promissan soldiers are stationed there. They would see any scouting mission on their soil as an act of aggression."

"Agreed," Clara chimed in.

Gregory sighed. "Then perhaps we should look to strengthen our own alliance with Tenebris."

The Dragon's eyes narrowed. "Go on."

Gregory leaned forward. "Your marriage already cemented our ties with the Republic of Innanis. Perhaps it's time we think more critically about Lady Moore's prospects."

My stomach fell. I had known this moment was coming, of course. The Dragon had, after all, been discussing my marriage since the day I'd sworn allegiance to Athenia. I wasn't sure I would ever feel ready for it to become a certainty, but even I had to admit that Gregory was right - marrying into Tenebris could secure an alliance against Promissa.

It was the most strategic choice.

The Dragon's sharp gaze locked onto mine, calculating, as if he was all at once weighing the feasibility of the proposal and trying to determine if I would protest. I wanted to, I did, but I kept my mouth locked tightly. Even when I felt the weight of Clay's attention on me, I stayed silent.

Finally, he cleared his throat. "Alright then, what are our options?"

Rosalia handed the Dragon a stack of folded parchment. "We've vetted three candidates, considering both their status and Hyraxian lineage. Clarn Freighter of Innanis has distant Hyraxian ties. Patrick Marshall of Promissa is a Water Wielder-"

"Avoid Promissan ties," the Dragon snapped.

Rosalia continued smoothly, unphased by his outburst. "Last, your nephew, Veric Starsen of Tenebris. He's a dragon, primarily descended from Zion. His power isn't particularly notable, but he has sizeable Hyraxian blood from his father's side."

The Dragon rolled his neck until it cracked loudly, his face pensive as he rubbed a hand thoughtfully over his jaw. "I hadn't realized my nephew had come of age."

Nephew?

My breath caught. They were discussing engaging me to Clay's *cousin*?

Next to me, Clay stiffened. A wave of heat suddenly radiated off him, and when I glimpsed at him from the corner of my eyes, I could see the flecks of gold flaring to life in his gaze.

"That is not a terrible idea," the Dragon mused.

Yes, it was. It was an absolutely, completely *terrible* idea.

Which meant it was definitely the one the Dragon was going to agree to.

"Confirm Veric's suitability," the Dragon instructed, meeting my gaze. "If all checks out, we just may have found our man."

Clay's silence was deafening. So was mine.

The Council meeting proceeded at an achingly glacial pace as the Dragon and Council members debated trade deals, kingdom taxes, and crop production in the western lands of Athenia. I did my best to focus, but my mind kept drifting to Veric. And to Clay.

I'd imagined a million scenarios about my arranged marriage. I'd imagined my future husband being older than me and then imagined him being younger. I'd imagined him being too quiet and imagined him being too loud. I'd imagined him being distant, ignoring me and living away from our home, and I'd imagined him being too close, never deigning to give me any privacy.

Not once did I imagine him being related to Clay.

Would we all have family dinners together? Sit around a fire with all our children running before us while Clay and I snuck heated glances at one another?

When the meeting finally broke two hours later, I hardly noticed until the room began clearing out.

The Dragon caught my gaze before leaving. "I'll have Emeryn begin planning the celebration for your Council Ascension. We must move quickly."

His message was obvious. My final trial would happen soon, and my initiation into the Council - and subsequent wedding - would follow shortly afterwards. I nodded in agreement, earning a knowing grin as his gaze flickered between Clay and me.

My stomach flipped unhappily as I'd realized what he'd done.

He hadn't invited me here just to witness and learn from a Council meeting. He had chosen this meeting specifically, orchestrated everything so that I would have to sit next to Clay while they decided my future engagement. The Dragon wasn't ignorant of his son's affections for me, and he would stop at nothing to tear us apart—he had made that abundantly clear to me.

When I first came to Athenia, he had been determined to secure my ascension to the Council. As the last Descendant of Hyrax, my induction would make Athenia the only government with complete representation from all the houses descended from the High Gods. I had thought that status was his greatest ambition.

I had been wrong.

Something mattered to him far more than a complete Council: preserving his bloodline.

Clay's feelings for me threatened that. Were we to be together, truly, it's possible that our children would inherit their powers from me, making them heirs to Hyrax rather than Zion. The Dragon couldn't risk such a deviation from his legacy.

This meeting had been just another way for him to remind Clay and me of all the reasons our relationship needed to stay strictly professional.

"Gods, I hate him," I muttered under my breath as the Dragon turned and exited.

Clay glanced at me suspiciously, eyebrow raised, but I only shook my head. No need to explain. "Let me walk you out," he commanded, standing.

"Do you think that's a good idea?"

"Do you think I'm asking?"

Of course not.

We exited the chamber and stepped into the ornate halls of the Dragon's wing. Golden furnishings, detailed with dragon wings and scales, lavishly adorned the chamber like the rest of the palace. Sunlight poured through large windows overlooking the forests beyond the palace. At the end of the hall, a marble sculpture of Zion stood, sword in hand. Paintings of past Dragons lined the walls, their stern gazes a reminder of the dynasty Clay would one day inherit.

"So that was... interesting," I mumbled as we turned the corner into the grand foyer of the castle.

I didn't know what to say to him. Were we supposed to talk about what had just happened in the room? Was he as disgusted by my marrying his cousin as I was?

The entryway, as always, bustled with courtiers. I wasn't sure how many had a permanent residence at the palace, but it was quite common for wealthy merchants or visiting Dukes who oversaw provinces within the Kingdom to stay within the palace during their visits to the capital. Their constant stares had been unnerving when I'd first started walking these halls, but I'd long since adjusted.

"I'm surprised you expected anything else," Clay murmured, his deep voice sending warmth radiating down my belly.

I ignored that particular feeling as I kept my eyes plastered on the path ahead.

"You had breakfast with Iris this morning?" he asked.

Apparently, we weren't going to acknowledge the engagement at all.

"How was she?"

"Different." I shrugged. "More reserved, I guess?"

He sighed. "I'm worried about her. She's gone through phases like this before – locking herself away, skipping meals, sometimes not getting out of bed for days."

I shivered, hating to think of her that way. "What usually helps?"

"Lorelai," he admitted, shoulders sagging under the weight of the name. "Lorelai helped."

The mention of Lorelai tightened my throat. Of course, Lorelai had been the one to help Iris. Lorelai had been everything to her.

"All we can do is to be there for her," Clay said, his voice resolute. "No matter how bad it gets, she needs to know she can count on us."

"Of course she can."

"There was one other thing I wanted to discuss with you." Clay reached for my elbow to stop me, pulling me aside so a group of courtiers could pass. "I've been continuing to look into your background."

My heart stuttered. "And?"

"Iris told me what you two learned about Zachariah Moore at Madame Stefania's."

Heat crept up my neck. Months ago, Iris and I had snuck out to investigate Zachariah, the man rumored to be my father. We'd found our way to an establishment known as Madame Stefania's, where we'd learned that Zachariah had favored male partners.

Clay smirked. "I have to admit, learning you had snuck out to a brothel brought up conflicting feelings for me. I'm not sure if I'm more irritated that you risked going into a dangerous area, annoyed that you didn't invite me, or curious about what your face looked like when you realized where you were."

"I'd rather not revisit that moment, thank you," I muttered, avoiding his gaze.

Clay chuckled, a grin dancing at the edges of his lips. I forced myself to look away from them.

"Can we get back to the point, please?"

"It seems Zachariah rarely took female partners. In group scenarios, he gave them little attention. Based on what I've learned, it seems unlikely that he's your father."

I sighed. It's not like I hadn't already suspected that, but hearing it confirmed still made my stomach drop. Clay must have seen my disappointment written plainly across my face, because he lifted his hand to trail his fingers across my cheek. His skin was soft against mine and for a second I let myself lean into that comfort until all too suddenly we both realized where we were and took a rushed step back from each other.

"Let's get you back to your room," he said a bit too quickly.

I nodded, falling into step beside him. "What do we do now?"

"I'm honestly not sure, Thea. My father has insisted on ending any further investigations into your background. He wants to focus on the ascension and avoid raising questions about your legitimacy as a Hyraxian Descendant."

"I'm sure the lack of a Mark on my chest only expedited that decision," I said dryly.

"If you want me to keep looking, just say the word."

I hesitated, my mind flickering to Hyrax. If I really wanted to find out the truth about where I came from, he was the person I should be asking. And yet the thought of that conversation filled me with an uncomfortable amount of dread.

"Maybe your father is right. Maybe we should just let it go for now."

"If that's what you want," he agreed, though I got the uneasy feeling that he still had something on his mind as he gazed at me from the corner of his eye.

"What?"

Clay frowned. "You know you can tell me anything, right?"

My chest tightened. "Of course."

Silence hung between us for a moment.

"It just still feels like your mind is somewhere else these days. Like there's something you're not telling me."

I swallowed down the guilt building in the back of my throat and opened my mouth to protest, but as we turned the corner into the Hall reserved for Descendants of Hyrax, I collided directly with Kent.

Kent reached out, holding onto my elbows until I had steadied on my feet. I nodded at him, then at Rankor, who stood slightly behind, grateful that their sudden entrance had stopped any further questioning from Clay. "Were you coming from my rooms?"

They wore plain clothes, which could only mean one thing: Rankor and Kent wanted to sneak out of the castle. We didn't leave the castle frequently. When we did, it was to spend the evening at a local tavern where Kent would perform with a group of other musicians. It wasn't a place considered appropriate for Clay and me as leaders of the country, but anyone who recognized us kept their mouths closed and the risk was usually worth it for a night away from all our responsibilities.

The last time we'd done it, though, we'd gone with Iris and Lorelai. We'd gone with Camilla.

"We're dragging Iris out tonight," Kent said with a wry grin. "It took some convincing, but I think it'll be good for her."

"Where is she?" I asked, looking towards the end of the hall with a naïve hope that she would appear in a bright gown with pink hair and a wide smile. I would do anything to see that version of her again.

"She'll be along soon. Last we saw her she was talking with –"

"A lady-in-waiting," Rankor interrupted. His tone was sharp, his gaze shifting to Clay with barely veiled animosity.

Clay, uncharacteristically, stepped aside and excused himself without another word.

"What was that about?" I questioned, as I watched him retreat at a furious pace down the hall.

Kent sighed, glancing at Rankor. For a moment, the two men only looked at each other, each seeming to communicate with the other silently.

"You'll have to ask him," Rankor finally muttered.

"Tell me a secret," Iris requested softly, twirling her glass of wine in her fingers.

Clay hadn't joined us at the tavern tonight, which admittedly seemed odd after he expressed such a desire to support Iris. His absence left me feeling a touch disappointed. Even though I knew I shouldn't, I had been looking forward to seeing my prince in a setting where he might let his guard down enough to actually laugh. Getting private time with Iris made the loss of that worthwhile, though.

We'd spent the first part of the evening upstairs, watching Kent sing and playing cards with Rankor. But after a while, the liveliness of it all seemed to drain Iris, and she'd grasped my hand and pulled me downstairs.

The lower level of the tavern was quieter. A long bar stretched across the wall and a single barkeep kept conversation with a young couple at the far end. A few other patrons sat scattered throughout the room, speaking in low tones and laughing softly. Iris and I found a corner bench near a fireplace, settling ourselves next to its dwindling embers.

I sighed, pondering her request. A secret. There were too many secrets between us, more than I cared to admit.

There was Hyrax, of course. And the time last year when I'd snuck out of the castle alone in search of a potion to restore my lost memories. That night had ended with me dosed with a drug that left me rather sensitive, and I had tried to seduce Clay while we stayed alone together in a dingy inn. Then there was the time I had visited Camilla after her capture, demanding to know why she had done the things she did.

Too many secrets.

"The Dragon threatened to send me oversees," I said finally, settling on one that seemed simpler than the rest.

"Because of Clay?" Iris surmised immediately.

I nodded, impressed by how quickly she figured it out. She really was brilliant. As a faerie, Iris had the unique ability to morph her appearance into anyone or anything else. The Dragon had capitalized on the talent and commissioned her to work as an Athenian spy. It wasn't just her magic that made her good at her job, though; it was the way she thought.

"How is that going, by the way?" She spoke in a detached tone, as if she didn't really care about the answer, but the simple fact that she asked seemed like progress.

I shrugged, uneasy. "I'm not sure I know what you mean."

She frowned, her gaze narrowing suspiciously.

A roar of applause sounded from the floor above us, and the music quieted. Kent must have finished his last song for the evening. Soon, we'd need to head back to the castle. I'd have to return to my rooms and pray to the Gods that I didn't slip into the Underworld again in the few hours of sleep that I allowed myself.

"There's nothing going on between us," I said, avoiding her eyes. "Nothing can."

She was quiet for a moment before finishing her wine in a single gulp. "You want my advice?"

Probably not, but I wasn't about to turn her down.

"Life's short, Thea. Too short to waste a single day ignoring your feelings for someone just because you think it's wrong. I've done that twice in my life, and both times ended in heartbreak. If I'd gotten over those fears sooner, then maybe Lorelai and I would have had the time we needed. And maybe, if we'd had that time, I'd have memories to look back on fondly instead of just regrets."

Her voice cracked, and my heart shattered for her. First, because of the tears welling in her eyes, and second, because I couldn't think of a single thing to say to her.

"I should have been faster that night," I whispered. "I'm so sorry."

Iris met my gaze, and the haunted look in her eyes sent shivers down my spine. "I'm not ready to talk about that night, Thea. I know you feel guilty, but I can't be the one to help you through those feelings. My own pain is all I can see right now."

I stood abruptly, crossing the space between us. Without asking if it was okay, I pulled her into my arms. She was stiff at first, but finally softened, her hands wrapping gently around my waist in return.

We didn't speak any further after that. We just sat in silence, the crackling embers the only sound, until Rankor and Kent came down to fetch us. They glanced between us with worried expressions as we headed for the carriage, uneasy by the silence.

When we all finally parted ways for the evening, though, Iris squeezed my hand twice and told me she was looking forward to breakfast in the morning.

I wasn't sure I'd ever felt more relieved.

CHAPTER FIVE

The next evening, Rankor and I ate dinner with Kent in his chambers. It was a meticulous space, carefully organized and always tidy. He arranged the books alphabetically on the shelf, always pulled the duvet up to the headboard of the bed, and kept his laundry out of sight.

It was as if no one truly lived here, which only made it seem more like Kent.

"I still can't believe you went between his legs." Rankor shook his head as he bit into his turkey leg. "That is *not* what I taught you."

"Yes, well, I'm sure you weren't the only one disappointed in that maneuver." I shrugged, leaning forward across the wooden table to grab the pitcher of ice water and fill my glass as I thought of my awkward conversation with Clay after my second trial.

"Still," Kent said, taking the pitcher from me after I finished. "You've completed two of the three trials already. How are you feeling?"

I thought over his words, letting them sit heavily in my mind. How *was* I feeling about it? Truthfully, it all felt a bit rushed. I'd spent a year knowing that the trials were coming, and then in the weeks after Camilla's imprisonment, my training had intensified tenfold. I'd spent every day of the past two months studying, training, and practicing for hours upon hours.

I'd had plenty of time to come to terms with what was waiting for me on the other side of the trials, but I still hadn't.

"I suppose I'm just focused on getting through the magic trial."

Rankor whistled through his teeth. "I do not envy you having to go through that."

I frowned. The magic trial was the one I knew the least about. Ryla helped me build my control over my powers, but only told me the magic trial wouldn't be announced in advance. The trial's surprise element would test my ability to use my powers spontaneously.

"What do you mean?" I asked with a frown.

"Clay's magic trial was brutal," Rankor said, wiping his hands and mouth with a napkin. "They tested his human form too. Chained him with iron and locked him in a burning building. He's fireproof, of course, but he had to break the chains and get out before the building collapsed on him. Then the second he got out, one of Ciclopia's beasts was waiting for him. He had barely a second to recover, shift into his dragon form, and fight."

My heart clenched just at *imagining* him in that kind of danger.

Kent nodded as Rankor told the story. "He nearly lost a wing in the process."

"And then there was Clara's son," Rankor continued, spearing a roasted carrot with his fork.

Kent's attention suddenly snapped to Rankor, and he slapped him sharply on the shoulder. "Don't tell her that!"

"Tell me what?"

The two men looked at me with matching sheepish expressions, forcing me to repeat my question.

Kent sighed heavily. "A few years ago, Clara's son was set to take over her seat on the Council. Everyone thought it was guaranteed, but for his trial, they abandoned him in the middle of a desert. He died three days later."

Gods. I gasped, stomach falling so suddenly that I had to clutch my belly to be sure that it was still there. On some level, I knew the trials could be fatal but to actually hear how easily they could end lives...

"But don't worry!" Rankor cried, holding his hands out towards me. "You're like terrifyingly powerful. I'm sure you'll do great."

I'm not sure if that was the kind of compliment he thought it was. I pushed away my plate, suddenly losing my appetite.

For the next half hour, I let them carry the conversation while my thoughts lingered on Clara and her son.

The Dragon wouldn't design a trial that could kill me, though?

He needed me to complete the Council. I was too valuable.

Right?

Unless...

Unless he'd saw Clay and I sneak off during my celebration dinner.

He'd made it very clear that he would prioritize his bloodline over a complete Council.

Oh, Gods.

My stomach churned, my skin prickling with cold. The room suddenly felt too small, too loud, my own heartbeat pounding in my ears.

I need to get out of here.

"I'm going to bed," I announced too quickly, pushing back my chair with a screech.

Rankor and Kent both shot me looks of confusion.

"Okay?" Rankor drew out the word.

Kent stood, brushing off his pants as he did. "Let me walk you out."

I nodded my thanks, and he guided me to the door with a respectful hand on the small of my back, stopping in the hallway once we were out of Rankor's earshot.

"Don't worry about the trial," he said softly, rubbing a hand supportively along my shoulder. "You're going to be fine."

"Right. Yeah." I forced a smile before backing away. "Thanks."

"Thea," he called after me sharply, and I turned back.

His expression was unreadable. Too careful. Too knowing.

"Is there anything else that has you upset? You seem off lately."

A shiver ran down my spine. There was a myriad of things that had me upset, and I couldn't talk to him about a single one.

I shook my head. "No, of course not. Just pre-trial jitters. I'll see you tomorrow. Goodnight."

*N*o.

I don't want to be here.

Music seeped through the realm, dark and melodic. The same grating chords he always played. The melody was maddeningly short and repetitive. I hated it.

I hated his music.

I hated this place.

I hated him.

Did he know I was here? Did he know I was standing at the edge of his river? I didn't even know how far his magic extended. Was he all-knowing here in this realm? It seemed ridiculous to think that I could avoid him here in the realm he had total dominion over.

In the distance, a low howl pierced the air, then another, and another. Hyrax's three-headed hound howled for him, and panic overtook me. Spinning on my heel, I broke into a desperate sprint. I didn't know where I was going; I just knew I couldn't stay here, couldn't face him.

I couldn't be the one to release him back into the Mortal Realm.

I wouldn't be.

"Wake up!" I screamed desperately at myself.

S omething wasn't right.

The air was too cold. A sharp chill bit at my skin. Winter drafts had begun creeping over the mountains lately, but I always closed my windows before bed. After this past year – after everything I'd been through – I had developed a careful ritual before bed. One that included no unlocked doors and no open windows.

I reached for the blanket, still half-caught in the haze of sleep, but instead of finding the familiar weight of my quilt, my arm bumped into something hard. Solid. I opened my eyes, and absolute darkness filled my vision. I froze, breath stuttering in my throat, every nerve in my body on edge.

Something was wrong.

Very wrong.

I pushed at the space around me, frantic, and my fingers scraped against the smooth wood. Walls. A ceiling? No, it was too close for that. My chest tightened, my breaths shallow and sharp. This wasn't my bed.

I was in a wooden box.

The box lurched suddenly, sending me crashing into the side. Pain flared in my shoulder as my body twisted uncomfortably in the tight space.

What in the name of the Gods was happening?

I blinked rapidly, desperate for even the faintest light to pierce the suffocating blackness, but there was nothing. No faint glow from a moonlit window. No flicker of a hallway torch. Only the crushing weight of dark and silence, pressing in on me.

I shoved against the wood above me, muscles straining, and it didn't so much as budge. My mind raced, but circled back to one terrible, unshakeable possibility.

It wasn't just a box.

It was a coffin.

Someone had locked me in a fucking coffin.

My magic surged, crackling hot and furious through my fingers. I clenched my jaw so tightly I thought my teeth might crack as dampness started seeping into the back of my nightgown as the coffin shifted again.

There was only one person in the kingdom who would dare to do this. Only one person was brazen enough, psychotic enough, to trap me here.

The Dragon.

Which meant only one thing.

This was my final trial.

The magic trial had begun.

CHAPTER SIX

I wondered how long it had taken Clara's son to realize he was going to die in his magic trial.

Had it been immediate?

Was he dropped into that desert and struck by the certainty of his demise right away, or had the truth crept in slowly—hours passing before he understood the Dragon would kill him?

Did he feel like I did now, realizing that I had already been locked in my own coffin?

Thick, foamy liquid rushed into the bottom of the box at a steady rate, the kind you'd only find in lakes or the open sea.

For the briefest of moments, a thought brushed across my mind. The idea of just... letting it fill.

If I drowned here and now, the prophecy wouldn't come true. Hyrax wouldn't rise from the Underworld.

A dead girl couldn't raise the God of the Dead into the Mortal Realm.

No.

I would not die here.

I would not give the Dragon the satisfaction of knowing I'd been that easy to kill, and I certainly would not let Hyrax and his duplicity be the reason I lost my life.

Shaking off the wave of despair, I forced myself to focus, pressing my hands against the wooden walls, searching for some kind of weakness.

Then, suddenly, the coffin slammed against something solid.

For a split second, the world seemed to hold its breath.

And then it tilted.

The box hit down, shattering on impact and splintering into jagged shards as icy water exploded around me. The sensation of it smacking against my skin was like a thousand tiny needles stabbing into me. I gasped involuntarily against the sharp, merciless cold of the water searing into my skin, choking on the bitter tang of salt and lake muck.

Gods, it was so cold.

I was nothing but flailing legs and thrashing arms as I searched for the surface, my thoughts little more than fragmented flashes of panic.

Up. Air. Move.

My leg slid across a splintered shard of the wooden box and the point of it sliced through my calf in a violent rush. I screamed, the water swallowing the sound, as I grasped onto my wounded leg.

The water around me turned red as blood bloomed around me.

Eventually, even the pain from the wound faded as the icy chill of the water took over every one of my thoughts. I couldn't think of anything, couldn't feel anything, but the cold and the way it sunk into every one of my bones. My fingers burned. My toes went numb. I was hollow, being drug down by the chill.

I kicked again, but my movements were sluggish now, uncoordinated. Useless.

This was it.

This was the moment where I would end.

It really would be that easy to kill me.

"*Y*ou're back again."

Hyrax sat at his dining table, Caldrius lounging in the seat at his side, looking far too relaxed with his hands crossed behind his dark head of hair. A modest spread of food lay before them, untouched, their focus entirely on each other—until I appeared, dripping wet and gasping for air.

"I didn't want to be back!" I snapped, chest heaving. I wasn't sure if I was more irritated with him or myself.

Caldrius chuckled softly, running a hand over his sharp jawline in a poor attempt to hide his amusement. My gaze snapped to him, hands planting on my hips as a flush of anger rolled through me.

"Do you find something amusing about this situation?" I hissed.

"Very much so." His eyes traced over me, slow and unhurried like he wasn't just looking at me, but memorizing me, seeing through me. Heat crawled up my spine as I glanced down at myself in confusion only to see that the water had left my silk nightgown practically transparent. I rushed to cover myself with an arm but Caldrius just kept staring, not even having the decency to attempt to hide where his attention was focused.

Hyrax, who had yet to acknowledge me, finally followed Caldrius' gaze. His eyes widened in horror, and he turned abruptly. With a wave of his hand, a thick black robe lined with plush fur appeared on my shoulders, heavy and warm.

"My dear," Hyrax chided, voice dry and sharp. "That is hardly appropriate attire."

"Well, it's not like I planned this little visit," I shot back, wrapping the robe tighter around me.

He rolled his eyes, muttering under his breath, "No, of course not."

"She thinks she's dying," Caldrius mused, his lips curving slightly. "Again." He didn't look at Hyrax when he said it. His focus stayed on me, unwavering. "Either you enjoy our company, or you have a terrible sense of self-preservation."

Gods, the way he looked at me. His attention was completely absolute, filled with more than just lust. Caldrius looked at me like he knew me. Like he had every right to study me, memorize every inch, as if I belonged to him in some way I didn't yet understand.

Hyrax laughed suddenly, snapping my attention back to him. "Haven't we been here before?"

I crossed my arms, glaring. "I'm not sure I understand your meaning."

"You came here the last time you thought you were dying," he said, waving a hand dismissively. "You didn't need me then and you don't need me now. Return to your realm, Theadora. You're more than capable of managing this silly trial."

I scoffed, somehow... offended at being dismissed by him. It's not like I wanted to stay in this realm any longer, but he'd never actually dismissed me before. And it stung in a way I hadn't quite expected.

"Oh, I'm sorry," I said, sarcasm dripping from my words. "Were you two busy?"

"Yes, actually." Hyrax's tone cut like a whip. "In case you've forgotten, I have other demands on my attention beyond you. I also have a wife who needs my care, an entire realm to oversee, and a meeting to conclude with my Supreme Lieutenant."

Supreme Lieutenant. I almost laughed aloud. What a ridiculous name for a position of authority.

"How do you even know that I'm in my trial?" I wondered aloud, stepping closer to their table. "How do you always seem to know what's happening in the Mortal Realm?"

Hyrax handed a stack of parchment to Caldrius, who flipped through it leisurely, signing off on a few with a nearby quill. Part of me wanted to crane my neck over to glance at them. Exactly what kind of business did the King of the Underworld find himself so preoccupied with?

"You're asking the wrong questions," Hyrax said, his tone clipped.

"And what, exactly, are the right questions, Hyrax?" I snapped back.

His eyes locked onto mine, an intensity in his gaze so fierce that I almost stumbled backward.

"Everyone in this room knows the questions you're longing for answers to," he said. "Your refusal to simply ask them directly is wasting my time. Believe it or not, my time is valuable."

Hyrax turned away from me, effectively dismissing me once more, and I fought the powerful urge I had to stomp my foot and demand his attention.

Caldrius stared at me, a challenge in his smile.

Fine. If they wanted me to ask, I would.

"Tell me what happened to my memories!"

Hyrax rolled his eyes, disappointment flickering across his face, and he remained silent, the emptiness of it stretching between us. I looked to Caldrius, who only leaned back in his chair and smirked.

"That's not the question he wants you to ask," Caldrius mock-whispered behind his hand.

I almost screamed in frustration.

"You don't have any memories, Theadora," Hyrax said finally. "There is nothing for you to remember."

The words struck like a blow. Ice flooded my blood, the coldness of it seeping through the warmth of the robe Hyrax had given me. The world around me blurred. The air thinned. I was about to wake up.

But now, I didn't want to leave.

"How is that possible?" I demanded, my voice rising. "Do you expect me to believe I just appeared on that bridge out of thin air?"

Caldrius chuckled, and my hand shot out instinctively, grasping onto the wineglass in front of me and hurling it at his head.

The bastard ducked with record speed, and all I earned for my trouble was another smirk and a cheeky wink. Gods, I hated him. I hated them both.

"I expect you to stop acting like a child," Hyrax snapped, slamming his palm on the table. The sound reverberated through the room. "And I expect you to face the truth. I will not explain to you what you are not ready to admit to yourself. Now go back to your realm, Theadora. We'll discuss the bridge when you're ready to admit who and what you are."

I could feel the dampness returning to my hair and skin.

"See you soon, Theadora," Caldrius called to me, his voice a silken promise.

I woke with a start, gasping for air.

My lungs only filled with frigid, salty water.

Choking, I thrashed blindly, arms and legs working as hard as possible, but it was useless. The lake dragged me down, cold and endless, pressing against my ribs, crushing. I kicked hard, forcing my sluggish limbs to move, but the weight of the water pulled me deeper. The light above shimmered too far away. My lungs screamed for air but I wasn't going to make it.

Magic suddenly surged in my veins, as if sensing my building panic, and for a moment I stopped fighting the pull of the water.

Of course. This was the magic trial, which meant I needed magic to survive.

The power inside me flared hot against the cold, raw and electric. I didn't even have to think—I just let go.

And unleashed.

Energy surged through me, shoving me upward like a bolt of lightning. My hair coiled wildly around my face as I shot through the depths, cutting through the water.

Then—air.

I broke the surface with a desperate gasp, choking, sucking in the frozen wind as I half-dragged myself onto the shore. Coughing up puddles of mucky water, I collapsed onto the earth, muscles trembling violently. Everything ached. My pulse slammed against my skull, my breath ragged as the world spun. The throbbing in my leg flared, no longer content to be ignored and blood seeped into the shore beneath me.

For a long moment, I just breathed.

Then—cheering.

Distant. Loud. Far above.

I blinked, forcing my vision to focus.

Rows of spectators loomed on the cliffs, perched safely behind stone barriers. The royal viewing box stood at the center, overlooking the shore.

The shore?

I pushed onto shaking elbows, my pulse hammering. Where the hell had they dropped me?

The air was crisp and sharp, carrying the scent of brine and cold.

Mountains loomed in the distance. Northwest.

If the mountains were northwest... then the castle would be southeast.

Which meant—

I stiffened.

I twisted toward the water.

The vast, dark expanse stretched into the horizon, eerily still, reflecting the overcast sky. A single ripple disturbed its glassy surface.

My stomach plummeted.

No.

Not here.

Anywhere but here.

A slow, creeping horror curled in my chest, a terrible certainty.

I spun toward the royal box, where the Dragon sat watching me.

"You dropped me in the middle of the fucking Great Lake of Athenia?" I yelled, my voice hoarse but furious.

He stood in place, far above, but even at this distance, I could see the smirk on his face. The way his eyebrow raised in a wordless challenge and a silent answer to me.

This was far from over.

The water behind me shifted.

The crowd went silent.

The ripples became waves.

A single deafening roar split the air.

The ground trembled beneath me, and I froze.

There was a reason people stayed away from this lake. A reason the stands were so far away from the water.

A shadow moved beneath the surface—huge. Unfathomably big.

Then a scaled head rose from the depths, water pouring off its emerald-green hide. Slitted golden eyes locked onto me, and a forked tongue flicked out to taste the air.

Then another head emerged.

And another.

And another.

The Hydraxan.

Ciclopia, the Mother of Beasts, had left one of her children here.

And now they wanted me to fight it.

Memorizing the beasts of Ciclopia had been part of my preparations for my first trial. Few of her children had lived into the modern era, but the Hydraxan was one of her deadliest creations - a beast that had survived thousands of years. A creature so deadly that not even the most powerful warriors in Athenia had killed it.

The center head of the Hydraxan dipped low, its forked tongue flicking out, tasting the air as it inhaled deeply as it's slitted eyes flicked to my injured leg.

It scented my blood.

I didn't move. Couldn't. Pure fear, colder than I'd experienced in a long time, was falling over me in waves.

All seven heads turned toward me at once, their slitted golden eyes narrowing, their massive necks tensing. Then—they roared.

A piercing, gut-wrenching wail that ripped through the air like a storm of sound, rattling my bones so violently I thought they might shatter. The ground buckled beneath me. The air itself trembled. The force threw me to my knees before I even realized I had fallen and my vision a blur of vibrating color.

Shit.

I scrambled to my feet, shoving past the fiery pain in my calf, and sprinted.

The Hydraxan struck instantly.

A head lunged from the left, snapping shut inches from my throat. Another from the right, fangs glinting as it aimed for my shoulder. I barely twisted in time, throwing myself low, dodging by a hair.

The beast was everywhere.

A third head lunged for my ankles, forcing me to leap—but before I could fully land, another head struck from above, jaws parting wide.

It was going to swallow me whole.

A burst of magic shot from my palm, slamming into the beast's open maw. The Hydraxan reeled back, but barely. It stumbled for only half a second before charging again.

No. No, no, no.

There was no outrunning it.

One of its heads rammed into my back, sending me flying forward. I hit the ground hard, landing awkwardly on a stone and the force knocked the air from my lungs. The pain was instantaneous, flaring through me as I *felt* my rib crack on the impact. Dirt filled my mouth, blood roared in my ears.

I barely rolled in time to avoid a head snapping where my throat had been.

Another lunged for my wrist—its venom-coated fangs bared.

I jerked my arm away at the last second, but the sheer heat of its breath scorched my skin. If just one of those teeth pierced me—

I would be dead.

Dear Gods.

A desperate surge of power exploded from me, slamming into the beast's chests. It staggered back a step—only one. But it was enough. I scrambled up, ignoring the searing pain in my ribs, my hands flying to my thigh—

For my dagger.

But it wasn't there.

I hadn't gone to sleep armed. The weapon that had become like an extension of me was still sitting in my bedchamber, useless.

Panic flared in my chest.

"Thea!"

Rankor's voice cut through the chaos.

I turned toward the stands. He was standing, his broadsword gleaming in the light as he held it high in the air.

Then he threw it.

Without hesitation, I reached with my magic, pulling the heavy blade through the air, into my waiting grasp.

The Hydraxan lunged again.

I planted my feet, twisted my hips, and swung.

Steel met flesh.

A clean, perfect slice.

A severed head crashed to the ground.

Blood sprayed in thick, hot arcs, coating the mud, the air, my face. The beast shrieked—another screeching, ear-splitting howl that sent the crowd gasping, covering their ears.

But before I could even catch my breath, the flesh moved.

The raw, mangled stump twisted.

The tendons rippled.

The blood stopped pouring.

And then—a new head regrew.

I blinked and a deep, sinking horror settled in my gut.

Of course, it wouldn't be that easy.

The beast turned back toward me, its many eyes narrowed. Great. I pissed it off.

Anger and frustration ignited inside me, hot and wild. I roared as I launched myself at the creature, hacking, slashing, unleashing every ounce of magic I had. I fought until I couldn't feel the pain of my injuries, until beads of sweat poured down my face, until my ears stopped ringing and all I could hear was pure silence.

And it didn't matter. Every strike was useless. Every wound healed. For every head I severed, another, angrier version replaced it.

I was burning through power quickly, blood pouring from my nose. And the Hydraxan wasn't slowing down.

My stomach churned. How was I supposed to win a trial that involved killing something that couldn't die?

I glanced toward the royal viewing box, desperate for a clue.

The Dragon was relaxed. Entertained. As if he were simply watching a show.

Next to him, the queen barely looked interested.

And then there was Clay.

Standing behind his father, tension radiated from his frame. His grey eyes locked onto mine.

He didn't flinch. Didn't breathe. Just watched me with eerie, unshaken certainty.

Like he already knew how this would end and he had complete confidence in me.

His hand lifted—slow, deliberate—and he made a fist in the air before he dragged a finger across his throat. Then he pointed directly at me.

I swallowed hard.

No

He couldn't mean—

Surely he didn't expect me to—

Could I even do that?

The Hydraxan launched toward me.

I blasted a surge of magic through my feet, propelling myself backward, soaring across the shoreline. I hit the ground hard, rolling violently, biting my lip as pain splintered through me.

Then, I stood.

This was a bad idea.

The beast charged.

This was a very bad idea.

I clenched my fists, reaching with my power—extending it, feeling for something deeper.

The connection snapped into place.

A bolt of raw awareness struck through me—absolute and terrifying.

I could feel the Hydraxan's heart.

I could feel its lungs expanding.

I could feel its hunger for me.

Its rage.

Its immortality.

"Thea!" Rankor screamed, panic sharp in his voice.

The beast was so close now. If this didn't work, I was dead.

I pushed, willing my magic to be stronger.

It leaped into the air.

I gritted my teeth and clenched my hand into a fist—

And squeezed.

And waited.

And prayed.

And, thank the Gods, the Hydraxan convulsed.

It landed on top of me, but I twisted away from its clamping jaws, my body shaking from the sheer effort of holding its heart in my grasp.

The creature shuddered, a soft growl escaping before its final head fell limply onto the ground.

Silence.

Then the world came back into focus. I could see the colors in the sky, hear the cheers of the crowd, taste the salt of my own tears.

It was over.

I had done it.

I had passed the final trial.

I was going to ascend to the Council.

Groaning, I pushed the beast off me and struggled to my knees, desperate to catch my breath despite the fact that each inhale felt like razor blades. I pushed onto one knee, struggling to stand. Struggling to focus. Struggling to...

Agony.

A sharp, burning pain tore through my wrist.

I gasped, my vision tilting and the world moved beneath me as my body went crashing back to the ground.

There was a gaping hole in my arm, the distinct impression of teeth marks carved into my flesh and the festering smell of the Hydraxan's venom suddenly surrounded me.

I screamed.

It spread like fire through my veins, a searing, unbearable torment that sent my body convulsing. My breath caught, ragged, and uneven. My muscles locked, spasming.

Screams tore out of me without reason or thought. Pain was too simplistic a word for what was exploding through me. It was complete and total obliteration.

Every nerve ignited. I was burning from the inside out. My own veins betrayed me, carrying the venom to my lungs – to my heart. I convulsed, torn apart from the inside and distantly I felt myself thrashing wildly, but I couldn't control it, couldn't control anything.

I tried to breathe, but I couldn't. I was choking - dying.

I knew what it felt like when a soul left its body to travel to the Underworld and I could feel mine slipping. My body was turning hollow. My vision was blackening at the edges. I could feel that oily pull to the Underworld.

The Dragon's voice shattered the haze. Cold. Cruel. Absolute.

"No one will help her. This trial is not over!"

No.

I did not go through all of this to die in front of an audience.

Not now. Not like this.

I had one chance.

I clawed for the last sputtering scraps of my magic, using the last of my sanity to do so even as my body fought against me every step of the way.

And when I finally had that power within my grasp... I *pushed*.

The venom screamed against my magic, resisting, scraping its claws into me, but I continued. I pushed harder, my own heartbeat stuttering as I forced it back out of the wound it had used to invade me.

I would not die like this.

My blood boiled, my body trembled violently.

And then—

Darkness.

CHAPTER SEVEN

P ain.

There was no end to it. Agony tore through me, unrelenting and raw, as if the venom had scorched every one of my veins. My muscles ached with unnatural heaviness, and my throat was raw, shredded by my screams.

I could barely think, barely breathe. The world swirled around me, indistinct and hazy, but I clung to the faint edges of consciousness, desperate not to slip away because I knew if I did there was a chance I might not return from the Underworld this time.

Then I felt it. The air shifting around me. The rush of movement—flapping wings, hurried footsteps—and the sound of voices breaking through the haze.

"Your Highness, she's managed to push out most of the venom herself, but some still remains. She needs immediate treatment!" a feminine voice demanded, urgent and sharp.

"The rules of the trial are clear. No one may intervene," came the Dragon's bitter reply.

An animalistic snarl rumbled near my ear, low and fierce, as strong arms slipped under my shoulders and knees. A moment later, I was lifted, cradled against a warm chest. The movement sent shards of pain slicing through my body, and I whimpered, curling instinctively toward the familiar cinnamon scent that enveloped me.

"Father," Clay's voice was tight, his anger barely contained. "The trial was to defeat the Hydraxan, something no Descendant has ever done. She passed your test. Are you really going to let her die here, on this field?"

"Others have died in their trials, Clayton! Why should this girl be any different?" the Dragon barked.

"Your Majesty," another voice interjected, steady and clear. Gregory Handel's tenor. "The Crown Prince is correct. The trial's objective was clear: kill the Hydraxan. Lady Moore succeeded where no one else could. If she dies now, so does the Council. Without her, there is no heir to Hyrax."

"Do you want your people to watch as you let her die?" Clay growled, his arms tightening around me protectively. "Do you think that will inspire their loyalty?"

Before the Dragon could reply, Clay turned, striding away with purpose. The cold air brushed against my tender skin as we moved, and the chill sent fresh waves of agony crashing through me. I gasped, another scream tearing from my throat, but Clay only held me closer, shielding me from the wind.

"Where do you think you're going?" the Dragon roared, his voice echoing across the field.

"You can find me in the Hall of Hyrax," Clay shot back without slowing.

"Kent and I can take her," Rankor's voice called, laced with concern and anger. "A Zion prince shouldn't be in the bedroom of a Hyraxian princess."

Fingers pressed against my back, too firm on my fragile, dying body, and the contact sent pain spiraling outward in violent waves. It started at my fingers and toes, radiating to my heart and back again.

I barely even recognized the sounds of my own cries.

I couldn't take much more. I wasn't strong enough.

Clay's voice came sharp and unyielding. "I don't care how many years of friendship we have, Rankor. You try to take her from me, and I'll burn you alive where you stand."

My body trembled, my breath faltering as the edges of consciousness blurred. Sleep beckoned, dark and inviting.

But I couldn't let go. I didn't want to.

I wasn't strong enough to fight anymore though.

"What do you mean?" Iris screamed, her voice shrill and thick with anguish. Was it her sobs that had pulled me back toward consciousness?

My body still wasn't my own. I floated somewhere between the Mortal Realm and the Underworld, neither offering solace, neither free from pain.

"We've done everything we can," a voice said, low and weary.

"Then do more!" Iris demanded, her tone cracking. "I won't lose her too. I can't. I can't lose anyone else—"

"Shh, Iris," Kent murmured, his voice soft and steady, though I could hear the strain beneath it. "Thea's strong. She's going to push through this."

I wanted to reach for her, to comfort her, to let her know I was still here, still fighting, but I couldn't. My body felt foreign, ravaged and brutalized, every nerve alight with fire and ice. Her frantic tears tore at my heart.

"Please," Rankor's voice broke through, rough with desperation. "There must be some other treatment. Something else you can try?"

A heavy silence followed, suffocating and absolute. Without distractions, I became painfully aware of my own body. My blood boiled beneath my skin, every cell screaming in agony. Sweat soaked through my clothes, clinging to my shivering frame, and my cracked lips begged for water even as my stomach churned at the thought.

"I understand how much you all care for her," the healer finally said, her voice heavy with resignation. "But no one has ever survived the Hydraxan's bite. It's remarkable she's lived this long—and only because of her quick thinking to expel the venom. It's in the Gods' hands now. We must return to the infirmary."

"No!"

Clay's roar shattered the quiet, more beast than man. The sound sent a shiver through the air, vibrating with raw fury.

"None of you leave this room until she wakes up!" he bellowed, his voice unyielding, commanding. "That's an order!"

The room fell silent again, thick with tension. Even in my haze, I could feel the weight of Clay's presence—his anger, his fear, his refusal to let me slip away.

I clung to that.

Through the pain, through the fog, I clung to the sound of their voices, their unwavering belief that I could survive this.

Because I had to.

A cool, damp rag pressed against my forehead, soothing the fever burning beneath my skin. Gentle fingertips followed, brushing away the damp tendrils of hair stuck to my face and neck. The touch was soft, comforting, pulling me closer to the surface of consciousness.

I clung to the scent of cinnamon.

"People will talk," Kent's voice murmured, low and steady, just above a whisper. "You've been in here for some time. Everyone saw your reaction on the field, and now the gossip's spreading. Something about you threatening to kill the entire palace infirmary staff if she died."

"She will not die," Clay said, his voice firm with conviction. The bed shifted slightly under his weight as he sat beside me.

"No, she won't," Kent agreed, his tone lighter but edged with a hint of warning. "Thea's far too stubborn for that. But when she eventually wakes up, you both are going to have to deal with the consequences of this, Clay."

"I don't give a fuck about the consequences right now!"

Footsteps echoed softly against the floor, and then the door creaked open and shut. Kent had left.

The room fell quiet, save for the sound of my shallow breaths and the rustle of Clay shifting closer. His hand brushed over my forehead again and his touch lingered for a moment.

"Just wake up for me, princess," he whispered, his voice raw, almost pleading. "I'll deal with whatever happens next. I don't care. I just need you to open those ocean eyes for me."

Time passed. How much, I couldn't say. Hours, days, an eternity—it all blurred together. The only thing I knew for certain was that a slow death was infinitely worse than a quick one. If given the choice, I would have gladly taken the blade a thousand times over rather than lie here, trapped in agony, listening to the quiet mourning of my friends.

I tossed and turned endlessly, desperate for relief, for escape, for something other than the fever ravaging my body. Someone would replace the cool towel on my forehead with a freshly dampened one every so often, yet that offered only fleeting relief. The fever burned on, relentless.

Sleep terrified me. Every time I drifted off, I feared I might not wake up. Sleep, as unwelcome as it was, offered my only fleeting moments of peace, though. I finally succumbed to it, lulled by the soft sounds of Rankor and Kent's snores and the low murmur of Iris and Clay talking nearby.

"I hate him for doing this to her," Iris said, her voice sharp and filled with barely contained fury.

"Not as much as I do," Clay replied, his tone heavy.

She snorted bitterly. "Then why haven't you done anything to stop him, Clay?"

"You know that I've done what I can."

"Come on, Clay! You're *still* just playing your part, even now."

There was a pause, thick with tension.

"You have no idea what I'm working towards."

"And you have no right to cry over her," Iris continued, her voice trembling with anger. "You've lost that right. For multiple reasons."

"I can't be with her, Iris!" Clay's voice rose, raw and defensive. "We can't be with each other. She reminds me of that every opportunity she gets."

"She's trying to protect herself!" The sound of fabric rustling and the creak of floorboards punctuated her words.

"Iris, I'm doing what I have to do as the next king of this country."

She laughed, cold and dark. "Funny. I imagine that's exactly what your father was thinking when he threatened her."

Silence. A heavy, suffocating silence.

Finally, Clay spoke, his voice low and dangerous. "He did what?"

Iris laughed again, but it was a bitter, joyless sound. "He told her that if she didn't end things with you, he'd remove her from the Council and send her to live overseas. I imagine he was just doing what he had to do as the king of this country."

"Please, Iris," Clay said, his voice cracking. "Try to understand—"

"Get out, Clay." Her voice was firm, resolute. "I don't want you here. And soon enough, she won't want you here either."

Cold sweat trickled slowly down the skin between my breasts as my body refused to stop trembling. I was hot and cold all at once, wide awake but bone-deep tired, ravenous yet nauseous. My body was a battlefield of contradictions as it fought the lingering traces of venom.

But at last, I was awake and sitting up.

Rankor slouched at the foot of my bed, snoring so loudly that the blankets shuddered under his head. Gently, I stretched my foot under the blankets and nudged his head until he snorted so loudly he woke himself and lurched to alertness.

"You're awake!" he exclaimed.

I grinned. "And you snore like a pig."

His face twisted in an expression of indignation. "I do not!"

He stood as I stretched wide like a cat, approaching me with concern before running his fingers across my forehead. "How are you feeling?"

"Like a mythical creature bit me," I replied grumpily, frowning as I tried to piece together my fragmented memories from the trial. "What happened?"

His brows lifted. "What do you remember?"

"Not too much after I killed it."

"The Dragon tried to stop anyone from helping, but we carried you back here and had the nurses examine you. You've been in and out of sleep for a few days with a fever. We weren't sure you would ever wake up."

I chuckled softly. "I'm basically impossible to kill at this point."

Rankor shook his head and leaned down to press an affectionate kiss on my head. "Don't jinx it. I'll go summon a nurse."

I relieved myself in the bathroom while I waited for him to return. The reflection that greeted me in the mirror had certainly seen better days. My hair was oily and matted to my head and my skin was paler than I had ever seen it before. With my muscles still aching though, all I could manage the strength for was to fold my hair into a simple braid before the nurse came to examine me.

"Remarkable what you did out there, Lady Moore," the nurse said as I settled back into bed. "You seem to be recovering well. The fever is to be expected, but I can already sense your strength returning."

"How long will the fever last?" Rankor asked, his brow furrowed with concern.

"Hopefully it'll break overnight. Try to get some more rest, my lady."

Rest was the last thing I wanted after two days of unconsciousness. What I really wanted, what I needed, was some roasted meat, peppered broth, and those little chocolates from the palace kitchen. My mouth positively watered at the thought, but the exhaustion weighing down my limbs kept me pinned to the bed.

The nurse left me with strict instructions to drink the tonic she'd prepared and offered Rankor a warm smile before departing. I let my head fall back against the pillows as she left, my eyes drifting closed despite my restless mind.

The brief reprieve didn't last long.

"Your Grace!" I heard the nurse cry out. "You startled me. I didn't expect to see you back so soon."

Rankor was out of his chair in an instant, nearly barreling into the nurse as he moved from my bedchamber into the parlor to block the doorway into the suite.

"Don't you have other matters to attend to, *Your Grace*?" Rankor asked, his voice sharp and uncharacteristically hostile.

"I'm not here to argue with you," Clay said, his voice trembling slightly. "I just need to see her. Please."

I could almost feel his concern, a palpable force radiating through the air.

"She should rest," Rankor insisted. "Why don't you go attend to all your princely responsibilities and wait to see her at tomorrow's Ascension with everyone else?"

Tomorrow. The word sent a wave of anticipation—and dread—crashing through me. After a year of preparation, my trials were over, and I was set to ascend to the Council tomorrow.

"It's okay," I called, struggling to stand.

The room fell silent as the two men turned toward me, their chests high. Rankor's face was a mask of fury, while Clay, with his overgrown hair and the shadow of a beard darkening his jawline, looked utterly ragged. Without a word, Rankor shoved past him, knocking his shoulder hard, before he slammed the door behind him.

"What's gotten into him?" I asked, my voice hoarse.

Clay didn't answer. His eyes roved over me, and a new kind of tension settled into the room.

"You wore that in front of him?" Clay's voice was low, his eyes sparking gold with intensity.

It was only then I realized how I looked. My fever had left me unbearably hot, and at some point, I'd stripped off my tunic and pants, leaving me in nothing but a thin white shift that barely grazed the tops of my thighs. My braided hair exposed my collarbone, and a rosy hue flushed my skin.

Clay's gaze lingered on the exposed skin of my legs, the anger in his expression shifting into something far more complicated. Jealousy was there, and concern, but beneath it all was fear.

"I'm okay," I whispered.

I took a step toward him, but my legs wobbled, and he was at my side in an instant, catching me before I could fall.

"Gods, Thea," he breathed, his grip firm and steady. "You scared me out there."

"I was a bit scared too," I admitted, breathlessly. "But I'm fine. It's just a little fever."

His hand moved to cup my face and slowly his thumb trailed over my bruised lower lip, pulling down the flesh slightly to examine where I had bitten into it during the trial. His eyes darkened and concern flashed on his features as he did, but the touch was so intimate, so sensual, that I nearly swayed for an entirely different reason.

"You shouldn't be here," I murmured.

His eyes closed, and he rested his forehead against mine. "Don't make me leave. I just—I just need to hold you for a minute. Please."

My stupid heart wrenched, wanting things it couldn't have. My trials were over. I would be engaged in a matter of days, married to another man in just a few weeks. I shouldn't be alone in my bedroom pressed against the Crown Prince.

And yet, there was something about the lingering terror in his eyes and the way he said please that made all my restraint shatter around me.

"I'm okay," I whispered again, needing him to believe it.

His arms wrapped around my waist, pulling me against his chest. He buried his face in my neck, breathing me in, holding me as though I might vanish. His grip was tight, almost desperate.

Clay had lived through an unspeakable amount of pain in his life, typically at the hands of his own father. He'd watched the Dragon murder his mother when he was just a boy, and now he had to watch his father continuously find new ways to torment me. He did what he could to protect me, but there was only so much that even he could do.

The trials were one of those things he hadn't been able to protect me from.

But the trials were over

And I *was* okay.

"Do people know you're here?" I asked softly, my mind returning to the consequences of this moment.

"You don't have to worry about that," he said, but the tension in his voice betrayed him.

"I do though," I said, thinking back to the Dragon's threats.

"I won't let him hurt you again," he vowed, pulling back to meet my eyes. The veins around his neck darkened, and his golden gaze burned with intensity. "You need to trust me on that."

I traced the veins with my fingers, watching as they faded under my touch. His expression softened, but his words still hung heavy in the air.

"You didn't answer my question."

He looked away. "I took a couple of the palace tunnels to get into this wing. The nurses know I've been spending time in here while you've been sick, though. Word has spread."

Panic flared in me, and I tried to pull back, but his grip tightened.

"Don't," he said firmly, holding me even closer to him. "Don't you dare tell me I should've been anywhere else. I know exactly where I should be—right here, with you. There's no version of this life where I wouldn't have been by your side, waiting to see you open your eyes again."

His declaration stole the breath from my lungs, filling me with warmth and dread in equal measure.

"Clay, you can't say that to me."

"I know that, Thea." He ran a hand through his hair haphazardly. "Gods, I know I can't say that. I know I can't even think it or feel it. I know very well that I can't crave you as much as I do, but…"

His voice trailed off as he met my gaze, as his eyes lowered to my lips.

My body was humming. All aches and pains were long ago forgotten. All I could think about now was how close he was standing to me, how much he smelt like cinnamon, how warm his fingers were against the back of my neck.

"But?" I whispered, sounding as needy as I felt.

The air was thick, tension coiling in the space between us, charging the air so intensely that nothing else seemed to matter.

Clay lifted his gaze from my lips, locking eyes with me again, staring so deeply that I wondered if he could see my soul.

"Fuck it."

He moved suddenly, taking hold of my face, pulling, and swallowing my words with the press of his lips against mine.

Gods.

Every thought, every concern, every fear was gone.

Clayton Vail was kissing me.

My body ignited with the feel of him until every part of me was singing and acutely aware of the places his fingers met my skin. His tongue darted over the purple bruise that lingered on my lower lip, soothing it with his gentleness, and I sighed against him, unable to stop myself from arching into his firm grasp. I fisted my palms into his shirt, not caring if I wrinkled his finely tailored black jacket.

He groaned into my mouth, the sound sending fresh heat through my fevered body as his hands snaked back to the nape of my neck to pull me closer to him, and I went willingly.

"I almost lost you," he whispered, pulling away to trail his lips across my jaw before pressing scorching kisses against the length of my throat. I arched, letting him support my weight when my weak knees couldn't do so on their own.

"I'm right here," I promised him. "I'm not going anywhere."

Truly.

I wasn't dying, nor was I planning on leaving his embrace.

My self-restraint fractured into tiny shards, lingering between us as months of tension and longing, and an overwhelming need for each other, could no longer be contained. I pulled his face to mine again, tangling my tongue with his, and I ran my hands through his silken hair.

A delicate throat clearing broke us apart as quickly as we had come together.

Nessira stood in the doorway of my bathing chamber, one hand over her eyes and the hint of a smile on her lips.

"I apologize, my lady," she said lightly. "I wasn't aware you had company, but I believe Miss Emeryn will visit shortly to discuss the Ascension."

Right.

Of course, Emeryn would be on her way. She had stopped by shortly after the completion of both of my previous trials to discuss the next steps. I should have known she would come to visit me today now that I had woken.

My body flushed brilliantly red, and I pulled the small quilt off my bed to wrap it around myself, suddenly aware of the fact that my shift was indeed rather revealing. I hadn't even heard the door as Nessira came in. Gods, anyone could have walked in on us and we wouldn't have even realized.

Reckless. We had been so idiotically reckless.

"Nessira." Clay's voice shook slightly as he smoothed his shirt. "I know I have no right to ask, but I would appreciate your discretion."

Her eyes sparkled with poorly concealed amusement. "I do not know what you're referencing, Your Grace."

"Right." Clay nodded and, with a fleeting glance back at me, backed out of my rooms and let the door fall heavily closed behind him.

The silence stretched for a moment before Nessira burst into laughter. Groaning, I flopped back onto the bed, pulling the quilt over my face.

That had been a mistake, one I couldn't risk making again.

Even if his touch on my face and neck would remain burned into my memory for the rest of my days in this realm.

CHAPTER EIGHT

My life is going to change today.

The idea had been running through my mind since the second I woke, on an endless repeat, no matter what I did to ignore it.

I shook my head as if to shake it out of my thoughts while I smoothed my thumb over the parchment before me. The slate pencil rested between my teeth as I shaded the delicate edges of a rose petal. My sketches were clumsy, uneven at best, but that was part of why I enjoyed the task.

It seemed like everything else in my life came too easily.

My status as a Descendant of Hyrax bestowed upon me riches, jewels, and high social standing. It had initially taken some time for me to gain control over my magic, but now it flowed through me easily. Power that others could only dream of commanding. Even fighting had come naturally, as if I'd been born knowing how to wield my body as a weapon.

But drawing was different.

I was absolutely terrible at it.

I'd been practicing every day, determined to develop a skill that was earned. And while I was still a long way off from painting any murals on the palace wall, the practice brought me a good bit of peace.

Peace that I desperately needed. Especially today.

Today, I would ascend to the Council.

Months of endless preparation had all led to this single day. What had at first been forced upon me had become something I wanted to embrace. Yet, as I sat here waiting for the ceremony, I felt strangely uneasy.

Something about this all felt... wrong.

It made little sense. I *belonged* on the Council. I was the last Descendant of Hyrax, the only one who could claim my family's seat. I had trained, studied, and sacrificed to be here. I was ready.

So why didn't I feel that way?

My emotions were all over the place. Desperate for Clay one day and rejecting him the next. Wanting to share all my secrets with Iris and my friends in one moment and being entirely unable to share my dreams of Hyrax the next. And all the while, I hated myself more and more.

"It's time," Nessira called, pulling me from my thoughts.

Worry pinched her lips, an expression she wore more often than not these days.

"Samsa, go prepare the bath for Lady Moore," Nessira instructed the young girl she had hired as my second Lady-in-Waiting.

When the girl's thin frame and pale blonde hair retreated to the bathing chamber, Nessira slowly approached me, crossing her arms unhappily across her chest as she eyed the remains of my breakfast from where it sat on a tray at the edge of my bed.

"You ate little," she noted.

"I wasn't hungry."

She nodded with a thoughtful expression. "You haven't eaten much at all recently."

"I'm fine, Nessira." I stood abruptly, brushing my hands together to rid them of pencil dust, and moved to walk past her, desperate to avoid this conversation. It was bad enough to deal with Dimitri, Rankor, and Clay constantly fretting over my health. I didn't need her piling on.

"My Lady!" Nessira's voice was sharp as she stepped in the way of my path.

With anyone else, her tone would have gotten her removed from her post.

"I'm worried," she said simply.

I sighed, running tired hands through the ends of my tangled curls. After spending days in bed with the fever, it had been too long since I'd brushed through it. It probably looked as hopeless as I felt.

"Don't be," I muttered.

"You're not eating or sleeping, my lady," she pressed, her voice softening. "It's plain to anyone with eyes you're still carrying the weight of Lorelai Pelland's death. Your sadness is unending, it seems."

"You speak as if I deserve to feel anything else," I snapped, the bitterness in my voice cutting through the air.

She looked away for a moment, and when she looked towards me again, the change was obvious. Her expression was no longer worried or angry.

She pitied me.

"Lady Moore," she said gently. "Lorelai's death was *not* your fault. You deserve to feel more. You deserve to feel all manner of happiness."

I laughed darkly. "Even if I were to excuse myself with the weight of her death, you assume I'm not capable of causing even greater destruction."

She frowned. "Why would you think that?"

The words hovered on the tip of my tongue, the truth begging to be set free. But the confession died on my tongue.

I couldn't share the prophecy with anyone. Not even Nessira.

After a long moment, I simply told her I was ready for my bath and strode into the bathing chamber.

She let the conversation fall away, thankfully, and left me to soak in the lavender scented water for longer than necessary while she and Samsa gathered everything they would need to prepare me for the ascension ceremony.

When they returned, long after my skin had pruned, they helped slide on my dress. It was unlike anything I'd ever worn before. The deep violet fabric rippled with sparkling embroidery. The sweetheart neckline showed my chest, where Nessira had carefully painted the Mark of Hyrax. Diamond pins adorned my elegantly twisted hair, their weight unfamiliar but regal. A massive fur-lined golden cape draped over my shoulders, its clasp heavy against my collarbone.

"You're ready," Nessira said, adjusting a stray curl.

Was I though?

Her eyes searched mine, and something in my face must have given her pause. She dismissed Samsa with a glance and disappeared into my closet, returning moments later with my dagger and thigh sheath.

"You know?" I gasped.

Nessira said nothing. She only helped me to lift my skirt and secure the blade into place.

I grasped onto her hand as she stood. "Thank you, Nessira. I appreciate your friendship."

With a small smile, she squeezed my hand in return. "And I appreciate yours."

The organ music was supposed to be uplifting. Traditionally played for ascensions, weddings, and coronations, it was meant to inspire awe and hope. Yet, as the heavy chords cascaded over me, I couldn't help but to find it all a bit ominous. From my place in the carriage, I could hear it faintly beneath the murmur of voices as the people of Athenia filed into the Temple of the Gods.

"Is it odd that the first time I've been to the Temple is for my ascension?" I mused aloud, almost to myself.

Across from me, Emeryn's head snapped up. She'd been silent for most of the ride, scanning her notes on the day's itinerary.

"You haven't?" she hissed. "Oh, that's no good. The optics are terrible. Try not to mention that to anyone. And don't gawk when you go inside."

Her words made me chuckle softly. The things Emeryn worried about always seemed so... trivial. Although, I supposed that's why they assigned her to manage my affairs. She cared about the details I couldn't bring myself to consider.

These days, that list was only growing longer.

If Hyrax and the Underworld didn't consume my mind, Lorelai and Iris preoccupied it. My mind constantly bounced from one dark thought to the next, only allowing me the briefest of moments to consider the Council or my ascension.

The air outside the carriage stilled, and a sharp tension settled over me.

It was time.

Emeryn tapped on the carriage door, signaling Dimitri. He opened it swiftly and helped her down before turning to me. His hand was firm as I stepped onto the cobblestone street, and after he was sure I found my footing, he released me, falling to one knee with his head bowed and one hand over his heart.

"It has been my honor to serve you, my Lady. I will be with you today and always."

My heart stuttered as my jaw fell slightly open. Instinctively, I wanted to tell him to stand, to insist there was no need for such a display, but Emeryn's sharp glare pinned me in place. Of course, he was bowing. This was my ascension, and that was the respect the ceremony required.

"Thank you, Dimitri," I murmured, my voice soft but steady.

He rose and followed as I climbed the marble steps toward the temple's grand wooden doors. They loomed before me, twice my height, with intricate stained-glass windows that told stories of Gods and legends. The wind stirred gently, brushing against my neck as I took in the towering structure.

Hyrax wasn't on the windows.

Of course he wasn't. There were no depictions of him.

"Are you nervous?" A familiar, melodic voice broke through my thoughts.

I turned to see Kent standing to my right, dressed in his finest military regalia. His orange jacket caught the sunlight, giving his tawny skin a warm glow, and medals gleamed across his chest.

"What are you doing here?" I asked, pulling him into a quick hug despite Emeryn's protests about my dress.

"Typically, a husband or relative would escort you."

"And I have neither of those."

"You don't," he agreed, offering his arm to me as we ascended the final steps. "But I have a great-great-aunt descended from Hyrax, so I volunteered."

"I didn't know that!" I squeezed his arm, grateful for his presence. "Thank you."

"You didn't answer my question."

I raised a brow, pretending not to understand.

"Are you nervous?"

For a moment, my stomach churned, and my thoughts flashed to my first appearance in Athenia. That day, I'd been terrified, a scared girl thrust into a world she didn't understand.

But I wasn't that girl anymore.

"No," I lied, fixing my gaze on the temple doors. "I just want to get this over with."

Kent's shoulders shook with quiet laughter, but he didn't acknowledge the untruth. "Very well. Let's go, then."

The heavy wooden doors creaked open and inside, an aisle lined with rose petals stretched before us, flanked by hundreds of Athenians standing shoulder to shoulder. For a heartbeat, the room froze, every gaze fixed on me. Then, in unison, they fell to their knees, arms crossed over their hearts in a gesture of reverence.

"I take it back. I can't do this," I muttered under my breath, overwhelmed by the weight of their devotion. My magic churned within me, wild and restless, as if rebelling against the moment.

"There's nothing you can't do, Thea," Kent said softly, tugging me forward. "You're the most powerful person I've ever met, and it has very little to do with your bloodline. You love these people, and they see that. This is the most widely attended court event in decades because of you, because they want you representing them. You're their chosen leader, and they didn't choose poorly."

Tears pricked at my eyes as I leaned into him briefly. With each step, the aisle seemed longer, the platform at the end farther away. I don't know if I would have been able to make it from one end to the other without the help of Kent's arm keeping me grounded, but I kept walking, and I held my head high, until we reached the raised dais.

The Dragon stood waiting, his expression inscrutable as his eyes raked over me. The other Council members—Clara, Gregory, and Rosalia—flanked him, their faces solemn.

Kent released my arm and bowed deeply. "I swear my heart, sword, and allegiance to you, Lady Moore, and to the House of Hyrax. Praise the Gods, and long may the Council prevail."

He stood, winked, and made his way to where Rankor and Iris sat in the front row. They were the words tradition dictated, the words everyone in this room would recite before the day was over, but they meant more from him. Kent meant those words because Kent valued me as a friend and not a Council member.

I turned to my friends, hopeful that I could express my gratitude in my expression alone, and stumbled back against the sudden rush of joy that overwhelmed me as I looked at them. Rankor's pride was undeniable. Kent nodded at me reassuringly. And Iris... Iris' hair was blue.

Iris'.

Hair.

Was.

Blue!

I could have screamed and jumped with elation upon looking at the cerulean waves that cascaded to her waist.

She wore a steel colored shift-style gown that clasped at her shoulders with two golden bangles and fell shapelessly to the ground. It was a far cry from her previous choices, which often included glittering fabrics, floral applicaes or sparkling gems, but it wasn't black. It was progress. She was coming back to me.

"Kneel," the Dragon commanded, his tone sharp enough to pull me back to the moment. "Lady Theadora Moore, you have come to this sacred temple for what purpose?"

I lowered myself, bowing my head as the ceremony began. The words fell over me one by one, each a link in the chain binding me to the Council.

"I wish to declare my intent to ascend to the Royal Council of Athenia."

"Do you attest to successful completion of the qualifying trials necessary to ascend the Royal Council?"

I shivered against the memory of Hydraxan venom fighting its way out of my system. Yes, I could certainly attest to that. Briefly, I lifted my gaze to the Dragon, who glanced down at me with a devilish glint in his eyes. No doubt he was remembering my agony as well.

"I do," I said through locked teeth.

"To serve on the Royal Council of Athenia is to serve the people of Athenia. Do you, Lady Theadora Moore, swear to protect this land and her people with your breath, magic, and soul from this moment until the moment you relinquish this role to your next of kin?"

"I do."

"And do you, Lady Theadora Moore, swear fealty to Athenia above all else and loyalty to this Council and no one else?"

"I do."

Each vow wrapped around me like an invisible vice, binding me tighter to the role I now held. The chamber was silent, the weight of the moment pressing down on every soul in attendance.

"And do you, Lady Theadora Moore, a daughter of Hyrax, swear that the House of Hyrax can continue this role in your stead should you no longer be able to fill this seat?"

There it was - the question I had been truly dreading.

The question was simple for other Council members. There were dozens, if not hundreds, of other family members that could step in and fill their shoes should they be unable. Swearing to this on behalf of their Houses was an easy promise to make, perhaps the easiest of the ceremony. For me, it was more. For me, I was swearing to create another Descendant of Hyrax.

There was no one else to fill this seat unless I continued the family line. That was the burden that had haunted me since the day I first arrived in Athenia. That was the necessity that had loomed over me while I tried to delay my engagement. That was what everyone thought was my purpose in this realm. I was the only Descendant of Hyrax, and they were asking me to swear that I wouldn't be the last.

"I do," I said, my voice echoing through the chamber.

"Then rise, Lady Theadora Moore, of House Hyrax, and begin your ascension to the Royal Council of Athenia."

He extended a hand to me and pulled me to my feet. I expected some untoward comment to be whispered to me as I made my way to the golden dish that sat atop a pedestal at the center of the platform, but his eyes were deadly serious and entirely focused on the task at hand.

The other Council members joined us, and together the five of us formed a circle around the pedestal. From his jacket pocket, the Dragon pulled out a golden dagger with a ruby-encrusted handle. Without flinching, he sliced the blade across his palm and let his scarlet blood trickle into the golden bowl.

"The blood of Zion!" he announced.

"Praise Zion!" the crowd cheered.

He handed the dagger to Rosalia next, who followed his lead. The only sign of her pain at the wound was a slight purse of her lips as her blood joined his within the dish.

"The blood of Delia!" she called, bringing her eyes to the crowd, who echoed her.

Gregory was next, adding his blood to the bowl on behalf of Herea before Clara did the same on behalf of Palaemon. And then, the existing Council members turned to me.

This was it. This was the moment everyone in the world had been waiting for.

It was time to complete the Athenian Council.

Clara passed the dagger to me with an encouraging smile, and I gripped it in my fingers, ignoring the nervous energy that overwhelmed me while I raised my other hand to meet the pointed blade. The metal pierced my skin with only the smallest amount of pressure, and I hissed through my teeth against the sting. After only a moment of hesitation, I dragged the blade down my palm until my scarlet blood rose easily and fell in droplets out of my hand into the bowl. I stared at it, watching as it mingled with the blood of the other Council members until it was impossible to tell which droplet came from who.

When I lifted my head, I was acutely aware of the attention that was on me. The air was thick with eager anticipation as the audience stared up at me with wanting smiles.

"The blood of Hyrax!" I yelled.

"The blood of Hyrax!" they called back to me. And as his name echoed in the temple around us, I could only wonder if he was in the Underworld, somehow aware that this was happening.

CHAPTER NINE

I needed to close my mouth. My jaw had been dangling open for far longer than was polite, but no matter how hard I tried, I couldn't seem to manage it.

I could only describe the scene in front of me as utterly perplexing. Everything I thought I knew suddenly seemed... wrong. I was witnessing something that seemed entirely contrary to every expectation I'd previously held.

"You're staring," Rankor chastised under his breath as he came to stand at my side.

My jaw snapped shut with an audible thunk.

"I can't help it!" I admitted. "It's just that I've never seen him—"

"Show a personality?"

Instinctively, I smacked his arm, earning a soft chuckle as he pulled me away from where I had been watching Kent play with his younger sisters.

"It's true," Rankor continued, tucking me into his arm as we paraded through the great hall.

The Dragon had thrown a proper ball in my honor. I had, of course, seen celebrations held in this space before, but none were quite as grand or as raucous as this one. The entire country was celebrating their Council. They danced and drank, laughed and ate. The people were happy, and that was what mattered. Now that I was officially a Council member, I needed to prioritize their happiness above the uneasiness that constantly filled me.

"Kent's always been a bit reserved. The only time he's not boring is when he's on stage."

"You're so rude," I scoffed, aware of the playfulness in his tone. Rankor loved Kent like a brother; that much was obvious to anyone with eyes.

"I only mean to say, he comes alive around his family. It's something special to see."

"They're Mortals?" I asked, searching for the signature of a Descendant's Mark on their skin but not finding it as Kent and the younger girls chased each other around their mother. She looked tired at first glance, but still happy.

"He's the only Descendant in the family. They thought all the blood had been washed out, but then he was born with his Mark. His dad was a fisherman in a small village along the shore, but he passed from a bad heart a year after the twins were born. His mom tried to get by, but when the military knocked on the door to scout him at twelve, Kent didn't hesitate. He promised he'd sign up on the spot as long as they made sure his mom and sisters were taken care of."

Twelve.

My heart stuttered. That was so young to be taken from your family. No wonder Kent had latched onto Rankor and the others. He'd needed a family.

Just like I had needed one when I first arrived here.

"And you?" I asked, scanning the room for other towering figures with dark hair and dimples. "Did your family come for the celebration?"

He shook his head, reaching for an apple from the fruit tray along the wall and biting into it eagerly. "My parents are both gone. My younger brother sends his congratulations, though. He couldn't get away from his sheep, but he's dying to meet you one day."

"He's a shepherd?"

Rankor chuckled under his breath, his eyes somewhere distant. "A damn proud one at that."

"And my parents refuse to step foot in this cursed land," Iris said, joining us with a drink in hand. "No offense to your Council, my Lady."

Anger rolled off her in waves as her heavy eyes scanned the scene. Her sour mood was at odds with the room's merriment, which only seemed to upset her more.

"Gods, some of these people should really take a dance lesson," she noted, watching a couple struggle to stay in time.

"Well, we can't all be effortlessly elegant," I teased, bumping my shoulder against hers.

She met my eyes with a small smile. "Am I supposed to congratulate you on signing your life over to that man?"

Her reference to the Dragon was obvious.

"I didn't have a choice."

"I know," she said, glaring at the Dragon from where he sat on his throne examining his cuticles. "You didn't. I just think it's time for people to start creating some other choices for themselves."

"Iris," Rankor said sharply, stepping closer. "Some thoughts are better kept in private quarters, before someone mistakes them for treason."

Iris turned away from him, not bothering to acknowledge the warning. Her gaze swept the room before locking on the center of the ballroom. Suddenly, she stilled, her shoulders rising as her jaw snapped shut. Without a word, she shoved her drink into my hand and practically fled.

I sighed, downing the rest of her drink in one fluid motion.

"Jeez," Rankor muttered, running a hand through his long hair. "I didn't mean to upset her so much."

"It wasn't you," I said, my gaze landing on the spot she'd been staring at. They had scrubbed the floor clean since the attack during Clay's birthnight celebration, but I couldn't forget that Lorelai's blood had stained the marble there.

"You ever feel like it's one step forward and three steps back with her?" Kent asked, joining us slightly out of breath. His sisters were now piling their plates with cupcakes at the dessert table.

"She's grieving," I said. "That's not an easy process."

"Still," Rankor said, passing Kent a glass of dark wine. "Seems like it's always just the three of us these days."

"It's okay to admit you like having my undivided attention," Kent teased, punching Rankor's arm playfully.

I was about to smile when it hit me. It was just the three of us here.

"Where's Clay?" I demanded, my tone sharp.

Obviously, things had been tense between us lately, but certainly his duty required him to be at the ascension of a Council member. As Emeryn would say, the optics of his notably being missing from today's events were terrible. Clayton was the Crown Prince. He would one day preside over the very Council I was now sitting on. This major ceremony and celebration surely required his presence.

So why wasn't he here?

Kent's face darkened as he stared at his boots. Rankor shifted with an irritated huff.

"Apparently not here," Rankor snapped.

"Alright, that's it!" I said. "What's going on with you two?"

Before I could press further, the sound of a knife against glass echoed through the ballroom. The Dragon was rising from his throne.

"Friends, family, and honored guests," he called as the room quieted. "It is my honor to welcome you into my home. Some of you have traveled very far, and I speak on behalf of the Council in expressing our sincerest gratitude."

A hand tugged my arm, and I tensed, power flaring in my fingertips.

"Calm yourself," Rosalia hissed, linking her arm with mine and pulling me forward. "When he speaks on behalf of the Council, we're expected to join him."

Right. I wasn't just Theadora Moore anymore. I was a Council member.

Rosalia deposited me at the Dragon's right, completing the line of five for the first time in years.

"Lady Moore—Thea," the Dragon corrected himself, his smile practiced. "Your arrival in our kingdom was unexpected, but it has been a joy to watch you blossom. We are lucky to have you on the Council. To Thea, to the House of Hyrax, and to the kingdom of Athenia!"

He raised his glass, and the crowd followed suit, shouting their praises. But as he leaned close, his smile twisted.

"I warned you not to continue this dance with my son," he whispered. "Now the Court has seen him openly defy me for *you*."

Panic rose in me.

"We are so lucky you call Athenia home," the Dragon continued to the crowd. "And tonight we have so many reasons to celebrate you. Not only has Lady Moore ascended to the Council, but she has given me her permission to deliver a very special announcement!"

And in two days' time, Lady Moore will set sail for Tenebris to meet her fiancé, my nephew Veric Starsen of House Zion."

The blood drained from my face. The crowd waited in silence. Time slowed.

"As of this morning, Lady Moore is engaged to be married to my nephew, Veric Starsen of House Zion. In two days' time, she will set sail for Tenebris to celebrate her engagement in her fiancé's homeland before they return home to Athenia!"

The Dragon smiled, lifting his glass toward me in mock congratulations and I did the best I could to paint a pleasant expression on my face..

This game he insisted on playing with me would have consequences—for the rest of my life.

CHAPTER TEN

I *hated to admit it, but walking through the cold, dusty caverns of the Underworld felt like a welcome reprieve from my waking life after the announcement of my engagement. Dealing with my lying ancestor was somehow preferable to watching the Dragon revel in my misery.*

I had known the engagement was coming, of course. I'd known it for some time now. Once I joined the Council, it was only a matter of time. Still, the announcement had caught me off guard. It had felt like the very floor had fallen out from under me. Undoubtedly, that had been the Dragon's intention all along. He'd wanted to see my shock, frustration, and despair. He'd wanted to see me blush. And I had given him exactly what he wanted.

I disgusted myself by letting him win.

As I swept open the doors to Hyrax's throne room, I braced myself for another patronizing, evasive conversation. Sighing, I stepped inside and froze.

He wasn't here.

That was odd.

Hyrax was always here. Every time I entered this realm, he sat waiting for me with wine in hand and that dreadful melancholic music playing. But now, the room was empty. The fire burned low in the hearth, casting fleeting shadows across the room and filling it with an eerie chill.

The silence was unnerving.

I had rarely been alone in this realm. My first visits had been clumsy and disorienting, marked by near-disasters and one too many brushes with danger. But now...

Well, if Hyrax wasn't here, what was a girl to do but explore?

I needed a distraction, after all. Something to pull me away from the weight of politics, councils, and unwanted marriages. What better distraction was there than seeing what this realm offered?

A mischievous grin tugged at my lips as my eyes scanned the room, settling on a door behind the throne. With a glance over my shoulder, I moved toward it, careful not to touch the bones that made up the throne. I didn't want to think about whether they were real.

The door opened into a winding hallway. Smooth gray walls replaced the rough stone tunnels I was used to, and torches lit the way with a soft, flickering glow. At a crossroads—door to the left, hallway to the right—I hesitated, chewing on my lip.

Was I in a castle?

Did this realm stretch beyond the caverns and throne room?

It had to. There had to be somewhere where the souls of the dead now lived.

"I'll meet with you in a quarter hour," a deep male voice called, shattering my thoughts.

Hyrax.

Panic surged through me as I recognized his voice, its resonance pulling at the power within me. His footsteps echoed, growing louder with each passing second.

What if he didn't take kindly to finding me wandering the Underworld on my own? He might be my ancestor, but he was still a god. And Hyrax wasn't a god anyone wanted to anger.

Turning to retreat, I sucked in a sharp breath as I realized his footsteps were coming from the direction of the throne room.

"What is it, my Lord?" another voice—Caldrius, perhaps.

"I sense Theadora," Hyrax sighed, his footsteps slowing.

Shit.

*He could **sense** me? What did that even mean?*

Without thinking, I pushed open the door to my left and stumbled into the room beyond, closing it quietly behind me.

The scent of smoke and bergamot filled the air as I took in my surroundings. The bedroom was dimly lit and disheveled, but its chaos felt oddly deliberate, as though the owner knew exactly where everything was. Dark tapestries depicting ancient battles hung on the walls, their fabric soft under my fingertips as I traced across them.

A four-poster bed with rumpled black sheets dominated one wall. Next to it, a small wooden desk sat cluttered with slate pencils and crumpled parchments. Drawn to it, I walked gingerly to the desk and lifted one of the crumpled papers, unfolding it carefully to reveal the sketch of a rose not entirely unlike the one I had attempted to draw earlier today. A far more skilled artist than I drew this sketch, but they must have been disappointed, given how carelessly they discarded it. I couldn't imagine why. It was stunning, perfectly accurate in its proportions, and expertly shaded.

"Find something you like?"

I jumped, smothering a yelp as I turned to see Caldrius leaning against the door, arms crossed and eyes focused on me as his lips curled in a teasing smirk. He wore a simple black shirt, noticeably covered in blood, unbuttoned low enough to reveal a tuft of dark hair.

Flustered, I stepped back instinctively, but my heel caught on the edge of a rug. Caldrius moved faster than I expected, a hand catching my elbow before I could stumble. Warm. Steady. Unshakable.

"Easy," he murmured, amusement flickering in his eyes. He didn't let go right away, and for a fraction of a second, the warmth of his grip was the only thing I could focus on.

I yanked myself free, heat flooding my cheeks. "Do you make it a habit to lurk in dark shadows and sneak up on unsuspecting women?"

He raised an eyebrow, smirking at me playfully. "I don't think one can lurk in their own bedchamber, love."

My heart lurched, and the parchment fell from my fingers, floating haphazardly back to the desk as I stepped back and smoothed my fingers against the skirts of my dress.

"My apologies, I hadn't realized."

"You know, if you wanted a private tour of my room, all you had to do was ask." His voice was thick with double meaning.

The warmth in my cheeks grew, spreading down the back of my neck as I scoffed at him. "Of course I didn't come here for that!"

"No?" He crossed the room, seating himself on the edge of the bed as he undid his boots. "So you make it a habit to break into rooms uninvited?"

I chewed on my lip, closing my eyes as I pinched my arm aggressively. Maybe I could just force myself to wake up and this would be over. I would no longer be trapped in a dark bedroom with a madman. If I could only wake up—

"It's fine if you want to hide out for a little while. He's looking for you, but I sent him toward the lake. I won't tell him you're in here if you don't want."

Frowning, I tilted my head slightly. "And why would you keep that from Hyrax? You're his second-in-command, aren't you?"

"I am." He nodded. "And you're obviously upset. So I won't tell him you're here if you don't want to see him."

I opened my mouth to respond, only for the words to fall helplessly between us. Truthfully, that level of kindness wasn't something I had expected from the man whose violence was so profound his own brother had had to flee from him and start a new country. The man who now was closer to Hyrax than anyone had ever been before.

Spare his wife Pasnia perhaps, but I had never actually seen her.

Caldrius smiled softly, as if he could sense how confused I was by him. He stood from the bed and pulled his shirt over his head in one smooth motion, dropping it on the sheets in front of him.

A strangled noise—something between a gasp and a very undignified squeak—escaped me as I spun away.

Too late. The image seared itself into my mind. Broad chest, golden skin dusted with scars, muscles carved like something out of a sculptor's dream.

Absolutely not. I needed to erase the last five seconds from existence.

"What are you doing?" I cried.

His dark laugh fell around me in waves. "I've spent the day dealing with some undesirable companions and am covered in blood. I'd like to change my clothes. No one said you had to look."

I wasn't looking.

I might have initially peeked briefly just to see if he had clothed himself once more, but I quickly turned again when he reached for the buckle of his pants.

"You're very indecent!"

"Not yet."

"Well, couldn't you at least have waited until I left?"

"No," he said simply.

I scoffed, huffing out my frustration and choosing to change the subject. "What kind of undesirable companions do you keep?"

"They're not friends of mine, I assure you. The Underworld is a realm not unlike yours, though. When my liege's subjects get out of line, it's my job to remind them that their existence can be ended anytime he wishes."

I tossed over his words. There wasn't much literature on the Underworld. It had been so many years since the gods had walked among us, and Descendants and Mortals only traveled here after our deaths, so it wasn't like we knew much about this realm in our lives.

"Where does a soul go if it dies here?"

"They don't go anywhere," Caldrius shrugged, stepping forward in loose trousers that hung low on his hips and an unbuttoned shirt. I shivered involuntarily. *"If Hyrax extinguishes a soul, it is a death of a final kind."*

Well, that sounded... unpleasant. Chewing on my lip, I wondered how many years Caldrius had spent here. He'd died centuries ago, of course, but how long had it taken him to get close enough with Hyrax to earn his current position?

"Can I get you something to drink?" He asked, passing in front of me as he made his way to the bar cart that sat near the fireplace. It was nearly empty, but he poked around at it until he pulled out a crystal decanter with amber liquid and held it high. *"Looks like all I have to offer is whiskey."*

"Whiskey is fine," I muttered, making my way to the couch that sat facing the fireplace. I didn't particularly love the idea of sitting and sharing drinks with Caldrius of all people, especially when he was still rather indecently dressed, but I seemed to have very little control over when I entered and left this realm and he was right—I was upset, and I didn't want to see Hyrax. So, I'd have to be okay with his Supreme Lieutenant instead.

"Tell me what's got you so riled up." He passed me a glass and moved to sit on the floor against the wall.

I cocked my head as I looked down at him, somewhat surprised. No one at court would dare sit on the ground so casually, but here I was with a former king who currently nursed his drink with one arm propped up against a bent knee while his dark eyes stared at me.

"I got engaged today," I admitted, tossing my head back to stare at the worn ceiling.

He chuckled, running a hand through the dark waves of his hair, even as dried blood lingered on his fingertips. He let his hair grow long, and it looked unkempt, as if he hadn't bothered to comb it.

Caldrius was so unlike the men I was used to seeing at court, who were so consumed by what others thought of them. He sat with me so casually, *comfortable in his space and in my presence. He was entirely self-assured, so much so that he didn't bother with formalities or titles, neither mine nor his.*

He sat with me as one might with an old friend.

"Not your choice, I presume?" He asked.

"No, it wasn't. Not that that fact matters to anyone but me."

"I refused my arranged marriage."

I jerked my head up so sharply that a cramp settled into the flesh of my neck as I met his gaze. He smiled sadly as I began kneading out the tension.

"My father wasn't happy with it. He had wanted me to marry some duchess or princess, but the day I met Isidore changed everything. Her parents sent her from the kingdom's outskirts to serve as my mother's seamstress. Her talents were undeniable, even as a Mortal, and so eventually she was tasked with making me a jacket for my engagement announcement. Tell me, Thea, do you believe in love at first sight?"

The air was suddenly too warm, too thick.

"I don't know," I whispered.

He chuckled. "Well, I can promise you it exists. Isidore became my sun, and everything besides her was total darkness. We left the palace that night and were married in secret."

"I didn't know you were married."

His eyes darkened as they looked through me, lost in another time and place. "You wouldn't. It wasn't written in most history books."

"What happened to her?" I asked with a frown. For a man who had loved his wife so much, he wore a terrible amount of grief, visible like a dark cloak around him.

And how could anyone in the Underworld experience grief?

This is where souls came after their death, so shouldn't his wife be with him here now?

His face contorted, pain turning to anger. To rage. "I know what they say about me in the Mortal Realm. They paint me as the villain."

"You were the villain," I blurted, unable to stop myself.

His dark eyes scanned over me, lingering on my lips before coming back to meet my gaze. I shivered involuntarily, as I so often did when he focused his attention on me. The intensity with which he looked at me stole my breath and left me uneasy and confused.

"Haven't you learned not to trust your history books by now?"

"Why wouldn't I?"

He shrugged. "You're the daughter of Hyrax. They haven't exactly painted him in the best light either."

"The fact that I descended from him doesn't change what he's done."

"You speak as if you were there. You know only what you've been told about him, about us both. Have you never questioned who's telling you the truth?"

I stood, leaving my emptied glass on the table as I made my way to the door. I wasn't sure where else there was for me to go in this realm, but I knew I couldn't stay here with him any longer.

"Hyrax says you're quite fond of that prince of yours?"

I froze, fingers clenching the doorknob tightly. "I don't see how that's your concern."

"I think he's probably related to me somehow." He ran a hand over his jaw, scratching the skin on his neck gently, as if he was considering it. "Maybe you should ask him about what happened to my wife."

I woke with a jolt, gasping as I lurched out of my bed. As the dream faded and the familiar sights and sounds of my bedchamber settled over me, I couldn't swallow away the unease that lingered. I didn't want to believe

Caldrius. I didn't want to believe that the history books misrepresented him and that he wasn't the monster they depicted.

Because if that were true, then I'd have to open my heart to the possibility that Hyrax was also a victim of falsified histories and I wasn't sure I was ready to forgive the God for lying to me.

As much as I didn't want to believe Caldrius, though, part of me wondered if I should. When he told me to ask Clay about his wife, sadness was visible on his face. He displayed a kind of sadness that couldn't be faked. It was palpable in the purse of his lips and the downcast nature of his eyes. After centuries, his heartache was so still real I could almost feel it myself.

Something had happened to his wife before she had been erased from history.

Which begged the question of *why* she had been erased?

CHAPTER ELEVEN

I laid awake for hours, tossing and turning as I tried to let sleep claim me once more, but it simply refused. My mind was too awake, spiraling with questions about Caldrius.

Nothing about him made sense.

He was a Descendant of Zion, a former king of Zion's line. Now, in death, he served Hyrax, though—not just as a follower, but as his Supreme Lieutenant. There was no one the God trusted more. I'd seen that clearly. But how could a Descendant of Zion, born to oppose Hyrax, become his most devoted servant?

And then there was the mystery of his wife.

Not to mention, Caldrius wasn't the only concern plaguing my mind. I wasn't going to be able to avoid Hyrax forever. I'd already learned the hard way that avoiding sleep wasn't a viable option and I couldn't just outrun him in the Underworld and hide away in secret rooms, not when he could sense my presence in his land.

What I really needed was answers. I needed to figure out why this was happening to me? Was this some twisted extension of Hyrax's power, or something more? Did this happen to all of his Descendants, or was it only me? And most importantly—what did he want with me?

"Ugh!"

I threw off my quilt and reached for the velveteen robe hanging by my bedside, unable to stand my racing thoughts any longer. I tied the sash tightly around my waist and shoved my feet into slippers. It wasn't the most dignified attire for a Council member, but no one would be awake at this hour.

At the last moment, I returned to my dressing chamber to grab my dagger and thigh sheath. Then I slipped out of the Hall of Hyrax, winding through the palace corridors until I reached the spiraling staircase with the golden dragon-scale banister.

I rolled my eyes as I ascended, my fingers brushing the cool metal. I hated that everything here screamed Dragons. Their egos were inescapable.

When I reached the door to Clay's chambers, I hesitated, my hand hovering over the wood. The time had come for me to be honest with him. The weight of these secret visits with Hyrax was crushing me. I couldn't bear another sleepless night, dreading the inevitable pull of the Underworld. Clay cared about me—or at least, I thought he did. We'd moved past suspicion and mistrust. He would believe me when I said I didn't *want* to be visiting Hyrax.

He would protect me.

Finally, I knocked softly, three times.

The door opened swiftly, and I frowned as I met the gaze of a small woman, exactly my height, who laughed at something inside the room before turning to me.

"Lady Moore," she gasped. "What are you doing here? Is everything alright?"

For a moment, I thought I had made a mistake—that this wasn't the Crown Prince's chambers, but someone else's. Then I saw her, *really* saw her.

Porcelain skin. High cheekbones. Full lips curved into a small smile. Her golden-chestnut hair spilled in loose curls around her face, and her silk robe clung to her frame, falling just off her shoulder.

And on her wrist was a silver bracelet that trailed into a ring on her fourth finger. A golden dragon carving glinted on the back of her hand.

My breath hitched as a piercing jolt shook through me.

"Who is it, Elaina?" Clay's voice called from within.

The woman—Elaina—laughed lightly before turning to the room. "It's Lady Moore."

Clay appeared behind her, his gray eyes widening at the sight of me. His chest was bare, his hair damp, and his trousers hung low on his hips.

Dear Gods.

"Thea," he said, his voice tight. A faint blush peppered his cheeks as his gaze darted between me and Elaina. He looked almost... guilty.

"I'm sorry," I stammered, my voice barely audible. My legs were heavy, rooted to the spot, even as every instinct screamed at me to run. I couldn't bring myself to look away from the bracelet locked on her wrist.

"Thea, this is..." His voice trailed off as he stared at me. I wondered if he could see my emotions written plainly on my face. From the odd way Elaina was looking at me, I suspected they both could.

"I'm Elaina," she said, extending her hand toward me. Her smile was dazzling, her tone impossibly kind, as if her presence in his room wasn't destroying my heart and leaving the broken mess of it lying on the floor at her feet. "Clayton's fiancé."

Fiancé.

The word echoed in my mind, but somehow didn't make sense. It couldn't.

I stared down at the hand she held between us. Even her nails were immaculate, perfect oval cylinders on top of her delicate fingers. She was absolutely the most stunning woman I had ever seen. Of course she was. Of course, Clay would be engaged to someone beautiful.

I stared at the bracelet again. The golden dragon carving.

Gods. He had proposed to her with that bracelet and she was holding it out to me like a beacon, waiting for me to grasp onto that hand in a friendly greeting.

"I should go," I muttered, magic sparking beneath my fingertips.

"Thea, wait," Clay said, his voice laced with concern.

The sour taste of bitterness filled my mouth.

Clay was concerned for me. Clay, who was standing half naked in his bedroom alone with his *fiancé*, had the audacity to show concern for my feelings.

He hadn't been concerned enough to find a single moment to tell me he was already engaged or that his fiancé was here in the castle. He hadn't been concerned that fact might bother me when he tangled his hands in my hair, swore he belonged by my side, and kissed me just yesterday.

Iris's voice suddenly echoed in my memory. *"You have no right to cry over her. You lost that right."*

She had known.

"Get out Clay. I don't want you here and soon enough she won't want you here either."

It wasn't just Iris, though.

This was why he'd been fighting with Rankor. This was what Kent and Rankor had been silently communicating about. They had known.

They had *all* known.

And none of them told me.

I was going to be sick.

The world spun around me as Clay stepped closer, and Elaina put a warning touch on his hand. By the Gods, she was touching the hand that had brushed back my hair so recently that I could almost feel it caressing me now.

I turned sharply and retreated down the hall without another word.

"Thea, please!" His footsteps followed me, his voice desperate, but I didn't stop.

I couldn't.

If I stopped, I might break.

My skin burned as magic coursed through me, fueled by the raging storm of my emotions.

It wasn't as though I had any right to be upset. Clay wasn't mine. He had never been mine, and he never could be. I had been the one to remind him of that time and time again. I had no claim to him—his heart or his body.

And yet, the sight of him with another woman was a blow that struck deeper than anything I had endured before.

I burst through the palace doors into the icy chill of the gardens. Frigid winds swept down from the mountains, carrying tiny white flakes that danced against my skin. Their icy touch did nothing to soothe the fire raging inside me though. My magic surged, wild and untamed, as uncontrollable as it had been that first night I'd used it.

That night, Clay had coached me through it. He'd handed me a single rose, his voice steady as he guided me. That memory had seared itself into my mind, vivid and sharp, alongside a hundred others of tender, stolen moments. Moments that felt like nothing now.

Moments that had never meant anything.

I should have known. I'd spent so much time dreading my own marriage, but it had been foolish not to realize that Clay's was inevitable, too. He was the Crown Prince, bound by the same duty and tradition that I was. I should have prepared myself for this.

Knowing something and seeing it unfold before your eyes were entirely different things, though.

This storm inside me wasn't just about his engagement—it was about the lies. He hadn't told me. Had they been engaged the entire time I'd known him? How long has she been walking the same hallways in the castle with me? How could he have left me to stumble upon Elaina in his bedchamber, extending a hand of friendship as if my world hadn't just fallen apart?

I didn't even know her and I hated her for the simple fact that she could have him and I couldn't.

Sprinting, I pushed through the gardens, my feet carrying me toward the valleys between the castle and the mountain. I was losing control. Months of learning to bend magic to my whim were meaningless now, when my emotions were so volatile, which meant I needed to get as far from the castle as I could before it erupted from me and tore down everything it touched.

I tried to steady my breathing, to calm myself, but every inhale brought fresh torment. I saw his hands in her hair. His body moving against hers. I saw him making those unbreakable vows to *her*. Their future together—her perfect, beautiful hand in his, their children laughing as they walked the palace halls right in front of me.

I was going to spend the rest of my life watching him love her.

The thought broke something inside me, and my control finally snapped. Magic coiled under my skin, building until it tore free from my body in a violent rush, so strong it knocked me off my feet. Pain lanced through me as I hit the frozen grass, gasping and trying to steady myself.

And then I froze.

Floating where I had stood moments before was a thread of brilliant golden light. It pulsed faintly, radiating power so familiar it sent shivers down my spine.

It felt like... me.

"What in all of creation did I just do?"

My voice was barely a whisper as I stood and stared down at my hand, as though it belonged to someone else. After everything—after all this time—there were still pieces of myself that I didn't understand.

The question wasn't just *who* I was. It was *what* I was.

A shrill, piercing screech tore me from my thoughts. My gaze snapped to the thread as it pulsed, growing brighter.

And then, clawing its way through the light, came a hand.

A milky white, decaying hand.

An arm emerged, then a leg followed it, until a creature tumbled from the thread and collapsed in a heap before me.

The stench hit me first—foul and rotting, so strong it made my stomach turn. The creature looked human, or like it had once been, but now it was nothing more than a grotesque mass of decayed flesh and exposed muscle, its reptilian eyes wide as it seemed to take in its new surroundings.

And then it turned to me.

It roared, revealing rows of jagged, pointed teeth, before lunging forward with unnatural speed. I barely had time to react before it slammed me to the ground, its claws raking down my arm. Pain flared, hot and sharp, and I screamed, blasting it back with a surge of magic.

I scrambled to my feet, wrestling my dagger from its sheath as the creature charged again, its jaw hanging grotesquely as spit flew into the air.

I darted forward, driving my blade into the underside of its jaw until the hilt met its flesh. The creature froze, its reptilian eyes glazing over before it collapsed, lifeless, at my feet.

Ripping the blade free, I panted, grimacing as its blood dripped onto the grass at my feet. My arm throbbed, the torn skin slick and wet beneath my robe.

Suddenly, the body twitched, and I squealed, instinctually wrapping my magic around it and throwing it back into the light.

The glowing thread of golden light vanished a moment later, leaving no trace of the magic—or the horror—that had emerged from it.

Trembling, I tucked my blood-soaked arm into the sleeve of my robe to hide it from any eyes I might pass on my way back to my rooms.

By the time I ran back through the palace halls and slammed the door shut behind me, all I could do was slide heavily to the floor, shocked by the undeniable truth of the past few hours.

Tonight hadn't just broken my heart. It had left me with yet another secret to keep.

CHAPTER TWELVE

I marched into the training yard, ignoring the biting chill of the air and the snowflakes beginning to drift lazily from the sky. Nessira had insisted I dress warmly before storming out of my rooms, her stern words forcing me into thicker leggings, a fur-lined vest, and sturdy leather boots. The cold bit at my face and hands, but the fury in my chest burned hot enough to keep me moving.

Rankor was demonstrating sword techniques to two young boys as I approached him. His thick coat was hardly battle-ready, but he moved with the easy confidence of someone who had wielded a sword in far worse conditions. When he caught sight of me and grinned, his breath fogging in the crisp air.

"Thea!" he called, sheathing his sword with an exaggerated flourish. "Perfect timing! These boys could use a lesson from someone with *real* skill."

"Sure," I muttered, my voice low and cold.

Without hesitation, I planted my feet, balled my fist, and twisted from the hips just as he'd taught me—then I punched him square in the jaw.

Rankor stumbled back with a strangled noise, clutching his face. "Ow! *Ow*! What in all of creation was *that* for?" He pulled his hand away to inspect the thin trickle of blood on his lip and gawked at me like I'd just set him on fire. "You *punched* me? In front of the children?"

I glanced at the two boys, who stood frozen, their wooden practice swords dangling from their hands. "Leave."

They bolted, their weapons clattering to the ground. Rankor gaped after them. "Cowards," he criticized before turning back to me. "You know, most people start a conversation with *words*."

"Pick up a sword," I ordered.

"What?" His brows furrowed. "I'm not fighting you, Thea."

"Pick up the sword," I snapped, magic flaring beneath my skin.

Rankor let out a long, suffering sigh. "Thea, I'm a *Brawn*. You can't outmatch my strength, and we both know it."

The sword at his feet jerked into the air, hovering ominously before whipping toward him. Rankor let out a strangled yelp and dodged just in time.

"You *might* be stronger," I said, my voice like ice, "but I'm more powerful."

Rankor muttered something under his breath that sounded like a prayer before bending to retrieve his own blade. "Fine, but make a note that I think there are several other ways we could entertain ourselves that do not risk bodily harm."

I didn't answer. Instead, I yanked the floating sword back into my grip and swung at him with a heavy downward stroke. Rankor parried, but his stan

ce was cautious, his movements slow.

"You knew," I hissed.

His brow furrowed. "Knew *what*? That you've finally snapped? Because that's becoming quite clear."

I struck again, forcing him back. The realization dawned in his eyes, followed by regret.

"So" he drawled, "I take it you met Elaina?"

"All this time, I couldn't figure out why you and Clay were fighting so much. How long have you all been keeping this from me?"

Rankor raised his blade defensively. "Clay wanted to tell you himself. He thought it would be better coming from him."

The pity in his tone made my rage flare. I swung harder. He deflected the blow but staggered back, his boots skidding in the snow.

"Clay didn't tell me," I spat. "Elaina did. When she opened his door half-dressed."

Rankor groaned, dragging a hand over his face. "*Gods above, man,*" he hissed, as though Clay could hear him across the palace. He barely dodged my next strike, his movements growing more frantic.

"Thea, why don't you put the sword down and we can *talk* about this?"

"Fight me!" I shouted, aiming a kick at his ribs.

The impact sent him stumbling, and he let out a wheezy laugh. "Are you *sure* you don't want to sit down and breathe deeply first? Maybe count to ten."

I advanced again, blade at the ready.

Rankor held up a single finger, backing away. "I'm beginning to think—hear me out—that maybe, just *maybe*, you should do some *inner work* on how to process difficult feelings."

Irritation flushed through me. I didn't want to talk or process my feelings. I wanted to punch and kick and hit away all the anger and sadness that felt like it was eating me alive.

I slashed my blade towards him. He barely avoided it.

"Or," he panted, ducking another strike, "perhaps a sparring match is exactly what you need. A *controlled* sparring match. With *rules*."

I lunged again, and he dodged dramatically, twisting his body like he was performing some kind of elaborate dance.

"Are you *mocking* me?" I snapped.

"Only a little bit."

I swung again, but this time he miscalculated, his boot catching a patch of ice. With an undignified squawk, Rankor went down, landing flat on his back. He blinked up at me, stunned, then groaned, sprawled in defeat.

"Well," he huffed. "I hope this was cathartic for you."

I pointed my sword at his chest. "Get up, Rankor. You're a war-hero. Stop pretending like anything I'm doing is actually hurting you."

He faked another wheeze. "Or I could just stay here and reflect on my life choices."

I jabbed the blade forward an inch, and he sighed dramatically before dragging himself to his feet.

Before I could swing again, Kent's voice rang out across the yard.

"Enough!"

The sharp command cut through the cold air like a blade. I turned, startled by the raw authority in his tone. Kent never raised his voice. From across the training yard, he approached us with measured steps, his jaw tight, his eyes burning with an anger I had never seen directed at me before.

"Take the boys back to their lessons," he instructed Rankor without breaking stride.

Rankor hesitated, his gaze flicking to me. For once, he didn't have a quip. With a frustrated sigh, he handed his sword to Kent and gestured for the boys to follow him toward the castle. Their protests faded quickly, leaving Kent and me alone in the yard.

I squared my shoulders. "If you're here to lecture me—"

Kent didn't let me finish. Without any warning, he swung the sword mercilessly toward me.

I barely managed to parry. The impact sent a jolt through my arms, and before I could reset my stance, he struck again—fast, sharp, relentless. I moved instinctively, forced to react with more precision than before. Unlike Rankor, Kent *wasn't* holding back.

"You're angry," Kent said, swinging the blade toward me.

"Obviously," I snapped, deflecting another blow.

"And you're lying to yourself if you think this is just about Clay."

His words hit harder than his sword. My grip faltered, my arms dropping slightly.

He took advantage of the opening. With a swift step, he hooked my ankle and swept my legs out from under me. I landed hard, the breath knocking from my lungs. The sky spun above me, framed by the snowfall.

"You rejected him," Kent reminded me, his voice implacable.

I gritted my teeth as I pushed myself upright onto my elbows. "He lied to me."

"No, he didn't," Kent countered, his blade steady at his side. "He made no claims about not having the same restrictions that *you* have when it comes to romantic entanglements. In fact, at least he was *honest* about his feelings for you. Can you claim the same?"

I rolled to my feet just as he leveled his next strike at me and his blade grazed the ends of my hair. Frustration boiling over, I lashed out wildly, my form unraveling.

"Now you're just sloppy," Kent observed, deflecting each strike with ease. "Did I strike a nerve?"

I had never seen Kent like this. He was always so reserved, so *careful*, always tiptoeing around emotions to keep from upsetting anyone.

He certainly wasn't being reserved now.

Right now, I didn't *want* to hear his logic, though. I wanted to be angry. To *stay* angry. I wanted to drown in my rage because as long as it consumed me, I wouldn't have to face what was lurking beneath.

If Kent refused to give me that, I would just have to find somewhere else to direct my fury.

I let the sword slip from my grip, turning on my heel toward the castle.

"We're not done here," Kent called after me.

"I *am*," I snapped, yanking my arm free when he reached for me.

His voice softened, but his words carried weight. "You're projecting, Thea. You have been for months. It's time to face what's really going on inside of you."

No.

I couldn't.

I couldn't think about all the secrets I was keeping, all the pain I had caused, the pain I *had yet* to cause if that prophecy was true.

I couldn't let myself dig into the feelings that were clawing at my ribs, because if I did they might just break me apart from the inside out.

Salty tears blurred my vision as I shoved him away, my magic lashing out instinctively—erecting an invisible barrier between us. As if pushing him back physically could keep him from sensing *too much*.

"Stop reading my emotions!" I shouted.

Kent flinched, his expression shifting—like I had just struck him with something far worse than magic. His eyes darkened, a rare flash of emotion passing over his usually measured features before he forced his focus back on me.

"I wouldn't have to if you just opened up to me - to any of us," he insisted.

"What do you want me to say, Kent?" My voice was hoarse now.

"We can start with why you're feeling so guilty."

The breath locked in my throat.

Guilt.

Of course, I felt guilty. I had so much to feel guilty for. So much that no one else knew about.

"Lorelai's death wasn't your fault," Kent called after me as I started marching away. "None of this has been your fault."

But he was *wrong*.

It was *all* my fault.

Lorelai's death.

The monster I had summoned last night.

And when Hyrax walked the Mortal Realm again, that would be my fault, too.

I had no right to feel betrayed by Clay.

Not when I was destined to betray them all.

CHAPTER THIRTEEN

I t took three men to load the trunks full of gowns and jewelry onto the ship bound for Tenebris. One shipman groaned loudly as he hefted the last case, his face red with exertion. I shot a sharp look at Nessira and Samsa, who stood off to the side, barely concealing their grins.

"I thought it best to bring options for you," Nessira said with an unapologetic shrug. "A woman should look impressive when she meets her future husband."

My stomach churned at her words.

While I longed to leave the kingdom and explore new parts of the world, especially now when I was eager to put some distance between my friends and me, this trip wasn't about adventure. Its sole purpose was to meet my betrothed, Veric, and bring him back to Athenia for us to be wed.

I had spent the past few days since the Dragon's announcement wondering what Veric would be like. Would he be as cruel as his uncle? Would he resemble Clay in any way? Would he find me pleasant—or utterly unremarkable? And what would I think of him?

Would he find *me* attractive?

Did that even matter?

No. Of course it didn't.

We had a duty to fulfill, and my feelings—and his—were irrelevant.

"It's time to board, ladies!" the captain called. "We're just waiting for one more passenger."

I frowned, confused. "Who else is joining us?"

"I am."

I never imagined two words could fill me with such immediate frustration.

I spun on my heels, my boots crunching against the frozen dock. Clay stood a few feet away, dressed down in simple trousers and a thick coat suitable for the voyage. Behind him, a palace servant struggled to balance the trunk he was carrying.

"Absolutely not!" I snapped, my voice sharper than I intended.

"You don't have a say in the matter," Clay replied, his eyebrow arching in challenge. "I have business to attend to in Tenebris, and this happens to be the most convenient option for me to get there."

His smile was infuriatingly cocky, and I had to resist the overwhelming urge to slap it off his face.

"And your *wife*?" I asked coldly. "Will she be joining us?"

Out of the corner of my eye, I saw Nessira shift uncomfortably. She inclined her head toward Samsa, silently instructing the girl to board the ship.

Clay's eyes flashed golden, his smile faltering for a brief moment before he replied, his voice low. "Elaina, my *betrothed,* will not be joining us. It's just you and me, princess."

"And me!" Nessira cut in brightly, linking her arm tightly with mine. "There is much to do to prepare you for meeting *your* betrothed, my Lady. You and I will spend most of our time together while we sail."

Her words were a clear warning. If Clay wanted to get to me, he'd have to go through her first. I don't know how I got so lucky as to be assigned Nessira as my lady-in-waiting, but I was going to thank the Gods for her every night for the rest of my life.

As we turned and made our way to the ramp of the ship I leaned my head gratefully against her shoulder. "Thank you."

She sighed, giving my hand a reassuring squeeze.

Behind us, Clay said nothing. He trailed after us in silence, his presence a heavy weight I couldn't ignore.

Turns out I wasn't just bad at drawing; I wasn't a particularly good sailor either.

The boat lurched to the left over a wave, and I heaved dryly once more. My stomach had emptied itself hours ago, leaving me to cough miserably over the side of the wooden railing.

"Oh dear," Samsa murmured, patting a damp cloth on my forehead. "Is there nothing I can do for you, my Lady?"

"Do you think I'm powerful enough to lift the boat out of the water and float it steadily all the way to Tenebris?"

I wasn't. I'd already tried that a few days ago when the first wave of seasickness convinced me I might die before arriving. It had only been three days on this cursed vessel, and there was no way I was going to survive the rest of the journey.

"You'll get yer sea legs soon enough, milady," a sailer said to me. "Takes some time, but ye'll settle, eventually."

"You said that yesterday, Cerl."

"And I might say it again tomorrow at this rate." He grinned toothily.

I wanted to respond, but the boat rocked once more, and I flopped my head heavily over the side again. This torment might actually be worse than Camilla's shadow monsters nipping at my skin.

"Thea." Clay's voice sounded from behind me. "Come."

Not a request from a friend.

An order from a Prince.

One I couldn't feasibly say no to.

Nessira's stomach had turned out to be just as weak as mine, so she hadn't been able to help steer him away from me after all. I'd avoided him for most of the trip through an array of excuses, ranging from needing to relieve myself to a sudden fascination with the mechanics of ocean navigation. And the only good thing about my raging nausea was that it had kept most people away from me, including the prince.

Until now.

"No," I groaned, unable to collect my thoughts enough to think of a new reason to escape his presence.

"Now."

Once my stomach had settled, I was going to give him a piece of my mind. If it ever settled, that is.

Pulling myself off the rail, I followed him downstairs to the chamber he'd been occupying during the journey. It was a small space with a simple single-person bed and a tiny wooden desk cluttered with open books and notes.

Clay avoided my gaze as he shut the door and locked us into the tight, damp space. He was in a vicious mood. He radiated irritation, and I had no doubt that he was angry with me for having stopped talking to him. Did he really expect us to proceed as we had been, though?

Did he expect me to carry on treating him as my friend even though every time I looked at him I pictured another woman's hand in his?

He went straight to the desk, gathering the parchments and tossing them into his trunk in exchange for a single candle. Without a word, he exhaled a quick burst of dragon fire, igniting the wick so that its flame flickered dimly between us.

"Make it float," he instructed, holding it in the air between us.

For a moment, I was back on that terrace with him.

He held the rose out to me, flat on his palm between us. A thornless rose, pulled from the shadows and held between a Descendant of Zion and a Descendant of Hyrax.

"What were you feeling?" he asked.

"Afraid," I whispered, acutely aware that even though I was alone with the Crown Prince—a man who had been nothing but ill-tempered with me—I didn't feel afraid anymore.

I shook my head violently to clear the memory away. "Clay—"

"Just trust me, Thea."

I glared at him. My trust was something he had lost the second Elaina answered his door.

He sighed and threw back his head, as if realizing how disastrous his own words were the second they left his mouth. "Please."

Gods.

My wretched heart had the audacity to flip when he said "please," as if it refused to understand reason. Although, it always had refused reason when it came to him. I'd fallen for Clay even though I knew it was wrong, even though we both knew it was wrong, and now my cursed heart was going to have to deal with the pain that came with that recklessness.

Wordlessly, I lifted my hand, grasping the candle magically and holding it steady in the air.

"Good." He moved to stand behind me.

Too close behind me.

I could feel the warmth radiating off his body, like an embrace around me. Slowly, his hands reached toward my wrists, holding them with a feather-light grip as he traced small circles on my skin.

His touch was far too soft and far too personal.

Warmth radiated down my spine, my body already softening and breath hitching. I felt my pulse like a steady drumbeat throughout my body. He was only touching my wrists, and that small touch was all I could think about.

"No," I protested, attempting to pull away even as my voice betrayed the effect he was having on me

"If you drop that candle," his voice was nothing more than a whisper against the shell of my ear. "This entire ship will go up in flames."

I gasped, realizing at the last second that my loss of focus had left the candle falling toward the wooden floorboards of the ship. My power lashed out, grasping it in the nick of time and raising it back into its position in the air. Clay only laughed and returned his fingertips to my wrist, beginning to trail them up the insides of my arm.

His fingers climbed further, their touch impossibly slow and tender. He traced the bare skin of my collarbone before resting his hands on my shoulders. When his thumbs pressed into the tender flesh there and began moving in firm circles, I almost moaned aloud.

Dear Gods.

"What are you doing?" I asked, hating how breathy my voice sounded.

Despite all the reasons I was angry with him, I was entirely unable to stop myself from relaxing under his touch as he began massaging out the tension I'd been carrying in my shoulders since first discovering my unavoidable seasickness. Somehow, that made me even angrier.

"I'm distracting you," he whispered, lips tickling my ear. "And I think it's working."

Well, yes. He was certainly distracting. With every delicious circle of his thumbs against my shoulders, my stomach quieted until the only feeling left for me to focus on was the heat in my lower abdomen and my irritation at feeling it.

Traitorous heart.

Traitorous body.

I didn't want to be so consumed by Clayton Vail, but he was my light in a midnight world. I was drawn to him like a moth to a flame, helpless to do anything other than fall hopelessly for him.

"You're wicked."

"You have no idea princess, but one day I am going to show you just how wicked I can be." He reached across my neck to pull my hair back. I shivered at the sensation of his fingers trailing across the delicate skin. "We need to talk."

"I don't want to."

"I'm sure you could convince me to distract you another way." His voice was thick with double meaning. "I would be more than happy to oblige you."

I turned, smacking his chest in frustration. "You're *engaged*, Your Grace."

"The flame, Miss Moore."

Without looking, I held out my hand, and the candle flew into it. I blew it out in a quick, angry breath and shoved it at him. "I believe I have finally found my sea legs."

Clay put an arm around my waist and pulled me close, pinning me against his chest. "We're on a ship, my dear. There's only so many places you can run. If you want to make a scene of forcing me to chase you, that's your choice. I will, however, catch you, and the entire ship can bear witness to this conversation then."

I lifted my leg and slammed it down, hoping to smash his foot, only for him to move it out of the way before I even got close. All I got for my effort was a breathy chuckle brushing the hair by my neck.

"Fine!" I huffed. "What do you want to talk about?"

"Elaina."

"She is quite possibly the last thing in all the realms I want to discuss, Clayton."

He rolled his eyes at my use of his full name but released me, allowing me to cross the tiny room and put some much-needed space between us. Distance was what I needed to cool the heat in my blood. My mind might have been well aware that I couldn't have him, and my heart might be finally learning that Clayton Vail brought me nothing but pain, but my stubborn body wanted him all the same.

And it certainly didn't help that his days at sea had been good for him.

Spending his time chatting on deck with the sailors had lightened his hair and tanned his skin. The farther we traveled from Athenia, the warmer the weather became. Which meant he had resorted to wearing loose cotton tunics, open low over his sculpted chest and rolled high over his muscled forearms.

He was beautiful.

And I probably looked a lovely shade of green.

Elaina probably didn't get seasick. Elaina probably looked stunning, with the sea air blowing through her thick hair. The extra sun probably brought out some cute freckles or highlights in her hair. Truthfully, though, Elaina would probably look stunning doing the most unglamorous of tasks.

Gods, this jealousy was going to eat me alive.

"We were engaged when I was barely over eight years old," Clay explained. "I've known her since I was a boy. She's been a friend to me through the years, but nothing more. She has never been anything more than that to me and I have never been anything more than that to her."

His words came out in a rush, as if he were desperate to convince me of their truth. And maybe it was the truth. Maybe they had never been romantic with one another.

But they would be.

They had to be.

That's why she was staying in his room. There was no need to keep them apart. There was no need for chaperones when they were expected to create an heir.

"And what have I been to you?" I whispered.

Anger, hurt, and desperation leaked into my voice like weights dragging me under. Shoulders that had just relaxed under his touch were now impossibly tight with tension once more. Clay stepped closer and tentatively lifted a hand to caress my cheek. His eyes were wild with passion and an emotion I wasn't brave enough to name, but was wise enough to recognize.

"You have been everything to me, Thea, and you very well know that."

I chewed on my lip as I stared up at the ceiling of the chamber, desperate to avoid those eyes. "And what would you have me be next?"

Clay froze. His mouth opened as if to say something before closing once more, just as I knew it would.

Until this moment, I might have been his everything, but in the future, he was hers. She was his future in a way I could never be.

"Thea, I—"

"Don't!" I held up my hand sharply, stopping him from saying the words that I knew in my bones he was about to utter. I couldn't hear those words, not when my eyes were already misty and my heart felt like it was being squeezed to death. Those words were nothing more than empty promises now, and anger was an emotion more easily dealt with than heartbreak. So I allowed myself to lose myself in that furious rush of frustration. "Don't you dare."

We stood frozen, both visibly upset and unsure of what move to make next.

"What I know, Clayton, is that there is nothing here for either of us. The longer we continue this dance, the worse it will hurt in the end. "

He looked away, running a hand over his jaw. When he finally turned back to meet my gaze, the longing in his eyes was enough to spur my tears to roll down my face.

"Just because I'm aware of the situation—of our roles in court—doesn't mean I won't spend every minute of the rest of my life wishing you were the woman who got to stand by my side."

That, at least, was a sentiment we could both share.

The boat rocked suddenly, but my stomach stayed steady. I brushed the back of my hands across my cheeks, wiping away my tears and pulling back on the mask of indifference I'd grown accustomed to wearing. Then I watched as he did the same.

And in just a moment's time, it wasn't Clay and Thea in this small room – it was the Crown Prince and the Hyraxian Council Member.

Two people who shared nothing more than a connected duty to their kingdom.

"If you'll excuse me, Your Grace." I cleared my throat, brushing my hands on my skirts to clear away the clamminess that had suddenly overtaken me. "I should probably go pick a gown to wear when we arrive. A woman should look impressive when she meets her future husband."

Each step away from him felt heavier than the last.

But he didn't ask me to stay, and I didn't want him to.

I had never seen anything as beautiful as a shoreline after days spent staring at the endless expanse of the open ocean.

As we approached Tenebris, I couldn't tear my eyes away from the foreign world unfolding before me. Even as the crew busied themselves docking the ship, I remained rooted at the railing, captivated.

"It's beautiful," Nessira whispered beside me, her voice soft with wonder.

The port was alive with vibrant energy. People moved in brightly colored clothing, the hues of orange, red, and gold catching the sunlight. Towering stone buildings lined the streets, their symmetrical facades adorned with elaborate mosaics depicting sunbursts, flowers, and mythical creatures. Many of the multi-story homes had overhanging balconies where women shook out linens and children leaned over the railings, watching the bustling courtyards below.

The Emperor and Empress had sent an envoy to greet us. A line of soldiers, resplendent in their brightly colored armor, stood waiting as we disembarked. Their orange breastplates gleamed under the light, each adorned with the emblem of the sun, and their capes billowed lightly in the breeze.

As I took my first unsteady steps off the ship, a man stepped forward and bowed deeply at the waist.

"Lady Theadora Moore," he said, his voice warm and steady, "it is my great honor to welcome you on behalf of the monarchs to the great country of Tenebris. I am Ashburn, and I will escort you to the Sun Palace."

Ashburn was tall and broad-shouldered, his brown skin glowing under the afternoon sun. He had neatly cropped, short, dark hair, and a long yellow cape flowed from his shoulders, distinguishing him from the other soldiers. When I nodded in acknowledgment, he gestured toward a small box resting on the ground.

The palanquin was exquisite. Its glass walls, outlined in polished gold, enclosed a bed of velveteen pillows. The top curved into a delicate dome, crowned by an intricate dragon sculpture. Orange and red ribbons streamed from wooden beams that extended from its base, fluttering gently in the breeze.

"Please, make yourself comfortable, and we will begin our journey," Ashburn said with a polite smile.

I blinked, surprised. "You wish for me to ride in that?"

"It is traditional for guests of great importance to be carried to the palace via a palanquin," he explained. "The monarchs would be honored if you would allow this."

"And what of my ladies?" I asked, glancing back at Nessira and Samsa.

"It is not a far journey," Ashburn assured me. "Several of our men have horses and would be happy to ride alongside your ladies."

"While your men are quite strapping, Ashburn," a familiar voice interjected, "I personally will not be sharing a mount."

Clay descended from the ship with the casual confidence only he could manage, a teasing smile tugging at his lips.

Ashburn's composure wavered, his mouth opening and closing before he managed a hurried bow. "Your Grace! The monarchs were not expecting you. I apologize for not having another palanquin available for you."

"That's all right," Clay said smoothly, his gaze sweeping over the bustling city. "I'll enjoy walking alongside your soldiers."

An awkward silence followed, but Ashburn quickly recovered, beckoning me toward the palanquin. I settled onto the velveteen cushions, the soft fabric cradling me as four soldiers took their positions at each corner. Nessira and Samsa were helped onto horses, their skirts carefully arranged, while Clay fell into formation with the soldiers, chatting amiably as we set off.

Through the glass walls of the palanquin, I watched the city unfurl around me. It was as foreign as Athenia had been when I first arrived, and I stared through the windows, unblinking as we made our way through streets alive with music, laughter, and the hum of a thriving city.

The journey was brief, no more than twenty minutes, before the palace finally loomed into view atop a hill.

We passed through a grand golden gate and along a long, mirror-like pool that stretched nearly a mile. The water shimmered under the sun, bordered by lush gardens filled with vibrant flowers and citrus trees heavy with fruit.

When we reached the palace courtyard, I found myself momentarily breathless.

The Sun Palace was a masterpiece. The structure, built of warm clay-colored stone, rose in perfect symmetry. Intricate floral patterns and inscriptions, alive in their detail, adorned its surface. A wide dome crowned its center, flanked by smaller domes atop spires that framed the building like sentinels.

The soldiers lowered the palanquin gently to the ground. One stepped forward, opening the door and extending a hand to help me out.

"Welcome to the Sun Palace," a voice said, but I barely registered the words. I fixed my eyes on the towering structure before me, its beauty eclipsing everything else.

CHAPTER FOURTEEN

Ashburn led us through the halls of the Sun Palace so quickly that I barely had time to take in my surroundings. Still, my eyes darted around, absorbing flashes of mosaic walls and colorful tiled floors. Windows cut into intricate shapes—flowers, suns, and stars—let in streams of golden light. Greenery and vines climbed the walls, inviting the outside in.

After a year spent in the pristine white marble of the Athenian palace, this explosion of color was overwhelming.

It wasn't just the decor that impressed me, though. The air carried the rich aroma of spices and fresh bread, wrapping around us like a warm embrace. My stomach growled loudly, and I flushed as heads turned my way.

"Do not fear, my Lady," Ashburn said, a soft chuckle in his voice. He glanced back at me, his expression warm. "Dinner is being prepared as we speak. The monarchs insisted on meeting you first."

He stopped before a set of large, ornately carved doors, holding one open and sweeping his arm forward in invitation.

I hesitated, glancing instinctively toward Clay. Despite this trip being arranged for me as a Council member, he was the Crown Prince. Surely he should step forward first to greet the monarchs of Tenebris? Clay, however, only met my hesitation with amusement. Leaning close to my ear, he murmured, "Don't tell me you want to delay meeting your fiancé?"

I fought the urge to smack him. Straightening, I stepped forward and led our group into the throne room.

My breath caught as I entered.

Forest-green tapestries with swirling patterns stitched in shimmering golden thread draped the walls. Velvet curtains of deep crimson framed the tall windows, and matching tasseled carpets stretched across the floor. To the left, a group of young women sat on pillows, laughing and sipping from delicate porcelain cups. Their gazes turned to us sharply as we entered, but their smiles were warm. To the right, two small boys chased one another, their golden circlets marking them as princes. And directly ahead, the Emperor and Empress rose from their thrones—towering, gilded seats upholstered in scarlet fabric.

Emperor Kamon stepped forward first. His long, dark beard matched the thickness of his hair, and his white coat shimmered with golden embroidery at the cuffs, echoing the swirling designs of the tapestries. A silk shawl draped casually over his shoulder, and his fingers sparkled with rings set with emeralds and rubies. His crown extended into five sharp points, so fine they looked as though a single touch could draw blood.

"Lady Moore, welcome to Tenebris!" he said, his voice booming as his grin revealed polished white teeth.

"And Prince Clayton," Empress Rani added, her expression more reserved as her gaze flicked over him. "What a pleasant surprise."

Empress Rani was every bit as grand as her husband. Golden pearls trimmed her crimson blouse, a fabric that fit snugly over her shoulders and beneath her chest. A flowing silk skirt, high-slitted, revealed a sliver of dark skin. A shimmering gold cloth draped her shoulders, and her neck and ears glittered with jewels. Her golden crown sat effortlessly atop her coiled dark hair.

Clay bowed deeply at the waist, his charming smile firmly in place. "I apologize for not sending advance notice, Your Majesties. Prince Damon and I have been corresponding, and I thought this was a perfect opportunity to meet him in person."

My heart skipped as I watched him. Every time I thought I knew him, he revealed another side. This Clayton Vail—the charismatic politician—was entirely new to me, a far cry from the man who'd kissed me in secret or the demanding prince who expected my deference.

Empress Rani's smile stayed tight, but she nodded her acceptance of his explanation.

The monarchs descended the steps of their dais, their joined hands a gesture so effortlessly affectionate that it struck me as foreign. After months of observing the tense interactions between the Dragon and the Athenian Queen, such tenderness seemed almost unnatural. Although, admittedly, much about Tenebris so far felt largely foreign. It was more than just the colors, smells, and clothing. There was no Council here to greet us. Tenebris relied solely on the leadership of House Zion, delegating the governance of their lands to the Descendants of the other High Houses.

Hence why they wanted to claim one of my future children as their own, even though I held less of a position of authority here than I did in Athenia.

I dipped into a low curtsy. "I am deeply grateful for your kingdom's hospitality, Your Majesties."

"It is our pleasure to host you," Emperor Kamon said, stepping forward to take my hand. He pressed a chaste kiss to my knuckles, his eyes gleaming with genuine warmth. "I only wish your visit could be longer. There is so much of our kingdom to show you."

The Dragon had allowed me a fortnight in Tenebris—long enough to meet Veric, solidify good relations with the monarchs, and celebrate my engagement with a ball. Then, it would be back to Athenia, this time with my future husband in tow.

"Veric will join us this evening," Empress Rani said, as though reading my thoughts. "Tomorrow, we have arranged for you both to tour the city together. In Tenebris, it is customary for a couple to spend ample time together before their wedding."

Emperor Kamon brushed her hair back from her face, his thumb grazing the hollow of her throat in a gesture so intimate it made my chest ache. "Yes, a marriage built on friendship is one that brings joy to both parties."

A marriage that brings joy is one a woman chooses for herself, I thought bitterly, but I kept the words locked behind a polite smile. I ignored the heat of Clay's gaze on my back as Emperor Kamon called forward to one of the women seated on the pillows.

"This is Saharn," he said. "She will escort you to your rooms. I'm sure you will appreciate the chance to refresh yourselves after your journey."

The Empress scanned her eyes down my body and added, "We have also provided traditional Tenebrisian garments, should you wish to wear them to dinner."

I nodded my thanks, following Saharn as she led the way out. Nessira, Samsa, and Clay fell into step behind me. Saharn, a tall girl in a burnt-orange dress, spoke softly as we walked, describing the palace and detailing tomorrow's itinerary, but my attention drifted to Clay. I slowed my steps to keep pace with him.

Nessira, the brilliant woman that she was, noticed my intentions and brushed forward past my shoulder. "Saharn, would you be able to help Samsa and I note down the details of the itinerary so we know how to appropriately prepare Lady Moore?"

Saharn glanced at Nessira over her shoulder and nodded enthusiastically. "Of course, I'm more than happy to-"

They trailed off into conversation as I turned my attention to Clay.

"Care to explain what business you have with Prince Damon?" I asked under my breath, my real question unspoken. Was this truly about diplomacy, or had he come simply to follow me?

Clay raised an eyebrow, the corner of his mouth curling into a smug smile. "Not particularly, but rest assured, it has nothing to do with you."

"I find it hard to believe you'd cross an ocean just for introductions."

He shrugged, his attention flicking to Saharn briefly. "Do you think everything I do revolves around you?"

I balked. "Of course not, but-"

Clay laughed softly, glancing at me from the corner of his eye, something that looked mysteriously like playfulness glinting in the depths of his golden flecked grey eyes.

"Are you –" I paused, struggling to find the words. "Are you teasing me?"

"I suppose. Although not in my preferred way." He lifted a brow as his attention dropped to my lips for a moment before focusing in front of us once more.

There was something about him that seemed different. Maybe it was the light in his eyes, glowing from something other than anger, or the appearance of a dimple in his left cheek that I had somehow never noticed before. Perhaps it was even just the simple fact that his shoulders sat half an inch lower than they did normally. Truthfully, it was *everything*. Everything seemed... lighter.

"You're relaxed here," I mused aloud.

He didn't meet my gaze even as I felt like I couldn't rip my eyes away from him. I so rarely got to see him like this. He never allowed himself to let his seriousness and strategical thinking slide away to just be a man, but when he did? Well, that was the version of him I liked best.

"Stop looking at me like that," he commanded, his eyes still focused ahead.

Blushing furiously, I returned my gaze to Saharn's back but my willpower only held out for a few minutes before I was tracing over his features again, memorizing every detail of him from his windblown hair to the shadow across his sharp jawline. Gods, he really was beautiful like this.

There were only a few more moments that I'd be able to soak him in before we'd be separated and forced to play our roles again.

"Seriously," he insisted, placing his hand on the small of my back to encourage me to keep walking even as my body slowed. "You cannot keep looking at me like that."

"Like what?"

"Like you're not actually angry at me anymore."

Finally, he met my gaze, and I nearly stumbled from the heat that lingered in his eyes. Heat that struck right through me, then slid down my spine at a torturously slow pace before settling right between my thighs. His eyes traveled my body, lingering over parts that should insult me but only made me feel even hotter.

Oh.

Is that how I had been looking at him?

I shook my head, as if I could shake myself loose of these feelings, and took a steadying breath to cool my overheated face. Right. I *was* angry at him. I *should* be angry with him.

But my anger was fading with every single day that passed while my logical mind reminded me that he hadn't actually lied, that it was ignorant for me to not realize he would be forced to marry a Descendant of Zion, and that I was actually the one keeping much bigger secrets between us.

I clenched my fists, digging my nails into my skin to stop myself from overthinking as I stared down at the floor in front of us. The floor was safe. When I looked at the tiled floor, all I could see of him was his boots. Boots were safe to look at.

Even if those boots were attached to thick muscular legs, wrapped tight in leather that hugged every part of his body, even his -

"Yes, I'm relaxed here," Clay admitted, pulling me out of a very dangerous thought spiral. "I'm not the heir apparent here. Obviously my every move still matters, and has implications for our people, but at least I don't feel like my every move is being watched and reported back to my father."

I thought over his words, feeling my own shoulders loosen as they settled. Yes, I suppose not having to deal with the Dragon was one very nice benefit of this trip.

"Now pay attention," he instructed, dropping his hand from my back and pointing instead towards Saharn.

"The Monarchs have reserved this hall for their guests," she said. "We've prepared this room for you, Lady Moore."

She handed me a small bronze key on a silver string, then gave a matching one to Nessira. "Your ladies will stay here." She gestured to the door beside mine. "There is an adjoining door inside. Prince Vail, we're preparing accommodations in the royal wing more suited to your station."

My jaw tightened, irritation bubbling under my skin. They were so desperate to claim my offspring but treated me as so much lower on the ladder of authority that I couldn't even stay in the same wing as the Descendants of Zion.

Clay glanced down the hallway. "Surely there's another room in this hall?"

Saharn blinked, startled. "Prince Vail, I assure you the royal wing is far more suitable. The rooms are—"

"This trip is for Councilwoman Moore," Clay interrupted, his tone firm and words purposeful. Not Lady Moore - Councilwoman Moore. It might not earn the same respect in this country, but it meant something in mine. "She is second only to the Dragon of Athenia. I'm confident that whatever room you deemed appropriate for her will suit me as well."

I stared at the floor, biting back a grin as warmth spread through my chest. Saharn sputtered, then bowed her head and stepped back.

"Will you-" Her voice was timid as she glanced rapidly between the two of us. "Will you need a chaperone for the evening?"

Clay's laugh was congenial, but I detected a level of amusement lying underneath it. "Do Tenebrisian customs typically require chaperones?"

They didn't. Tenebris only concerned itself with the heirs of House Zion. The presence of chaperones was an Athenian custom since our nation depended on the heirs of all High Houses.

Saharn's nervous eyes bounced between Clay and I rapidly, as if she didn't know how to respond. Nessira only rolled her eyes dramatically and took her key from the girl's hand.

"I think that will be all, Saharn," Nessira announced. "Surely I can serve as a chaperone this evening."

"Surely," Clay agreed, mischief coloring his gaze.

Nessira met his eyes without fear while Saharn retreated down the hallway. When it was finally just the four of us, she turned to me, a question on her face. Sighing heavily, I nodded, inclining my head in a silent instruction for her and Samsa to head inside. She was hesitant to leave at first, her eyes filled with silent warnings, but eventually they went into their suite, leaving Clay and I alone in the hallway.

I turned my icy glare on him.

"Come now, there's no need for hostility," he teased.

"Why do I feel like you're hiding something from me?" I asked, crossing my arms over my chest.

His gaze darkened, all playfulness suddenly fading away. "Funny, I've thought that same thing about you for months now."

"**I**ris would love this," I thought to myself as I gazed at my reflection in the mirror, picturing how her eyes would sparkle upon seeing the gown I had received.

Tenebrisian fashion was worlds apart from Athenian styles.

Nessira grumbled for nearly an hour about wasting her time packing gowns, only to find an entire closet of silks and jewels already awaiting me here. One look at the difference in style made it clear I'd stick out like a sore thumb if I wore anything we had brought with us from Athenia.

And so, the transformation began.

Nessira and Samsa drew a bath for me, scrubbing my skin and hair until the calming notes of jasmine and lilac replaced the lingering scent of salt and sea. Powders and creams filled the bathing chamber—some left my skin sparkling, others brought color to my cheeks, and still more smoothed the flesh of my legs.

When they deemed me sufficiently pampered, they selected a gown for the evening. The dress, pale pink and layered in shimmering chiffon, flowed to the floor, its fabric split into two daring slits over my thighs. Two narrow strips of fabric met at my navel and clasped over my shoulders in a plunging v-neckline, leaving my back, sides, and much of my chest exposed.

They wove my long blonde hair into intricate braids reminiscent of Saharn's, incorporating sparkling jewels into the strands. More jewels adorned my ears, neck, and wrists, catching the light with every slight movement.

I looked at myself in the mirror and barely recognized the woman staring back—a dazzling, vibrant stranger who felt both delicate and powerful.

It was all a bit fun, actually. It was as if I was playing dress up and existing in a version of life where every decision I made, every gown I wore, and every word I spoke didn't have to be carefully planned ahead of time. I could simply choose a gown that I liked because the color was delicate and the cut of the fabric made me feel confident without having to worry if the Dragon would think it was the best representation of my House.

So far, my time in Tenebris had been terribly contradicting.

All at once, this visit was the culmination of everything that was forced upon me by being a Council member - politics, diplomacy, marriage, alliances - and yet it was the first time in so long that I actually felt able to breathe. The first time that I truly felt like myself and not just the puppet of my kingdom.

"The dresses here are certainly a bit more... revealing than at home," Samsa murmured, smoothing the sheer blue fabric of her own gown. It was nearly translucent, with a faint underlining that offered just enough modesty.

Nessira, by contrast, wore her amethyst skirt and cropped blouse with ease, a golden sash draped elegantly over her shoulder.

"The Tenebrisian people are much freer than Athenians," she said, catching my glance. "You'll find many things are different here."

"Have you traveled here before?" I asked, fastening my dagger to my thigh. The slits in the skirt were so high that wandering eyes might spot the weapon, but I couldn't bring myself to leave it behind. Nessira's gaze flicked to the dagger perceptively, but she said nothing. Once again, I was grateful for her understanding.

"My mother's family is from Tenebris," she explained. "She met my father while he was here on business. They built their lives in Athenia, but we visited often when I was a child."

That explained her ease in this foreign palace, the way she seemed entirely comfortable in her revealing gown while Samsa awkwardly shuffled to cover exposed skin

I glanced at my reflection again, both awed and unsettled by what I saw. I somehow looked both delicate and powerful, beautiful and strong. And yet, all I could focus on was the false Descendant's Mark Nessira had painted onto my chest—a reminder that my would-be husband would one day discover the truth.

"We should go, my Lady," Samsa whispered, her voice hesitant, as though reluctant to pull me from my thoughts.

Sighing heavily, I turned to face them, my stomach twisting as I met their serious gazes. Even though Samsa was new to me, there was no need for pretense between us. We all understood how much I wanted to avoid this meeting.

Meeting Veric, putting a face to the name of the man I was to marry, would make the arrangement unbearably real.

"You don't have to do this," Nessira said softly, ignoring the alarmed glance Samsa shot her.

I wanted to laugh. I wanted to cry. I wanted to throw myself out the nearest window and run as far as my legs would take me.

"This is my duty," I said, my voice quieter than I intended. "This is what I was born to do."

Nessira's mouth twisted into a frown. "I don't think you believe that."

The truth was that I wasn't sure what I believed anymore.

None of it mattered, though. My king had declared I would marry Veric Starsen, and so I would. Now, I only had to meet the man.

CHAPTER FIFTEEN

Saharn greeted us outside my room as we began making our way to dinner. Clay had already gone ahead, she explained, but she was happy to escort us to the banquet hall. In Tenebris, large feasts were traditional for celebrating important guests and joyous occasions—like an upcoming engagement, for example. Tonight, the monarchs and Veric invited both friends and family to dine with us.

The sounds of their celebration carried down the winding hallways, which were open to the outside air. The humid heat was oppressive, and I instantly understood why the Tenebrisians wore such minimal clothing. One step outside was enough to make even the most modest want to strip away their layers.

"I will announce you," Saharn said with a warm smile, stopping just short of the dining hall.

There was no door, only a single oversized archway through which I could already see men and women of all ages laughing and sharing food. My eyes scanned over the crowd, lingering on every eligible young man, wondering if one of them might be Veric.

Saharn must have noticed my unease. Perhaps it was the way I gripped my hands together to keep them from shaking. She paused briefly, offering me a moment to collect myself. "You look beautiful," she assured me before leading us forward through the archway.

The room quieted as hundreds of eyes turned toward us.

"Allow me to present Lady Theadora Moore of Athenia, the last remaining daughter of Hyrax!"

My stomach churned violently, and I had to wipe my damp hands against my skirt to keep from trembling.

Then, all at once, the room rose to its feet, a cacophony of applause echoing as the Tenebrisians welcomed me into their home. I slipped my practiced mask into place, tucking my nerves away behind a polite smile, and made my way to the long dining table at the room's head.

Clay sat to the right of the monarchs, dressed in a russet-colored Tenebrisian-style jacket with gleaming red buttons. He was engaged in conversation with Damon, the Imperial Prince seated beside him. To Clay's left was an empty seat, likely meant for me. Beside it sat—

"Lady Moore," Veric said, standing and clearing his throat. His smile was warm as he extended his hand. "It is a pleasure to meet you. I am Veric Starsen."

I stared at his outstretched hand for a moment too long, frozen in time as my mind tried to process what was happening.

He was here. He was real.

I was staring at the man I was going to have to stand by for the rest of my life, whether I liked it or not.

Unblinking, I drew my gaze from his outstretched hand up to his structured face. Veric was tall—nearly a foot taller than me, even with my heeled slippers. His sun-kissed skin glowed golden, and his striking blue eyes sparkled against his tanned complexion. He had neatly shorn his dark hair at the sides, tousled slightly on top in a deliberately messy style. As he smiled wider, extending his hand closer to me, I couldn't help marveling at his impossibly sharp jawline.

He was beautiful.

And I felt absolutely nothing for him.

I couldn't. Not when every part of me was so attuned to the dragon prince behind him, whose golden eyes burned into every inch of my exposed skin.

I risked a glance at Clay.

My prince's heated eyes, glowing brilliantly, traced over me—from the crown of my head to the exposed skin of my thighs peeking through the slits of my skirt. His gaze lingered, lips curving into a slight smile and my pulse quickened as I realized he'd noticed the dagger strapped to my leg. I shifted slightly, trying to hide it.

Gods, it was too warm. My cheeks flushed, and I prayed the crowd would chalk it up to the nerves of a new bride rather than my complete inability to ignore Clayton Vail.

Nessira gently cleared her throat behind me and all too suddenly time fell into place again, as did the sudden awareness of all the eyes that lingered on the awkwardness of his hand waiting suspended in the air between us.

I sputtered, "It's a pleasure to meet you at last, Veric," and threw my arm forward to grasp his hand.

My smile was tight as he bent forward and brushed his lips against my knuckles, eyes holding mine. "You look beautiful."

Plenty of people had called me beautiful before. It was one of the easiest, most superficial compliment you could give someone. Usually, it didn't phase me too much. And yet, when Veric said it, a weight of uneasiness settled over me.

When Clay said it, my blood practically sang with awareness, and need, and-

No.

There would be no thoughts of Clay tonight.

Veric grinned and rounded the edge of the table to come stand at my side, gently placing a hand at my waist to guide me to my seat. His touch was gentle and reassuring. Not firm enough to be overly personal, but not delicate enough to seem awkward for two people who were to be married. Everyone in the room watched our movements, and only after I sat—conveniently between Veric and Clay—did Emperor Kamon rise to announce the start of the feast.

Everything blurred around me. The world carried on while I remained frozen. Within moments, everyone returned to their conversations, the buzz of laughter and music filling the space. Musicians played lively, unfamiliar tunes on an array of instruments, while servers passed around trays of roasted meats, spiced vegetables, and dipping sauces. Without asking, someone heaped food onto my plate.

I felt as if something had removed me from my body. I felt fully aware of my surroundings, but strangely detached.

Clay, on my left, had turned his back to me, his focus entirely on Damon. Perhaps that was for the better. I wasn't sure I would be able to carry on a conversation with Veric without making it abundantly obvious that Clay was the only person in this room I really wanted to talk to.

"So," Veric began tentatively, "my mother tells me you enjoy the gardens at the Athenian palace?"

I blinked at him. "They were a great comfort when I first arrived in Athenia," I replied, unsure how to follow up. Should I ask about his interests? That seemed like the polite thing to do. One should try to find out details about their betrothed. I should know about his hobbies, beliefs, family-

"Your mother is the Dragon's sister?" I blurted, desperate for a new topic. "Clay's aunt?"

I snapped my mouth shut, mortified. Why was I bringing up Clay?

I had left Athenia enraged and determined to distance myself from him and now I was practically humming with the awareness that his thigh was only inches from mine. I was entirely unable to stop thinking about him. Had I left all of my senses behind on the shores of my kingdom?

My prince shifted beside me, that leg brushing against mine for a brief moment before jerking away, and I knew instantly that he was listening to every word of our conversation. Even while totally focused on speaking with Damon, his attention still lingered on me.

"Yes," Veric said, his tone growing awkward. "Though I haven't seen my uncle or cousin in years. I was actually a bit surprised to see him here. Are you two... close?"

"Not at all," I said quickly, forcing a sweet smile and pulling my leg further away from him. "We work together on the Council, but beyond that, we hardly know each other."

"I see." Veric's expression softened as he opened his mouth and closed it again, debating what to say. "This is a bit strange, isn't it?"

I frowned, tensing slightly. "What is?"

Veric spooned a bit of mashed potato into his mouth before dabbing his lips clean with a napkin. "You and I. We are to be married and we are only just meeting."

"That is the way of High Houses," I said, choosing my words carefully.

He watched me closely, blue eyes focused entirely on me. "Of course. I mean no disrespect."

"What do you mean?"

A bit of a flush colored his tawny skin as he ran a hand over his jawline. "I'm sorry. I'm not saying this right at all. I only meant to say that I hope you and I can have the chance to really get to know each other. I'd rather not feel like my wife is a stranger."

Picking up his utensils, he began cutting into the meat on his plate, but I left mine untouched. My stomach was far too uneasy to eat a single bite.

"And what *would* you like from your wife?"

Veric glanced up at me and sighed, a wrinkle forming in the space between his dark brows as he turned in his seat to face me more fully. He rested his arm on the back of my chair comfortably. "Well, I want a partner, Lady

Moore. I understand that you have to prioritize heirs, and I'm honored to have the privilege of furthering your line, but for me, marriage is for more than just children. I want a friend in my wife, someone who I can laugh with and trust completely."

I felt frozen again, unable to move a single part of my body or even take a deep breath in. My chest was tight, palms so clammy I had to brush them against the fabric of my dress. "I don't give out my trust easily."

Veric stared at me before nodding softly. "I'm not asking for it right now. I'm just saying that I hope that's a place we can get to. Someday."

I met his gaze, searching for some sign of malice or duplicitousness, but found none. He looked genuine enough. Could I really trust myself enough to be a judge of that, though?

How many times in the past year had people I assumed were genuine betrayed me?

Veric cleared his throat, turning back to his dinner. "Anyway, did the Empress mention tomorrow's plans?"

"We're touring the city?"

It didn't matter how many shallow breaths I forced into my lungs, I couldn't seem to stop that heavy feeling on top of my chest.

"Indeed." Veric sipped his wine, his tone warming. "The streets outside the Sun Palace are alive with beauty and culture. I'm looking forward to seeing them through your eyes."

"Have you lived in the city for long?" I asked, noticing the way his eyes lit up as he spoke about it.

Veric grinned, his expression playful and full of pride. "For as long as I can remember. I can't wait to share it with you. The food, the people, the music—everything here is so vibrant. It's unlike any other place in all of creation."

I shifted in my seat, still feeling trapped in the awkward formality of our meeting. "It will be lovely to spend the day together."

Veric's eyes sparkled as he took in my words. He opened his mouth as if to say something more, but hesitated, sighing softly before leaning closer to me. His voice dropped to a conspiratorial whisper. "Actually, I think I have an idea for tomorrow."

"Yes?"

"In the name of building trust, what if, just for a day, we forget about the marriage and the alliance and simply enjoy exploring the city together? I'll take you to my favorite shops, and we can do or say whatever we like without worrying about politics or expectations. You'll just be you, I'll just be me, and we'll focus on having some fun. Then, when we return to the engagement ball, we can go back to being diplomatic and responsible. Until then, I want us both to feel comfortable enough that we can simply be ourselves."

His suggestion took me by surprise, and even though I still had plenty of misgivings, I couldn't stop the small smile spreading across my lips. If he was being honest about simply wanting to build a friendship between us, then perhaps spending our first day together free of expectations could be... nice.

Because if he was being genuine about wanting a partner in his wife, then I could admit that it would be nice to have a partner in my husband.

"I think I would very much like that, Veric."

His smile widened into something remarkably radiant, a perfect white grin that made him seem even more approachable. He squeezed my shoulder affectionately just as a young man approached him, calling his name fondly. Veric turned to greet the newcomer, who spoke to him as though they were old friends. Veric introduced me briefly, and I nodded politely, but my thoughts lingered on our conversation.

And then, as was always the case, I thought of Clay and wondered if he had heard all of that.

"They will probably expect us to mingle shortly," Veric whispered under his breath, his tone conspiratorial. "Truthfully, I've never been fantastic at feigning interest in small talk."

"Well, in all honesty, neither have I."

"I believe that is part of your job description, Councilwoman, is it not?" Veric's eyes glinted mischievously, a playful spark lighting his features.

I blinked at him, momentarily surprised. It took me a moment to recognize the teasing in his tone.

First, he offered me a reprieve from formalities, and now he teased me as though we were already old friends.

It was becoming obvious that Veric was nothing like I had feared he would be.

I wasn't sure what was worse: being chained to a cruel man or having an incredibly kind, likeable man chained to me while my affections were so obviously somewhere else.

"It's a new position," I said, smiling sheepishly. "You could say I'm learning as I go."

He extended a hand to me as he stood. "Perhaps we should go learn together, then."

This time, when I offered him my hand, it wasn't because I felt obligated or because an entire room was watching. It was because I wanted to.

We moved through the room together, mingling with guests, as others drew us into different conversations. Everywhere we went, Veric was careful to introduce me first and include me in every discussion. When one of his friends mentioned a recent harvest of dates, Veric stopped to ask if I liked the fruit. When a young woman proudly spoke of her work teaching mythology at a new school, he turned to me, curious about my experiences learning mythology at the Athenian castle. Each time we moved to another guest, his hand on my waist was a steady, reassuring presence.

His behavior was... remarkably perfect.

"Would you like to dance?" he asked suddenly as the band transitioned into an upbeat melody, the string instruments humming with life.

My gaze shifted to the center of the hall, where guests had begun to rise and fall into step with practiced ease. Women twirled in quick circles around their partners, their feet kicking lightly before their movements culminated in graceful lifts. The men shuffled them effortlessly between their arms, the steps both intricate and elegant.

"I don't know the steps," I admitted. "And truthfully, I'm a terrible dancer."

Veric took my hands gently, leading me to the outskirts of the dance floor. "It's simple, really," he said with a warm smile, lowering his voice to count the rhythm for me. "See? One, two, kick. Three, four, hop. We repeat that three times. On the fourth, I'll lift you."

A nervous laugh escaped me as heat crept up the back of my neck. The steps looked effortless when performed by the others, but Veric's instructions seemed anything but simple. "I may step on your toes."

His grin widened. "I would be honored."

After a quick burst of nerves, I nodded my head softly, accepting the invitation. Wrapping one hand around my fingers and pressing the other at the small of my back, he pulled me to him. Though not too close, thankfully. We began moving together, awkwardly at first, our steps out of sync with the tempo of the music. But gradually, the routine became more familiar, the rhythm easier to follow. By the fourth repetition, I was moving with confidence—well, mostly.

"You're doing great!" Veric said, squeezing my waist gently as he lifted me into the air in time with the others.

The rush of air through my hair was exhilarating, and for a moment, I let myself enjoy the dance. I threw my arms up with a laugh, only to lose my balance as the motion threw off my timing. Veric's hand slipped from my waist, and I scrambled to grab his shoulders, my feet landing unsteadily back on the ground.

We froze, staring at each other in shock before I burst into a fit of giggles. "I am *not* doing great," I admitted between laughs.

Veric was slow to gift me with his smile, but before long, his laughter joined mine. "So, minimal dancing at the wedding?"

"Do you think we could do away with dancing entirely?"

His shrug was playful. "You're the bride, and a Council member at that. If you say no dancing, they'll have to listen."

"Perhaps Lady Moore would find the dances of her own nation easier to manage," a deep voice interjected from behind me.

Too close behind me.

I turned to meet the brilliantly bright golden gaze of Clayton Vail, who, though he spoke to Veric, kept his attention focused solely on me.

"It seems it's my turn to protest that I don't know the steps," Veric laughed, his tone light, though his expression held a flicker of tension.

"I'm not proficient enough to teach you," I replied quickly, trying to mask the nerves building in my chest. "Besides, we'll have plenty of time to learn Athenian dances together when we return."

Veric nodded, his smile returning, but before he could speak further, the band transitioned into a slower, more familiar tune. Clay's hand wrapped around my elbow before I could stop him.

"Come now, surely you'd like to prove to your fiancé that you're capable of dancing without injuring him," Clay said with a smirk, his charisma laced with something sharper, something that didn't leave room for nego-tiation. "I'm happy to serve as your partner for this one dance."

No.

The last thing I needed—or wanted—was to be dancing with Clayton Vail. He was the man who left me flustered with anger and longing, the man who lied to me, the man who expected me to carry on as though nothing had happened when he showed up unannounced on this trip, seemingly determined to throw me off balance.

I simply could not dance with him. Not when he had a fiancé at home and I had one standing right next to me.

"Prince Vail," I said, my tone carefully measured. "That's kind of you, but Veric and I have so little time to get to know one another before our wedding. As I said, he and I will have plenty of time to learn the Athenian dances together."

Clay didn't let go of my elbow, even when I gently tugged. Instead, his heated gaze shifted to Veric, his expression tight with unspoken authority.

Veric hesitated, glancing between the two of us, before he nodded and stepped back. "The Prince is right," he said smoothly, though his smile faltered slightly. "This celebration is as much for you as it is for me. Enjoy the dance—I'll look forward to hearing about it."

He pressed a kiss to my knuckles before stepping away, leaving me alone with Clay, whose arm slid easily and far too comfortably around my waist.

"Are you out of your mind?" I hissed under my breath, my irritation boiling over.

"You might say that," he admitted, golden eyes scanning over my face and lingering on my lips.

"People will talk."

"They might," he replied with a shrug, his tone maddeningly casual as he glanced around us. "But you'll find the Tenebrisian court is far more discreet than ours."

The room blurred around us as Clay began to move, guiding me effortlessly through the familiar steps of an Athenian dance. My body betrayed me, following his lead as if it had been waiting for this moment.

"See, you don't dance horribly," he pointed out, twirling me away before pulling me close so that my back was pressed firmly against his chest. "You just need the right partner."

"You're insufferable," I muttered, spinning out once more.

"You like it," he replied, his grin infuriatingly charming as he pulled me back towards him.

When I stepped on his foot, it wasn't entirely accidental.

Clay chuckled softly, his grip on my hand tightening slightly as he ran his thumb slowly over my palm. His eyes, still that magnificent shade of gold, trailed down my body, lingering on the slit of my skirt where the blade at my thigh was visible once more.

"I have to admit," he murmured, his voice low and intimate, "the dagger on the thigh is an interesting accessory, but I don't think it's having the effect you intended."

"And what effect do you think I want it to have?" I shot back, my tone sharp despite the heat blooming in my cheeks and the tension curling low in my stomach.

"I suspect you want to remind people you're not someone easily killed," he said, his gaze flicking to my face. "I suspect that even though you put on a brave face day in and day out, the things you went through left scars, and now you need that blade to scare off anyone who might think of trying to hurt you further."

I titled my head back, momentarily forgetting about the room around us as my body flushed with heat. "And are you not afraid of me?"

He leaned closer, his lips just brushing the shell of my ear as he whispered, "Princess, I'm terrified of you."

My knees weakened at his words, and he felt it. His grin widened as his arm tightened around my waist, holding me upright as he continued to guide me through the dance. Around us, the room was insignificant; the music, the laughter, the murmured conversations all faded into the background, as it so often did when he was this close to me.

Clayton Vail had always seen me—truly seen me—in a way no one else ever had. And for that, I hated him. But there was something else I felt for him, something deeper that I refused to name, that burned just as hot as my anger when he said things like that.

"But as I was saying," he continued. "That dagger is having a very different effect on me than the one you intended. So you'll have to excuse me for stealing you away for a moment. I had planned to stay out of your way tonight—I really did. I even told myself I wouldn't look at you but then you walked in, wearing this dress, with so much of your perfect skin on display and a blade strapped to your thigh, and you looked like a Goddess in a room full of Mortals. After that, I couldn't help myself. Spending the night watching you, dressed like this, on another man's arm was not a form of torture I had been prepared for."

My breath caught in my throat, and I stumbled slightly, breaking step. Clay's arm tightened again, steadying me, his expression unreadable.

He was jealous.

The realization struck me like a blow. Clayton Vail was jealous. The knowledge sent a rush of emotions surging through me—satisfaction, confusion, and something that felt dangerously close to hope.

Although what I was hoping for was beyond me.

"I'm sorry," I whispered, staring up at him.

He held my gaze, not even blinking. "For what, princess? You've done nothing wrong."

"You haven't either, not really."

Clay raised a brow, and I knew what he was thinking without him having to say the words.

"Yes, you should have told me about Elaina sooner, but that engagement isn't in your control any more than this one is in mine."

I sighed heavily, unhappily. Dancing with him was easy, effortless. How could something feeling so incredibly right be so terribly forbidden? It simply wasn't fair.

"Sometimes, I think about how things would be different if it were in my control," he admitted.

"And what would you change?"

"A lot," Clay laughed darkly before looking down at me again, the fire in his eyes sending waves of heat down my body. "But for starters, you wouldn't be sleeping across the hall tonight."

The music slowed, the melody winding down to its final, lingering notes. We came to a stop, standing far too close, our gazes locked. I opened my mouth to speak, to say anything that might break the tension crackling between us, but no words came.

"Clay, I—"

"Lady Moore, perhaps I might trouble you for the next dance?" Emperor Kamon's voice interrupted from behind me, startling me back into the present.

I turned quickly, my heart still racing as I forced a smile onto my face. "Of course," I replied, stepping away from Clay and taking the Emperor's offered hand.

As the music picked up speed again, returning to the fast-paced string melodies favored by the Tenebrisians, Emperor Kamon began speaking animatedly about the musicians and their skill. I tried to focus on his words, but my attention kept drifting back to Clay. He stood at the edge of the room now, his wineglass in hand, watching me with an intensity that set my skin aflame.

Then, without a word or a glance in my direction, he turned and strode out of the room, leaving me alone with the lingering echoes of his touch.

CHAPTER SIXTEEN

Veric kindly walked me back to my room at the end of the evening. He animatedly pointed out his favorite aspects of the palace's architecture as we walked. He truly came alive while talking about Tenebris, his passion awe-inspiring but also somewhat disheartening. It had only taken a single night in his presence to see how painfully clear it was that he was going to miss this place terribly.

And I felt downright awful that I was the reason he was being dragged away.

After bidding him goodnight, I lost myself in my thoughts as I sat in front of the mirror, combing out my hair. There had to be a way to ensure some semblance of his happiness in Athenia. Surely, I could use my funds to redecorate Hyrax Estate. While I couldn't rebuild the manor in Tenebrisian style, I should be able to add brightly colored textiles and pillows like those common here. We could even hire a chef familiar with Tenebrisian cuisine. Perhaps I could find a temporary cure for my sea sickness, allowing us to return to Tenebris regularly. We could build a home here to visit when the air got cold in Athenia.

Veric had been nothing like I'd expected, and I couldn't help feeling disappointed in myself for not considering him more deeply before tonight. I had been so consumed by my hatred for this arrangement that I hadn't stopped to think about the fact that he, too, was being forced to marry a stranger. And if that wasn't difficult enough, he was also being uprooted from his home, his family, and the culture he so clearly adored to spend the rest of his life in Athenia—with me.

This arrangement wasn't just hurting me.

If there was a way to make this easier for Veric, I would find it—for him and for both of us. And maybe, just maybe, after enough time, I could grow out of the burning want that consumed me every time I met Clay's eyes and learn to show a fraction of that affection to Veric.

I wasn't expecting any more company that evening, so the gentle knock at my door startled me. Jumping from my seat, I clutched my chest. Tentatively, I called my magic to my fingertips, and grasped the dagger in my hand as I approached the door, relaxing only when a familiar voice called my name.

"Thea, let me in."

I pulled open the door quickly, glancing at him in confusion.

Clay was alone, leaning against the doorframe with heavy-lidded eyes and a lopsided smirk. His disheveled hair dangled slightly in front of his eyes, and I felt an overwhelming urge to brush it back even as he chuckled at the dagger in my hand.

"Are you going to stab me?

"What do you want?" I asked with exasperation, pulling my rust-colored robe tighter around me.

His grin widened, more playful than usual, as he held up a bottle of wine like an offering. "I want help finishing this."

Gods. *That* was the cause of the playfulness and the mischevious smirks. He was drunk.

I frowned. "It's a bit late for a visit, don't you think?"

His head tilted to the side and he pulled his lower lip across his teeth. "No one has to know."

"It's improper."

"So what?"

Who was this man and what had he done to the Clayton Vail from last year who had insisted on decorum at all costs?

This was a terrible idea. Allowing Clay into my room, drunk, alone, in the middle of the night was a *terrible* idea. There was no way I could let this happen.

"I'm still angry at you!" My voice raised an octave as I struggled to find an excuse to turn him away, and I wondered if he could hear it for the lie it was.

"Exactly. That's why I'm offering to split the finest wine in this kingdom as an olive branch."

"Well, what would your fiancé think of that?" I shot back.

He groaned, holding a hand to his chest as he rocked back on his heels, but his smile didn't falter. "Trust me," he said, "she'll be thrilled to hear about this."

That... was intriguing.

And I was definitely running out of excuses to stop myself from grabbing his shirt and pulling him inside. Want for him coiled in my stomach as I stared at him, at the line of his jaw and the fullness of his lips and the effortless confidence of his stance...

No.

Clay wasn't exactly sober and one of us had to be responsible. Getting drunk with him was *not* responsible.

His expression turned serious for a moment, his gaze trailing to where my hand rested on the door. "He's going to chain you tomorrow."

I froze, the words hanging ominously between us. That couldn't possibly mean what it sounded like... could it?

"It's a tradition of House Zion," Clay explained, stepping forward so suddenly that I stumbled back. "Instead of the typical marriage bracelets, we use the Chains of Zion. They're forged by Dragonfire. During the ceremony, the magic hardens them, making them unbreakable until one spouse leaves this realm."

I thought of the bracelets I'd seen the Queen of Athenia wearing. I had, of course, known they were symbolic of her marriage to the Dragon, but I hadn't realized they were so *permanent*.

"It's meant to symbolize the strength of the union," Clay continued, his voice quieter, "in honor of Zion's unbreakable love for his wife Isidore. Tomorrow, at the engagement celebration, when you accept his proposal, Veric will chain your left wrist. At the wedding, he will chain your right wrist. Those chains will stay there for the rest of your life."

A coldness settled over me as Clay's eyes grew distant, focused entirely on my hand.

"Why are you telling me this?" I whispered.

He chuckled, raising an eyebrow. "Don't you want to know what to expect?"

We both knew that wasn't why he was here. It wasn't why he'd shown up at my door with a bottle of wine. It wasn't why he'd moved his room to the hall where I was staying. It wasn't why he'd insisted on coming on this trip in the first place.

He sighed, sensing my frustration. "I'm telling you this because tonight is the last night you'll be just Thea. Here, in Tenebris, you're not a Councilwoman. No one cares if I come into your room or if we stay up all night talking. But tomorrow? Once that chain is on your wrist, you'll be Veric's fiancé. Everything will change. So I'm asking you to spend one night with me before that happens. Nothing more, nothing less."

I wanted to remind him that while Veric's chain wasn't on my wrist yet, his was most certainly on Elaina's. We weren't just Thea and Clay. We couldn't be.

But I couldn't move past the looming dread his words had inspired. He was right. Tomorrow, once that chain was on my wrist, there would be no going back. Everything *would* change.

Well, fuck. I supposed I deserved a night off from being responsible.

Reaching out, I took the wine bottle from his hand. I held his gaze as I brought it to my lips and drank deeply. His smile grew, and I stepped aside to allow him to walk into my room.

Tenebrisian wine must have been far stronger than anything back home, because a single glass had my head spinning.

Admittedly, there was something... nice about just sitting and laughing with Clay. He was still so shockingly relaxed here. I savored every moment I got to see him like this, comfortable and happy. Lounging back on the on the floor, leaning against the couch with an elbow propped on his knee, he smiled softly as he recounted a story about some mischief he and Iris had gotten into as children. His gray eyes sparkled as he stared up at the ceiling, his expression distant yet content.

"Play a game with me," he said suddenly, his gaze snapping to mine.

I took another deep drink from the bottle, eyeing him warily. "What kind of game?"

A game felt...risky.

Perhaps it felt that way because we were alone in my bedroom, me curled in a blanket on the foot of my bed and him only a few feet away. Perhaps it was the glint in his eyes. Or perhaps it was the heat lingering between us ever since we had danced together despite both of us being engaged to others.

His face lit up with a genuine smile, the kind so rare it left me momentarily stunned. I could probably count on one hand the number of times I'd seen him smile like that and I remembered them all because they had all amazed me with their utter beauty. The fact that my mere willingness to humor him had earned it made my chest tighten.

I would play any game he asked to see that smile again.

"I'll ask you a question," he explained. "And you answer truthfully."

My stomach sank and faces flashed in my mind—Hyrax's and Caldrius'. This was indeed a risky game for someone with as many secrets as I had.

"And the fun of this game?" I teased, narrowing my eyes.

"We take turns."

I should say no.

But then again, I hadn't ever been very good at saying no to him.

Curling my feet beneath me, I sat up and tossed my hair back over my shoulders, catching the way his gaze followed the strands. "Fine. You start."

He didn't hesitate. "What's your favorite food?"

Of all the questions he could have asked, that was not one I'd expected. It was hardly prying or invasive. Wasn't the point of this game to dig for truths?

"That's your question?" I asked, incredulous.

He shrugged. "I don't know the answer, and I want to."

I eyed him suspiciously, but answered. "The little chocolate tarts from the kitchens that are usually reserved for your father."

His eyes widened. Those tarts were infamously the Dragon's favorite dessert, and he'd made it clear they were to be prepared only for him.

Those tarts were guarded like they were the finest jewels in the kingdom.

Except the kitchen boy had a crush on Nessira and would give her the shirt off his back if she asked for it.

"How do you manage to get them? I can't even get my hands on those!"

I grinned triumphantly. "That's another question."

Clay laughed, holding up his hands in mock surrender before taking the bottle from me and gesturing for my turn.

"What do you do for fun?" I asked.

A furious blush spread across his cheeks, and he rubbed the back of his neck. "I enjoy mystery stories. Heroes seeking justice and all that."

I'd known that—seen the novels in his room last year—but there was something endearing about hearing him admit it aloud. It was nice seeing Clay as himself.

"What do *you* like to do for fun?" he countered.

Frowning, I leaned my head back against the bed. "I haven't had much time for fun over the past year," I admitted.

"When you have?"

"I liked when we went riding before you took me to Hyrax Estate."

Clay laughed, his gaze distant with the memory a smile lingering on his lips. "I don't think Netta enjoyed it as much as you did."

Several months ago, he'd been the one to first escort me to my ancestral home. We'd raced our horses to get there, and though I'd clearly won, he'd insisted I cheated when my powers accidentally lifted my horse, Netta, into the air. Perhaps it hadn't been my best display of sportsmanship.

I considered my next question. "Do you want to be king?"

Clay tilted his head, as though the question had caught him off guard. He pulled the bottle to his mouth, drinking deeply before answering.

"Truthfully, yes. It's probably more diplomatic to say something about hating the role and only wanting to serve the people, but I was bred and raised to wear that crown. It's the only thing I've ever known. I've worked hard to prepare myself to be a good king. I care about my people—about keeping them safe and fed. As the Dragon, I'll be able to make sure they're taken care of. There are things I'd like to change one day, things I want to revolutionize."

"What things?" I interrupted.

"That's another question," he teased, raising a brow at me. "It's my turn now. What's your favorite color?"

"Orange," I answered quickly, again puzzled by his choice of a rather simple question.

But as I prepared to continue my previous line of questioning, another thought surfaced. "Last year, you told me the story of Caldrius stealing the Bident of Hyrax for Zeus before the Gods raised the Veil."

He furrowed his brow. "Yes?"

"What happened to him after? Did he have a family - a wife?"

Clay passed the bottle to me and leaned back against the couch, stretching out his long legs and crossing them at the ankle. "What made you think about that?"

I shrugged, feigning innocence. "It just popped into my head."

He stared at me for so long, I wondered if he knew I was lying. If he did, though, he didn't call me on it.

"I'm not sure," he said finally. "Most information about Caldrius has been erased from the Zion family records. He's not exactly celebrated. I believe he had a wife, but I don't know much about her."

The room seemed heavy with unspoken words. I swallowed down the awkwardness with another gulp of wine.

"Tell me what you think of Veric," Clay said softly. It wasn't a question—it was a command.

I sighed. "He's been kind so far. Friendly. Easy to talk to. There are far worse men to be engaged to."

He took the bottle and drank deeply, staring at it for a moment before nodding in agreement. "That's true."

I took the bottle back. "Tell me about Elaina."

"Elaina is... going to be an incredible queen. We've been engaged since before we could walk. Neither of us is the other's first choice." A pointed look in my direction. "But she's kind. Like me, preparing to rule is all she's ever known. She speaks several languages, has traveled the world, served the poor, and studied under renowned healers. She'll be a wife in name, but a queen by birthright."

Jealousy churned miserably in my stomach. Sweet, perfect Elaina. A wonderful woman. A better queen. Everything I could never be.

"Why do you always keep roses in your suite instead of other flowers?" he asked, breaking my spiraling thoughts.

I rolled my eyes. "Surely there are more exciting questions."

His expression sobered as he stood. Silently, he walked towards where I laid sideways across the bed, head propped up by my bent elbow. Clay never looked away from me as he came to stand right in front of me and lowered himself to his knees so that we were eye level.

"You are exciting to me, Thea," he breathed, reaching up to trail his fingers down my cheek and jaw. "Your likes, dislikes. The way your mind works. Your sense of morality. Your body, especially in the fashions of this kingdom, I might add. It all excites me. Yes, there are parts of you that I don't yet know, but I want to. I want to know your favorite food, flower, color. I want to commit it all to memory because it *all* excites me."

My heart sputtered and stalled. I knew it. He had been listening in earlier, when I'd told Veric we weren't friends and hardly knew each other. I'd said it partly to anger him, knowing the words would frustrate him, but I hadn't expected this answer.

"Roses are my favorite," I finally answered, breathless as he leaned closer, as he focused so completely on my lips I thought he might just close that inch of space between us and kiss me. "Because they remind me of you."

His attention on me was absolute. The air between us thickened, every sensation heightened. Warmth was crawling up my body, bringing with it an overwhelming awareness of every place my clothing touched my too-sensitive skin.

He wrapped his hand around the back of my neck. "I've never wanted anything as much as I want you."

This game had been very, very risky.

The adjoining door creaked open suddenly. Nessira entered, carrying washcloths and a flickering candle. Her sharp gaze scanned us, even as we jerked apart, then flickered to the now empty bottle on the floor.

She cleared her throat aggressively. "I've brought towels, my lady."

Flushing deeply, I pointed toward the table. "Leave them there, Nessira."

"It's quite late," she said pointedly, her tone laced with accusation as she glanced at Clay.

Clay stood, taking the bottle. "I should let Lady Moore rest. Big day tomorrow."

Nessira watched him go with arms crossed impatiently across her chest. As the door clicked shut behind him, she turned to me, muttering something about déjà vu before wishing me a good night and leaving me alone with my thoughts.

CHAPTER SEVENTEEN

I opened my eyes in Hyrax's throne room. He sat alone at his dining table, apparently waiting for me, as he used to do so often. Tonight, he wore freshly pressed, immaculate clothes, dark fabric accented by silver embroidery at the cuffs. He had neatly combed and styled his gray hair and beard. He looked every bit as impeccable as one might expect of a God.

When his gaze met mine, he smiled pleasantly and gestured to the chair at his right, silently inviting me to join him.

A part of me wanted to reject him outright—to stomp my feet, curse him for his lies and misdeeds, and force myself awake and out of this realm. As much as that temptation burned within me, though, his words from our last conversation still echoed in my mind, his declaration that I simply didn't have any memories to recall. I'd been tossing it over for days, tearing myself apart, trying to piece together what that could possibly mean.

If it could be true...

Hyrax was the only person who had ever spoken about my past with such finality. His words carried no doubt, no speculation. As much as I wanted to deny him, I couldn't ignore the possibility that he might hold the answers I'd been so desperate to find.

Reluctantly, I crossed the room and sank into the chair at his table. His blue eyes sparkled as he regarded me.

"This is nice," he remarked, summoning two glasses of wine with an easy wave of his hand. He pulled his to his mouth, smelling deeply before drinking with an appreciative hum. I left mine untouched. "We used to do this more often."

The memory stirred something uneasy in me. "Things were different then."

Back then, I hadn't realized I was visiting the Underworld. I hadn't known that the mentor I had come to trust was the God who had tried to enslave the Mortal race. I hadn't realized the only reason he was showing me kindness was because of some prophecy that I was the key to his release. That had been back when I valued him, when I trusted him.

It wasn't the first time I'd been burned by trusting someone I shouldn't.

Hyrax nodded, his expression pinched in thought. "So you say. Tell me, who exactly did you think you were speaking to in those days?"

I sighed and shrugged. "I don't know. Some specter of my imagination, maybe? Or a face from my past that I'd forgotten."

"I told you," he said firmly, "there are no memories from your past."

There it was again—that same confident declaration, hanging in the air between us.

Somehow it made even less sense now than it had the first time I'd heard it.

"I don't understand," I admitted, my voice quieter as I leaned my elbows forward onto the table. "How can a person simply have no memories?"

Hyrax traced circles along the rim of his crystal glass, his expression pensive. "It's difficult for me to explain."

"What in all of creation could make it difficult to answer basic questions?" My irritation spilled out in sharp words. After all this time, why was he still insisting on keeping these secrets from me? Secrets about me I had every right to know the answer to.

"You must be ready—not only to hear the truth, but to accept it as well."

My frustration erupted. My glass flew from the table, shattering against the stone wall. Shards of crystal glittered as they scattered across the floor. Hyrax didn't flinch. He simply watched, infuriatingly calm as ever, while I struggled to steady my breathing. It had been a long time since I had lost control of my magic like that.

His lips twitched into a faint smirk. "As I was saying, you don't seem ready for that."

Anger burned through me like molten fire, searing every nerve. Just as I was about to unleash the full force of my rage, the door creaked open, and the echo of boots against the stone floor cut through the tension.

Caldrius strode into the room, his dark hair gleaming in the light of the roaring fireplace. He paused when he saw me, dark eyes flicking between Hyrax and me before he offered a polite bow.

"Theadora," he said smoothly with a lopsided grin, "how lovely to see you again."

"Caldrius," I replied, my mind flashing to that night in his chambers.

His knowing gaze lingered on me, as if he could sense the unresolved tension in the room—and where my thoughts had drifted.

"This evening's reports, my liege," he said, walking forward and resting his hand against the back of my chair as he leaned forward to give a stack of parchment to Hyrax with a bowed head. The tips of his fingers traced lightly against my back, barely a touch, yet somehow searing. A slow, absentminded gesture, like he wasn't even thinking about it. Like it was natural. A shiver ran up my spine before I could stop it.

"The new arrivals are waiting outside for you," Caldrius continued.

I frowned. "New arrivals?"

They both glanced at me, their expressions confirming my suspicion. Recently dead souls had arrived.

"Do you greet them personally?" I asked Hyrax.

Rising from his seat, he smoothed his jacket and glanced down at the parchment. It was a list, each name meticulously recorded, with a specific time and date. Their times of death.

"I am the ruler of the Underworld. It is my duty to welcome all souls to their place of rest and determine their future in the realm."

Curiosity itched at the edges of my irritation. Despite my frustration with him, I couldn't suppress it. "What does that mean, exactly?"

There wasn't much written about the Underworld. No one knew what it looked like or how it operated. It wasn't a place you could travel to and learn about until after your death.

...unless you were me, of course.

Hyrax's gaze flicked toward the door, his shoulders tensing slightly.

"You should go, sire," Caldrius said, his tone calm and measured. "I know you dislike keeping them waiting."

Hyrax's gaze lingered on me, conflicted, as though something about me unsettled even a God. Finally, he nodded. "Perhaps we can continue this conversation on your next visit. I would like to share the Underworld with you."

I opened my mouth to respond, only to close it once more entirely. The offer left me speechless. In all of my months visiting this place, Hyrax had never invited me to learn about this realm before. Even in those early days when we might have been friends, he had only ever asked about my life. Then, once I'd realized who he was, I simply assumed that learning more about the Underworld might be forbidden for me, a living soul.

Caldrius' voice broke through my stunned silence, his hand giving my shoulder a gentle squeeze. "I'd be happy to give Theadora a tour while you're occupied, sire."

Hyrax hesitated, his gaze shifting between us, before nodding. "Yes. That would be nice, I think."

*A*s Caldrius led me through the winding tunnels of Hyrax's castle toward the exit, a rush of excitement rolled through me at the thought of exploring this unknown realm.

Caldrius walked beside me with a confident grace, gesturing subtly in the correct direction whenever we reached a crossroads. His dark clothes were simple yet tailored from fine fabric, fitted against his tall frame. His hair, just as dark, fell in thick waves that curled around his ears and the base of his neck. As we walked, I studied him, trying to decipher the man beneath the polished exterior.

"Why are you staring at me?" he asked, a smile playing on his lips even as he kept his gaze forward.

"Why did you offer to do this?"

"Do you always answer a question with a question?"

"Do you?"

His laugh echoed around us, rich and unrestrained. When we finally reached a dark stone door, he pushed it open, and the crisp night air rushed over my skin, wiping every thought from my mind.

The world outside was magnificent.

The night sky stretched endlessly above, scattered with stars so abundant they illuminated the landscape, casting everything in a silver glow. My pale skin, dulled by too many days spent indoors, seemed to radiate under their light. Surrounding the castle, countless flowers bloomed in vibrant shades of red, purple, and orange, untouched by the chill in the air.

And the castle itself...

I spun around to take it in, though its full expanse was impossible to grasp from this close. What I could see mirrored the dark, gothic architecture of

Hyrax Manor. The stone facade stretched high into the sky, crowned with multiple iron spires. Tall windows, framed in intricate ironwork, glinted in the evening starlight.

"You're smiling," Caldrius remarked, his voice soft.

I turned sharply to meet his gaze. "It's beautiful."

"I know," he replied, his eyes locked on mine. "Come."

He offered his arm. After a brief hesitation, I looped my hand through his, allowing him to guide me down the stone stairway that descended the mountain Hyrax's castle rested on. In the distance, the twinkling lights of fiery torches and buildings glimmered like a mirage. Music floated on the breeze, mingling with the unmistakable sound of laughter.

"What is that?" I asked, nodding toward the lights.

"One of the Villages of Life. There are several across the Underworld, each filled with reunited families and loved ones who spend eternity together."

I glance over the expanse of land, the blocked off sections of square patches of land surrounded by dirt-filled wheelbarrows and tools. "They farm?"

He nodded. "They farm, fish, and share all they gather. Food is plentiful here, as is merriment. Villages of Life are a happy place for souls. Living here is their reward after a life well-lived."

I stared at the rolling fields in stunned silence as the sounds of joy grew louder with each step toward the village. From the distance, I could see women laughing and dancing together, children chasing each other through the streets, and men playing lutes while singing.

These souls weren't being tormented or enslaved. There weren't monsters roaming around inflicting terror.

There was joy.

"This isn't what I expected," I admitted.

"You imagined doom and gloom?"

Heat rose to my cheeks, and his grin widened.

"All souls come here, good and bad," Caldrius explained. "Those who deserve happiness in eternity find it. Hyrax is not a monster, Theadora. He frequently visits these people, ensuring their well-being. They love hosting him whenever they can."

"And the-" I paused, unsure of how to best phrase my question. "What of the bad souls? What happens to them?"

Caldrius' steps slowed, and I slowed with him, my hand still tucked in his arm. He looked down at me, a shadow in his eyes as he sighed heavily. He tensed briefly. "Hyrax does nothing. When souls arrive, they judge themselves. They face their misdeeds. If they fail to come to terms with their actions and forgive themselves, their guilt consumes them."

"What happens to them, then?"

Caldrius nodded toward a stretch of wilderness to our left. Dead trees stretched miles high into the sky, their branches twisting unnaturally. Wind whispered through the grove, breathing in the life from the nearby village and exhaling frigid air. I shivered, and Caldrius stepped closer.

"They go there, where their guilt eats away at them. It's... gruesome."

I frowned, staring at the ominous patch of forest. Shadows lingered at the edges of the clear divide between the wooded area and the vibrancy of the space we stood in.

"How gruesome?" I asked.

"They waste away until they're mindless creatures, harming anything in their path. The villagers call them the Undone. I've had to eliminate several who wandered too close to the Villages of Life. It's not a part of my duty I enjoy discussing."

Wordlessly, he untangled my hand from his arm and wrapped it between his fingers instead, tugging firmly and stepped away, effectively ending the conversation. I stumbled after him, not quite matching his hurried pace at first.

"Did you have to go to the forest when you first died?"

A line formed between his brows as he looked down at me. "Why would you ask me that?"

For a moment, a pang of regret coiled in my stomach. "I guess I assumed you would have had to face what you did in the Mortal Realm."

Caldrius was quiet, so quiet that I thought he might not answer me at all until he shifted his arm gently, the motion pulling me closer to him as he looked down at me. "No Thea, I didn't go there. I didn't have to because I felt no guilt for what I did when I was alive."

Ice prickled the back of my neck and raised the hairs on my arms. Caldrius was responsible for the deaths of hundreds of people. How could he feel no remorse for that?

"You may not understand my actions," he whispered, moving us towards the village again. "But the world was different when I was alive. The Gods walked freely in the Mortal Realm, and their presence, their power, changed everything. When I stole Hyrax's Bident, I was serving my God. There was no greater honor."

"And afterwards?"

The end of my question hung in the air between us.

How did he justify becoming such a tyrant that his own brother had to flee across an ocean?

A shadow passed over his face. "Let's just say when the the Gods raised the Veil, they didn't just remove themselves from the Mortal Realm. They took pieces of our world with them, pieces I wasn't able to live without, but I was helpless to stop them. Tell me, who is more culpable - the madman or the God that drove him there?"

I chewed on my lip, unsure what to make of his words, but thankfully, he didn't seem to need a response.

He tapped my hand gently before pointing to the flower bushes lining the road to the village. "Hyrax's castle doesn't have gardens like you're accus-

tomed to, but flowers are plentiful. I can identify them for you as we walk if you want."

He wanted to change the subject, to divert our conversation away from the horrors of the past to instead focus on the beauty that was laid out in front of us. Wanting to shy away from negative memories was something I was all to familiar with.

So, I let the conversation fade away.

"I think I would like that," I told him.

For the next twenty minutes, he spoke no more of Gods or ancient histories.

Our conversation dwindled as we finally reached the pathway leading into the village. I took the opportunity to watch him as he walked slightly ahead of me. Caldrius moved with a balance and grace that belied his height, his sharp jawline faintly reminiscent of Clay's. It struck me how self-assured he seemed—both as a former king and as someone intimately familiar with this path.

As we passed under the archway into the Village of Life, he tugged me forward just as a petite woman with caramel-colored curls and golden skin stepped into view, her wide smile radiating warmth.

"This is Alma," Caldrius introduced. "Alma, this is Theadora, Hyrax's—"

"Oh, I know who she is!" Alma interrupted, rushing forward to clasp my hands in hers. She bowed her head and pressed a kiss to my knuckles.

"Gods, you don't have to do that!" I exclaimed, trying to free my hands.

Alma smiled up at me through dark lashes, her lips quirking playfully. Keeping one hand clasped around mine, she gently tugged me forward. "Nonsense! We're honored to have you here, Theadora. Allow me to show you our home."

As Alma led me through the village, she pointed out the tall, colorful buildings, their stone facades painted with stunning murals of flowers, animals, and idyllic landscapes. She introduced me to every soul we passed, and *each bowed to kiss my knuckles despite my protests. Vendors insisted I sample their baked goods, while children darted between us, plucking flowers from nearby gardens to weave into my hair.*

"This one too!" a little girl called, tugging at the fabric of my skirt. She held up a dandelion, reaching to add it to the growing crown atop my head.

Alma laughed, scooping the girl into her arms. "That's a weed, Amalia! The princess doesn't want weeds in her hair."

Amalia's pout deepened, her lower lip trembling in the unmistakable prelude to a tantrum. Alma sighed, bracing herself.

"Nonsense!" I said quickly, plucking the dandelion from Amalia's small fingers and tucking it behind my ear. "It's beautiful."

Amalia's eyes widened in surprise before she squealed with delight, clapping her hands. "Pretty!"

I laughed, turning to Alma. "Is she yours?"

Amalia's pale skin and light eyes bore little resemblance to Alma's golden complexion, though their hair colors weren't entirely dissimilar. Still, their differences were striking enough to make me curious.

"Oh no," Alma replied, setting Amalia down. The child immediately darted back to a patch of dandelions, giggling. "Amalia arrived a few months ago. She died of a fever. Her parents are still in the Mortal Realm."

"So, who takes care of her?"

Alma tilted her head at me, a surprised smile on her face and her eyes dancing. "We all do, of course. This is the Underworld. Here, we're all family."

*A*fter what felt like hours playing with the children in the Village of Life, Caldrius and I found ourselves on a hill overlooking the bustling village below. I sprawled back in the grass, letting the soft strands thread through my fingertips, while he sat nearby, one arm draped casually over his raised knee.

"This isn't at all what I expected," I said for the second time that night.

The wind tickled my cheeks, carrying the faint scent of flowers mixed with the earthy undertones of the grass beneath me. From below, the sounds of the village floated up to us—snippets of laughter and the distant strumming of lutes. Overhead, the stars stretched endlessly, their light glinting down on the two of us.

Caldrius glanced at me, his expression unreadable. "I'm not surprised."

"It's nothing like anyone in the Mortal Realm would imagine," I continued.

He let out a low chuckle. "I doubt the Mortal Realm's views of the Underworld have changed much since I was alive."

I rolled to my side and propped my head on my hand to see him better. He wasn't looking at me, his gaze fixed on the horizon, lost somewhere I couldn't follow.

"Can you blame them?" I asked, breaking the silence. I had intended to stop asking him about the past, at least for a little while, but somehow we always found ourselves back here. In the place where he always seemed to know more than he was willing to tell me. "Hyrax tried to enslave the Mortal Realm."

Caldrius turned then, his dark eyes meeting mine with unsettling intensity as he pivoted to face me fully. "You still don't trust him."

"I don't see why I should."

His jaw tightened, and for a moment, he remained silent. Then he spoke, his voice laced with frustration. "Has it ever occurred to you that everything *you know about the Underworld—about Hyrax—is nothing more than a story crafted by frightened Mortals to justify their own ignorance?"*

The sharpness in his words caught me off guard. I sat up fully, blonde hair spilling haphazardly over my shoulders. Caldrius's gaze flicked to the strands, softening as if he regretted his outburst.

"I know what Hyrax is capable of," I shot back.

*"You know what he **was** capable of. Do you not think people can change? Surely, you must admit that the Hyrax you've met is not the monster your realm has painted him to be."*

I chewed on my lip. Truthfully, I wasn't sure what I believed about Hyrax. He had lied to me and he had been kind to me all at the same time.

"And if you're not ready to admit it about Hyrax," Caldrius continued, "are you at least ready to admit it about me?"

My stomach somersaulted and I met his eyes. "What do you mean?"

"I know what your realm thinks of me. I know what you thought about me when we met. But now? After all the time we've spent together, do you still agree with them? Or is part of you now questioning those stories? Do you wonder what could have driven me to the choices that led to my death?"

The wind tousled my hair, and this time he reached out, tucking the unruly strands behind my ear. The gesture sent a strange warmth rushing through me and he let his hands linger on the base of my throat before pulling away slowly.

"So what was it, then?" I asked, imploring him with my eyes to finally cease being vague and actually let me in. "You want me to trust that you're not a monster? Prove it to me then. Tell me what happened to you."

He looked away, his eyes unfocused for a moment and I was just about to stand, frustrated at his avoidance when he finally spoke.

And it all poured out.

"I was Zion's favorite—his grandson, his chosen heir, his most trusted confidant. He'd been in my life since I was a child. When he came to me with

his plan to steal the Bident, I didn't question him. He was a God, after all. Who was I to question his judgement? I should have, though. In all those years that he had been with me, he watched me fall in love with Isidore. When my father nearly disowned me for rejecting my marriage, Zion was the one who told him to show me mercy."

Caldrius' lip pulled back from his teeth in disgust and he leaned back heavily onto his hand. He seemed entirely lost in his memories until a shudder rushed through me from the chill in the air, suddenly pulling his focus back to me. Without stopping his story, he shrugged off his jacket and passed it to me.

"Before my father died, Zion told him to not pass into the Underworld with anger in his heart. He said that Isidore was far too beautiful to stay away from. I had thought he was defending me. I thought he loved me. Turns out, he just wanted her. And when a God wants something, there is no asking. No denying. He saw her, he decided she was his, and by the time I realized what had happened, she was already gone. While I was stealing Hyrax's Bident, Zion was stealing her. The next day, the Veil rose, and I lost her forever."

A memory scratched at the back of my mind, but it slipped away before I could grasp it.

"I was out of my mind with grief," Caldrius continued, his voice thick with emotion. "And as the closest relation to Zion, my power was unmatched in the Mortal Realm, especially with the Bident in my possession. My brother thought that made me dangerous. Truthfully, I think deep down, he just wanted a crown of his own. So, after Zion became the first of my blood to betray me, Ennoss became the second. He stole the Bident, fled to Athenia, and left me to the assassins he hired. They killed me simply because my magic was stronger than theirs."

A chill swept through me, my thoughts scattering like leaves in the wind. I wanted to speak, to respond, but no words came.

"You don't believe me," he murmured, turning his gaze back to me. His voice was calmer now, but his dark eyes burned with conviction. "But deep down, you know I'm right. You've seen how quick they are to fear anyone more powerful than themselves. You know they look at you with that same fear."

A shiver crept down my spine, unbidden. He wasn't wrong. I had seen it. That day in the ballroom, when I'd brought an entire room of assassins to their deaths with a simple thought, those that were left standing had stared at me with terror etched on their faces.

"Even your prince," Caldrius added, his tone softening to something almost coaxing. "Do you think he'd be willing to accept what he doesn't understand? Imagine how he'd react if he knew you were here... if he knew you were with me."

His hand found mine, his fingers curling around my own in a gentle squeeze.

Numbly, I stared at our intertwined hands, my mind drifting to Clay. What would he think if he knew where I was? Who I was with? Would he even listen long enough for me to explain? And even if he did, what could I say to justify any of this?

My fingers twitched in Caldrius's grasp, but I didn't pull away.

"You know I'm right," he pressed, his voice a whisper now.

I lifted my gaze to meet his, the weight of his dark eyes pressing into me. For a long moment, I couldn't find the words to respond.

And maybe that was answer enough.

CHAPTER EIGHTEEN

I woke suddenly, my blood still rushing from the memory of it all.

I sat up and finger-combed through my hair while a small grin played at the edges of my lips.

Despite the ominous conversation with Caldrius that ended my visit, this might have been my most enjoyable trip to the Underworld yet. I never could have imagined the world that existed beyond the cold, imposing walls of Hyrax's castle. Even now, I doubted anyone would believe me if I tried to tell them about it.

Although, I supposed that simply proved Caldrius' very point. Hyrax was a villain by all Mortal accounts, so naturally we would expect his realm to be nothing more than a nightmare given form.

And yet, it wasn't.

For those who had earned eternal happiness, he had created a paradise. The Underworld was a place where everyone could live and work together peacefully, where every soul was accepted and celebrated. Hyrax ensured that while all souls came to the Underworld, not all had to suffer.

The suffering was reserved for the Undone alone. Caldrius had looked… haunted when he described them. And if a man whose legacy was infamous could look that way, what kind of creatures could inspire such a reaction? The thought clawed at the edges of my mind, refusing to let go.

And then there was how we ended things—his warning about Clay.

Caldrius had been certain Clay wouldn't accept my relationship with him, whatever that relationship even was. But there was also the insinuation that had lingered under his words. He wasn't just warning me that Clay wouldn't accept my friendship with him; he was warning me that Clay wouldn't be able to accept *me*.

But that didn't make any sense.

Clay already knew my powers were far greater than anyone else realized. He knew I'd survived the power-stripping ritual unscathed. He knew I could kill an entire room with a thought. He knew and accepted all those things without hesitation, without fear.

Clay knew I wasn't a monster.

I trusted him completely.

A sound jolted me from my thoughts. Footsteps. Slow, measured, deliberate. Purposefully quiet. My hand flew to the dagger stashed under my pillow, and I pulled magic to my fingertips instinctively. Whoever was in the hall didn't want to be overheard.

Which wasn't a good sign.

My pulse quickened as I rose silently from my bed, gripping the dagger tightly. Anxiety coiled through me, tightening my muscles and sending my heart racing, but I moved anyway, tiptoeing to the door.

The steps stopped just outside. A latch clicked softly, followed by the faint creak of a door swinging open.

"You're late," I heard Clay whisper.

CHAPTER NINETEEN

Without daring to breathe, I pressed my palm against the door handle, twisting it slowly and pulling it open just enough to peer into the hallway.

I had only a second to glimpse the stranger before he slipped past Clay and into my prince's suite. Clay looked down both ends of the corridor to check if his guest was followed, and then he shut the door behind them with a hollow click.

But that second that I had watched them had been enough. Enough to notice the finely tailored clothes, so distinct from Athenian styles. Enough to recognize the tall stature, tanned skin, and dark hair of the Imperial Prince of Tenebris.

What was Prince Damon doing sneaking into Clay's room in the middle of the night?

Was this the mysterious business that had led Clay to join me on this trip?

My heart thundered as I crept into the hallway, each step deliberate and soundless. The floor beneath me seemed louder than ever, creaking faintly as I moved. I reached Clay's door, breath catching in my throat, and pressed my ear against the wood.

"Have you any updates on what I proposed?" Clay's voice was low but insistent.

"What you proposed is impossible," Damon replied, his voice taut with restrained frustration. "My father will never go against his current alliance with the Athenian Dragon."

"Your father is currently opening his borders to Promissa. That seems like going against Athenia to me."

A heavy pause followed.

"They could arrest me for treason for even having this conversation."

"Which is why I ensured my rooms were far from prying ears," Clay countered, his tone sharp despite the hush.

In the guest hall. Seperate from the Royal Wing.

He hadn't stayed here to be close to me, he'd stayed here to have this meeting in private.

The irony wasn't lost on me. In his effort to avoid spies, he had unwittingly placed himself right next to me—the very person who *was* spying on him.

"Yes, well this conversation is unavoidable. We're no longer boys, Damon."

Damon sighed, and for a moment, silence filled the space between them.

"My father has always talked out of both sides of his mouth," Damon said finally. "He says what he must to appease both Athenia and Promissa, but he will never risk another Great War. He won't support you."

"I didn't come here for his support," Clay said, his voice steady.

"I just told you—"

"I didn't say the Emperor in question had to be your father."

Another silence fell, heavy and sharp. A slow, icy shiver crept up my spine.

"Surely, you are not suggesting what I think you are," Damon said, his voice trembling, whether with anger or fear. I couldn't tell.

"Of course not," Clay reassured him smoothly. "My plans will take time to set into motion, but it's no secret that your father's affection for his goblets is drawing him ever closer to death's door."

Damon grunted, a sound that felt like reluctant agreement.

"You and I both know that you will become the next Emperor far sooner than I will become the next Athenian Dragon," Clay continued. "You've met my father, Damon. You know what he's capable of. We cannot allow him to destroy everything my ancestors fought to build. Every day, he drives us closer to ruin. The people are starving, our borders are crumbling, and Promissa is circling like vultures. I've seen what happens when a kingdom falls, Damon. I won't let it happen to Athenia."

"What is it you want from me, Clayton?"

"I want your word—not just as a friend, but as the next monarch of Tennebris. I want your assurance that when I overthrow my father, your armies will be ready to support me if the need arises."

"What you ask for is no small thing," Damon said, his voice tight with unease. "You know I love my country, but betraying my father? Risking everything for this alliance? Do you have any idea what you're asking of me, Clayton?"

"I'm aware. I must ask it, nonetheless."

There was a long pause, then the unmistakable sound of two hands clasping in agreement.

"I suppose this is my first official alliance," Damon said.

Clay laughed softly. "And I suppose this is mine."

The creak of furniture signaled one of them rising. My heart lurched, and I darted back into my room, sliding under the covers without making a sound. My chest heaved as I lay still, staring at the ceiling, my thoughts racing. There was only one explanation for that conversation coming to mind.

Clay was planning a coup.

My thoughts tangled in a storm of confusion and dread. This was *treason*. The justification of his reasons didn't matter. If the Dragon found out, he would have Clay executed without mercy and have one of his younger sister's named as heir.

Footsteps echoed in the hall, retreating until I could no longer hear them. Until all I could hear was the realization repeating itself like a mantra in my head.

Clayton Vail was a traitor.

And the Dragon would kill him for it.

I laid in the dark, staring aimlessly as my heart refused to slow for what felt like an eternity. In truth, it must have only been a few minutes before my door creaked open and Clay stepped inside though.

He moved through the shadows without a word, his footsteps soft but his presence heavy. Sitting at the side of my bed, he leaned forward, resting his elbows on his knees with a heavy sigh. His shoulders slumped under the weight he carried, a burden that seemed unbearable even for him. And I didn't have the slightest idea what to say to him.

We sat like that for a long time and the silence stretched between us, taut and unyielding. Neither of us knew how to begin, how to bridge the yawning chasm that had grown between us.

I wanted to hug him and throttle him all at the same time.

Which was, honestly, how I felt about him most of the time.

"You heard."

It wasn't a question. It didn't have to be.

"How did you know?"

He laughed softly, a bitter sound almost swallowed by the quiet. "I'm always aware of you, Thea. Sometimes, I can't tell if your scent is real or just a figment of my mind, but that floral aroma of yours... it was too strong to deny this time."

I frowned. "You can smell me?"

A slight nod. "It's a Dragon thing."

"Then why didn't you stop the conversation?" I demanded, my voice tight with emotion.

Part of me admired him—admired the strength it took to attempt what he was planning. I had always known Clay would make a better ruler than his father ever could. The fact that he was willing to risk his own life for the good of his people spoke volumes about the kind of leader he would be.

But did that make him a good man?

Because I may be hiding things from him, but I wasn't the only one. More often than not, over these past few months, he too had kept secrets from me. He'd lied to me. And now, this was one more betrayal to add to the growing list.

It didn't matter if we couldn't be together because of our bloodlines.

We couldn't be together because it was becoming apparent that we didn't trust each other.

"I suppose I didn't mind if you happened to find out," he breathed. "I couldn't bring myself to tell you—I didn't want to put you in that kind of danger—but I hated the idea of something else lingering between us."

"I've been in danger since the moment I showed up," I reminded him sharply. "You still should have told me. Who else knows?"

"Iris. A few members of the Guard I trust. And now Damon."

Iris. An invisible fist wrapped around my heart with an iron-tight grasp. Of course she was involved in this too.

My arm snatched out, grabbing his wrist. "He'll kill you, Clay. He'll kill anyone who helps you."

Finally, he lifted his head, meeting my gaze. I expected fire in his eyes, the burning passion that usually lurked there, but all I saw was a heavy sadness as he twisted his arm to take hold of my hand.

"I'm aware of what I'm risking," he said, his voice low and steady. "But I have to do what's right. It's not just his cruelty, Thea, or the abuse of the women at Court. It's the way he taxes the poor to keep them in need of his support. Then he withholds that support to manipulate them into submission.

"He appoints the most deplorable of his friends to be dukes, even though they show no regard for the well-being of their provinces. There are parts of this country you haven't seen, Thea. Good people who are dying in poverty because he wants them to. He wants them to feel like they need him. He wants them to fear how much worse it could be without the crumbs he throws their way."

The sheets slipped to my waist as I sat up, my thin nightgown brushing against my skin. I didn't care, and he didn't even seem to notice. His words hung in the air between us, too heavy to ignore.

"And you will change all those things?" I asked, my voice soft but firm.

He paused, letting the tension coil tighter, pulling me closer to the edge of understanding. A shiver raced down my spine, the weight of his answer already pressing down on me.

"I will change so many things, Theadora," he said at last, his voice a promise as much as it was a challenge.

"Like what?"

"Like the Council," he said, his tone sharper now, more resolute. He squeezed my hand gently. "I'm going to change everything about the Council."

C lay didn't stay to explain what his proposed changes to the Council were. He simply told me to get some sleep and left, pulling the door closed tightly behind him. As if sleep was possible when those words turned over and over in my mind.

Surely, the changes he referenced weren't about... *Council marriages.*

There were plenty of other reforms he could have meant. Perhaps he wanted to change the Trials? Or question the tradition of the most powerful family member from the High Houses being appointed to the Council. Maybe he intended to expand the Council to include Descendants from other Houses.

There were countless possibilities Clay could have been mulling over long before he ever met me.

But I knew Clay. Deep in my soul, I understood him in a way I didn't understand anyone else. My gut was telling me he wasn't talking about any of those other ideas.

The thought gnawed at me. Even when he left my room, sleep evaded me, and lying in bed only made my thoughts spiral further—Councils, magical realms, marriages, politics. I was so fucking *tired* of thinking about politics.

Eventually, I abandoned my bed and settled at the desk, tracing idle shapes as my mind wandered. I let myself drift to simpler things: the feel of sunlight on my skin in the Village of Life, the way the laughter there had felt warm and real. It had been more of a home than any other place I'd known—more than Hyrax Manor, more than the halls of Athenia.

The shapes on the parchment began to meld together, almost unconsciously, until I realized I was staring at the likeness of Caldrius.

I blinked, startled, and something bubbled inside of me—something absurd and ridiculous. Laughter erupted from my throat, unbidden and uncontrollable.

"Oh Gods," I groaned, dropping my head into my hands.

It wasn't a bad depiction of him, in all honesty. I suspected he'd have opinions about my shading, but there was no denying it was him. The dark curls that framed his ears, the large, expressive eyes, the full lips curved into that too-knowing, teasing smile. It was undeniably Caldrius.

Supreme Lieutenant of the Underworld. Second in command to Hyrax, God of Death. The Descendant King responsible for the tragedy that had birthed Athenia.

He'd refused his arranged marriage.

But he'd also lost everything because he chose love over politics.

"One day, these secrets are going to eat me alive," I whispered to the drawing, folding the parchment neatly before tucking it into the bottom of my chest of belongings.

CHAPTER TWENTY

I stared at my reflection in the mirror as Nessira twisted my long blonde waves into intricate braids, tucking them away from my face. My lip ached from the constant chewing as I worried over what Clay had said the night before, but I couldn't seem to stop.

His plans didn't even matter, anyway.

Based on Clay's conversation with Prince Damon, his plans wouldn't be coming to fruition anytime soon. My marriage to Veric, however was imminent. Whatever Clay had intended for the Council—whatever sparks might have lingered between us—were irrelevant now. If Clay was planning to change the laws, it wasn't for us. It was for the next pair of star-crossed lovers who would finally be able to allow themselves to embrace the spark that secretly burned between them.

"You seem distant this morning, my Lady," Samsa noted as she slipped my feet into the hard-soled shoes I'd be wearing today.

I glanced down at her, then met Nessira's eyes in the looking glass as she stepped back to admire her handiwork. I stood, smoothing my skirt with trembling fingers, and took a deep, cleansing breath.

"All is well, Samsa," I said, my voice steadier than I felt. "We should go. Veric is likely waiting for me."

Clay was a future that didn't exist for me. I needed to embrace the one I would have.

Veric stood by the exterior palace doors, waiting as we descended the last steps from the guest rooms. His gaze met mine, and his wide smile softened something in my chest.

"You look absolutely stunning, Theadora," he said, taking my hand and bowing deeply. "Tenebris suits you."

Once again, Nessira and Samsa had chosen an ensemble from this country's fashions for me to wear. The cropped blouse, fitted beneath my breasts, displayed intricate beading and embroidery on the dusty rose fabric. Its neckline was scandalously low, requiring extra preparation time for Nessira to paint the Mark of Hyrax across my chest. My matching skirt flared with golden flowers expertly embroidered along the hem. Dangling gold earrings completed the look, along with a delicate veil folded seamlessly into the braids of my hair.

"Thank you, Veric."

Veric himself looked striking in a long white tunic with elaborate golden thread work and a high collar. His bare arms—exposed to adjust for the heat—were impressively defined. In the daylight, his thick hair shone darker, his eyes even brighter. And he grinned at me with a genuineness that made my heart ache.

He tucked my arm into his, keeping that smile plastered on his face as he led me outside into the warm embrace of the day. The heat wrapped around us like a heavy blanket as Nessira and Samsa followed at a respectable distance.

As we reached the edges of the palace property, I frowned, glancing around. "Will the guards be joining us?"

Veric tilted his head, his confusion mirroring my own. "Why would they?"

"I'm a Princess of House Hyrax," I said simply. There hadn't been a single day in my life that I didn't have a guard attached to my hip.

Veric's grin widened, his voice dropping to a conspiratorial whisper. "I suspect your Crown Prince will be displeased when he finds out, but let's just say the guards owed me a favor."

"You convinced them not to come? *How?*"

"I meant what I said last night," he told me earnestly, his grip on my arm tightening slightly as he tugged me to continue our walk. "I want to know my future wife, not my future Councilwoman. That distinction is important to me."

Exploring Tenebris with Veric by my side was exhilarating, if only because I got to see it through his eyes. Every corner we turned ignited his excitement, his voice animated as he rattled off facts about the history and architecture of every street, building, and monument.

He walked me to the school where he had mastered his magic and introduced me to the elderly mentor who had taught him. He showed me the courtyard where he and his friends had spent their boyhood afternoons, laughing as he recounted stories of pranks and mischief. His life unfolded before me, piece by piece, and I listened to each story with rapt attention, allowing myself to see the world the way he did.

Eventually, we found ourselves in what Veric called the market district, a labyrinth of vibrant streets filled with colorful stalls. Merchants sold everything from rich textiles to elaborate pottery, fragrant spices, and shimmering jewelry. Each step brought a new scent—grilled meats sizzling over open flames, the sweet bite of cinnamon and cardamom wafting through the air.

Artisans lined the narrow paths, displaying leather goods, carved wooden figurines, and delicate beaded veils.

Veric's passion for it all was infectious. He moved from stall to stall, his energy boundless as he asked questions, teased the vendors, and insisted I sample their offerings. His admiration for his homeland shone through every word and gesture.

And yet, as we walked, I couldn't shake the image of the Village of Life from my mind. Despite the warm welcome from the Tennebrisians—some bowing, others inviting me to dance or sample their wares—the connection I felt to them didn't compare to what I'd experienced the night before.

Still, Tenebris was undeniably beautiful. Even here in this bustling market corridor, where people darted in and out of shops and homes, the buildings towered elegantly. Their sparkling windows and wide arches glinted in the sunlight, and every stone seemed to glow under the warm air. Even the streets themselves were works of art, painted with intricate murals of gods, mythical creatures, and sprawling landscapes.

After nearly an hour of strolling, Veric noticed me staring at one of the street paintings and glanced at me, curiosity etched on his face.

"Do you recognize it?" he asked.

I chuckled softly, my gaze fixed on the image of a beast with multiple heads, each one more venomous than the last. "I killed it."

Veric slowed to a stop, tilting his head in disbelief. Then he laughed.

"No, I mean it," I insisted.

His brows shot up. "You killed the Hydraxan?"

"During my magic trial. And believe me, it wasn't easy. I nearly died."

His expression shifted—confusion giving way to disbelief, then to something that almost looked like admiration. He whistled softly, taking my hand and leading me onward.

"You know something?"

"Hmm?"

"You're somehow equal parts terrifying and awe-inspiring. It's not at all how I expected you to be."

I snorted, feeling a blush creep up my cheeks as we continued our path through the market. As we walked, I let my attention wander to a nearby cart, where an older merchant displayed an array of blades and weapons.

I approached slowly, not letting go of Veric's hand as I studied the collection. None of the weapons seemed particularly formidable; many needed polishing or sharpening, but the hilts were beautifully carved with elaborate swirls and lines.

"They're mostly decorative," Veric explained as I lifted one, testing its weight with a frown. "Used to signify status or worn during special occasions."

"Like what?"

He took the blade from my palm and twirled it effortlessly between his fingers before holding it up to the vendor. "Two silvers."

Fishing the coins from his pocket, Veric handed them over and extended the blade to me, hilt-first, with an elaborate flourish and a bow.

"For you."

"You didn't have to," I laughed, accepting the gift.

"Well, they're worn on occasions like our party tonight. It's a tradition for the groom's father to etch the handle of his sword."

"And is it tradition for the bride to have a weapon?"

He met my gaze conspiratorially. "No, but I suspect that might be a tradition you're willing to start."

Nessira took the dagger to carry for me while Samsa helped with the box of spices and teas Veric purchased on my behalf. At first, he'd frowned when I asked for them, insisting he could get me anything I wanted—that just further up the street were the finest bakeries and dressmakers in the country.

But I'd only shaken my head. "The spices and tea are exactly what I want."

He seemed suspicious as we passed a cart of sparkling jewelry that stole Nessira's attention, but I held firm. Spices and tea were practical things that I could easily bring back to Athenia. I'd save them for a time when Veric felt particularly homesick and surprise him with the familiar flavors.

It wasn't much, but it was something. It wouldn't give him the life he wanted here in Tenebris, but perhaps it would ease the ache just a little.

We got along well enough. Veric had made me laugh several times throughout the day, and he was always kind and considerate. He matched his pace to mine and consistently offered breaks for rest or food. He shared everything he could with me, teaching me about his culture and his place within it.

Truthfully, I liked Veric.

It wasn't the same passionate intensity I felt for Clay—the kind of connection that could either set us ablaze together or burn down the realm around us. Glancing at Veric didn't send tingling anticipation racing through my veins. Holding his hand was nice, but it didn't leave me acutely aware of every place our skin touched.

But it was *something*. There were much worse men to be married to. So, I would commit myself to nurturing that companionship for the rest of our lives.

As the sun climbed higher, the streets became more crowded and the noise of the market district began swelling around us. People jostled past, their voices rising in a cacophony of bartering, laughter, and chatter. Veric guided me through it all, one hand wrapped around me and the other firm on my back, but there was a growing sense of unease prickling at the edges of my awareness.

I couldn't pinpoint it at first. A shift in the air, maybe, or the way certain merchants glanced nervously at the edges of the square. Even Veric seemed more alert, his amiable smiles fading as he scanned the crowd.

Then came the distant sound of boots. Heavy, measured, and growing louder.

The first soldier appeared at the far end of the square, his dark uniform a sharp contrast to the colorful stalls. Then another. And another.

The merchants fell silent first, their voices trailing off as the soldiers pressed forward. Shoppers paused, their gazes darting between the guards and each other. The festive energy of the market evaporated in an instant, replaced by tension so thick it was suffocating.

"What's happening?" I whispered, gripping Veric's arm.

He didn't answer immediately, his expression darkening as more soldiers poured into the square.

Then chaos erupted.

"What are you doing?" Samsa cried, clutching the glass of tea leaves just as a soldier grabbed her arm.

The jar shattered on the stones, splintering into shards that cut into my ankles.

"Let go of her!" I demanded, reaching for the blade at my thigh.

My magic surged as I focused on the soldier holding Samsa, forcing his grip to loosen. She stumbled free, running into Nessira's arms. But even as I acted, more soldiers closed in, their shouts ringing above the chaos.

"What is the meaning of this?" Veric demanded, his voice sharp as a soldier seized him.

It all happened too fast. Hands reached for me, for Samsa, for Nessira. They were ripped backwards away from me.

And suddenly I wasn't looking at my ladies. I was seeing red hair, a hand wrapped around a throat, a floor covered in the blood of my friend.

Veric was dragged away, his protests drowned in the rising noise.

My magic split, wanting all at once to protect him and Nessira and Samsa, but I couldn't do it all. Especially not with this many people in the square and with the guards moving so quickly. They surrounded me, their distrust obvious. Magic crackled in the air between us.

I ripped my power up from the depths of my gut prepared to unleash it when a sharp jab in my neck stopped me cold.

The syringe emptied, its contents icy as they spread through my veins. My legs gave out first, and I collapsed into the waiting arms of a soldier. My arms went numb next, and the dagger slipped from my fingers, clattering onto the stones with a loud clang.

I felt my magic fighting against the poison, pulsing desperately to defend me, but it was no use.

The last thing I saw before darkness consumed me was a shimmering golden thread, glowing faintly in the air before it disappeared into nothingness.

CHAPTER TWENTY ONE

I knew immediately that someone had moved me. The air around me was damp and stale, heavy with the scent of stone and earth. As I slowly blinked my eyes open, the dim lighting stung as my vision struggled to adjust. Slowly, the shapes around me came into focus—a dirty stone wall, a rough dirt floor.

I slumped against the wall, my body leaden and unresponsive. Whatever drug they had injected into me still coursed through my veins, leaving me entirely paralyzed. I couldn't move, couldn't speak, couldn't even scream. All I could do was stare down at my body, at the shackles clamped tightly around my wrists and ankles.

Panic rose like a tide, threatening to consume me.

This couldn't be happening. Not now. Not after I'd been so diligent in being the person they wanted me to be. I'd done everything anyone had asked of me. And yet, here I was, locked away, just as I had been on that very first day in Athenia.

Memories clawed their way to the surface: burns on my arms, explosions shattering the world around me, shadows ripping my skin apart. They assaulted me, each one sharper than the last, until a strangled gasp finally escaped from deep in my throat, the first sound I'd managed since waking.

I wanted to scream, to cry, to force the panic back down, but my body betrayed me.

Then a voice cut through the chaos.

"Thea, breathe!"

Clay.

The sound shocked me out of my spiraling terror. My eyes darted across the cell, and there he was, slumped on the ground opposite me. His face was hollow, his breathing labored, and his body lay at an awkward angle, as if he'd tried to move toward me but hadn't been able to make it far.

"You're going to be okay," he promised, his voice strained but steady. "I swear, but I need you to stay calm for me."

I didn't care about my own well-being, though. Not anymore. All my fear, all the memories, faded the moment I saw the newly purple bruise across his jaw.

But my mouth wouldn't cooperate enough to tell him that.

I sat there, trapped in a body that felt like it wasn't my own, focusing all my effort on forcing my quivering lips to form words. My head throbbed with the effort.

Finally, I managed to whisper, "What in all of creation is happening?"

Clay's expression softened, relief flickering across his face. "Are you okay?"

"No, I'm not okay!" The words tumbled out in a rush, each one a little less of a struggle. "One minute I was trying pastries, and the next I'm being stabbed with some mysterious drug—for the *second* time in my life, I might add—and I couldn't do anything to stop it! What's the point of having so much power if I can't—"

"Theadora!"

His sharp bark cut through my ramble, urgent and intense. My breath hitched as his eyes locked on mine, scanning me desperately. Veins pulsed in his neck as he strained to lift his head higher, inching closer despite the chains binding him.

"I need to know you're not injured," he said, his voice breaking slightly.

"I'm fine, Clay," I said, my tone softening. "I'm unharmed. Just angry."

A dry chuckle escaped him as he let his head fall back to the ground. "You're not the only one."

"What happened?" I asked.

"I was with Damon, playing cards, when the guards rushed in shouting something about the Zion Archives being raided. Before I knew it, the syringe was in my neck." His jaw tightened, and he exhaled shakily. "I put up as much of a fight as I could because I knew if they were coming for me, they'd already gotten to you. But whatever it is that they used... it's not Mortal blood. I'd wager it's magically engineered—something mixed with Mortal blood."

His explanation faded into the background as those first words hit me like a hammer.

The Zion Archives had been raided.

"Clay," I said slowly, the pieces of the puzzle already falling into place, "who would do that? Who would raid the Zion Archives?"

His brows knit together as he frowned. "I don't know. Magical dealers, maybe? Looking for wares to sell. Usually, they don't go anywhere near official archives of the High Houses. Especially not House Zion. We don't take kindly to that sort of thing."

Of course not. To raid the Zion Archives would mean taking an enormous risk—one no one would dare without a powerful reason.

Unless, of course, someone promised protection to whoever conducted the raid. And if the person offering that protection was powerful enough to ensure their safety, that might make it worth the risk.

But what was inside the Archives?

"Clay," I said, my voice low and purposefully quiet. "Where is the Sword of Zion?"

His frown deepened. "What do you mean?"

Zion's Sword was his God-forged weapon, like Hyrax's Bident. His power was stregthened when he wielded it.

"Does Zion have it? In the Upperworld?"

Silence stretched between us. His gaze darkened, and when he finally spoke, his voice was cautious. "I'm not supposed to say, Thea. House Zion has never revealed the location of the sword since the Veil went up."

He didn't need to say anything else.

His hesitation told me everything I needed to know.

The Sword of Zion was here, in this realm. And whoever had raided the archives hadn't done so at random. They were looking for it.

And I had a pretty good guess why.

A bubble of laughter rose in my chest, bitter and mirthless. The laughter turned into a groan as I let my head fall back against the wall, the implications crashing over me like a tidal wave.

My secrets had finally caught up with me.

Who would want Zion's weapon? A weapon only usable by Zion himself—or perhaps by another God of similar power?

Perhaps his twin brother.

I looked at Clay, feeling sensation slowly return to my fingertips as my magic stirred weakly in my veins. I couldn't avoid this confession any longer.

"I have to tell you something," I said, my voice shaking with the weight of what I was about to say.

The words came easily. Once the first one escaped my lips, the rest tumbled out in a flood—an endless, unrelenting waterfall of tragedy and secrets that I had locked away for far too long.

I told Clay about the night I first arrived in the Underworld, about the eerie stillness of that awful lake and the chilling welcome from Hyrax's hound. Then, I told him about meeting Hyrax for the first time, and then about every meeting afterward. I described the way Hyrax spoke, the calculated grace of his mannerisms, the subtle power behind his words.

Through it all, Clay sat quietly, his golden eyes fixed on me as he slowly regained enough strength to prop himself against the stone wall. His face remained unreadable, save for a flicker of emotion when I admitted to going to see Camilla while he had been in the infirmary. By the time I recounted the prophecy, however, that fleeting expression had disappeared, his features once again impassive.

In that dimly lit prison cell, our bodies still weighed down and immovable, I told Clay everything. Every detail that had been buried deep within me spilled into the stale, dusty air. And when I finally purged the last of it from my system, I met his steady gaze.

"You think Hyrax is behind this somehow?" he asked after a pause.

"He's trapped in the Underworld," I said, shaking my head. "I don't know how he could be, but this all feels a little too coincidental, don't you think?"

I wasn't sure I believed in coincidences anymore—especially not ones involving my godly ancestor.

Clay was silent for a moment, his gaze distant as he worked through my words. "Do you know what he would want the sword for?"

Caldrius' past had made it clear that no one but Hyrax could wield his Bident safely. But perhaps that restriction applied only to those with Mortal blood. Maybe the Gods weren't bound by the same limitations.

"Maybe he's able to use its magic somehow?" I suggested.

"Why wouldn't he just go after his Bident?" Clay countered, frowning. "That's in the Mortal Realm too."

The question stuck in my mind, its implications unraveling. The Bident was Hyrax's chosen weapon, the ultimate symbol of his power, and it was currently sitting unguarded at Hyrax Manor. Why wouldn't he seek it out first? Why would he want his brother's sword instead?

I shook my head softly, unease coiling in my chest. Maybe I was reading too much into this. Maybe Hyrax had nothing to do with any of it.

Then again, there was an easy way for me to find out.

I could always just ask him directly.

"When exactly were you planning to tell me about all of this?" Clay's voice cut through my thoughts like a blade.

The air in the room shifted. While I had gotten lost in my own theories, my confession had settled between us. Clay had taken it all in, processed it, and come to terms with how he felt. And from the fire in his eyes, I could tell exactly what that feeling was.

He was furious.

I flinched instinctively, but the words that escaped my lips were bitter and defensive. "I couldn't tell you."

Clay rolled his eyes, a low snarl escaping him. "You not only could have told me, you *should* have. All this time, I knew it—I knew you were keeping something from me."

A dark chuckle rose in my throat before I could stop it. How dare he. How dare *Clay*, of all people, accuse me of withholding secrets?

"What exactly is funny, Miss Moore?"

"Frankly, you are, Mr. Vail," I snapped. "As if you have any right to criticize me for keeping things from you."

He scoffed, his eyes narrowing. "How long are you going to punish me for not telling you about Elaina? I've already told you she means nothing to me."

I stiffened, surprised. "I was actually referencing your secret little plans with Prince Damon," I shot back, my voice dripping with venom. "But thanks for reminding me it's actually twice you've left me in the dark."

"And both were for your best interest!" he countered, his tone rising.

"That's not for you to decide, Clay! You should have trusted me."

"Just like you should have trusted me enough to tell me about the Underworld! Damn it, I could have helped you, Thea. You didn't have to carry this burden alone."

"It isn't your burden."

"That isn't the point," he growled. "I have spent every day for months knowing that the person I care about most is hiding something from me. I watched you wither away. Watched you spend days without sleeping. Walked the palace halls looking for you, only to learn you'd been at Hyrax Manor for over a week. You fought an invisible battle by choice. I fought one you forced upon me."

My mouth snapped shut, the audible click of my teeth echoing in the cell.

Damn him.

He was right.

We sat there in silence, both of us breathing heavily, until the tension in the air grew too thick to ignore. But this tension wasn't just born of anger. It was something deeper, something far more complicated.

Clay broke the silence first, his voice quieter but no less intense. "Thea, what you're saying... you're suggesting that you have the ability to travel across the Veil."

I stared at him, studying every detail of his face. The way his blonde hair fell messily over his brow, the tight line of his jaw, the flicker of something behind his golden eyes. I memorized it all because I knew this might be the last time I saw him as my friend.

I think we both knew the significance of what I was suggesting.

Clay studied me, his brow pinched as his mind turned with thoughts he wasn't willing to say aloud.

"I didn't tell you because I was afraid." I finally admitted, the words ripping out of me like shrapnel. "Terrified that you'd look at me like some kind of monster. Like I was just another pawn in Hyrax's game, because yes, I do understand what I'm suggesting."

His golden eyes softened, but the tension in his jaw didn't fade. "Thea, I could never—" He stopped himself, shaking his head. "This isn't just about you, though. You may be the most powerful person in this realm, but if my father finds out about that prophecy, if anyone else finds out—"

"I know the risk," I whispered. "Do you think I haven't lived with it every day?"

A tense silence settled between us, heavy and suffocating. Clay's eyes flicked to the cell door, his head tilting slightly as if he'd heard something.

"Do you hear that?" he murmured.

I strained to listen, but the pounding of my heart drowned out everything else. Then the sound of heavy boots echoed in the hallway, and my breath hitched. Torchlight flickered, and the faces of several Tennebrisian guards appeared beyond the bars.

Ashburn stood at the front, his face downcast, his shoulders tight with tension. He wore the same armor he had donned to welcome us into his country, but now it carried the weight of betrayal.

"The paralyzation should wear off soon," he said, his tone formal but edged with unease.

Clay's glare was sharp enough to wither stone. "Do you understand that drugging and imprisoning the Crown Prince of Athenia is an act of war?"

Ashburn flinched, his bravado slipping for just a moment. He bowed his head respectfully, but his voice wavered as he said, "We were attacked, Your Grace. Actions needed to be taken to ensure the kingdom was safe from enemies."

"And we are your allies," Clay growled.

Ashburn only nodded solemnly. "We hope you understand the need for precautions."

"Now what?" I rasped, my throat dry and raw.

"The monarchs wish to discuss the attack with you both. My men will help you to the throne room."

The thought of being carried, limp and helpless, through the palace hallways made my stomach churn. I could probably float myself with magic, but one look at Clay told me he already knew what I was considering—and disapproved.

He was probably right.

Terrifying the Tennebrisians any more than we already had wasn't the best idea.

"This isn't over," he muttered as the guards approached us. "You and I are going to have a very long conversation about trust when we get out of this."

"If we get out of this," I muttered, my voice tired.

CHAPTER TWENTY TWO

As we landed on two pillows in the otherwise empty throne room, the monarchs awaited us. Empress Rani sat rigidly on her throne, her posture so stiff she seemed carved from marble, while Emperor Kamon paced restlessly before her. His gaze flickered to us only briefly before returning to the ground, his hands clasped tightly behind his back.

Clay's rage was palpable, radiating from him in waves. Even in his weakened state, I could sense the heat simmering beneath his skin. For a fleeting moment, I was glad that the dose of Mortal blood they had given him was muting his Godly magic. Part of me wondered if he would set the entire palace ablaze with Dragonfire if he had access to it.

The other part of me didn't want to find out.

"I suggest you start explaining why you had an Athenian Prince and Councilwoman incarcerated," Clay said, his voice low and razor-sharp.

Kamon stopped pacing, his eyes locking with Clay's. Whatever Kamon saw in my prince's burning gaze made him hesitate. I saw it there too—Clay wasn't just a spoiled prince from a foreign court, here to gamble and drink with Prince Damon. He was a ruler, both by birth and by sheer force of will. If not in title, then in action and intention. He was already acting like the

King of Athenia. And he had no qualms asserting his authority on behalf of his nation.

I realized then how foolish I'd been to think Clay was idly following the Dragon's commands all this time, just waiting for his time to inherit the throne. The signs of his plan had been there all along.

Clay hated his father, as a man and a ruler, and he had long before I ever showed up.

This was who Clay had always been—a man willing to do whatever it took to protect his people.

"What did you inject us with?" I demanded, breaking the heavy silence.

"It's something we've been developing," Empress Rani said, her voice cold and precise. "A dose of Mortal blood to dull your powers, infused with the icy stillness of Water Elemental magic."

"I'm intrigued to know what other weapons you've been developing," Clay hissed, his words laced with venom. "And for what purpose?"

"It's a method of self-defense," Kamon said, his tone clipped. "Nothing more, I assure you."

Clay's hand twitched, then his leg, as he fought to regain control of his body. Despite his struggle, he kept his gaze locked on the monarchs, his focus unrelenting.

Empress Rani rose from her throne and moved gracefully to a golden table near the dais. She poured a glass of water from a crystal decanter, her movements slow and deliberate, before stepping toward me.

Careful not to spill a drop, she held the glass to my lips in a silent question.

"Thank you," I whispered hoarsely. She tilted the glass, letting the cool water trickle down my throat.

Clay watched the entire interaction with predatory intensity, his golden eyes tracking every movement. If Empress Rani had so much as twitched toward me in malice, I had no doubt Clay would have found a way to retaliate—even in his current state.

"Start talking," Clay growled, a dangerous rumble emanating from his chest.

Emperor Kamon stopped pacing and sank heavily onto his throne, his shoulders sagging. "We don't know much," he admitted, his voice heavy with frustration. "Our Zion Archives are located along the shore of Lake Treyon. Early this morning, we received reports that the manor housing the archives had been ravaged, its contents raided. Admittedly, we thought the attack might have been orchestrated by Athenia, given your presence in our dominion."

"What changed your mind?" I asked.

Kamon's eyes darkened. "There are reports of archives being raided in your kingdom as well."

Ice traveled down my spine. That had to be connected.

"What's missing?" Clay asked sharply.

"Nothing, as far as we can tell," Empress Rani replied. "Ashburn himself led the investigation."

"What about witnesses?" I asked, forcing my voice to remain steady under the weight of their scrutiny.

The monarchs exchanged a brief, tense glance before Empress Rani stepped forward towards us, her hands clasped tightly behind her back and her shoulders tight.

"That's the oddest part," she said, her voice quieter now, almost hesitant. "Not a single soul from the nearby town is alive."

My heart jolted painfully in my chest. "The thief killed them all?"

"No," Emperor Kamon said with a heavy sigh. "Their wounds appear... self-inflicted."

The words struck like a blow, cold and sharp. I wasn't sure if the icy chill that spread through my veins came from their drug or from the sheer horror of what he was suggesting.

What in all of creation could have driven an *entire town* to do something like that?

"Thea," Clay said, his voice cutting through the thick silence. He looked to me, his gaze fierce and unyielding, burning right through me. "We need to return to Athenia."

Given the late hour by the time we finished talking with the monarchs, Clay had decided we would need a good nights rest before heading home. So, when feeling returned to my body I carried myself heavily to my room, each step weighed down with the remnants of the drug and the heaviness in my heart.

Veric found me in my rooms later that evening, his eyes wide and filled with worry as I opened the door.

"Are you all right?" he asked in a rush, eyes scanning over me.

I managed a small, sad smile. "I am. I apologize for the scare."

He stared at me like I had two heads as I stepped aside to let him in. "What are you apologizing for? You didn't imprison yourself."

No, but I might be responsible for other, much worse, aspects of this crisis.

I gestured toward the couch, encouraging him to sit while I took the chair opposite him. He still wore the same clothes from earlier, though his hair was disheveled, likely from running his hands through it in frustration.

"The Empress told me you'll be leaving in the morning."

I nodded. "I'm sorry we won't be able to have that grand engagement party."

Veric let out a soft laugh, rubbing a hand over the stubble on his jaw. "I suppose I should get used to Council matters taking precedence over our personal lives."

The Council had taken precedence over everything since the moment I woke up in that infirmary bed. Still, I wasn't sure even I had adjusted to it.

I hesitated before speaking again, needing to discuss something that had been on my mind since that first night we'd danced together after meeting. "You know, if this isn't what you want, I won't force it on you. Bearing heirs of House Hyrax is my responsibility, not yours."

His gaze held mine, unwavering. "I love Tenebris. Truly. If marrying a beautiful woman and giving her children is the way I can serve my kingdom, then I'll do that." He exhaled slowly. "I know I'm not your first choice."

"That's not—"

He lifted a hand to cut off my protest and leaned forward, resting his elbows on his knees. "It's fine. I get it. You can't help who you love, and there are so few people in the world who share that kind of cosmic pull. The way you and Prince Vail look at each other... it's like watching two halves of a whole. He moves, you move. He smiles, your eyes light up. It's actually somewhat endearing to watch."

I bit down on my lip so hard that there was a flash of pain as I balled my hands into fists in my lap. I hadn't realized we'd been so obvious. How unbelievable cruel it was to come to take him from his kingdom while I made my affections for another abundantly clear.

Guilt curled deep in my stomach. "I'm so sorry, Veric."

He gave me a sad smile. "You have Clay. I have Tenebris. We'll just have to find the space between those truths where our relationship can exist. If you need me to be a husband in name and a stranger otherwise, we'll do that. If you need a friend, I can be that too. We'll take it one day at a time when the time comes."

I frowned. "When the time comes?"

His eyes flicked toward my wrist. "No engagement party. No chain. We're not locked into this quite yet. I know what your Dragon has ordered, but if you need time to decide if you can accept that, we wait."

I only wished it were that simple.

He wasn't from Athenia. He didn't know that when the Dragon commanded something, there was no turning him down.

"What now?" I asked softly, pulling at my fingers in my lap.

"You go home," he said. "And we give it that time. When you're ready, if you're ready, you send for me, and I'll come."

"**Y**ou cannot be serious!" I screeched, barely recognizing the frantic, high-pitched sound as my own voice.

Clay had arrived in my rooms at dawn, all but dragging me from bed. He'd demanded I dress in leathers and leave with him immediately, offering no explanation beyond "*Trust me.*" Now, after hours of climbing sand dunes under a merciless sun, here I stood, sweat pooling under my too-warm jacket, as he declared the most absurd plan imaginable.

And there he was—smirking over his shoulder, pulling off his shirt like this was the most reasonable thing in all of creation.

"I would never kid about this, princess."

For a heartbeat, my brain stalled as I stared at him. He was tanned and carved like something out of legend, every muscle a testament to his years of training. And there, just barely visible above the low-cut edge of his trousers, curled the Mark of Zion—the tip of a Dragon, its head dark and ornate.

"Were you finished with the conversation?" Clay asked with the arch of a smug brow. "I expected a little more attitude."

I snapped my mouth shut, mortified at my staring.

"No!" I crossed my arms over my chest, forcing my gaze firmly above his neck. "I am *not* doing this."

"Yes, you are."

"Clayton, be *practical*."

"Theadora, I *am*." He turned then, his voice tight with exasperation, but something beneath it—stress, maybe even concern—made me pause. "We need to get home. If Hyrax is after the Sword of Zion, we can't waste a fortnight on a ship."

"And why can't *you* go home and let me meet you there?"

The look he gave me could have turned a man to stone. "I'm not leaving you alone in a foreign country, Thea."

I opened my mouth, closed it, then opened it again. We'd already been at this for too long, and I'd yet to come up with a valid excuse to sway him. Desperation clawed at me. "Well... what about Nessira?"

Even I heard how whiny I sounded.

Clay raised a brow, crossing his thick arms over his bare chest to mirror my stance. "Nessira and Samsa will both be on a ship tonight back to Athenia. I can't carry all three of you."

"I am *not* going to ride you, Clayton!"

My cheeks flushed red at the sound of my own words, and Clay's eyes darkened as they traced down my body. Slowly, he stepped toward me, every inch of him humming with a predatory calm that made my heart flutter. His heat flushed over me.

"I am your Crown Prince," he reminded me softly, tucking a loose strand of hair behind my ear. "It is my God-given responsibility to ensure your safety. And right now, I need to return to my kingdom. There is no way in all of creation I'm leaving you behind. So yes, Theadora, I am going to shift into my Dragon form, and you are going to use those very special powers of yours to stay seated on my back the entire flight home."

"This is ridiculous," I whispered, though my voice lacked conviction.

"This, princess, is the first time I've ever let anyone do this." He stepped back a pace, smirking again as he reached for the laces of his trousers. "But for you, Thea, consider riding me a standing offer."

I yelped and spun around, clapping my hands over my blazing face as his low laughter rolled behind me. "You are insufferable!"

The air shifted—warm and heavy—followed by a low rumble that shook the sand beneath my boots. I turned cautiously and nearly staggered back. Where Clay had stood moments before, a golden dragon now loomed, scales shimmering like liquid sunlight. He watched me with slitted, impatient eyes, his head level with my shoulders, as if to say *well*?

"I hate you for this," I muttered as I trudged past him to grab the pack.

He snorted, sending a puff of smoke curling around me, and bent low, extending one massive front leg like a ladder.

"You want me to just walk up your leg?" I blinked at him.

The Dragon's head bobbed.

"What if I hurt you?"

He arched a scaly brow—if Dragons had brows—and gave an exasperated huff, the sound so human it startled a laugh out of me.

Still, I hesitated. He was massive, easily twenty feet tall, and there was no feasible way I could clamber up without looking completely ridiculous. I glanced up at him, the steady rise and fall of his belly, the gleam of sharp, dangerous claws only a few feet away. My nerves tangled into a tight knot.

Clay stomped his leg in irritation, snapping his jaws just shy of my head. "Oh, hush! I'm thinking!"

He huffed again, softer this time, smoke curling lazily around his snout.

Drawing a breath, I pushed my magic downward—through my chest, down my legs—until it lifted me in one sudden, buoyant rush. I landed awkwardly atop his back, gripping his scales for balance as he shook slightly beneath me, his body vibrating in what might have been Dragon laughter.

"See? That was easier for both of us," I said, patting his warm, golden scales affectionately.

His head turned, one slitted eye watching me with smug satisfaction. He shook out his neck, wings unfurling wide like the sails of a ship.

"Wait—" My voice pitched higher as I realized what he was about to do. "Clay, don't you da—"

The world dropped out from under me. My scream ripped through the air as Clay pushed off the peak, his wings slicing through the wind with a deafening crack. I threw my magic out instinctively, anchoring myself like a strap to his back as the ground fell farther and farther away.

The first few moments were sheer, unfiltered terror. The rush of wind whipped at my face, tore at my hair, stole the breath from my lungs. My heart hammered wildly, and I squeezed my eyes shut, refusing to look down.

But then, slowly, the panic ebbed. The rush of flight turned exhilarating, and I cracked one eye open.

The desert sprawled beneath us, the golden sand dunes rolling on for miles, glowing in the morning sunlight. I grinned despite myself, lifting my head to feel the wind on my face.

"*This is insane*," I called out, though I knew he couldn't hear me.

Somehow, I felt his response anyway.

You love it.

And, annoyingly, he was right.

CHAPTER TWENTY THREE

Clay landed in a clearing outside the palace, and I kept my back to him as he shifted and dressed. I focused on the familiar silhouette of the castle in the distance. It looked exactly the same as it had before we left—its spires cutting into the grey sky—but somehow, everything felt different.

Wrong.

Every breeze that brushed my cheek carried with it a shiver of unease, like the wind itself whispered a warning I couldn't quite hear.

"Come on," Clay said softly, stepping forward and taking my hand.

His fingers entwined with mine, and his thumb traced soothing circles across the back of my hand. It was a thoughtless gesture—one I doubted he even realized he was doing—but it pulled me out of my haze of dread, forcing me back to reality.

He was engaged. I was engaged.

As much as I enjoyed that feeling of his hand in mine, I would never have more of him than that.

Clay tugged me gently forward, oblivious to the knot of unease tangling itself in my chest. We hurried through the palace halls, his grip firm, his mind clearly elsewhere. The courts people, on the other hand, weren't as distracted. They stared openly at our intertwined hands, eyes widening, whispers curling through the corridors like smoke.

We were most certainly not in Tenebris any longer and the people of this country wouldn't be as unphased by us walking the line between friendship and something... more.

"Clay." I dug my heels in, tugging on his hand to stop him.

He turned to me, brow furrowed, as though only now realizing I'd been dragging my feet. His fingers remained tight around mine—unyielding, as if he couldn't let go.

"Maybe you should talk to your father alone."

The suggestion seemed to catch him off guard. His frown deepened, suspicion clouding his golden eyes.

"This is a matter for House Zion, don't you think?" I kept my voice low but firm with unspoken meaning. *We can't share everything with him.*

No one could know what I'd told Clay. Not about Hyrax. Not about the prophecy. And certainly not about my ability to cross the Veil. His father would only see it as another reason to be rid of me. It was far too dangerous.

And besides, I needed a reason to get away from Clay for a little. I had a plan, one that he would most certainly not approve of.

Finally, he exhaled sharply, his grip loosening as he stepped back. "You're right."

Relief washed over me—too soon.

"Promise me you'll go to your rooms and stay there," he said suddenly, his voice softer now, but no less serious. "Until we know what *he* wants, we can't be sure you're safe."

Oh, my poor, worried prince. I bit back a smile, though my chest tightened at the sight of him—tired and worn, but still trying to carry the weight of the world. *If only you knew.*

If Hyrax had wanted to hurt me, he'd had a thousand opportunities over the past year. For all his devious games, his cryptic words, and his secrets,

Hyrax had never done me harm. If this was part of the God's plan, I had to believe I could handle it.

I clasped my hands together to hide the tremor in my fingers and forced a reassuring smile.

"Don't worry," I teased lightly, though my voice shook just a bit. "I smell like a Dragon. I'm going straight to my rooms for a bath."

He studied me for a beat longer than I would've liked, as though he could see right through me, as if he could sense my unease. Then, finally, he nodded.

"Good," he said, though he didn't sound convinced.

I turned quickly, hurrying down the hall before his concern could morph into suspicion. My pulse pounded in my ears as I rounded the corner, slipping into the shadows of the corridor.

I lied to him.

Again.

I didn't have a choice, though. There was one more thing I had to do—one more secret I wasn't ready to share.

Not yet.

I shivered against the chill in the air, forcing myself to take a steadying breath. It was hard to tell if the cold was truly biting into my skin or if the weight of what I was about to do had my nerves on edge.

I never thought I'd stand here again—outside the palace dungeons, chewing my lip, trying to summon the courage to step inside.

It was almost painful to admit, but once again, I needed *Camilla*.

The woman who had spent months trying to kill me. The woman responsible for Lorelai's death and the trauma that still haunted Iris. Of all the people in all the realms, she was quite possibly the last I wanted to speak to. But, as much as I hated it, she might also be the only one with answers.

After all, she'd been the one to unearth that damned prophecy about the daughter of Hyrax lowering the Veil.

I'd wanted to dismiss it. I'd wanted to believe I could ignore it.

I couldn't anymore, though. I had to face the fact that the prophecy might be real if I wanted to find a way to break it.

"Can I help you, Lady Moore?"

The guard at the door frowned as he took in my appearance. My leather attire—dirty from travel, far too battle-worn for someone of my station—only deepened his confusion. In Athenia's courts, women didn't dress like this. Not ever.

I should have changed. I'd surely just sparked a hundred rumors about the ill-dressed Hyraxian Descendant skulking into the dungeons. The Dragon would hear of it by morning.

But that was tomorrow's problem.

"I'm here to see a prisoner," I said, keeping my voice even.

The guard tilted his head, fiery red hair flopping over his ears. He knew exactly which prisoner I meant. He shifted awkwardly, crimson spreading across his cheeks. "I'm not sure that's wise, Lady Moore."

"I wasn't asking for your opinion."

"The Dragon hasn't granted her leave for visitors."

Ah. There it was. The protest I'd expected.

The Dragon's command had been clear: no visitors, no exceptions. He had given me permission to see her once—months ago, but clearly that exception had long since expired.

Time to play my first card.

"I'm a Councilwoman," I reminded him. "Would you defy me?"

He stiffened, jaw tightening. I watched his jaw work, watched him avoid a question that demanded an answer. Even if that answer was that he had to listen to the Dragon's orders, as a Councilwoman he was still a lower station than me. He had to answer me.

So why wasn't he?

His eyes darted toward the hall beyond the door and his fingers twitched. That's when I realized it. The twitch of his fingers betrayed him. He wasn't just following orders. He was hiding something.

"What's your name?" I asked sharply, trying to peer over his shoulder into the prison.

He rubbed a hand against the back of his neck. "Gertrand, my lady."

"Gertrand." I let his name hang in the air like a weight. "Why are you trying to stop me?"

Still, he said nothing. The silence stretched between us, heavy and unyielding.

Fine, if my status wasn't enough to convince him to let me in, then I would have to move onto my next play.

It was all a bit... ironic. The palace dungeon guards, selected for their ability to contain the kingdom's worst enemies, were widely respected for their strength and power. Yet here I stood, nearly a year after I had been locked in those very cells, and Gertrand couldn't stop me.

Not anymore.

I didn't even raise my hand. My magic surged forward in a single breath, sending him stumbling back as the heavy door blasted open with a resounding crash.

I stepped inside, forcing my movements to stay slow. Deliberate. My boots echoed on the stone as I approached the last cell on the left—the one I knew far too well.

And then I saw her.

Camilla lay crumpled in the corner, a shriveled figure soaked in blood and filth.

Gods.

Her sun-kissed skin had gone pale, the fragile blue of her veins visible beneath its surface. She faced me, one arm outstretched, as though she had reached for help that never came. Bruises mottled her skin—handprints circling her forearms like shackles. If not for the faint rise and fall of her chest, I would have thought her dead.

The stench of festering wounds hit me, sharp and nauseating. I slapped a hand over my mouth, bile rising as my chest tightened in fury.

They brutalized Camilla until she now laid there helplessly.

Beaten.

Bloodied.

Gods knew what else.

Shock and confusion rolled through me, strong enough to make my knees weak.

Then disgust.

Then utter, overpowering rage.

Magic filled me, flowing easily from that deep place in my gut into every inch in my body. It consumed me until I felt more like shimmering energy than I did corporeal.

I spun toward the entrance, locking eyes with Gertrand, who stood at attention—still and silent. For all his bravado, even he flinched when my magic flared.

"What in all of creation happened to her?" I shouted.

Gertrand sighed, infuriatingly casual. "She is a prisoner, my lady."

My chest rose and fell heavily as I worked to breathe through the inevitable explosion building in me. I knew that if I let it out, that if this mass of pure power escaped me, the entire castle would crumble around me.

"She is a prisoner," I repeated, voice like death. As though that excused it. As though that made this acceptable.

"Who did this?"

"I cannot say," he replied, avoiding my gaze.

Dark laughter spilled from my lips, low and humorless.

The Dragon.

"He's been here?" I didn't need to specify who I meant.

"He sends visitors. That's all I can say. I am sworn to his service."

He deserved to die in the most painful brutal manner possible. For Camilla. For me. For all the women who had fell victim to his brutality. The Dragon had to pay.

I turned back to Camilla's cell. She hadn't moved—not an inch.

"Let me in."

Gertrand hesitated. I shot him a glare that left no room for argument, and he waved a hand with a resigned pinch of his brows. The glass barrier vanished.

I stepped inside and rushed to Camilla's side, pressing my palm to her forehead. Her skin burned under my touch, heat radiating from every infected wound. She wouldn't survive much longer like this.

If she died, I wouldn't get the answers I needed.

I turned back to Gertrand, my voice firm, cold. "No one else sees her."

"My lady, I cannot—"

"Gertrand." I rose to my feet, still feeling that raw power in every part of me as I brushed the dust from my knees and stalked past him toward the dungeon door. "You know who I am, don't you?"

He nodded, fists clenched.

"And you know what I've done?"

Another nod.

I stepped into the torchlight, letting just the smallest bit of that power escape. I let it rattle the door behind me. Let it knock over some of the beds in the empty cells. I even let it squeeze gently against his heart, just the tiniest bit, just enough to cause that heart to skip a beat, just enough to let him know how *easy* it was for me.

His face paled as he rubbed his chest with one hand.

"Then you know that on the day I arrived in this kingdom, I stood at the center of an earthquake I caused. You know I killed an entire room of people without lifting a finger. And you know that I am the only being to ever survive the bite of a Hydraxan."

Gertrand swallowed hard, the bob in his throat rocking.

I paused at the threshold, glancing back over my shoulder. My voice dropped, seething with quiet menace.

"Tell me, Gertrand. Are you more afraid of what the Dragon will say to you, or what *I* will do to you if another hair on her head is touched?"

His head dropped, his silence answer enough.

The door slammed shut behind me as I left, stomping through the castle without caring who saw me or what they thought. That magic still pulsed wildly in me and a single thought echoed in my head.

Camilla wouldn't survive in that dungeon.

Which meant I would have to break her out.

And I was going to need some help to get her out successfully.

CHAPTER TWENTY FOUR

*C*aldrius wasn't in his room when I searched it, and the embers in the hearth had long since gone cold. The silence of the space gnawed at me, the faint scent of ash lingering in the air. The bed remained neatly made, the curtains drawn, as if he hadn't disturbed the room, as though he hadn't been there for days.

My frustration swelled with each passing moment. I didn't have time for this. Camilla needed my help as soon as possible, and Caldrius might be the only one who could give me the answers—or the means—necessary for me to save her.

I stormed through the echoing halls of the castle, my boots slapping against marble as I made my way toward Hyrax's throne room. The massive doors loomed ahead of me, their ancient wood carved with twisting vines and bones, yet when I pushed through them, the chamber beyond was empty. My pulse quickened, impatience bleeding into something sharper. Something frantic. I was running out of time.

"Where are you?" I whispered to the vast emptiness, my voice swallowed by the cavernous room.

Retracing my steps from when Caldrius had given me a tour, I hurried through the dim corridors, chasing the faint flicker of lantern light as it danced against the walls. The castle felt different tonight—hollow. The torches sputtered weakly, as though even their flames had grown tired. The shadows were darker, and the marble walls felt colder. I glanced toward the massive windows as I passed, where the starlight bled in silver streaks across the floors. It was beautiful in an eerie, unsettling way. Too quiet. Too still.

When I finally stepped out of the castle, the chill of the night sank into my bones. I broke into a run, skidding down the hillside toward the woods Caldrius had mentioned before—the cursed trees where the Undone roamed. The world blurred around me as I sprinted, every thud of my boots punctuated by the pounding of my heart.

"Caldrius!" I called from the edge of the woods, my voice ringing into the abyss. A biting wind curled around me, slicing through the leathers I wore, carrying with it a damp, metallic scent that made my stomach twist.

Nothing.

No answer.

I swallowed, my throat dry. The trees stretched ahead of me, their dead limbs tangled like a nest of skeletal fingers clawing at the moonlight. The air here was heavy, pressing against my chest, and the cold... it wasn't natural. It wasn't the cold of winter or even of death—it was the kind of cold that seeped into your soul, something that whispered of misery and madness.

Nothing good waited for me in those woods

"Caldrius?" I called again, softer this time.

The silence that followed was absolute.

My stomach dropped, fear threading through me. I stepped forward on instinct, testing the ground beneath me as though it might shift beneath my feet.

The silence deepened.

I could feel it now—something watching me. A presence, oppressive and suffocating, curling like smoke in the shadows.

"Okay," I muttered under my breath, my voice trembling despite my effort to sound steady. "You can do this."

I took another step into the trees, then another. The moment my foot crossed that invisible threshold into the wood, it was like the world closed in around me. The sound of my own breathing became deafening but no footsteps echoed, no wind stirred the branches overhead. It was like the forest itself swallowed every other sound, every breath, every trace of life.

I turned to glance behind me—only to find the path had vanished. The castle, the hillside, the world beyond these trees was... gone. All that remained was an endless, twisted forest. My pulse raced, panic flaring in my chest.

I gripped the dagger at my thigh, its cool weight grounding me.

I could do this. I had to do this.

Then I heard it.

A groan—low, wet, and guttural.

I spun sharply, the dagger raised, my heart hammering in my chest.

They emerged from the shadows like nightmares given form. Two figures, crawling low to the ground, their limbs twisted unnaturally, like spiders. Pale, white skin clung to their frames in torn, peeling patches, exposing raw, blackened flesh beneath. Saliva dripped from their gaping mouths, pooling into the dirt as they hissed and snapped. What little hair they had clung to their skulls in sick, oily strands.

But it was their eyes—neon green and glowing—that froze me in place.

I knew this kind of creature. I had seen it before.

The creature on my left—a girl, once—lunged for me, her bony fingers clawing at my ankles. I slammed my boot into her forehead, recoiling as her skin stuck to the leather.

"Oh, gross," I muttered, my voice faint as nausea rose in my throat and I tried to kick the flesh off my shoe.

The second—a man who had been older, his face half-rotted—launched at me with a snarl, his skeletal hands latching onto my arm. Pain shot up to my shoulder, and I cried out, dropping my dagger.

"That's enough!" I snarled, shoving my magic outward. The creature flew backward, slamming into a tree, but it didn't stop. None of them stopped.

Two more emerged from the darkness, their groans rising into an unholy chorus. My dagger yanked itself back to my hand, and I spun, slicing into the neck of one as its claws tore through the leather at my side.

They just kept coming.

Then a blade sliced through one of the creatures as it lunged for me. It's head fell heavily and rolled in the dirt.

"What in all of creation are you doing?" Caldrius' voice thundered as he appeared at my side, his face streaked with blood, his sword dripping black gore. He looked furious—wild, like the battle had ignited something ancient inside him.

"Oh, thank the Gods," I gasped, stumbling backward as another creature charged.

"Behind you!"

I ducked just as his blade sliced through the air, decapitating the creature looming over me. Its blood splattered across my back, warm and acrid. My stomach twisted in sudden nausea.

*"Oh, Gods!" I squealed. "That is **disgusting**!"*

"That's what you're worried about right now?" Caldrius barked, incredulous.

"I can't kill them!" I cried, pointing at the severed head still blinking on the ground.

Caldrius shot me an exasperated look over his shoulder. "They're already dead."

"So what do we do?!"

"We start by not wandering into cursed woods in a foreign realm!" he snapped, swinging his blade to take down another Undone.

I rolled my eyes, jamming my dagger into the throat of one of the creatures. "Very helpful advice right now, thank you."

"Come on," he growled, grabbing my hand and pulling me forward.

"The woods don't end!" I protested, trying to keep pace.

"They do if you've lived here for hundreds of years and know your way out."

Fair point.

I let Caldrius lead the way, my breath coming in ragged gasps as we ran through the twisted landscape. The trees seemed to stretch endlessly, but finally, the darkness thinned, and we broke free from the cursed wood, stumbling into the open realm beyond. I staggered, clutching my side as I gasped for air.

Caldrius spun on me, his sword still dripping with black gore, his chest heaving from the fight. His eyes—dark, blazing, electric—locked onto mine before scanning over me. He gripped my shoulders tightly before spinning me to examine my backside for injuries.

"I'm fine!" I barked.

"You most certainly are not!" He released me, allowing me to turn back and face him. "You must be deranged to have gone in there alone and unprotected."

Not deranged. Desperate.

Similar enough, and yet entirely different.

"Explain what you were doing in there," he growled, his voice low and dangerous. "Now."

My pulse still roared in my ears, nearly drowning out his words but I straightened, stilled my trembling muscles, and met his gaze head-on.

"Looking for you!" I shot back, still trying to catch my breath, trying to ignore the way his own chest heaved, not with exertion but with the lingering concern he seemed to have felt for me.

*"**Why?**" he roared.*

I chewed on my lip, before placing my hands on my hips and forcing myself to stand to my full height. "I need your help."

"You need my help?" He echoed, as if the words didn't seem to make sense, as if they were entirely illogical.

I swallowed as I nodded, a sudden breeze pulling my hair into the air.

"With what?" he snapped.

I hesitated, then finally said, "I want to steal the invisibility bangle from Hyrax."

*I*t had taken far less convincing than I'd expected to get Caldrius to help me on this mission. Before I knew it, he'd grabbed my hand and pulled me back toward Hyrax's castle, his pace quick and unrelenting, seemingly unfazed by the blood still drying on our fingers.

Caldrius moved with purpose, cutting through the winding rock halls with such determined strides that I struggled to keep up. The castle twisted and turned around us like a maze, any hope of remembering the path evaporating with each step. Finally, we stopped in front of a massive set of wooden doors—easily twenty feet high—carved with intricate depictions of Hyrax and what I assumed was his wife, Pasnia.

Caldrius glanced over his shoulder, scanning the shadows to ensure we were alone. He pressed his ear to the door, listening intently as the silence stretched on, thick and heavy. Then, satisfied, he pushed the grand door open with a grunt and gestured for me to follow him into Hyrax's bedchamber.

"What will he do if he finds us in here?" I whispered, my voice barely audible.

"*Less talking, more looking,*" he muttered, already rummaging through the drawers of a chest against the far wall.

The room wasn't what I expected. For a God's private sanctuary, it was shockingly normal. Thick, rumpled obsidian sheets covered the massive, round bed, as though Hyrax had just risen from it. Weapons lined the wall—daggers, swords, maces—all perfectly displayed, except for the gap where his Bident should have been. I felt the empty spot with my fingers, a stark reminder that Hyrax's greatest weapon remained locked in the Mortal Realm.

Near the hearth, faint embers cast a reddish glow over two upholstered chairs and a small table. A half-finished game of chess sat between them, frozen mid-battle. The strange domesticity of it unnerved me. This wasn't the chamber of a monster—it was a place of quiet, perhaps even rest.

"*You're not looking,*" Caldrius snapped, dragging me from my thoughts.

I shot him a glare but turned my attention to the vanity, where jars, scrolls, and oils sat scattered. "*Where is Pasnia?*" I asked, though I hadn't meant to say it aloud.

Caldrius stilled. The tension in his shoulders was immediate, and when I turned, I saw the flicker of something troubled in his expression. "*Her highness is preparing for the Eternal Slumber.*"

I froze. "*What does that mean?*"

"*She's dying,*" he said simply, his voice quieter than before.

"*How?*"

"*She's been ill for some time. Not even Gods can live forever. Keep looking.*"

The weight of those words settled deep in my chest. Gods could die. The Eternal Slumber wasn't just some poetic phrase—it was death. And if Pasnia, the Goddess of Madness, could die, then Hyrax could, too.

"*What will happen when she... slumbers?*" I asked.

He didn't look at me as he sifted through the contents of the chest. "Someone new will rise. Her vessel may fade, but her power will find a new host. That's how it works."

It didn't make sense. "How do you know all of this?"

Caldrius paused, his tone tight. "The Book of the Gods explains it. Or so the legends say."

"The Book of the Gods?" I repeated, frowning. "What is that?"

He glanced at me like I'd just asked something ridiculous. "It's an ancient spell book. Written by the Gods themselves. It's said to contain the spell that raised the Veil. When they raised the Veil though, the book vanished into the Mortal Realm somewhere."

I blinked, trying to process it. "There's still so much I don't know."

Caldrius' movements slowed, his fingers skimming over something deep inside the chest, his entire frame going still.

My pulse spiked. "What?"

A beat of silence. Then, excitedly—"Got it!"

He lifted the bangle, the iron etchings gleaming faintly in the dim firelight.

I jumped, my heart leaping into my throat. "Be quiet!" I hissed.

He smirked unapologetically, stepping toward me with his find—a thick iron-clasped bracelet. The etchings across its surface glimmered faintly, humming with power as he placed it in my outstretched hand.

"One invisibility bangle," he said. "Courtesy of Hyrax."

I turned it over in my palm, the weight of it heavier than I'd expected. It was a weapon fashioned by a God, one that hadn't been good enough for Hyrax to value. I wouldn't make the mistake of underestimating its usefulness though. I smiled, pleased to see the same satisfaction on Caldrius' face.

"How do you plan to get it out of here?" Caldrius asked, his expression turning serious.

I swallowed, the moment I'd been dreading finally upon me. Time to reveal another secret I'd been holding too close. "Can I trust you?" I asked softly.

His expression didn't waver. Instead, he closed the space between us, his voice dropping lower. Quieter. More certain.

"I will never harm you, Theadora." His gaze locked onto mine, unwavering. "You can trust that."

It was a vow—one that felt far heavier than I'd expected. A knot tightened in my chest, but I forced it aside. "Then watch," I said, lifting the bangle in my hand. "I'm going to open a door to the Mortal Realm."

Caldrius' brows shot up, but he said nothing. Instead, he simply stepped back, crossed his arms over his chest, and did as he was told. He watched.

I closed my eyes, centering my focus on the golden thread I'd seen so many times before. The power inside me stirred, crackling through my veins like lightning. I focused on the pull, on the image of the portal—small but strong. The magic built and built until, with a sharp exhale, it burst outward with a rush of release. When I blinked my eyes open, I saw it. A golden thread shimmered in the air before us, small but bright.

"Can't say I've ever seen anything like that before," Caldrius murmured, his tone tinged with wonder. "You are full of surprises."

"Is that a compliment?" I teased, though my focus remained fixed on the thread.

"Always," he said, the words quieter than before.

I held the bangle up to the thread, my breath catching as I tossed it through. It vanished instantly, disappearing into the Mortal Realm. I could only hope it had landed where I intended—on my bed in the palace.

Caldrius circled the golden thread, his eyes narrowed as he inspected it. "What now?"

"Now," I said, letting my shoulders slump with exhaustion, "I wake up and go save the person who tried to kill me."

He snorted softly. "You know, you have a strange way of living, Theadora."

I glanced at him and shrugged. "You're one to talk."

For the first time since we'd stepped into the castle, Caldrius laughed. It was short and low, but real. And as the golden thread faded into nothingness, I realized that, for now at least, we were both in this together.

CHAPTER TWENTY FIVE

I woke with a gasp, bolting upright, heart hammering in my chest. For one disorienting moment, I wasn't quite sure where I was. I saw the familiar drapes of my bed looming like shadowed specters, but my mind was still tangled between the Mortal Realm and the Underworld.

Then it all came rushing back to me.

My hands flew to the sheets, fingers scrambling, searching for something—anything—as I tore through the tangled fabric with frantic urgency. A tremor of panic licked at my spine until my fingertips brushed under the pillow, closing around the cool, solid shape of the bangle.

I froze. My pulse seemed to halt entirely as I held it up, the metal glinting faintly in the silver glow of moonlight that streamed through the window. My breath stuck somewhere between disbelief and triumph.

It had worked. *It had actually worked.*

A weapon from the Underworld now sat in my hands... in the Mortal Realm. An object that should have been bound by the Veil, a boundary so absolute that not even the Gods could breach it, now existed *here*. This single act, this impossibility, shattered every rule I thought I understood.

My thoughts tumbled, cascading with the weight of it. But now wasn't the time to linger on the implications. There would be time yet to worry about all the lingering questions in my mind. For now, I had to focus.

I had to move. I had to save Camilla.

The silence of the palace was heavier at night, like it carried the secrets of a thousand slumbering souls. My bare feet met the cold stone of the hallway, grounding me, forcing me to focus. I crept like a shadow through the corridors, keeping my grip tight around the bangle in my pocket. Some irrational part of me feared it might dissolve back into the Veil if I let go, as though the rules of reality could reclaim it.

Gertrand still stood guard at the palace dungeon. His red hair was even more disheveled than before, dark shadows under his eyes betraying his exhaustion. He slumped lazily in his chair, staring blankly at the ceiling, his foot tapping a dull rhythm that echoed faintly off the stone.

I hesitated only long enough to pull in a deep breath, shaking out my shoulders as though I could shrug on a sense of urgency. Then I stumbled forward, exaggerating my panic as I rushed toward him. "Oh, thank the Gods!" My voice broke just the right way, high and breathless.

"Lady Moore!" Gertrand jerked upright, fumbling to steady me as I nearly collapsed into his arms. His hands gripped my wrists, his face alarmed. "What's wrong?"

"Oh, it's dreadful!" I wailed, twisting my hands in his grip as though too distraught to focus. "My necklace—it's missing! My betrothed gave it to me in Tenebris; I must have dropped it somewhere. I've searched *every-where*—the banquet hall, the library, even the gardens. This is the only place left! I *know* it must be here."

The guard relaxed slightly, though his hands still hovered awkwardly, unsure whether to comfort or restrain me. He sighed, clearly relieved to be dealing with a frantic noblewoman rather than the cold threat I'd been hours before. "My Lady, I'll help you look for it. You don't need to—"

"Are you sure?" I widened my eyes, my voice a mixture of pleading and surprise. "Wouldn't that mean abandoning your post?"

His brow furrowed as the words registered. I watched his hesitation take root and grow.

"Well, I suppose that would be a breach of protocols..."

I sidestepped around him with practiced ease, pressing myself to the dungeon door.

"I'll only be a moment!" I insisted. "Back before you even realize it. It'll be our little secret!"

Before he could protest and further, I pushed into the dungeon and the heavy door clicked shut. Immediately, I summoned my magic, forming an invisible tether between Gertrand and I. I felt as he took a tentative step forward, hand reaching for the door to follow me in, and I focused my energy on that connection between us, slowly tightening it until his breathing hitched. The faintest sounds of choking carried down the hall before silence fell.

The pull of unconsciousness hit him quickly, slumping him back against the chair.

"Sorry, Gertrand," I muttered under my breath, pulling the dungeon door open again to look at him.

A faint noise echoed down the corridor—a door creaking somewhere far away, or maybe footsteps. My heart slammed against my ribs. Gertrand twitched slightly, his brow furrowing as his unconscious body leaned forward in the chair. I tightened the thread of magic, holding my breath as he stilled again. As quietly as I could, I wrapped my power around him and dragged him into the dungeons. His body floated limply beside me as I hurried down the corridor toward Camilla's cell. She was in the same position as earlier and I pressed Gertrand's hand to the barrier, flinching as the glass rippled and vanished, and the stench hit me like a physical blow.

Rot. Blood. Sweat. The kind of smell that clung to the back of your throat, refusing to let go.

"I cannot believe I'm doing this," I whispered, gagging as I stepped into the cell and made my way towards her.

Camilla looked no better than before—crumpled and fragile, like a hollowed-out version of herself. Her labored breaths rattled unevenly as I crouched beside her. Kneeling, I lifted her trembling hand and carefully slid the invisibility bangle onto her wrist. The second it touched her skin, her body flickered and vanished, leaving only the faint pull of my magic to guide me.

I wrapped my power around her like a cacoon, enveloping her and pulling her up, only for my hold on Gertrand to slip. His unconscious form fell, and I barely had time to catch onto him before he slammed into the ground.

"Gods," I groaned, struggling to support both of them in the air. I had underestimated the effort it would take to carry them both. My energy wavered under the strain, black dots floating on the edges of my vision, but I gritted my teeth and pressed on. The guard's body floated back to his post, settling into his chair where he would wake later, none the wiser.

Then it was just me, Camilla, and the yawning palace halls.

I kept my pace steady and even as I walked through the halls, just in case prying eyes were lingering somewhere in the shadows, but when I finally made my way out into the night air, each step was getting a little more difficult than the last. I struggled to keep her body supported, but could feel my magic flickering softly, needing a break.

When we finally reached the palace stables, dawns first streaks of light were painting the sky. I swung myself onto a horse, gripped the reins tightly, and maneuvered Camilla's weight behind me, locking her down onto the horse the same way I had strapped myself to Clay's dragon form.

We rode hard, the wind ripping against my skin as I pushed the mare harder. There was no time to waste.

By the time Hyrax Manor rose into view, sunlight spilled over the estate, golden and soft. I nearly collapsed off the horse as I guided Camilla inside, still holding her weight with my magic and gritting my teeth against the dull headache that was forming from the exertion.

I rushed inside, propping up her body by the hearth and lighting a fire to warm her. The next moments blurred. I found a basin, filled it with the cleanest water I could, and knelt beside her, scrubbing the filth from her skin. Blood swirled into the water, staining it crimson, but even after minutes of scrubbing she hardly looked any better. Her wounds were bad—too bad for me to fix with any skill I possessed.

"Gods damn it!" I muttered, pressing a cloth to the fevered flesh around her ribs. The infection had spread, the wound's edges angry and inflamed. "I don't know what I'm doing."

"I must be dead," Camilla rasped suddenly, "If you're admitting to any weakness."

I jerked, nearly dropping the cloth as I met her barely open eyes. "You're awake."

"Apparently," she groaned, her voice brittle. "Where am I?"

"Hyrax Manor," I answered, brushing damp hair from her forehead. "You're safe."

"It's freezing."

"You're near the fire," I said softly, dread curling in my stomach. "Just rest. You'll be fine."

She didn't argue, though her breathing faltered. Her voice dropped to a whisper. "I'm not. I'm going to die soon."

"No," I said fiercely, pressing my thumb to her wrist, searching for the faint pulse. "I won't let you."

Her pulse was weak, though, barely even perceptible.

"Not even you're powerful enough to keep me here," she murmured, lids fluttering shut again.

Her breathing grew fainter, the pulse beneath my thumb dangerously slow.

She was right. I couldn't fix this by myself.

My chest tightened as I whispered, more to myself than her, "Then I'll find someone who can."

And with that vow, I rose, determination pounding in my veins.

I pounded on the door, my fist connecting with ringing force each time it struck the wood.

When it finally swung open, Clay stood there, blinking at me in half-sleep before taking only a heartbeat to assess my frantic eyes and blood-splattered clothes. His hand reached out instinctively, hooking gently around the back of my neck as his gaze scanned over me, searching for some unseen injury.

"What happened? Are you hurt?" His voice was low, steady, but threaded with concern.

He wore nothing but loosely tied silk pants that hung low on his hips, his chest bare, the warmth of sleep still clinging to him in the tousled mess of his hair, but his eyes were wide, sharp with alertness, darting over me desperately.

I placed my hands firmly against his chest and shoved, forcing him back into the room. This wasn't a conversation to be had in public castle halls.

He yielded without resistance, his grip slipping from my neck as I stepped inside and closed the door sharply behind me.

"I'm fine," I said quickly, the words tumbling out as I cast a glance around the room. It was quiet, intimate. The hearth held only dying embers, their warmth barely reaching the nearby couch. Atop it pillows sat stacked, slightly indented as if a head had been lying there. On the armrest sat a tossed aside quilt.

"I need help," I said, forcing my voice to steady.

Clay's frown deepened as he studied me, his gaze lingering on the dried blood staining my dress. He hesitated only a moment before nodding. "Anything. What do you need from me?"

His response hit me harder than it should have, something in the quiet conviction of his tone catching me off guard. I ignored the way my heart flipped at his words, at the weight of his unquestioning loyalty. The Clayton I'd met a year ago would never have reacted this way. He would have demanded explanations, chastised me for barging into his chambers without warning. He would have analyzed and weighed every detail before acting.

But now? Now he didn't even need to know why. He was willing to do whatever I needed without a single question.

And I was about to ask for far more than he would ever expect.

"Not yours," I whispered, the words barely audible as they left my lips.

His frown deepened, confusion flickering across his face. But before he could speak, a soft rustling came from the doorway behind him.

Elaina emerged from the bedroom, tying the sash of a golden robe around her waist. Her honey-brown hair spilled over her shoulder in a loose braid, her face free of any cosmetics, effortlessly radiant in the dim morning light. She moved with ease, the casual confidence of someone who was entirely comfortable in Clay's personal space.

"What's going on?" she asked, her tone mild as her gaze shifted between us.

My stomach twisted. For a moment, I couldn't breathe, couldn't think. I met her eyes—the woman set to marry the man I loved—and the weight of it all hit me like a physical blow.

I hated her.

I hated the way she looked so effortlessly beautiful, so composed. The way she fit seamlessly into his life, into his room, as if she belonged there. The way she was the one standing beside him in the quiet hours of the morning, while I stood here covered in blood and secrets.

She was his queen. I was an unwelcome intrusion.

I hated everything about her.

But I forced myself to swallow it—all of it. Every shard of pride, each razor-edged fragment of bitterness and jealousy that threatened to tear me apart from the inside. I buried it deep, letting the hatred twist and knot in the pit of my stomach, where it could fester unseen.

Because this wasn't about me. Not right now.

"I need her help," I said finally, my voice flat, the words scraping against my pride like sandpaper.

Elaina blinked, startled by the request. Clay's confusion shifted to something sharper, his eyes narrowing as he looked between us.

It didn't matter. There was no time for explanations. No time for the tangled mess of emotions swirling beneath the surface.

Camilla was dying. And Elaina had trained with healers.

Camilla had spent a year trying everything in her power to end my life, and now I was willing to risk everything to save hers. Even if it meant asking for help from the woman who had everything I wanted.

CHAPTER TWENTY SIX

To her credit, Elaina didn't ask any of the questions that were clearly burning in her mind when we burst into Hyrax Manor and I pointed her towards Camilla's slumped body in the parlour. She simply grabbed her bag of medical tools and set to work.

"You're lucky you came to me when you did," she muttered, inspecting the angry gash along Camilla's ribs. Her brow furrowed as she leaned in closer, the firelight casting sharp shadows across her face. "The infection has already spread too much."

"But you can help her, can't you?" My voice barely rose above a whisper, tinged with desperation I couldn't hide.

Elaina glanced over her shoulder, her expression grim as she sliced a blade cleanly across the scabbed wound, blood welling up instantly. She quickly packed the open wound with clean cloth, her movements precise. "It would be easier with a healer's magic," she admitted, her tone clipped, "but I'll do what I can."

I hovered nearby, watching her work with a mix of awe and dread. My magic simmered just beneath my skin, itching to help but unsure how to direct itself without making things worse. The room felt stifling, too hot despite the cold air outside. Clay's gaze burned into my back, his silence far louder than any words could have been.

He hadn't spoken since I told him what I'd done—how I'd snuck into the dungeons, taken Camilla, and brought her here. He hadn't chastised me or yelled, not yet. Silently, he'd simply thrown on a cotton shirt, led us to the stables, and set a punishing pace to Hyrax Manor. Now, though, his quiet fury radiated off him like the heat of his dragonfire, simmering, dangerous.

He wouldn't be able to keep quiet for much longer.

Even without looking at him, I could feel the weight of his judgment, the questions he didn't need to voice. When I did chance a glance his way, his eyes blazed with restrained anger and something else—unease, perhaps, or the careful calculation of someone trying to solve a puzzle they didn't want the answer to. It left me on edge, my already frayed nerves stretched thin.

Elaina wiped sweat from her brow and glanced over her shoulder, her tone clipped. "I need you out."

The words stung, but I couldn't blame her. I nodded and turned to leave, only to pause when she spoke again.

"No, I need *both* of you out," she clarified. She didn't even glance up, her hands steady as she packed more cloth into Camilla's wound. "The tension in here is unbearable—I don't know if it's Clay's temper or whatever energy is buzzing off of you, Thea, but it's suffocating me."

Oh.

Clay's gaze snapped to mine, and for a moment, we just stared at each other. I expected him to argue, to push back, but he gestured toward the door with a sharp tilt of his head, silently ordering me to lead the way. He lingered for just a moment longer, watching me, before following me out into the dim halls.

The air outside the room was cooler, but it did little to soothe the tension coiling in my chest. I led him through the twisting corridors of Hyrax Manor, the familiar stone walls pressing in on all sides. The faint light of dawn seeped through arched windows, casting the halls in a muted glow. The shadows seemed longer here, heavier.

I led him to the room I'd claimed as my own during the nights I'd spent here, away from the castle. Shadows cloaked the space, even in the early morning light. Tall, arched windows lined one wall, casting twisted patterns onto the stone floor as thin beams of light slipped through the ironwork. Heavy velvet drapes in deep crimson and navy hung beside them, thick enough to keep most of the daylight out, leaving the room in a cool, muted glow.

At the center of the room stood a four-poster bed, its dark wood carved with twisting vines and mythical creatures. Layers of heavy fabrics draped from the canopy over plush pillows and blankets, left in a careless mess from sleepless nights.

I barely had time to close the door before Clay's voice cut through the silence like a blade.

"Do you have any idea what you've done?"

So, we were jumping straight to the argument. No pleasantries, no easing into it.

I sank onto the edge of the bed, curling my legs beneath me as I forced myself to meet his gaze. "I know I should have talked to you first—"

"Talked to me?" His voice was sharp, slicing through the space between us as he spun away, running a hand through his already messy hair. He paced to the far side of the room, his movements agitated, restless. "Thea, you think your only mistake was not mentioning this reckless little plan to me?"

Frustration bubbled up, and I gritted my teeth. Magic crackled at my fingertips, slipping free and knocking over a candlestick on the nearby desk. The clang echoed sharply, cutting through the charged silence. Clay's jaw tightened, his eyes darting to the fallen candlestick before locking back on me.

"I was doing what I thought was right," I said, my voice low but steady. "Camilla might be the only one who understands what's happening to the Veil—what's happening to me."

"Right." He let out a harsh laugh, turning to face me, his expression twisted with anger. "And the Gods know you want an explanation for that more than you care about anything else. So you thought it was a brilliant idea to sneak behind my back, into the dungeons, and free a prisoner—a woman who has tried to kill you multiple times."

"I'm aware of what she's done."

"She's the reason Lorelai is dead!" His voice rose, raw with anger, and the words hit me like a blow.

"I know that!" I snapped, the words harsher than I intended. Of course I knew that.

He scoffed, shaking his head as if he couldn't believe what he was hearing. "Do you ever stop to think what your actions mean—not just for you, but for the rest of us who actually have to deal with the consequences?"

"Look," I said, forcing my tone to soften as I stood. "Once she tells us what we need to know, we'll put her back in her cell."

"Put her back in her cell," he repeated, his tone dripping with disbelief. "You really think it's that simple?"

I threw up my hands, exasperated. "Well, it was easy enough to get her out—"

"That's not the point!" He walked to me until he was towering over me, his heat pressing in like a physical force. "You think you can just do whatever you want, like the rules don't apply to you. You've always thought that and you've *always* failed to see the world around you! She's been missing for hours, Thea. I guarantee someone has already noticed her absence so it's only a matter of time before they realize you were the last person to see her."

"And what would you have had me do, Clay?" I demanded. "Let her die?"

"Not lie to me!" he roared, his voice cracking under the weight of his fury. "You looked me in the eye and told me you were going to bed."

"I couldn't just let her die," I argued, my voice quieter now, trembling.

"And is her life worth yours?" he shot back, his tone raw. He took a deep breath, jaw working as the veins in his neck momentarily darkened. "Do you have any idea what my father will do when he finds out? He'll kill you, Thea. He'll kill you, and there's nothing I can do to stop him this time."

The words cut deeper than I expected, and for a moment, I couldn't breathe. I needed space, needed air between us.

"He can try," I snarled, turning my back to him as I walked towards the window and stared out.

There would be consequences for this. I knew that. I couldn't deny it even if I wanted to. After all this time, though, after everything I'd been through and done, the Dragon didn't scare me anymore. He shouldn't scare Clay, either.

We could fight him. Together.

Clay's voice dropped to a low growl. "You'll start a war."

"Isn't that what you've been planning all this time, anyway?" I spat, the venom in my voice surprising even me as I glared at him over my shoulder.

His face hardened. "I have been preparing to remove my father from power for years, and you've thrown all of that into chaos with one reckless decision. One you're not even sorry for."

I could have denied it, asked for forgiveness, pretended to regret my choices. But he was right. I wasn't sorry—not for seeking out the one person who might hold the answers I needed. Even if that decision forced him to move up his timetable. Even if it forced him into a position neither of us had been willing to accept.

Silence stretched between us, thick and charged. Our harsh, unsteady breathing filled the air for a moment, as the reality of my actions—and his loyalty—settled heavily upon us.

I walked towards him, stopping when there was merely feet between us.

This was the moment we'd been building toward since the day we met.

It was me or his kingdom.

He had a decision to make.

"So what are you going to do about it, Your Grace?" I whispered.

He watched as a tear rolled down my cheek, his jaw clenching, his fists tightening before he looked away, beginning to pace as he weighed his options. Finally, after what felt like an eternity, he turned to me.

There was no princely mask on his face now, only resignation. "I'll send for my allies in Tenebris and Inanis. It'll take time for them to arrive, but there are soldiers that are loyal to me. I'll have Rankor send the orders. You'll need to stay here until we're sure its safe for you."

"I'm not hiding!"

"You'll do what I tell you to," he barked. That darkness was stretching up his arms, climbing higher by the minute.

Fury surged through me as I stormed forward, grabbing his arm to make him face me. "It has never worked like that between us, and you know it."

"Because you think you're above the rules that the rest of us have to follow!"

"And because you're a pompous ass!"

A knock at the door shattered the charged silence, and for a moment, neither of us moved. We stayed locked in our silent battle of wills until I finally turned and went to open the door.

Elaina stood there, her eyes downcast. When she looked up, her gaze flicked to Clay, then back to me. "I'm done," she said. "Camilla will need rest, but she should be fine."

Relief washed over me, and I exhaled a shaky breath. "Thank you."

Elaina's lips lifted in a faint, fleeting smile, and she held up her bloodied hands. "Is there somewhere I could wash up?"

Clay's presence loomed behind me, his heat radiating as he brushed past us both, muttering something about needing to fly to clear his head. Elaina and I watched his figure disappear down the hall, his steps heavy and unyielding. The sound of them eventually faded down the hall, but the weight of his words stayed. He was furious with me but beneath the anger, there was something else - a fear I couldn't quite name.

"Of course," I said to her, my voice quieter now. "Follow me."

"The manor doesn't currently have any staff," I explained, setting the pail of water down in front of Elaina in the washroom. I pulled fresh washing cloths from a nearby closet, setting them beside her. "Emeryn told me I could hire some, but honestly, I prefer the solitude."

Elaina raised an eyebrow as she glanced up at me. "I suppose that's not surprising."

She had a measured tone, but there was something unspoken in the way she watched me. I turned away, busying myself with tidying the space as she stripped off her soiled clothing and began scrubbing the dried blood from her hands and arms. The sound of water sloshing against the basin filled the silence.

"What do you mean by that?" I asked, finally breaking the quiet.

She met my eyes briefly before returning to her task. "I know they kept you under careful guard during your first months in Athenia. If I'd spent that long being constantly watched, I think I'd savor every moment of privacy I could get."

Her words hung in the air, the truth of them cutting sharper than I'd expected. I busied myself with pulling together some extra clothes—a simple skirt and long-sleeved tunic—and handed them to her. She accepted them with a small, appreciative smile that felt almost too kind.

"Aren't you carefully watched in your own kingdom?" I asked, trying to shift the focus away from myself. After all, she was high-born enough to be engaged to the future King of Athenia.

Elaina shrugged lightly. "I spent most of my childhood away, studying in private academies. Later, I trained with the healers. They treated me like any other acolyte—no guards, no special treatment. It was freeing, in a way."

Her words surprised me. I'd assumed her life would have mirrored mine—structured, scrutinized, suffocating. Instead, there was a quiet strength in her tone, one that hinted at a life lived on her own terms.

I stayed silent as she finished washing, her movements methodical, and glanced around the room. It wasn't grand like my suite at Hyrax Hall, but it was functional: a copper tub in one corner, shelves of cleaning serums and cloths, and a large window overlooking the ocean. The morning fog blurred the horizon, muting the world in a gray haze. Faintly, I could make out the shape of two massive golden wings cutting through the mist.

"He'll be back soon," Elaina murmured, her voice soft but certain.

When I turned, I found her watching me, now dressed in the borrowed clothes. A playful smile tugged at her lips as she dried her hands. "He can't stand to be away from you for long. He practically worries himself into a frenzy."

I froze, her words catching me off guard. My chest tightened, unease coiling low in my stomach. This was not the conversation I had expected, nor one I was prepared for. "I'm sorry—"

"Don't be," she interrupted, raising a hand to stop me. Her tone was gentle, but there was a firmness in her gaze as she gestured toward the adjoining bedroom. Reluctantly, I followed her, settling onto the chaise she indicated. It felt strange, like this was her space and not mine.

"This isn't exactly how I imagined I'd finally get a private moment with you," she said, folding her hands neatly in her lap. Her voice was light, almost teasing, but there was an undercurrent of seriousness that set me on edge. "But I've been hoping to have a conversation with you for some time."

My pulse quickened as I swallowed hard, her words stirring a mix of anxiety and curiosity. Elaina laughed softly, clearly picking up on my unease. She reached out, taking my hands in hers, and gave them a reassuring squeeze.

"I'm sure Clay has told you that our relationship is one of friendship and nothing more," she began gently.

I chewed my lip, unsure how to respond. "And how do you feel about that?"

Elaina chuckled, her eyes glinting with amusement. "Oh, my dear, I am no scorned lover. Trust me."

"But he is to be your husband," I pressed, my voice hesitant.

"A fact neither of us had much say in," she said simply. She looked toward the window, where we could see the faint silhouette of the Dragon circling closer to the manor. "Theadora, I want you to know that I hold no ill will toward either of you for your feelings. Quite the opposite, in fact. I've known Clay since we were children, and I've never seen him so devoted to anyone."

Her words struck something raw in me. I pulled my hands from hers and stood, putting distance between us. "It doesn't matter," I said, my voice breaking as tears stung my eyes. "It can't matter."

"Doesn't it?" she asked softly, her voice barely above a whisper.

I pivoted to face her. "How could it?"

Elaina rose slowly, her movements deliberate. Her gaze softened as she approached me. "Theadora, what you've done tonight changes everything." She reached for my hands again, her touch grounding. "You and Clay have both endured more than anyone should, and the depth of your feelings for one another is painfully obvious to anyone with eyes. Why not allow yourselves a chance at happiness? Don't you want that?"

Gods, I wanted it. I wanted that happiness more than I wanted my next breath.

Tears slipped down my face, and my voice cracked as I whispered, "How can you say this to me?"

Elaina's laugh was warm, almost amused. "As much as Clayton Vail may seem irresistible to you, he's far from my type."

I blinked, the words taking a moment to register. "What?"

She smiled, her expression wry. "I prefer my lovers a bit more... feminine."

Oh. *Oh.*

The realization settled over me, easing some of the weight pressing on my chest. "Why wouldn't Clay just tell me that?"

Her smile turned knowing. "It's not as accepted in my kingdom as it is here in Athenia. I imagine he wanted to give me the respect of sharing that information myself."

Before I could respond, a heavy boom shook the air—the unmistakable sound of a beast landing outside. We both startled, turning toward the window as the Dragon's shadow loomed closer. The tension between us shifted as we turned back to face each other.

"He's here," she said simply. Her voice was steady, but there was a quiet finality to her words. "I'd give him some time to brood. He'll come to you when he's ready. In the meantime, I can raid your cuppards and make everyone something to eat?"

My smile was small, but genuine. "That would be very kind."

With a gentle squeeze, she released my hands and started toward the door, but I called after her before she could leave.

"Elaina!"

She paused, glancing back with a raised brow.

"I'm sorry I hated you for so long. You're actually... really great."

Her smile widened, her laughter soft and warm. "Of course I am. Great people are often the most hateable."

With that, she slipped out of the room, leaving me alone with my thoughts. For the first time in what felt like forever, a small, tentative smile pulled at my lips as I waited for Clay to arrive.

CHAPTER TWENTY SEVEN

When Clay finally came to me, after what felt like an eternity, the sun was already beginning to set. I'd spent most of the day attempting to read and dozing off when I couldn't bring myself to pay attention to the words on the pages in front of me. Even after those short bursts of rest, my body still ached from how long I'd been awake worrying.

When I heard his soft knock at the open door, I turned rapidly from where I'd been brushing out my hair to meet his gaze, a rush of anxious energy flowing through me.

His grey eyes trailed over me from where he leaned heavily against my doorframe. He'd thrown on the same clothes from earlier, though they were notably more rustled than before. And even though he looked just as tired as I felt, with dark circles under his eyes, he was undeniably handsome, body lean but with corded muscles visible from where his arms crossed over his broad chest.

"You look more relaxed," I said, noting the way his shoulders sat a little lower than they had earlier when he'd stormed out of the house.

He pursed his lips and nodded before pointing towards the small set of chairs before the hearth. "May I?"

My pulse raced as I inclined my head towards them and stood to close the bedroom door as he took a seat. He didn't look angry anymore, which was some small relief. Now he just looked tired - of the day, of the fight, of everything that still lingered between us.

"I'd offer you a drink, but I don't actually have anything worth drinking here in the manor."

A small breath of air escaped as he laughed through a stressed smile. "Now that might be the worst crime you've committed yet."

I thought of Camilla in my living room. Then I thought of the times I'd taken lives, the day I'd gone to an illegal drug dealers party, the time I'd allowed Iris to take me to one of those sex houses. I had committed far worse crimes, and we both knew it.

Taking my time, I lowered myself slowly into the seat across from him, watching his every breath. Despite my conversation with Elaina, despite her insistence on Clay's feelings for me, I suddenly felt... doubt.

It was an odd sensation. I'd never had to doubt the way Clay felt about me before. From the moment I'd overheard him telling Iris that I intrigued him to the moment I'd knocked on his door the day before and asked for his help, he'd always made his intentions, impossible as they may be, abundantly clear. I'd never had to worry that he didn't find me beautiful or that he didn't enjoy my company.

But that had been before I'd allowed so many secrets to linger between us, and now it seemed so clear that we weren't standing on level ground anymore.

"What happens now?" I finally asked softly, unable to bear listening to the silence any longer.

He looked up at me from where he'd been staring at the embers in the hearth, his body here but his mind far away. "I'll return to the palace in the morning. Tell Rankor and Kent to gather the men that are loyal to them.

Iris should have some members of the Order that will join us as well. Then we'll go to my father."

"He's not just going to surrender his kingdom, Clay."

He folded his hands together, leaning forward on his knees. "I know that."

Clay had been right when he'd pointed out earlier that he wasn't ready to make this move yet. Gaining control of a kingdom wasn't easy. It was a bloody, messy, war-filled process. Maybe if Clay had the time he needed to gather all his allies, to follow his plan the way he'd intended to, innocent lives could be spared.

And the only thing standing in his way of doing just that was... me.

"There is another option," I whispered tentatively, my heart not wanting to give life to the plan that my mind knew was a reasonable enough course of action.

His eyes flashed to mine.

"I could go to Tenebris. Or Promissa, even. I'm the last Descendant of Hyrax, either kingdom would happily take me in and protect me and-"

"You want to leave Athenia?"

I stilled, heart falling through my stomach at the tone of his voice. We sat for a moment, simply looking at each other before I finally steadied my breathing enough to choke out, "No. I don't."

Athenia was my home.

He was here, of course, but Iris, Kent, and Rankor, too. They were my family and being sent away from them had been my biggest fear for so long.

I had something new to fear now, though.

Maybe my being here was causing more chaos in their lives than my presence was worth.

"You think leaving would fix this?" His voice cracked, the words landing heavier than I'd expected.

"You're talking about starting a war, Clay. People will get hurt. People we love could die. You said yourself you're not ready to fight that war, and I don't want to be the reason you lose your kingdom."

My voice cracked, and he stood instantly, moving to my side before kneeling in front of me and taking my hands in his. Silently, he reached up and brushed aside the tear that rolled down my cheek before tucking my hair behind my ear and running his finger down the length of the strand.

"You *are* my kingdom." His hands traveled down my forearms until they held my waist. The future King of Athenia, descended from Zion, bowed before me with an expression filled with such adoration it made me only want to cry harder. "War will always come with casualties. I know that better than most, Thea, but everything that means anything to me is right here in this room. I would burn my own kingdom to nothing but embers if it meant I could protect you and have you with me. I'm not afraid of war. I'm afraid of losing you."

"Our bloodlines-"

"It's *just blood*, Thea. It only holds power over you if you let it."

"I don't know how it can't," I confessed. "You'd be a King from House Zion, and I..."

My voice trailed off, not willing to give sound to what we both had already realized to be the truth.

"And what if we weren't?"

My brows pinched together in confusion. "I don't understand."

He looked away, battling some internal frustration. "I'm tired of always having to think like a king, especially when that means we can't just be honest with each other about what this is between us."

I shivered. "So, be honest with me, Clay."

"You want honesty?" He leveled his eyes on mine. "I'm terrified I'll never measure up to what you deserve, but I'll never forgive myself for letting this kingdom's expectations stop me from trying."

He stood and pulled me up, stepping closer as his hands brushed my hair over my shoulders and cradled my face. "Tomorrow, I will lead a rebellion that will make history, and when I have finished and I sit on the Athenian throne, I want you to be the woman sitting next to me."

It was a pretty vision, us together, treated as equals and free to simply be with each other and live as we wanted with no ridiculous rules or arranged marriages keeping us apart.

It felt impossible, it always had.

But Clay was right.

What he was about to do could change everything that this kingdom deemed possible.

"That's what I want," he whispered, his fingers warm around the back of my neck. "Last year I told you that you didn't know what you wanted, that you never had."

I laughed through my tears, recalling the moment he'd shouted those words at me and stormed off, each syllable feeling like a stinging blow against my skin. "I recall."

He lifted my chin, forcing me to meet the eyes that glowed golden with emotion. "So now it's your turn to be honest. Do you know what you want now?"

Thick emotion filled every part of me, making me both hot with passion and frozen with fear all at once. It was all I could do to simply nod up at him.

"Then tell me," he demanded, his voice dropping. "Tell me what you want."

Words felt impossible. My throat felt too clogged with emotion for any words to pry themselves free, even if they were swimming in a frantic swarm in my head. There were so many things to say, so many things I finally wanted to allow myself to tell him. I wanted to admit that I'd realized something important.

The problem between us had never been that Clay wouldn't choose me over his duty. He already had time and time again. The problem was that I had been unwilling to let go of the role that had been forced upon me, because giving it up meant I'd have to truly accept who and *what* I was.

With him, though, holding me like this in the privacy of my home, maybe I finally felt safe enough to accept it all.

When I met his eyes and saw him gazing down at me with such unguarded vulnerability, I wasn't able to stop myself from simply pushing forward and pressing my lips against his, allowing my body to provide my answer. I poured every ounce of doubt and longing into the kiss. And for the first time all day, everything else fell away.

When I kissed him, it wasn't just an answer - it was a choice. To trust him with all of me, even the parts I was still afraid to face.

The kiss was gentle at first, nothing more than a tentative press together before I pulled away.

"You," I whispered. "I want you."

My hands lingered on his waist and his remained tangled in my hair and for a moment we just stayed there in that blissful meeting until all too suddenly, the tension that had been building to this moment for so long suddenly snapped.

Clay's fingers around the back of my neck tightened and my own fisted in his shirt, grounding me in him. He pulled me back towards him, and his lips moved against mine, all at once teasing and desperate. He took my bottom lip between his teeth, not enough to hurt me but possessive enough to make it clear that he wanted me too, that he wanted to mark me in a way that no God ever could and that set my soul positively on fire. A feminine moan moved through me and Clay's hands were suddenly under my thighs lifting me against him and I locked my ankles around his hips, savoring the feeling of his body between my legs.

He carried me to the bed, not breaking our kiss for a single second, even as I gasped when his tongue invaded my mouth, stroking into me possessively. As he sat, he angled me on top of him so that I straddled him tightly and he pressed my hips down onto his hardness, rocking me back and forth. I followed his lead, savoring the friction against my needy core.

Gods, it was all so overwhelming. The room was sweltering, heat rising steadily from Clay's magic, and his skin was possibly burning my own, but I couldn't help but find that all the more intoxicating. My own magic was just as unruly, flying out of me in tiny bursts that knocked over books and unlit candles.

Clay's hands strayed up my back, igniting every nerve in my body as they trailed towards my breasts and he grasped at them over my dress, rubbing his thumbs against the hardened peaks. My body responded instantly, back arching into his grip, desperate for more, desperate for him.

"Is this alright?" He pulled away from me to ask, his eyes glowing brighter than I'd ever seen them before.

Always so thoughtful, so considerate. He didn't want to push me too far or too fast. Clay knew this was all so new to me and even though his need for me was evident in the thick length of him that pressed against my most sensitive place, his priority was my comfortability.

Warmth surged in my heart.

This man.

I wanted to give him all I had.

I'd wanted to for so long and had never allowed myself to open my heart to him. I'd spent so many days and nights terrified of the inevitable heartbreak that I kept myself from the sheer beauty that would be the joy of us *together*.

I didn't want to fight these feelings any longer.

Never breaking eye contact, I stood and reached for the laces of my corset.

"Is *this* alright?" I challenged, working the straps loose.

Clay leaned back on the bed, watching my every move with undivided attention, his gaze heated and trailing to the swell of my breasts. "Would you like some help with that, princess?"

I smirked, hands stalling on the laces. "That would be the gentlemanly thing, don't you think?"

With a smug smile, he rose and pulled at the hem of his shirt, ripping it over his head in one clean motion and exposing the expanse of his muscled chest before coming to stand behind me and take over the job of undoing the laces.

"This will be the last thing I do tonight that will be considered gentlemanly, Miss Moore." He pushed my hair over one shoulder, leaving a trail of tingling flesh everywhere his fingertips touched before he began pressing kisses along the line of my spine while he undid the corset and pulled it over my head.

"Oh?" I gasped, my voice breathy and uneven.

He grabbed my waist suddenly, pulling me back sharply against the firm expanse of his body, and it was like being pulled into a stone wall. "I have thought about this for so long, Thea. I've wondered what it would be like to find all the little places that you like to be touched. Planned out all the things I would do with you. Dreamed of what sounds you would make while I made you come for me. I intend to have all those questions answered before the sun comes up."

Suddenly, I couldn't breathe.

His fingers traveled to my shoulders, hooking under the fabric of my dress and easing it down. He went slowly, painfully so, lingering over every inch of skin until the cotton lingered right over the tips of my hardened nipples and even though I couldn't see him, I felt his attention as he pulled and exposed my breasts to the warm air. The rest of the dress fell shortly afterwards, leaving me in nothing but my white lace panties.

The room was silent, the only sound that of my own shuddering breath as he trailed his touch along my bare skin, leaving a wake of chilled skin in his path as he found his way to my breast and squeezed the pebbled tip.

"Oh," I gasped, throwing my head back against his chest, which shook with gentle laughter.

I angled my head towards his, longing for the touch of his lips on mine again and he happily leaned down to meet me, tracing my bottom lip with his tongue and guiding my hips to turn so that my front pressed against the bare skin of his chest.

Gods, I loved it. I loved the feeling of his firm body like an unmoveable wall holding me in place. I loved the touch of his hands, one trailing to squeeze the muscle of my ass and the other circling the back of my neck, holding me in place while his thumb traced a maddening path up and down my pulse. And it wasn't enough.

"I need more," I confessed, pulling away to look up at him and committing the sight of him with wild eyes and swollen lips to memory.

His groan was the only sound he released before his mouth was on mine again, tongue dipping in and out in a tantalizing rhythm. He eased me back further so that he could crawl into the bed over me, and before I knew it, he had tucked a thick leg between my thighs, hard against the point at which they joined. My need was too strong to be understood, but instinct drove me to shamelessly rock myself against that leg, seeking the slightest bit of friction to ease the growing tension in my core.

He nipped at my chin and throat, the pain sharp at first but instantly soothed by the dart of his tongue. I gasped out loud, body arching towards him. His chest shook slightly as he chuckled again and the motion against my breasts left them heavy and aching for his touch. Like a mindreader he complied, grasping onto them and pulling one between his lips, tongue darting out as he suckled me.

Gods, I felt like I was about to die in the most beautiful way possible.

He lifted his head, keeping his attention trained on my body, while his tongue darting out over his lower lip as he trailed a finger down my body, circling the delicate tip of my breast before continuing down with impossible gentleness and maddening slowness. I whined my protest. The sensation was entirely satisfying and entirely not enough. Twining my fingers through the softness of his overgrown hair, I pulled him to me once more, needing his mouth on mine again. That hand continued its path, choosing now to climb upwards on the bare skin of my thigh, towards that place of burning need.

"*Yes,*" I whispered, shocked by the shameless need that coated my voice in heaviness.

I remembered briefly when he had touched me there the first time we kissed at the Hyrax archives. That had been over the thick material of my riding pants and had still felt indescribable. I wasn't sure I could handle it with just the thin lacy scrap of undergarment between our skin.

His fingers traced gentle circles there, and it took only a minute for me to feel like I was about to lose my mind. Without meaning to, I gasped his name and his mouth was suddenly there to silence me as he pulled aside the lace and placed his fingers against my bare flesh, each circle sending pulses through every part of my body. I followed his touch, rocking my hips against his fingertips as I chased that unbearably sweet pressure.

"I want to have you," he whispered, pulling back to watch me as I writhed against his hand. Slowly a finger pushed inside me, then another, the sensation foreign but positively delectable. "Gods, you're so fucking wet for me, princess."

He looked down at me, the question in his eyes.

It was the last barrier that existed between us, the final decision that had to be made before we officially reached a point that we could never come back from. And though I knew it would change absolutely everything, I no longer cared about anything but Clay and how badly I wanted his fire to consume me.

His fingers kept their rhythm as I nodded up at him, my heart seizing at the way he grinned before removing himself from the crux of my thighs. I whimpered, unconsciously locking my legs around his hips to keep him tight against me, only to completely still as he brought his fingers to his mouth and sucked off the taste of me.

"Is that one of the things you dreamed about?" I whispered.

His expression was positively devilish. "And you taste sweeter than my most unspeakable fantasy."

I was momentarily curious about what exactly said fantasy entailed.

Clay stood, hovering by the bed for a moment just to look at me before his hands undid the belt of his trousers and in no time the Crown Prince of Athenia stood before me, naked in all his glory, tall and muscular. And *incredibly* well-endowed.

There was no way I was prepared for this.

And there was no way I was saying no to it.

"Lift your ass for me, princess," he instructed, hooking his fingers under the waistband of my panties. I did as I was told, lifting my hips so that he could slide off the fabric.

Somewhere inside me, I was aware of the nerves that swam in my stomach underneath the layers of desire. The awareness that I didn't have the slightest idea of what I was doing, or what I *should* be doing. My hesitancy must have been visible on my face because Clay got to his knees on the bed and wrapped a hand around the back of my neck, lifting my chin to meet his gaze.

"Relax," he told me. "Just be with me. Don't worry about anything else. We can stop whenever you want."

My wanting it wasn't necessarily in question. Heated anticipation was firing in waves from my core, desperate and needy. "I don't know how to-"

He shushed me with a gentle press of his lips against mine as he guided me to lie back and pushed my thighs apart with a knee. "Princess, my enjoyment of this evening is not something you need to question. And if for some unimaginable reason you doubt how much I think you are the most stunning fucking creature I've ever seen, then trust that we will have plenty more opportunities for me to teach you every single way we can love each other. For now, just lay back and let me worship at your altar."

A wave of emotion overcame me, filled with longing and trust, desire and friendship, passion and... something I hadn't given voice to.

Clay hooked his hands under my knees, raising my thighs as he positioned himself at my entry. There was one last pause, one last questioning glance, before I whispered, "Yes," and he pushed himself into the deepest part of me.

I gasped out, shutting my eyes against the sudden sting of pain, breathing through my nose and Clay was still, allowing me the time I needed to adjust to the feeling of him and open my eyes again.

"Okay?" He asked, running a thumb comfortingly over my cheek.

"Perfect."

He kissed me, slow and tantalizing, both a promise of what was to come and a vow that I was safe with him. As his lips worked against mine, his tongue and teeth running against my bottom lip, his hips began to rock, moving in and out of me with gentle carefulness.

And it was... *sensational.*

My core clenched, locking tightly around him as he moved and he groaned, the sound only spurring me on. With every push and pull of his body, that pain faded, leaving searing pleasure in its wake. His pace quickened, his head thrown back for a moment in his own pleasure, and my toes began to curl, that high building with every movement. It clouded my mind. Every thought and fear faded from existence and my breath became cries that sounded around us.

"Open your eyes," he commanded.

I hadn't even realized I had closed them.

Clay stared down at me with such total and utter devotion that there was no doubt at all of whether he was enjoying this. There was no doubt that what he was feeling went far beyond the sexual ecstasy we were both lost in. I knew the words before he gave life to them, and this time I didn't stop him from saying them.

"I am in love with you, Theadora," he whispered, pausing his movement only to wipe away the tear that slid down my cheek.

Words failed me.

Thoughts failed me.

But my feelings for him never did.

"And I love you."

His hips shifted, penetrating me impossibly deeper, and I moaned, savoring the bite of pain in the new angle. Clay's forehead pressed against mine as he thrust into me, each movement more frantic than the last. I raised my hips to meet his, hating every second he wasn't fully inside me.

"Again," he commanded through gritted teeth.

"I love you."

"Again."

Over and over. I said it until my words turned to screams. Until the pressure built so high that the world shattered around me in sparkling perfection that left my body shaking. Until the furniture itself rattled as magic exploded out of me. Until he groaned my name and stilled inside me, filling me.

And when everything was quiet, after he had slowly slipped out of me and pulled me against his chest, I said it again.

"I love you."

His fingers traced their way through my hair. "Always princess, no matter what comes next."

CHAPTER TWENTY EIGHT

I traced my forefinger around the dragon Marking Clay's hip. The beast stretched its neck high above his pelvic bone, its tail winding down his thigh - a permanent reminder of the God that gifted him his power.

"I used to wonder what this looked like," I murmured, watching the subtle twitch of his body under my touch. I circled that spot again, just to the left of his pelvic bone, and his fingers tightened on my back.

With one hand propped under his head, he lifted his gaze to the Mark. "Does it meet your expectations?"

"Everything meets my expectations."

He grinned and rested his head back once more. "I aim to please, Miss Moore."

Clay gently guided my head to rest on his chest, his fingers weaving through my hair. Hours had passed in this quiet contentment, lying wrapped together beneath the sheets, lost in each other's warmth.

But morning would come eventually.

"What happens now?" I whispered.

He sighed heavily. "I suppose we should talk to Camilla. I'll summon Rankor and Kent in the morning. They should be here for that conversation."

"Not Iris?"

The thought of explaining this to Iris - of admitting that I'd freed the woman responsible for Lorelai's death - churned in my stomach. That conversation was unavoidable, though. Better to face her sooner than later.

"Not Iris." Clay's voice was stern, inviting no further argument.

I shifted up, meeting his gaze even as he tried to avoid mine. "We have to tell her."

Clay reached up, brushing back my hair. "After we talk to Camilla, I'll go to Iris and speak with her myself."

"She's my best friend, Clay. I should be there for that conversation. I'm the one who freed Camilla."

His expression hardened with frustration as he looked away. "Iris is one of the deadliest people I know - second only to you, princess. I'm not letting her anywhere near you until I know she'll control herself."

I frowned. Clay could turn himself into a giant winged beast. Rankor and Kent were deadly war warriors, trained in their own unique abilities. Iris was... just a faerie. What danger was there in shifting your form into that of another?

The memory of our conversation from earlier flitted through my mind briefly. He had said that Rankor and Kent would have allies and that Iris would also have associates who would join our cause.

"What is The Order?" I asked, recalling what he had said.

Clay's thumb stroked my cheek before he guided me to lay back down again in the space above his heartbeat. Moving his hand from under his head, he entwined my fingers with his own. "They're an elite group of assassins."

"I thought she was a spy?"

"They're often one and the same." He squeezed my hand gently.

A million questions popped into my mind, demanding immediate attention, but Clay's dismissal of the topic was clear in his voice. He wasn't ready to talk about it, and I supposed there would be time enough for questions and discussions tomorrow. For now, if this was my only night to simply be here with him, I wanted to savor every second.

"No more secrets," He said suddenly, breaking the comfortable silence. "If we're going to do this together, I don't want anymore secrets between us. Next time you go to the Underworld... you tell me."

I'd held my secrets like armor for so long. Surrendering them felt like stepping into thin air and just trusting Clay to catch me. Trusting him not to abandon me, regardless of what he learned.

"No more secrets," I agreed, the words as much as vow to him as they were to myself.

"Sleep now," he murmured, a soft command. "We'll figure out the rest later."

I pressed my lips to his chest, moving up to straddle his hips, his length firm between my thighs as I began to rock. His hands gripped my thighs, his eyes blazing gold as he gazed up at me.

"Sleep later," I reasoned, smiling. "For now, I want to show you how quick of a learner I can be."

I woke hours later than normal, the sun already hanging high in the sky. Clay kept me up all night, so I wasn't surprised my body craved extra rest.

Thankfully, my exhaustion led to a peaceful night's sleep without any unexpected travels to foreign realms.

Clay wasn't in the bed beside me, though, when I blinked my eyes open. His half of the bed was already cold, which meant he had already gone to the castle.

And so it begins.

I took my time in the washroom, pulling on a robe and rinsing my face. The woman who stared back at me in the looking glass didn't appear any noticeably different from she had the day before, spare some swollen lips, and yet everything inside me felt new.

I loved. And I was loved.

Finally, admitting it to each other had lifted a weight off my shoulders that I hadn't even realized had been weighing me down. And what we'd done...

Well, that had been beautiful.

It was the culmination of a magnetic pull between us that had always felt far too strong to be natural. I hadn't thought it possible to feel more for Clay than I already did, but somehow, what we'd said and shared last night had elevated everything. I was practically floating with happiness, despite all the reasons I had to be worried.

By the time I made my way down the staircase, I found Elaina sitting in the sunlit room near the entryway, sipping tea and staring out the window at the ocean.

"It's a beautiful view," she commented, noticing me with a soft smile.

"It really is." I joined her by the window, enjoying the quiet before she motioned toward the tea.

"I made you some tea," she offered, filling a cup for me before settling back in her seat. "Clay went to the castle early this morning. He said he wanted to let you sleep."

I felt warmth creep into my cheeks. She had all but given us her blessing last night, but still, she was technically his fiancé. His bracelet remained locked around her wrist.

"So," she drug out the word, obviously sensing the awkwardness of the situation. "I'd ask how your evening was, but it was obviously *very good.*"

Oh gods. I sat the tea down and let my face fall in my hands, desperate to hide my furious blush. "Did we... keep you up last night?"

Elaina laughed, a carefree sound. "Not at first, but it is hard to sleep soundly when every so often the entire house starts to shake."

My power had taken on a life of its own last night. I was really going to have to work on getting that under control if Clay and I were going to do that again.

And I most definitely wanted to do that again.

"I am really sorry," I sighed, lifting my head to meet her smiling gaze.

Elaina waved her hand at me, brushing off my apology. "Nonsense. You should never apologize for an evening as remarkable as last night must have been."

My blush was most definitely turning the entirety of my face bright red. Elaina chuckled softly before clearing her throat awkwardly. "So I found many of the herbs for the tea in your garden. I left some extra in the kitchen. I would recommend drinking it once a week moving forward."

It took a moment for her words, and the meaning under them to settle in, and I glanced down at the mug in my hands as understanding dawned over me.

"Thank you," I whispered.

Baby dragons were the last thing we needed right now.

Just then, the sound of heavy hoofbeats sounded outside, and we both glanced toward the door before Elaina gave me an encouraging nod. "Go. I'll check on our patient."

I didn't hesitate, rushing outside into the winter air without a second thought about the fact that I wore nothing but a thin silk robe. Sure enough, Clay was dismounting, with Rankor and Kent following behind.

My eyes found Clay's instantly, a sense of relief and something deeper washing over me as he strode toward me.

Gods, this man had wrapped his entire hand around my heart.

"How was the ride?" I breathed, barely hiding the real question beneath my words.

Are we still okay in the morning light?

He grinned, his gaze straying towards my lips before answering, "Fast."

His answer was obvious in his body language. *We're perfect.*

Relieved, I turned to greet Rankor and Kent – only to notice Kent's face twisting into a look of horror. His eyes darted between Clay and me, widening before he muttered something under his breath and made a beeline for the house, looking faintly green.

"Excuse me," he mumbled, barely making it through the door before disappearing.

Before I could ask, Rankor's gaze started bouncing between Clay and me, a puzzled frown forming on his face before it split into a knowing, triumphant grin. He threw open his arms in celebration. "So you two finally fucked, huh?"

Oh. My. Gods.

"Go inside, Rankor," Clay commanded, sounding every bit like the King he was about to become, though his lips twitched in amusement.

Rankor started walking, his smile never fading for a minute. "No, really, I think it's great. At least I hope it was great. Well, who am I kidding? Look at you two. You're two attractive people. Of course it was great."

If a portal to the Underworld opened right there beneath me, I would have gladly jumped right into it and never came back.

"Inside!" Clay barked, giving him a gentle shove towards the manor while I hung my head.

Despite my raging embarrassment, Clay seemed unbothered; he grinned and pressed his hands against my hips to pull me towards him for a tantalizingly slow kiss.

"Will Kent be okay?" I breathed when he pulled away to cradle my face.

"He's always been that way. He get's a little awkward when he senses certain things."

"Like love?"

Clay kissed me again, this time longer and filled with unspeakable motives that made my toes curl inside my boots.

"I think he might have been picking up a slightly different emotion from me."

I chewed on my bottom lip and he stared at the small motion. "And what *were* you feeling, Your Grace?"

"Well, I was thinking about how good you looked when you were riding me last night, and imagining bending you over backwards the second I get you alone. So, you can probably imagine."

My cheeks flamed, but I pressed myself closer to him. "Poor Kent."

Clay's mouth started a trail of kisses along my jaw, finding their way to nibble on my earlobe. "Lucky me."

"Hey lovebirds!" Rankor's voice shattered the moment. He stood on the porch with his arms crossed over his broad shoulders, his grin replaced by a furrowed brow. "She's awake."

CHAPTER TWENTY NINE

The room felt like it might crack under the weight of unspoken tension.

Kent stood by the window, his back to us, fingers gripping the sill with a force that made the veins in his arms stand out. He hadn't said a word since we arrived, hadn't even spared Camilla a glance. Rankor, in stark contrast, leaned forward in his chair, his sharp gaze fixed on her like a blade pressed to her throat. Neither moved, but the energy between them was sharp enough to cut.

Clay stood near the hearth, his arms crossed tightly over his chest, his arms nearly completely black. His breath came slow and controlled, but the twitch in his jaw betrayed the restraint it was taking to keep from exploding.

It was Elaina who lingered closest to Camilla, her hands deft and deliberate as she adjusted the cloth on her forehead. She didn't look at any of us as she murmured, "She's stable enough. You can ask her questions." But the way her shoulders squared and her body angled slightly toward Camilla made it clear—she was prepared to shield her patient, no matter what.

No one moved. No one spoke.

Camilla herself lay motionless on the couch, her gaze heavy-lidded but sharp as it slid over each of us. Her expression was unreadable as she looked at Rankor, at Clay, at Kent, and then, finally, at me. Her eyes lingered, dark and unsettling, before drifting closed again.

Clay caught my eye and gave a subtle nod, a silent command to take the lead.

I exhaled shakily, stepping forward and lowering myself into the seat across from her. My fingers tightened into a knot in my lap, the tension in the room pressing down like a hand around my throat. I took one last steadying breath, then spoke.

"There are things I haven't told you all," I began, feeling the eyes of Rankor and Kent lock on me. "There are aspects of my powers that are... unprecedented. Historically, it seems, there hasn't been another Descendant as powerful as I am."

Kent frowned, confusion etched on his face. "We know this."

"Let her finish," Clay commanded.

I took another steadying breath, my gaze fixed on the intricate patterns woven into the rug at my feet. "A few months ago, I visited Camilla. I... I asked her to explain why she'd done what she did."

All eyes turned to Camilla, a shell of the beauty she'd once been. Her once-vibrant form was now frail and diminished, her dark hair dull and thinning, her skin sallow and pulled taut over her bones.

Her voice was barely more than a rasp. "I found a prophecy. It foretold of a Descendant of Hyrax who would lower the Veil."

"That's not possible," Rankor protested, tightening his jaws.

"That's what I thought," Camilla replied. "Until -"

"Until I arrived," I interjected, lifting my gaze. "Until I showed up out of nowhere with no explanation for how I got here."

Silence fell as Kent shook his head slowly. "I don't believe it. You wouldn't do that."

"She couldn't!" Rankor echoed, his gaze flicking between us. "*It's not possible.*"

"It's not true!" Camilla snapped, pushing herself to sit up. Elaina rushed to her side, helping her and propping a pillow behind her back before she continued. "When I found it, I was practically out of my mind. I'd been hearing things, seeing things that weren't real. Then I found that damn prophecy and my grandmother convinced me I had no choice but to turn to shadow magic to kill Thea."

"I'll have her head," Clay growled, sounding more beast than human.

Camilla let out a bitter, hollow laugh. "Too late. She's already dead."

My breath hitched. "What?"

"I tried to tell you," she said, her voice barely a whisper. "I tried to tell the guards, but they wouldn't listen. They ignored me every day, until one day they didn't ignore me anymore..." Her voice trailed off, her eyes hollow as her throat tightened with memories.

Clay's jaw worked in controlled anger. "I will hold them accountable for their actions. No woman should be treated that way, regardless of her crimes."

Camilla's lips trembled, tears shimmering in her eyes before she angrily pushed them away. Elaina touched her shoulder gently as Camilla steadied herself, her gaze meeting mine with a dark resolve.

"What did you need to tell me?" I asked, dread curling in my stomach.

She looked right at me, blocking out the men in the room. "After you left, *she* came to me. She told me everything, that it was all a lie. They forged the prophecy. She drove me out of my mind, knowing all along that I would never succeed in killing you. It was all a plan to get your blood."

My skin turned cold, a chill crawling up my spine. It couldn't be true. It couldn't.

"Who?"

Camilla picked at her fingernails, the thin skin fraying and starting to bleed. "Alina wanted me to marry Clay so badly, but the Gods wouldn't answer her prayers. So, she... she found a way around it."

"A loophole?" Clay's voice was a dangerous growl, his body tense as he came to stand between Camilla and I.

"*She* promised Alina the power to make me pregnant if Alina sacrificed her mortal body."

"Alina sacrificed herself?" Kent questioned, horror evident in his words.

I could barely hear him, though. I couldn't breathe.

It wasn't true.

"*Who, Camilla?*" I screamed, shattering the tension in the room with my desperation.

Clay was at my side in an instant, a hand coming to my neck, concern etched on his face, but I couldn't look at him. I couldn't focus on anything my Camilla.

Her voice trembled, her eyes darting to mine. "Pasnia. Alina sacrificed herself to let Pasnia take control of her body. The Goddess of Madness is here in the Mortal Realm."

Pasnia. The Goddess who had been absent during every one of my visits to the Underworld. The Goddess who was apparently so ill she was close to death—and yet, somehow, she was here. In the Mortal Realm.

The wind slapped my face, cool and biting, as I sat on the steps at the back of the manor. I'd bolted outside without explanation, barely hearing the others as I left. Power had surged in me so suddenly that the ocean had risen in a towering wave before crashing back down with a thunderous roar. Now, I barely noticed my legs give way as I sank onto the stairs, struggling to breathe through the tempest in my chest.

The storm in my mind was louder than the crashing waves.

Clay's presence reached me before I saw him, a steady warmth that seemed to anchor the chaos spiraling inside me. He draped a quilt around my shoulders and settled down beside me, close but not suffocating. He didn't flinch when the ocean swelled and roared again, but his gaze lingered on me, steady and unreadable. His jaw was tight, and for a moment, I couldn't tell if it was worry—or something else.

"You doing okay?" His voice was low, gentle, as though he was afraid a louder tone might shatter me.

I almost laughed, a bitter sound that never fully escaped my lips. Okay? Nothing about this was okay. Nothing had been okay since I'd ascended to the Council. "Do I have a choice?"

"With me, yes," he said, his tone soft but resolute.

I turned to look at him, and the concern etched into his expression made my defenses waver. He meant it. If I wanted to fall apart right now, he'd let me. He'd hold me together, so I didn't have to do it myself. But that wasn't who we were—neither of us. We didn't fall apart.

We endured. We fought. We led.

And I wasn't about to start backing down now.

"So," I cleared my throat, trying to steady my voice. "Pasnia's the one who's looking for the Sword of Zion."

Pasnia's the reason that the town of innocents is dead. They were driven to madness by her magic.

Clay's gaze shifted to the horizon, the endless rhythm of the waves reflected in his steady demeanor. He folded his hands together and nodded. "It would seem so. But something doesn't add up. I've been looking into it, and according to everything we know, only the God bonded to the weapon can use it. Neither Hyrax nor Pasnia can harness the Sword's power."

The words echoed the suspicion gnawing at the edges of my mind. There was still something we were missing. If Pasnia couldn't use the Sword, why go to such lengths to find it? Why risk everything for something that wouldn't serve her purpose?

Unless... the Sword wasn't the purpose at all.

A chill crept down my spine as the thought settled, dark and heavy. What if the Sword of Zion was just a distraction? A means to cover her true goal? Camilla had been insistent that the prophecy was a fabrication, a manipulation by Pasnia to lure me into her schemes. But what if it wasn't entirely false? What if I *was* the Descendant destined to lower the Veil? I'd already proven I could breach it—maybe not permanently, but long enough to traverse realms.

That couldn't be a coincidence.

What if every scheme, every sacrifice, every twisted game was part of Pasnia's plan to make me lower the Veil? To free Hyrax?

The realization settled like a stone in my gut, hollow and unrelenting. My chest tightened as I grasped the truth I'd been avoiding for so long.

"I need to talk to him," I whispered, my voice barely audible over the crash of the waves.

Clay sighed, his shoulders sagging slightly, as if he'd been waiting for me to say those words. He reached for my hand, threading his fingers through mine with the same steadiness that had kept me grounded time and time again. "Yes, you do."

"I've asked him for answers before and he won't give them to me. He's vague. It's like he's holding back until I give him something in return."

Clay squeezed my hand. "Maybe I'm not the only person who's seeking honesty from you."

His support was like an anchor in the storm, a grounding force when I felt like I might be swept away. Not even he could erase the reality I faced, though. This wasn't something he could stand beside me for. This wasn't a battle we could fight together.

This was mine.

And mine alone.

Worse than that, this wasn't a battle I could win unless I finally gave Hyrax the truth he had been trying to pry out of me.

Clay closed the bedroom door with a soft click, crossing the room to hand me a small cup of water. I accepted it gratefully, the cool solidity grounding me. His eyes swept over me, lingering just a moment too long before a teasing smirk tugged at his lips.

"You should wear that every day for the rest of your life," he remarked, his voice low and suggestive.

I glanced down at myself, suddenly aware of the snug fit of my protective leathers. The sleek black ensemble hugged my frame like a second skin, the long-sleeved tunic reinforced with crossing straps across my torso. The fitted pants laced tightly along the sides, molding perfectly to my legs. It was practical, armored elegance—battle-ready, just as I needed to be.

Clay moved to the hearth, and with a breath so casual it seemed second nature, flames bloomed to life. The warm glow cast flickering shadows over his features as he adjusted the logs. Then, in a single fluid motion, he tugged his shirt over his head and tossed it onto the armchair, revealing the lean, corded strength of his chest. He turned back to me, entirely at ease, while I fought to keep my composure.

"I explained everything to Rankor and Kent before they left," he said, his tone calm and measured, though his eyes remained fixed on me.

"Everything?" I arched a brow.

He stepped closer, brushing my hair back over my shoulders with practiced ease. "Everything," he confirmed, his voice dropping an octave. "They'll spread the word about the rebellion and should be back tomorrow with updates. Now that we know Pasnia is in the realm, I also asked them to talk to Iris. I need to know she's safe, too."

I let my head rest heavily against his chest, savoring the steady rhythm of his heartbeat. He wrapped his arms tightly around me. "That was the right decision."

He tilted my chin up with a gentle hand, his expression softening. "So, how does this work?"

I hesitated, chewing my lip. "You're not going to like it."

A dark laugh rumbled in his chest, the sound both amused and resigned. "I don't like any of this."

I took his hand, guiding him to the edge of the bed and pressing gently on his shoulders until he sat. His hands found my waist instinctively, grounding me as if to hold me here, to stop me from slipping away.

Which, to be fair, I was about to.

"Usually it happens accidentally when I sleep, but it's not always predictable."

He frowned. "So, we just go to sleep and hope for the best?"

My stomach twisted in nerves. "I actually think I might be able to open a door."

Clay's gaze flickered with unease, which I didn't entirely blame him for, but eventually he nodded his acceptance.

"I don't know how long I'll be gone," I admitted, my voice trembling slightly despite my best efforts to keep it steady. "But I'll come back to this room. Try to get some sleep while I'm gone."

His lips twitched into a wry smile, though it didn't quite reach his eyes. "That's unlikely."

The levity faded quickly, replaced by a quiet intensity as he looked up at me. Gold flecks ignited in his eyes, and his voice lowered. "I don't feel good about letting you do this alone."

I brushed my fingers through his hair, then cupped his cheek, forcing his gaze to stay on mine. "I've been traveling to the Underworld alone since the day you met me. It's not new."

"That doesn't mean I have to like it," he growled, his grip tightening on my hips.

My hand trailed down his jaw, resting it on his shoulder. "I don't even know if I can bring someone back through the Veil. I'm not willing to risk your soul to find out."

His jaw tightened, his expression hardening briefly before he nodded, resigned to the truth we both understood. "We all have roles to play," I reminded him softly.

Clay leaned forward, capturing my lips in a kiss that lingered far longer than it should have. It was deliberate, an unspoken plea, as if he were committing the feel of me to memory. When he finally pulled back, his expression was unreadable, but his movements were methodical as he reached for my dagger. With quick, practiced efficiency, he tucked it into the sheath on my thigh, pulling the straps snug. His hands lingered, brushing against my leg in a way that sent heat rippling through me.

Then he leaned back, arms braced behind him, legs spread as he reclined on the bed. His torso gleamed in the firelight, lean muscle carved in shadow and light. A playful smirk tugged at his lips, though the tension in his eyes betrayed him.

"Show me what you've got, princess," he drawled, his voice teasing but edged with something deeper.

Suppressing a grin, I turned away, lifting my hand as I conjured the image of Hyrax's throne room. I let the power rise within me, raw and electric, before releasing it in a steady, controlled rush. The air in front of me shimmered and twisted, splitting apart to reveal a golden thread of light. It wove itself into a glowing portal just tall enough for me to step through.

"Impressed yet?" I quipped, throwing a glance back at him over my shoulder.

But Clay wasn't looking at the portal. He looked only at me, and the softness in his eyes stole my breath.

"You've always impressed me," he murmured, his voice quiet and full of sincerity. "Now go. Be quick and be safe."

Commanding as always.

I took a moment to steel myself, drawing in a deep breath before stepping forward. The golden light of the Veil enveloped me as I passed through, leaving the warmth of Clay and the Mortal Realm behind.

The bitter cold kissed my cheeks, but the protective leather clinging to my body kept it from sinking into my bones as my boot touched down on the stone floor of Hyrax's throne room. The darkness here felt different—thicker, heavier. Shadows pooled in the corners like restless, living things, their edges shifting as if breathing.

Hyrax sat atop his throne of skulls and bones, the onyx crown glinting on his silver hair. The jagged peaks cast shadows over his sharp features, his piercing blue eyes locking onto mine with a knowing familiarity that sent a shiver down my spine.

Nearby, Caldrius stood by the massive dining table, polishing his sword with slow, deliberate movements. The scrape of cloth against steel halted the moment he noticed me, his dark eyes narrowing with quiet attention.

The portal shimmered behind me for only a moment before it winked out of existence, leaving me alone with the two most powerful beings in the Underworld.

"Well," Hyrax drawled, one brow arching in lazy amusement. "That was quite the entrance."

I stepped forward, each movement deliberate, the sound of my boots echoing softly against the cold stone floor. My gaze never wavered from his. "I'm ready now."

Hyrax rose from his throne with a deliberate grace, descending the dais step by excruciating step. He didn't need to ask what I meant. The words hung unspoken between us, understood by all in the room. He knew why I'd come. So did Caldrius, his stillness charged with anticipation. They'd been waiting for this—waiting for me to accept the truth I'd been avoiding.

"Say it, then," Hyrax challenged, his voice smooth, calm, yet edged with burning expectation. "Speak the words, and I will happily answer any questions that remain."

Caldrius sheathed his sword across his back with a practiced ease. His leather armor, strikingly similar to mine, glinted faintly in the dim light. He moved to stand slightly behind Hyrax, a silent sentinel, his presence commanding yet unintrusive. His gaze stayed locked on me, unwavering.

I swallowed against the tightening in my throat, my chest a battlefield of turmoil. I fixed my eyes on Hyrax, the God whose Mark had once been seared into my chest. The God with blue eyes that looked so much like my own, I'd been stupid to not realize it sooner.

"You're my father."

Hyrax's lips curved into a faint smile, satisfaction bleeding into something deeper—something almost human. "Yes," he said simply, his tone void of mockery, laced only with certainty. "I am."

The air left my lungs in a rush, not in panic but in an unexpected calm. The ground beneath me felt steady, yet the weight of the moment made the world seem as if it had tilted, spinning on an axis I couldn't control.

"Which begs the question, my dear," Hyrax said, stepping closer, his silver hair catching the faint light as it gleamed like woven starlight. His gaze sharpened, tilting his head to study me. "What does that make you?"

The answer surfaced before I could even think, rising from somewhere deeper than words. My power responded instantly to the realization, surging through me in an untamed flood. It was more than magic—it was pure, raw creation. I felt my very essence shift, less flesh and blood and more unbound energy.

"It makes me a Goddess," I said, the words reverberating through the chamber like a ripple of thunder.

CHAPTER THIRTY

*H*yrax motioned toward the table, his hand brushing lightly against my back to guide me forward. "Sit. There's much to discuss. Caldrius, leave us."

"He stays," I snapped, the authority in my voice surprising even me.

Both men stilled, turning to look at me with mirrored expressions of shock. Caldrius's lips curved into a wry smile, and he inclined his head in acknowledgment before taking a seat at the table. Hyrax raised a brow, clearly intrigued, but he followed suit, summoning food with a lazy wave of his hand. The rich aromas of roasted meats and spiced wines filled the room, but my stomach churned.

I stayed rooted where I was, every muscle taut, barely trusting myself to breathe.

"I want answers, Hyrax," I said sharply, the tension in my voice cutting through the air like a blade. "No more half-truths or skirting the questions. I want the truth. Now."

Hyrax didn't rush, slicing into the meat on his plate with maddening calm. "I suspect you already have many of the answers you seek. You know how you arrived on the bridge that day?"

The bridge. The memory surfaced, jagged and raw.

That wasn't the day I'd lost my memories.

It was the day my memories began.

It was the day I'd been created.

"Did you know I'd control the Veil?" My voice rose, sharp and demanding. "Was that the plan all along?"

Hyrax chewed slowly, his eyes gleaming with amusement. "That was a surprise, actually. One moment I was pouring magic into you, and the next, you were gone. The Goddess of the Veil has a nice ring to it, don't you think?"

The words hit me like a blow. **Goddess of the Veil.**

I, Theadora Moore, was the Goddess of the Veil.

Except that wasn't even my name. Moore belonged to a man the world had assumed was my father because the truth was too impossible to imagine: that Hyrax, God of the Dead, had a daughter.

"Why now?" I demanded, my voice trembling with barely contained fury. Hyrax had taken Mortals for lovers before, that's how his Descendant lines had come about after all. But he'd never fathered another God in his millennia of life. Why now?

Hyrax sighed, setting down his fork, shadows flickering over his face. "My wife is very ill, Theadora. She has been my companion for a millennium, and soon, she won't be. It was her idea, actually, for me to create you."

I stiffened, my stomach churning. "Pasnia's not my—"

"The Goddess of Madness cannot have children of her own," Caldrius interjected, his voice calm yet cutting. It was the first time he'd spoken since I arrived. He, too, hadn't touched the food Hyrax had summoned. Instead, he sat perfectly still, his fingers tracing the rim of his wineglass as his dark eyes stayed locked on mine.

"So how did you—" My voice faltered as the pieces fell into place, each one more horrific than the last.

Each God had a signature weapon, accessible only to them.

Except for Hyrax's Bident.

While the other Gods might not have been able to wield its power, I had felt its magic course through me in the Hyrax Archives. It had mingled with my own power, familiar and intimate, like it recognized my magic.

Because it had.

"Ciclopia's final two beasts," I murmured, working through the revelation aloud. "Tyron and Eckna. When Tyron died, you used one of his bones to fashion the Bident. There's no record of what happened to Eckna, but after all this time…"

Hyrax's expression didn't shift, but his attention on me was suffocating.

"…the beast died a little over a year ago. Didn't she?"

Hyrax leaned back, his smile faint, but satisfied. "You are as brilliant as I hoped."

Rage bubbled beneath the surface, threatening to boil over. "You created me out of the bones of a monster?"

Hyrax waved a dismissive hand, as though my anger was trivial. "There are worse origins, my dear."

"This is insane," I muttered, pacing away as my fingers clawed through my hair. The walls seemed to close in, the horror of it all spinning out of control.

A hand landed on my shoulder, and my power lashed out instinctively. The force of my power sent Caldrius sprawling backward, crashing into the table before he recovered with startling ease. He raised his hands in mock surrender, his dark eyes steady on mine.

"You should have told me!" I shouted at him, my voice raw with betrayal as I pointed an accusatory finger at him. "All along you knew, didn't you? You let me trust you while you lied to me!"

Caldrius stepped forward, his voice low and even. "You never would have believed me. You had to get here on your own."

My hands shook with the force of my anger – the sting of his betrayal. "I trusted you!"

Hyrax sighed, his tone dripping with impatience. "Thea, you're being too hard on the boy. He was essential to your creation, after all."

The air seemed to still; the room frozen in time as his words sank in. Slowly, I turned to Hyrax, dread pooling in my stomach. "What?"

Hyrax gestured toward Caldrius with a lazy flick of his hand. "His sketches were invaluable to shaping you."

No.

Oh gods, no.

That's why Caldrius had always looked at me with such familiarity, why his gaze lingered too long, tinged with something I didn't want to name. He had told Hyrax what I should look like.

He told Hyrax to make me look like someone he had once known.

Someone he had once loved.

My stomach churned as I turned to Caldrius, the silence stretching between us like a chasm.

"I look like her, don't I?" My voice trembled, my hands balled into fists at my sides.

I didn't dare look away from him, begging him with my eyes to deny it, to insist it wasn't the truth.

Caldrius's lips tightened, his jaw clenching as his fists opened and closed. He didn't answer.

"Do I look like your wife, Caldrius?" I screamed.

He avoided my gaze, clenching his fists so tightly the knuckles were white. "Visually, yes. You bear a resemblance, but I assure you the similarities end there."

None of it was real. He wasn't my friend. He never had been.

I was just a replacement for the woman he lost.

Magic surged within me, too angry on my behalf to stay silent, and a crack echoed through the room as the floor split apart.

All this time. I've been living with a stolen name. I'd been looking in a mirror and seeing a stolen face. Nothing - **nothing** *- about my identity was my own.*

"Thea-" Caldrius stood, as if making to come towards me, and I snapped.

Power surged through me, wild and violent. The throne of bones shattered, plates clattered to the ground, and Caldrius was hurled against the far wall with a force that cracked the stone. The air rippled with heat and fury as the room trembled around me.

"Theadora!" Hyrax bellowed, standing abruptly.

"I'm not letting you out of the Underworld," I hissed, my voice like steel. "I'm not letting either of you out. And when I find Pasnia, I'll drag her back here myself, and all three of you can rot for eternity."

"Pasnia's in the Mortal Realm?" Hyrax's voice was barely a whisper, his sharp gaze cutting through the chaos.

I didn't answer. I couldn't. My tears blurred my vision as I summoned a portal, the golden thread blazing to life before me.

Without another word, I stepped through, leaving their lies and betrayal behind.

CHAPTER THIRTY ONE

I stepped into my bedroom, desperate for Clay, the words pouring out of me as easily as the tears streaking down my cheeks.

"It's true," I choked, my voice trembling. "I mean, I think somehow I knew it was true, but hearing him confirm it was—was something else entirely. He created me out of the bones of Eckna, Clay. The fucking monster that Ciclopia created."

I stopped short. Clay hadn't turned to me. He hadn't even acknowledged my presence. He stood across the room by the windows, where the faint starlight caught the shimmering golden scales crawling over his back and shoulders. His claws, long and black as obsidian, flipped through one of the discarded books I'd left on my desk.

"Clay?" I whispered, taking a tentative step closer, unsure if I was speaking to my lover or the dragon within him.

When he finally turned, the breath left my lungs. Veins along his neck pulsed with inky blackness, his face framed by scales that glinted in the dim light. His eyes, glowing gold and slitted, bore into me with a predatory intensity that made my knees weaken.

"What happened?" I asked, fear knotting my stomach.

He lifted a page that had I had tucked inside the book and held it up between us. It trembled in his clawed hand as he stepped toward me, his voice a low, guttural growl. "What is this?"

It was a sketch—my sketch.

I felt the blood drained from my face. The likeness was unmistakable: Caldrius, his sharp features rendered with meticulous precision. The waves of his dark hair, the commanding set of his jaw, the piercing intensity of his eyes. Looking at Clay holding it, it was impossible to deny the family resemblance, no matter how far removed they were. They had the same arched brows. The same pointed jawline.

"I can explain," I stammered, my voice barely above a whisper.

"Please do." His tone was a venomous lash. He held the sketch higher, shaking it as he stepped closer, heat radiating off him. "Explain to me how you managed to create a perfect drawing of a man whose image has been erased from existence. The only images of Caldrius are locked in the Zion Archives—images I've only seen once in my entire life. So tell me, Thea. How can you explain this?"

The words clogged my throat, too heavy to admit.

"I've... met him," I finally admitted, each word sinking like a stone in the air. "In the Underworld."

Clay recoiled. His hand trembled, crushing the paper between his claws. "You've what?"

"I've met him," I repeated, my voice cracking. "Shortly after I realized it was the Underworld, Hyrax introduced us. Caldrius is his second in command."

"And you what? Spend time with him?"

I chewed on my lip, unease curling in my stomach. "He's helped answer questions for me. He helped me find the bangle I used to free Camilla."

He turned away, his shoulders rising and falling with labored breaths. "After everything we've been through," he said, his voice low, barely restrained, "after last night, why keep *this* from me?"

The truth tangled in my throat. I'd wanted to tell him, intended to tell him—but I hadn't, and I wasn't entirely sure why I had left Caldrius out of the story when I started telling Clay the truth.

Maybe I'd feared this exact moment, this exact reaction. Or maybe I hadn't wanted to admit that I'd trusted Caldrius. That I'd seen a side of him that history had erased.

"I don't know," I confessed, my voice a broken whisper.

"Is he..." His voice trailed off as he turned back to me, claws flexing, while he considered his next words. "Do you have feelings for him?

The question hit me like a slap. "No! Gods, no."

He scoffed, bitterness twisting his lips. "Is that such an outrageous question? You went to him for answers, Thea. Confided in him long before you were ever forced to be honest with me."

I went to him, grasping his hands despite the heat of his skin. "Yes, it is a ridiculous question! I love *you*, Clayton. Only you. It's only ever been you."

I stressed each word, needing him to hear them, to memorize them, to feel the truth of them in his bones.

He looked down at our hands—mine pale and trembling, his blackened and clawed. He pulled away, his expression a mix of fury and heartbreak.

"Every time I think we're finally moving forward, some new lie comes to light that sets us backwards again," he said, voice heavy with pain. "First it was sneaking out of the castle. Then you hid the limits of your powers. Then it was freeing Camilla. I forgave it all because you promised me there would be no more secrets, Thea. But here we are. Again."

The sharp crack of his words shattered something in me. My chest ached, tears blurring my vision. "Caldrius is nothing to me, Clay. Maybe at one time I considered him a... friend, but I know better now. He's a liar, just like Hyrax. I feel absolutely nothing for him."

He leveled his eyes on mine, jaw tight, searching my gaze and understanding the meaning that was hidden under my vow. "But he feels something for you."

There was no sense in denying that—not anymore.

"I look like someone he lost," I breathed, my voice trembling. "That's all."

Clay's jaw tightened, his claws flexing as he stared at me, his voice breaking when he finally spoke. "And you didn't think I deserved to know?"

Tears streamed down my face. "I didn't know how to tell you."

"Did you think it would matter to me? I've stood by you through everything. I knew the moment I watched you kill a ballroom full of people without even moving that there was something more to you. You told me you were prophesied to free Hyrax and my only concern was protecting you. Even tonight I sat here all night worried for your safety, even though I watched you tear through the unbreakable Veil that protects this realm. What is the point of keeping things from me now? Haven't I proven myself to you?"

I swallowed against the building tightness in my throat. "You don't have to prove anything to me. I just - I didn't know how you would react. I didn't know what you would think."

Clay looked away, clenching his jaw against his own emotions as he took a step back away from me. "Then, after all this time, you simply don't trust me."

"It's not that-"

"It is!" he insisted. "I don't know how many other ways I can say this to you, Thea. *I love you.* I choose you. Over everything. Over my kingdom. Over my own life if it comes to it. But your secrets are going to tear us apart."

My heart twisted painfully, his words cutting deeper than any blade. "I don't want to lose you."

"Thea, if you haven't given me all your secrets, then you haven't given me all of your heart either."

Clay turned away, breathing deeply until the scales retreated into his skin. He ran a hand over his face and moved toward the door, pulling his tunic over his shoulders. "Rankor and Kent should be back soon with Iris. I should be there to greet them and discuss battle strategies. That's what I'm good at."

"I'll come with you," I offered, desperate to mend the fragile threads between us.

He held up a hand, avoiding my gaze. "No. Just… stay here, Thea. Please. I just need some time."

The door slammed behind him; the sound reverberating through the silence that followed.

I stood there, alone, my chest hollow, the broken pieces of my heart scattering at my feet.

I must have cried myself to sleep because I woke suddenly, eyes crusted over, to the sound of Elaina screaming my name. Panic surged through me as I bolted upright, still fully dressed in my battle leathers. I rushed out of the room and practically flew down the stairs to find Elaina by the window, her knuckles white as they gripped the edge of the sill. Camilla was behind her, propped up on the couch, her eyes wide and alert despite the strain evident on her face.

"What is it?" I demanded, skidding to a stop beside Elaina.

Camilla answered, her voice grim. "Iris is here."

My stomach dropped. Outside, Iris moved like a storm, her blades flashing under the early morning light as she cut through Rankor's and Kent's defenses. For all their size and skill, she handled them with deadly ease, her movements fluid, her slight frame deceptively powerful. She didn't even look winded.

"I didn't know she could do that," I whispered.

"Of course she can," Elaina said, her voice tight with a mixture of fear and admiration. "She's a member of the Order."

A pained groan from Camilla snapped Elaina's attention back to her patient. She rushed to Camilla's side, pressing her down onto the couch. "You need to stay still," she said firmly. "You're going to reopen those wounds."

Camilla's gaze flicked back to the window, resignation etched into her features. "I hope you got the information you needed," she hissed. "Because she won't stop until she kills me."

Just then, the front door flew open with a thunderous crash. Iris strode in, her scarlet hair streaming like blood down her back. Dressed in black leather, her blades gleamed like an extension of her own hands. Her piercing eyes locked on Camilla, burning with unrelenting fury, as she surged forward.

"Iris, stop!" I screamed, throwing up a hand instinctively.

My power flared, and an invisible barrier sprang up between her and Camilla. Iris rebounded off it with a growl, her gaze snapping to me.

"Put it down," she snarled, her voice a low, dangerous command.

"I can't do that," I said softly.

Her eyes narrowed, and she took a threatening step toward me, one of her daggers twirling effortlessly between her fingers. "Put it down!"

Clay rushed inside, stepping between us, his commanding presence shifting the air in the room. "Enough!" he ordered.

Iris paused, blade stilling in her fingers as she glanced between the two of us. Slowly, she laughed, the sound brittle and bitter. "Oh, this is rich."

Clay stepped toward her, reaching for the blade, but she danced out of his grasp. "Iris—"

"The irony of it all!" she spat, her voice dripping with venom. "A year ago, you were begging me not to join the Order. And now? Now you want my skills. Now you want me to convince half of my legion to abandon their sworn cause to help you steal a throne. Only you're not asking me to do it for the betterment of the kingdom. You're asking me to do it to save the woman you love." She pointed the blade accusingly at me. "Because she freed the bitch who killed the woman *I* loved."

Camilla flinched, tears slipping down her face. "Iris, I—" she began, her voice trembling.

"You don't get to speak to me!" Iris roared, lunging again. My barrier held, and she slammed against it with a scream of frustration.

"If you want someone to blame, blame the Goddess of Madness!" Elaina's voice rang out, sharp and cutting. All heads turned toward her as she stood by Camilla's side, her posture protective, her eyes blazing. "If any of you had taken the time to actually listen to Camilla, you would understand that Pasnia has been in this realm longer than any of you realize. She poisoned her thoughts, literally drove her out of her mind."

"You think that excuses it?" Iris growled.

"I think it means Camilla was a victim, too," Elaina said, her voice softening but no less resolute. "And we have a bigger enemy to deal with."

Clay's gaze shifted to Kent, a silent command passing between them. Kent nodded and began to hum a soft tune so quiet that only the three of us could hear it. The magic took effect, visible in the way some of the tension left Iris's shoulders. After a moment, she tucked her blades away into the belt across her hips and folded her arms across her chest.

"Fine," she spat through clenched teeth. "How do we find her?"

I drew on what I knew of Pasnia from my nights studying in the library upstairs. "Pasnia's magic has an animus that's visible when she's nearby."

"A butterfly," Camilla said hoarsely, her voice breaking the tense quiet. "It's a butterfly."

Clay nodded, his expression grim. "Then we keep watch. If anyone sees a butterfly, report it immediately."

"And then what?" Rankor asked, resting his hands on his hips.

"And then I send her back to the Underworld," I said firmly.

A heavy silence settled over the room. Kent sank into the chair by Camilla's feet, his brow furrowed. "This would be a lot easier if we knew what she wanted."

"She wants to lower the Veil, obviously," Iris said flatly.

"But why now?" Kent pressed.

"Because she's dying," I said, the words heavier than I'd expected. Every eye turned to me. "She doesn't want to leave Hyrax alone. That's why he created me."

Iris let out a bitter laugh. "So once again, we're back to you being the problem."

"Iris," Clay growled, his voice a sharp warning.

She turned to him, her gaze icy. "She's the only thing that can lower the Veil. You all know it. If Pasnia's planning to drop it, she's betting on Thea helping her."

Her words hit like a blow. She was right—I was capable of lowering the Veil. Hyrax hadn't even known Pasnia was in the Mortal Realm though. In all her time here, she'd never come to me, never seemed remotely interested in me.

So what if I wasn't the only thing capable of lowering the Veil?

"She wants the Book of the Gods." The revelation escaped me in a whisper.

"What?" Rankor asked, frowning. "What is that?"

Clay looked at me suspiciously, as if he somehow knew who had told me about the book. "It's a spell book, created by the Gods. No one really knows whats in it, but it's rumored to have the spell they used to raise the Veil."

I looked around the room. "What if Pasnia had been looking for the Book of the Gods in the Zion Archives and not the Sword of Zion? A spell in that book raised the Veil. What if there's a spell to lower it?"

"That could make sense," Clay nodded slowly, "but we've never had that book; it was lost centuries ago."

Camilla cleared her throat, avoiding Iris's stare as she interjected. "I might know someone who could find it. He used to sell crystals to my grandmother."

Iris turned to Rankor and Kent. "Then let's move. We'll head back to the castle and strengthen our defenses. Camilla sends word to her contact. Clay and Thea find Pasnia and deal with her. Then we take the throne."

Rankor smirked. "All in a day's work."

Kent went to Iris, clapping a hand on her shoulder and trying to lead her away before her temporary calmness wore off. She lingered a moment longer, settling her icy gaze on Camilla.

"I hope you are sorry. I hope her face haunts the rest of your dreams. It's a fate much worse than death."

I watched her go, her presence leaving a stifling tension in the room. It only heightened when Clay stormed away without another word. Elaina followed, promising she'd talk to him and get him to calm down.

Left alone with Camilla, I sank into a chair across from her.

"Never thought the day would come when you defended me from Iris," she said softly, seriousness in her voice. "Thank you."

I nodded. "Elaina was right. It's not your fault that Pasnia made you do those things. She's the real villain."

Camilla stared out the window as Iris, Kent, and Rankor rode away. "Still, Iris will never forgive me."

"No, she won't."

"And your friendship with her will never be the same."

"No," I agreed softly. "It won't."

Everything had already changed.

CHAPTER THIRTY TWO

By the time the afternoon sun rose high in the sky, the manor had long since gone quiet. Camilla dozed on the couch, her body still demanding rest as it healed. Clay and Elaina had yet to return, leaving the house heavy with an uneasy stillness. I lingered for as long as I could before I couldn't bear to sit still any longer. Wrapping a heavy cloak tightly around my shoulders, I wandered outside, the crisp winter air biting against my skin.

The gardens at the castle had once been my sanctuary, one of the few places I'd been able to find peace. My gardens here at Hyrax Manor hardly compared. The cold had stripped the crops and flowers of their vibrancy, leaving them withered and fragile. Even in the height of spring, though, the gardens had never possessed the same luster as the palace's carefully tended pathways.

Maybe when all this was over, I'd find time to come out here myself and spend my days ensuring that the garden got the love it deserved.

A sudden gust of wind whipped through the trees, rattling their bare branches. It sliced across my cheeks like tiny blades, but even that couldn't compare to the icy hollowness in my chest. How was it possible to feel so much in so little time? In a matter of days, I'd gone from the most exquisite of heavens to the darkest depths of loneliness.

Perhaps this was my curse.

I was a lone Goddess walking among Mortals.

There would never be anyone in this realm who could stand beside me as an equal. No one who could truly understand what it felt like to carry this weight, this power. No one would ever feel the same responsibility or utter isolation.

My knees sank into the cold, brittle grass as I lowered myself to the ground. I ran the dry blades between my fingers, letting their rough edges ground me as the steady wave of the ocean roared in the distance.

Chewing my lip, I tried to clear my thoughts, to push all my fears and doubts and *desperation* down. There would be time to deal with it all. Right now, there was work to be done. If I couldn't focus, people I loved would die.

A terrifying truth, dark and inevitable, crept into my thoughts.

"I'm going to watch them die either way," I whispered to myself, the overwhelming truth finally escaping.

I could endure with being the only one of my kind. Being a Goddess wasn't just about power or isolation - it was about time and the endless expanse of it that stretched before me.

I would have an impossibly long lifespan.

While my friends aged, matured and moved through the finite chapters of their lives, I would remain the same. Eventually, I would watch them all die.

One day I would watch him die.

And I would have to keep living without them.

A tremor shook my hands as I dug them into the frozen earth, the storm inside me far worse than the snow that was beginning to fall.

Iris was right.

There were fates worse than death.

When I returned to the manor, I found Clay in the kitchen, his hands busy preparing a meal. I hesitated in the doorway, unsure whether I should speak. He looked calm, his movements precise as he chopped herbs, but there was an undercurrent of tension in the set of his shoulders. I watched silently until his eyes flicked up, surprise briefly softening his features, when he noticed me.

"How long have you been there?" he asked, his voice steady but distant—the kind of calm that came before a storm.

"Not long," I lied. "I didn't know you could cook."

"You assume just because I was raised as royalty, I didn't learn any other important skills?" He gave me a wry grin, one that didn't quite reach his eyes, before dusting his hands off and passing me a biscuit. "Try it."

I took the offering and bit into it, unable to stop the soft moan that escaped as the warm, buttery flavor melted on my tongue. "Gods, that's incredible."

His lips quirked slightly, but he returned to chopping. "Sit," he commanded, his tone leaving no room for argument. He gestured toward a stool at the counter. "You haven't eaten all day."

I frowned, thinking back. Had it really been that long? My stomach growled loudly in answer, and I clenched a hand against my middle in embarrassment. I didn't know what was more surprising—that I'd simply forgotten to feed myself or that Clay had noticed.

Or that he still cared enough to cook for me.

He passed me a bowl of soup and another biscuit, which I took gratefully, savoring the first sweet taste. It was loaded with spices, savory at first, then settling into something unbelievably comforting.

"Thank you," I mumbled. "You didn't have to do this."

He shrugged, still avoiding my gaze. "You've been sitting out there for hours in the cold. I don't want you getting sick."

The bitter words escaped before I could stop them. "Can I even get sick?"

Was that possible? Did Gods get colds?

The knife paused mid-chop, and his hands stilled. For a moment, the only sound was the faint crackle of the hearth behind us. He straightened slowly, finally meeting my gaze, his expression unreadable.

"I don't know, Thea," he admitted, his voice quieter now, almost resigned. "But I'd rather not test it out."

I focused my attention on the bowl in front of me. "Why not?"

He arched a brow at me, suddenly looking very much like the stubborn prince who used to annoy me to no end. "Excuse me?"

"Why do you care?" I said louder, the words spilling out before I could stop them. "You made it very clear that you don't think this is working between us, Clay. You walked away from me. So, why do you care whether I've eaten or whether I get sick?"

"Because I love you, Thea." He said it as if it were an obvious fact, like saying the sky was blue or water was wet.

"You love me, but you don't trust me."

"And you love me, but you keep secrets from me," he shot back, stabbing the knife point-down into the cutting board.

"This is a ridiculous thing for you to be angry about! Do you need me to tell you about every single soul I've met in the Underworld?"

"It's not the same, and you know it!"

The sound of a throat clearing made us both jump. We turned to see Elaina standing in the doorway, with Camilla leaning heavily on her arm. The former greeted us with a soft smile.

"Camilla's feeling a bit better," Elaina explained. "We thought we might try to go for a walk."

Clay and I stood in awkward silence, watching them make their careful exit. Only after they disappeared did Clay shift his focus back to me. We both took steadying breaths, the tension in the room crackling.

"I need you to understand why I'm upset," Clay said sharply, breaking the silence. "I'm tired of being the one you trust the least. I'm tired of watching you take risks that you don't let me share in."

"I made a choice to keep it all a secret," I admitted, forcing my voice to stay even. "That might not have been the ideal decision in your eyes, but if you love me, then you have to accept that I'm not always going to make decisions you like."

He scoffed, shaking his head with a rueful smile. "You've made decisions I don't like since the day I met you, Thea. That's hardly the issue."

"Then what is?"

"How am I supposed to protect you if you insist on keeping me in the dark while this kind of stuff is happening?"

So that's what this was about. Clay's incessant need to play the white knight—the morally irrefutable prince, always ready to swoop in and save everyone, even those who didn't want saving. He couldn't accept that he'd finally met someone who didn't need his protection. Someone stronger than him.

"I didn't ask for you to protect me," I snapped, crossing my arms. "And I don't need your protection. I am a Goddess, remember?"

"I'm very well aware of that."

"Do you think I wanted this? Do you think I want to constantly have to control magic that can kill as easily as lifting a finger? Do you think I want my father to be the God of Death? I hate it, Clay."

He rolled his eyes, leaning backwards against the kitchen counter. "No, you don't. Since the day I met you, you've had no qualms reminding people you're powerful enough to stand on your own."

I wanted to scream, to lash out and shake him until he understood how frustrating it was to watch him pull away from me over something I had no control over.

"Why don't you just admit it, Clay?" I challenged. "You're not afraid of the secrets; you're afraid of me. You're afraid of what it means that I'm a Goddess."

"You think I'm afraid of your power?" His voice broke, raw and unguarded. "If anyone is afraid of the significance of your powers, it's you. I, on the other hand, have known you were extraordinary since the moment I met you. I've never doubted your strength—not for a second. What terrifies me, though, is that you still don't trust me enough to let me stand beside you and because of that one day you'll decide you don't need me anymore and leave me behind."

I opened my mouth to respond, but the lump in my throat silenced me. He wasn't wrong—not entirely. But he wasn't entirely right, either.

I stepped towards him, not daring physical touch, but close enough for him to be able to sense my sincerity.

"I never meant to make you feel like I don't need you," I whispered, each word trembling with the weight of my confession. "But it's hard, Clay. It's so hard to let someone into this chaos when I don't even know where it's going. Death and destruction have followed me since the second I was created. It's not that I don't want your protection, but maybe you need to be protected from me."

"You don't get to make that choice for me." His tone was sharp, but his eyes softened as he stepped closer. We were sharing air now, just inches apart. "I love you because you're built of fire and steel, because you challenge me in every way that matters. So if loving you is dangerous, it's a risk

I'll happily take. But I can't keep standing here watching you carry this weight alone while you push me away."

"I don't want to. But if I lose you—if something happens because of me—then how do I survive that?"

"You won't lose me, Thea."

His hands finally reached out to cup my face, and I leaned into him breathing in his scent. His touch was steady and grounding. Familiar. *Right.*

"We can't do this if you don't let me in—if you keep deciding for both of us what I can and can't handle. I'm not asking you to trust me because it's easy—I'm asking because I need you to believe in us enough to try."

"I can't do this without you," I whispered, needing to say it again.

He wrapped his arms around me, pulling me into his chest as if he could shield me from every danger, every uncertainty.

"You'll never have to," he vowed, and then his lips were on mine.

Our kiss was desperate, a mingling of salty tears, desperate fears, and burning desire. Not just for each other's bodies, but for each other's hearts.

I wrapped my arms around his neck and pulled him to me, needing to feel his warmth against me, wanting to be swallowed entirely by it. His hands roamed up my back, tugging tightly on the low-hanging strands of hair down my back, which sent pulses of need flying to my core.

Clay pulled that hair once more, forcing me to tilt my throat so he could set his sights on the delicate skin there, sucking and nibbling with such fever that my knees went weak.

Gods, I wanted him. Now, tomorrow, and every day after that. For as long as I could have him.

He took the lobe of my ear between his teeth and I sighed, pulling him to my mouth again. I needed that delicate push and pull of his tongue darting over mine again. He kissed me like it was our first and last time all at once, like he couldn't ever get enough of me, like he burned for me as desperately as I did for him.

As if I needed that confirmation, I dipped my hand between us, stroking across the thick length of him over his trousers. Clay groaned and leaned into my hand, head falling back softly before he set his sights on my jacket, working to undo the many clasps and buckles that kept it strapped on my form.

"Never wear this again," he growled.

"I thought you liked this outfit," I pouted, breathless.

He grinned when he undid the last clasp and slid the leather off my shoulders so that it fell to the floor with a heavy smack. In an instant, he wrapped one arm behind my waist and another under my knee, lifting me onto the countertop with ease.

"I like you better naked."

And then his mouth was on me, lips sucking and tongue darting over the peak of my breast while his fingers toyed with my other exposed nipple.

"Oh, Gods," I leaned into his touch, desperate for more, gasping sharply when he pinched that delicate tip between his fingers even as a pulse of desire coiled through my core.

"I see no Gods here," he said, his voice thick with passion as he pulled back and wrapped his hands through my hair. "Just one fucking perfect Goddess."

My fingers grasped the hem of his tunic, needing it off him, and he let me take control, sliding it off with impossible slowness. Unblinking, he watched me as I explored the expanse of him, running my fingers across the bands of tight muscles, delicately tracing the thin faint scar lines that crossed his skin at odd angles. I lingered at one particularly large scar across his side, the shape a half moon.

The scar from Camilla's shadow beast nearly killing him when he fought for me.

"I'd do it a million times over," he swore, reading my thoughts.

He tugged me off the counter, reaching for the waistband of my pants to pull them to the floor, only so that he could trace his way back up my legs with kisses pressed into my flushed skin. I tangled my fingers in his unruly hair, grounding myself in his silky strands and breathing in his cinnamon scent.

When he arrived at the apex of my thighs, he pressed a gentle kiss there before his arm was around my waist and he was lifting my back onto the counter, fingers replacing where his mouth was, ripping out tiny breathless cries from me as he ran his touch from my entrance to that explosive spot I craved him most.

"My perfect Goddess," he mused again, dipping inside me with aching slowness. "So fucking warm and wet for me."

I whimpered, rolling my hips to chase his touch, imploring to go faster, harder.

"So needy," he chastised, watching me as his fingers pumped in and out, building me to that place where the world faded from existence, but not quite letting me get there. "You're so beautiful, far too beautiful for this realm."

My eyes slammed shut as the muscles in my core locked around his fingers, only to cry out in anger when the feel of him disappeared. He stepped back, loosening the ties of his pants and shedding them without ever breaking eye contact.

Purposefully, I did not try to hide when my eyes trailed his body, lingering over the parts of him that made my pulse quicken. *He* was beautiful. And perfect. And everything.

He was everything.

"Come to me," I commanded, and he obliged, stepping forward again into me, mouth slamming into mine as his fingers wrapped around my ankles and lifted, pushing them onto the counter so that I was spread open for him.

The position was entirely exposing, evoking enough vulnerability that my stomach flipped for a moment before his tongue darted over his bottom lip as he looked down at me.

"Fucking perfect," he said, almost to himself with a shake of his head before he aligned himself to my entrance and gently pushed in.

I cried out, clinging to shoulders for support as I adjusted to the impossible fullness of him. I let him stretch me until the shock of pain faded into the most exquisite of sensations. Clay rolled his hips, slowly working into me, each motion sweeter than the last. I fell back, grasping onto the wall behind me for leverage to push my hips up to meet him, our bodies finding a perfect rhythm together.

He watched me with burning passion clear in his gaze, the muscles in his abdomen clenched and his jaw tight. Each movement sent me closer and closer to oblivion, my cries becoming more frantic by the minute.

"More," I panted. "Faster."

He obliged, grasping onto my hips and pulling me onto him to meet each thrust, the length of him reaching impossible depths inside me.

I was so close.

"Look at me," he barked. I met his gaze, the pure abandon on his features sending another rush of warmth to my core that left me clenching around him. He breathed in sharply as he felt it, but kept his steady pace in and out of me. "This is what I can offer you, Thea. This is the place I can bring you that no one else can."

Oh Gods, yes.

Fuck yes.

"*Yes,*" I cried as his thumb dipped to circle that bundle of nerves and every muscle in my body clenched. I screamed his name as shockwaves of bliss pulsed through. My magic roared, filling every part of me with impossible energy while Clay continued to circle and thrust and whisper sweet words while the shockwaves slowly ebbed and steadied.

I was limp and spent, my body hardly able to handle the ecstasy but desperate for me, desperate for him to find that same release.

He reached for me, pulling my head to his shoulder.

"Hold on to me," he instructed, and I did as I was told, wrapping my arms firmly around his neck, nails digging into the skin as he let go of all sense of control.

His hips pounded into me, measured movements abandoned for frenzied thrusts, each harder than the last. He lost himself in me, growling as scales erupted down his spine. His head fell back, exposing the vulnerable line of his throat, his golden eyes blazing with unguarded emotion and in that moment, he was entirely mine, unraveled and laid bare. His fingers dug into my hips, pulling me onto him until with a final deep thrust he exploded, an animalistic snarl escaping as he stilled deep inside of me.

We stayed like that for a moment, panting sweaty messes, clinging to each other. I watched as the scales slowly sank back into his skin again.

"We should do that again sometime," I mused dreamily.

Clay laughed, pulling back to press his lips against my forehead before reaching to collect my clothes and pass them to me.

"We will, princess. Believe me when I say I want to do that with you every chance I get."

I joined Clay as he continued preparing dinner, following his instructions for chopping the onions and laughing as I mangled the process entirely.

"An all-powerful Goddess who can't cook a single meal," he quipped, taking the knife from my hands with a kiss to my forehead. "You're lucky you're cute."

I giggled. "Careful, don't piss off a Goddess; it's typically not recommended."

Clay chuckled but didn't respond, pushing me aside instead so he could take over the task. The back door creaked, and I turned to watch Elaina and Camilla step inside, bringing a burst of frosty air with them. Elaina smiled warmly at us, gently guiding Camilla forward. Camilla walked tall, her dark eyes sharp and alert even with a hand pressed gently to her side.

"How was the walk?" Clay asked over his shoulder.

"It's definitely cold, but the snow is quite lovely," Elaina responded, unhooking her cloak.

"It was torture," Camilla grumbled, slowly making her way through the room.

"She's a bit of a whiner," Elaina whispered to us, with exaggerated drama, ignoring the gesture Camilla shot over her shoulder. "With enough rest and food, though, she'll be back to full strength in no time."

"We'll get some stew ready for you both," I told her.

Elaina offered a grateful smile, placing a hand on Camilla's arm to steady her as they turned toward the living space.

"I'm not eating a damned thing until every surface in that kitchen has been scrubbed clean," Camilla called over her shoulder.

"Camilla!" Elaina scolded, a grin obvious from her tone.

I laughed softly as they left, pulling out two bowls in the cupboard and slowing when I looked at Clay's furrowed brow.

"What's wrong?"

He glanced up at me briefly, the corners of his mouth tugging down-ward. "It's nothing."

I nudged him with my elbow as I began ladling the stew for Elaina and Camilla. "I thought we just covered the no more secrets thing."

He sighed, setting down the knife and tugging the ladle out of my hands before pulling me flush against him. His arms circled my waist, the warmth of his embrace soothing against the winter chill still clinging to the room.

"I'm just realizing how lovely it is to be living in a house with my former lover, my betrothed, and the woman I'm now sharing a bed with."

I laughed so hard I snorted, hand flying to my mouth in embarrassment.

"It's not funny," he deadpanned, though the corner of his mouth twitched upward.

I grinned. "It's *kind of* funny."

"Oh yeah," he agreed sarcastically, brushing a stray strand of hair from my face. "It's every man's dream."

CHAPTER THIRTY THREE

After we had a solid meal in our bellies, we dressed ourselves for the winter, pulling on cloaks and gloves. Camilla was about my size and easily able to wear the extra items I had in the manor. Elaina was slightly taller, but she accepted what I had with a grateful smile anyway.

"How do we even know this will work?" Clay muttered, voice filled with obvious skepticism. He was less than happy with my plan.

"It'll work," I assured him.

He glanced down at me, stepping closer to tighten the clasp of my cloak. His fingers lingered longer than necessary. "You should save your strength for Pasnia, not this."

Camilla smacked his hands away with a roll of her eyes. "She's fine, you big Dragon baby. Unless you want to waste three days trudging to Eagirton on horseback, in the freezing cold I might add, just let your bedmate use her very plentiful magic to speed this process along."

A chuckle escaped me, and Clay shot me a disapproving glare. "I like the fact that you two are actually getting along *less* than I like this plan."

"Oh, *come on* already." Camilla grabbed my hand, pulling me towards the door. Clay followed reluctantly, his boots crunching on the snow-covered ground. Outside, Elaina stood waiting for us with her head turned up to the sky, her cheeks pink and a serene smile on her face.

"The snow reminds me of home," she confessed.

"Yes, yes, that's lovely Elaina," Camilla sighed, though her voice lacked any real annoyance. She turned her attention to me as we came to stand by Elaina. "So, how does this work?"

I hesitated under their combined attention. "Well, I've never really done it before."

The glare Camilla gave me could have frozen the dessert.

"Okay fine," I sighed, thinking. "Describe to me where we're going."

"I told him in my letter to expect us," Camilla explained. "I suppose the dining room will be easiest."

I nodded. "Tell me what it looks like. Be specific."

Camilla folded her arms, thinking. "There are chandeliers. Two of them. The walls have dark paneling and there are tons of paintings. Expensive ones."

"Stolen ones," Clay interjected under his breath, earning an eyeball from Camilla, who ignored him and continued on.

"The table is long, made of dark wood, always polished so it shines, and the chairs are high-backed with white upholstery."

I closed my eyes, forcing myself to picture the space as she described it. I painted the image in my mind's eye with every detail she provided, pulling my magic toward it like a thread through a needle. When the space felt tangible enough to touch, I reached out with my power and tore open the distance between us.

I knew it had worked when Elaina gasped softly.

"I wish I knew I could do that before that awful boat ride to Tenebris," I mused, blinking my eyes open to admire the shimmering golden portal.

Clay's hand squeezed my hip in silent reassurance. "Everyone in. Be prepared for anything."

He darted a quick glance at my dagger, ensuring I had it firmly in hand, before stepping through the portal first. Camilla followed, her movements slower and still difficult. Elaina hesitated only a moment before following. With a steadying breath, I stepped in, sealing the portal tightly behind me.

The sensation of traveling through a portal in the Mortal Realm was different from stepping into the Underworld. While that felt instantaneous, this felt like a journey. The air roared in my ears, rushing past me, before my boots landed on the soft carpet of the warm dining room.

Camilla's contact sat casually at the head of the table, his glass of wine glinting in the firelight. He was obviously tall, even while seated, with a carved jawline and strong arms. And even though Clay and Camilla both had warned me he was dangerous, I couldn't help but notice how beautiful he was. He tucked his russet hair neatly behind his ears, and his green eyes danced with amusement as he appraised us.

"Well, that is something you don't see every day," he said smoothly, his eyes lingering on me for a moment too long. Clay stepped closer, his presence sharp and protective.

"Nikolai," Camilla greeted him, before forcefully clearing her throat. Her voice was firm, but a flicker of unease passed across her face. "We need to talk."

He gestured broadly to the table with a roguish smile. "Sit down, dear. We'll talk over drinks."

Nikolai Legum's reputation preceded him. Known for illegally trafficking magical goods, relics, and secrets, he was one of Athenia's most infamous criminals. After murdering his only real competition in the months before I arrived in Athenia, he was now the undisputed king of the criminals, and I had no doubt that he could rally a small army against us if we managed to piss him off.

I didn't even want to know how Camilla and her grandmother had gotten involved with him.

He refused to speak until servants had brought each of us a drink and offered all of us something to eat. None of us touched a thing. I looked down at the wine in front of me suspiciously, not willing to trust it.

"I typically don't conduct my business with the wayward granddaughter," Nikolai pointed out to Camilla, his tone teasing as he studied her.

She pushed her long hair behind her ears, her posture defiant. It was actually quite... refreshing to see her looking so impetuous again after being on the brink of death for the past few days.

"Alina is dead," she told him.

Nikolai's lips pursed, a faint smile pulling at their edges. Did this man take anything seriously?

"Well then, I officially do business with the wayward granddaughter," he announced with playful formality before glancing at Clay and I. "Although I am surprised the royals wanted to be present for this little rendezvous."

"We're not here to cause you trouble," I assured him, though the low growl rumbling from Clay's chest said otherwise. I reached out, placing a hand on his arm in a silent plea for restraint. Nikolai caught the motion, his sharp eyes lingering, his expression too knowing.

"Then what are you here for, Councilwoman?" He asked, his voice smooth as silk.

I cleared my throat. "I'm looking for something. An artifact. I was hoping you could help."

His brows rose, and he pulled the glass of wine to his lips, drinking deeply as he appraised me. "If I was the kind of person who could help with that, which I'm not admitting I am, I'd be a fool to get into bed with a Council member."

Clay stiffened next to me, just the mention of Nikolai in bed with me upsetting him. Even if it was just for the sake of a phrase.

"We're very aware of your dealings Nikolai," Clay told him, voice hoarse from the fire building in his lungs. "What we need supercedes the Council. Supercedes Athenia."

Nikolai only glanced at the prince before returning his narrowed eyes to me. "And what kind of artifact might you be looking for?"

My stomach someraulted. "I'm searching for a book."

He waved off my words with a dismissive hand. "I have dozens of books. Hundreds even. You'll have to be more specific."

I glanced at Clay from the corner of my eye. His jaw was tight, tension radiating from his shoulders. "What we're about to discuss does not leave this table."

Nikolai's amused smile faded slightly as he met the prince's eyes without fear. "You don't command me, prince. Not here."

"Nikolai, please," Camilla said, eager to diffuse the tension. "We have reason to believe that someone is looking for the Book of the Gods. Someone who intends to use it to free Hyrax from the Underworld."

Nikolai stilled, the playful light dimming in his eyes as he turned to Camilla slowly. His grasp tightened on the glass of wine and, for a moment, I readied my magic, prepared to defend my people if he moved against us.

"You cannot expect me to believe that," he drawled.

"We do," I replied evenly, working to appear calm even as my stomach tied itself into knots.

"Why should I?"

"Because Hyrax is my father," I announced, voice steady as the weight of the truth settled between us. Clay tensed beside me, his disapproval with my disclosing that information unspoken but palpable. I reached under the table, squeezing his knee in silent reassurance.

Nikolai's sharp gaze bore into me. There was neither fear nor awe in his expression as he assessed me, even knowing that I was a Goddess. His face just bore calculated interest. "There have been rumors," he murmured softly. "Of an unnatural power living in the castle."

Unnatural was a bit harsh.

He leaned back in his chair, pulling the napkin from his lap and tossing it onto the table. "I don't have the book."

I deflated. Air rushing out of me in a disappointed exhale.

"But," he continued, "I might have some ideas of where to look. I'll put people on it immediately. I expect the compensation will be commensurate with the size of the task."

Clay's lip curled back. "Your compensation is me not arresting you right now."

"Not good enough," Nikolai said simply with a shrug.

"We'll handle it," I interjected him, cutting off Clay before the situation escalated and we lost this shaky alliance. Even if I had to go to the Underworld to retrieve some random magical artifact that he would accept as payment, so be it. The only thing that mattered right now was getting that book before Pasnia.

Nikolai nodded, smoothing a hand over his jaw. "Very well. I might also have information on... other useful items. I'll keep you informed if I learn more."

"Thank you, Nikolai," Camilla said softly, a flicker of relief in her tone.

Clay rose from his chair first, waiting until Camilla and Elaina crossed the room to join him before turning his back on Nikolai, clearly eager to leave.

"Hey, Dragon Prince," Nikolai called, halting our exit. His tone was playful, but his eyes glinted with something sharper. "How's that cousin of yours? Still happily killing people?"

Clay froze, his body taught with tension. "Count yourself lucky she didn't come with us."

Nikolai chuckled under his breath, watching as we stepped through the shimmering golden portal. "Oh, I do," he mused softly.

The frozen lawn of Hyrax Manor crunched under our boots as Clay and I emerged hand in hand. The cold air burned against my cheeks, but Clay's arm around my shoulders was warm and steady.

"Does he know Iris?" I asked quietly, Nikolai's parting words gnawing at me. Something about the way he'd asked about her, the way his playful tone carried an undercurrent of seriousness, set me on edge.

"Only by name," Clay assured me. "A year ago, the Order sent her to kill one of his rivals."

I nodded, pondering it, pondering Nikolai himself. "I didn't quite like him."

Clay chuckled, and he tightened his arm around me. "I'd feel offended if you had."

I grinned, stepping towards the manor and dragging him along with me, eager to shed these cold clothes and spend the evening warming each other between the sheets of my bed.

"Clay!" Iris' scream fractured the air around us and we spun.

She sped towards the house on horseback, Rankor and Kent close behind her.

And an army close behind them.

CHAPTER THIRTY FOUR

"Form a perimeter!" Kent commanded, leaping off his horse with practiced ease. "Archers, find the high ground. I don't want anyone within a mile of this property!"

The grounds of Hyrax Manor were pure chaos. Soldiers scrambled to find their newly assigned posts, women and children hurried into the house, and men hauled weapons from massive caravans. Iris and Rankor strode toward us, their expressions grim, as Kent continued barking orders.

"What's happened?" Clay demanded, his voice cutting through the din with unflinching authority.

"Your father," Iris panted, her chest heaving with exertion. "He knows Thea took Camilla, and he knows about the rebellion. He's readying for war."

Clay's jaw tightened, but he didn't falter. Without hesitation, he ushered us into the manor and into the nearby study, slamming the door shut behind Kent, Elaina, and Camilla. Disarray filled the room—maps and parchment lay scattered across the worn wooden table, and books lay in chaotic piles on the shelves. Bracing his hands against the tabletop, Clay leaned forward, his shoulders taut with tension.

"How?" he growled. "Who flipped?"

Iris shook her head, stray tendrils of red hair escaping her intricate braid. "Hardly anyone knew. This was already in motion before we started spreading word about making our move."

"The civilians?" Clay pressed, his tone sharp and unyielding.

"Your father's started killing anyone he suspects of being a sympathizer," Kent spat, his crossed arms emphasizing the menace of the twin swords strapped to his back. "No trials, no interrogations—just swinging blades. We got out as many as we could and brought them here."

"He's acting like a madman," Rankor rumbled as Elaina moved to tend a gash on his arm, her hands steady and focused. "More than usual, anyway."

I stared at the table, the weight of Rankor's words settling uneasily in my gut. When I finally lifted my eyes, they locked with Camilla's. The same horrid realization flickered in her gaze, and she gave me a subtle nod.

"No one told him," I breathed, the resignation in my voice palpable. "It's Pasnia. She's at the castle."

Clay straightened, gaze sweeping over me as his mind worked out what I was suggestion. His expression darkened. "She's infecting him with madness."

An eerie silence, thick with tension and fear, fell over the room.

"That's... not good," Rankor muttered.

"Believe me," Camilla murmured, her voice low and haunted. "It's worse than you could imagine."

Iris' glare shot toward Camilla, but for once, she said nothing. There was no time for bickering, not with the fate of the Mortal Realm teetering on the edge.

"Did you find the book?" Kent asked quietly, his voice tense.

I shook my head. Even if Nikolai had started looking right after we left, there was no time to hope for it. "We have to go into this without it."

"And what?" Camilla asked sharply, her frustration bubbling over. "Just pray she doesn't have it already?"

Elaina reached for her, attempting to calm her, but Camilla shrugged her off. "Am I the only one who thinks this feels like a trap?"

"You would know," Iris snapped, her words cutting like a blade.

Clay shot Iris a warning glare, and she turned away, rolling her eyes heavily.

Camilla was right, though, even if Iris didn't want to admit it. Even if none of us wanted to believe it. Pasnia wasn't bothering to hide her involvement—she was practically daring us to come for her. A trap seemed inevitable.

And a Goddess wouldn't lay a trap unless she was confident she could catch her prey.

"Trap or not," Clay said firmly, his tone brooking no argument, "we can't just let our people die. If we stay here, they'll come for us, anyway."

The room fell into a tense silence as we collectively took a moment to breathe, steeling ourselves for the inevitable battle ahead.

I'd known this was coming, but somehow I still thought we'd have more time.

I stared at each of my friends in turn, taking in every detail of their somber faces as if it was the last time I would see them.

"What's your command, Your Grace?" Kent asked, his voice polished and formal.

"Majesty," I corrected instinctively, the word slipping from my lips before I could stop it.

The room turned toward me, confusion etched across their faces. Even Clay, who had so naturally taken command, frowned in surprise.

"You're officially fighting for a new king," I said, my voice resolute.

The revolution had begun.

Clay was our Dragon now.

The weight of my words settled over the room like a heavy shroud. For a heartbeat, no one moved. Then a grin tugged at Rankor's lips, followed by Iris' knowing smirk. Even Kent gave a slight, satisfied nod.

"Long live the king," Iris quipped, her voice tinged with dark amusement.

Clay ordered Camilla to get the civilians settled and Elaina to tend to the injured before leading Iris, Rankor, and me outside. Rankor brought us to a grizzled man with thick, carrot-colored curls. His polished armor bore the scars of countless battles, and he greeted Clay and me with deep bows as we approached.

"This is Commander Harland," Rankor introduced. "I've placed him in charge of logistics and troop movements."

Clay nodded sharply, offering his hand. "Commander."

Harland clasped it firmly. "It's an honor to serve you, Your Grace."

"Majesty," Rankor corrected, a sly grin tugging at his lips.

Harland's eyes darted to Rankor briefly before inclining his head. "Very well. Your Majesty, I've started coordinating with some of the men we brought from the villages surrounding the castle. We've got around two hundred fighters at your disposal, but they're largely untrained."

"They'll have to do," Clay said, releasing Harland's hand. "How are our defenses?"

"I've set up supply lines and communication runners. I've also identified potential choke points around the manor to keep the civilians safe while we push toward the castle."

Clay's gaze swept over the gathering forces, his jaw tight. This was a version of him I didn't entirely recognize—a prince who had led legions to victory during the Great War.

"What about the cavalry?" he asked. "Do we have enough mounted fighters to break their front lines?"

"Around fifty riders," Kent answered, joining us. "They're capable, but I'd recommend sending scouts ahead to avoid ambushes."

Clay nodded sharply. "Ranged support?"

"We stationed archers on the ridges around the manor," Rankor told him, gesturing toward the high ground. "Not many, but they're excellent shots."

"Leave them to defend the perimeter here," Clay instructed. "Harland, I want a full breakdown of our numbers, weapons, and supplies by nightfall. And scouts on every route to the castle."

Harland nodded. "As you command, Your Majesty."

We watched as the commander strode off, barking orders at the nearest group of soldiers.

"Do you trust him?" I asked Rankor, keeping my voice low.

His expression was uncharacteristically serious. "With my life. I fought with him during the Great War. He knows his way around a battlefield."

Clay took a deep breath, a spark of determination lighting his golden eyes. "Good. We'll need every edge we can get."

"What now?" Iris asked, her tone clipped.

Clay's lips pressed into a thin line as he considered. "Let's get inside. Everyone eats and rests. Come nightfall, we ride. The cavalry will hit first by land, and I'll attack from the sky. Iris and the members of the Order that are loyal to us will stay back to protect Thea. Thea only goes into the castle when I'm sure the pathway is safe."

I whipped my head toward him, my voice sharp. "What?"

"You heard me."

"I'll be on the front lines," I snapped.

Kent cleared his throat, exchanging a look with Iris and Rankor before jerking his head toward the gathering soldiers. "Let's... uh... give them a minute."

Rankor grinned faintly. "Good idea. Come on."

Clay waited until they'd moved out of earshot before grabbing me by the arm and pulling me back toward the manor. "Thea—"

I yanked free, fire flaring in my chest. "I'm the deadliest weapon you have, and you know it. Forcing me to stay behind is a waste of your resources."

He let out a heavy sigh, running a hand through his hair. "I also know that the last time you exhausted your magic, you were unconscious for two days."

"I'm stronger now."

His hand slid to the back of my neck, grounding me with a firm but gentle grip. "I know that, princess. You're also the only one who stands a chance against Pasnia, though. If you burn yourself out on the battlefield, who will stop her?"

The reality of our situation crashed over me like a wave, cold and relentless. For a moment, all I could see was the image of Clay falling from the sky during the battle with the shadow beasts. Fear twisted in my chest. I couldn't go through that again. "I don't want to leave you."

His eyes softened, his thumb brushing the base of my neck. "I know how to take care of myself."

Maybe he could.

But only for so long.

If I didn't successfully send Pasnia back to the Underworld, it was only a matter of time before they all died.

"What if I can't stop her?" The question escaped me in a trembling whisper.

His lips brushed my forehead, lingering just long enough to steady me. "There's no time to think like that, Thea. Right now, we just keep moving forward."

He nodded toward the house, taking my hand in his and tugging me gently. "Come on. Let's get you fed and in bed—as your king ordered."

With a wry grin, I looked at him from the corner of my eye. "I think I might need some help falling asleep. I'm really on edge."

Clay smirked and pulled me closer. "I think I know just the thing to help you relax."

I 'd never been in battle before. Never seen war unfold from the battlefield. Never faced the possibility of saying goodbye to my friends without knowing if they would come back.

An ominous stillness hung over us as we positioned ourselves atop the mountain overlooking the castle. Below, palace soldiers lined the ground in rigid formation, their weapons gleaming in the faint light. They were ready for us. Ready to meet us. Ready to kill us. Even the air seemed afraid to move, not a single breeze daring to interrupt the tension between the opposing forces.

Clay strode toward me, his hair mussed and shadows dark beneath his eyes. Despite his command that we all rest before the battle, he hadn't slept. He'd spent every second visiting the injured, refining battle strategies, issuing orders. And yet, even now, he moved with sharp, unyielding focus.

When he reached me, he didn't hesitate. His hands framed my face as he pulled me into a kiss—desperate and consuming. I melted into him, momentarily forgetting what we were about to do.

When he pulled back, his golden eyes searched mine, as though memorizing every detail. "Keep her safe," he said to Iris over my shoulder, his voice hard and commanding.

Then his gaze softened as he spoke to me. "I'll see you in my chambers when this is all over, princess."

"Count on it," I whispered, trying—and failing—to keep my voice steady.

He was gone as quickly as he came, tearing his shirt from his body before shifting. Wings erupted from his back, his form expanding as he soared into the sky. His battle cry split the silence, a feral sound that echoed over the valley.

From her perch atop a rock, Iris scoffed. She twirled a long blade between her fingers, the ruby in its hilt catching the light. "You're the Goddess here. He should tell you to protect me."

I raised a brow. "Do you need me to protect you?"

She scoffed again, brushing off her pants. "Of course not."

There was a time when I would have teased her, when she would have smacked my arm and grinned. But those days were gone. The ease between us had fractured.

Another roar from Clay tore through the sky, a feral command that sent shivers racing down my spine.

That was the cue.

It was time.

I met Iris' gaze, seeing that same tension in her eyes.

The world froze.

And then...

"Charge!" Rankor's voice thundered, cutting through the stillness like a blade. He spurred his horse into a gallop, the sound of pounding hooves reverberating through the earth.

Kent surged forward at his side, his twin swords gleaming in the faint light. The soldiers behind them shouted out in a chorus of defiance and desperation as our rebellion hurtled toward the enemy echoed their cries.

The clash was cataclysmic.

The ground trembled beneath the weight of two armies colliding, the force of it rattling through my chest. Fire rained down in molten streams as Clay dove from the heavens, his massive wings cutting through the sky, his flames consuming the enemy in searing waves. The air filled with acrid smoke and the metallic tang of blood, stinging my nose and burning my throat.

The sound was pure chaos.

Steel met steel with shrieking ferocity, the clash of blades ringing out like thunder. Screams of pain and rage mingled with the guttural cries of men fighting for survival. Horses reared and whinnied in panic, their hooves striking the ground with desperate force.

And above it all, Clay's roars reverberated through the battlefield, primal and unrelenting.

It wasn't just noise. It was carnage given a voice.

I clung to the sight of him, a fiery beacon in the chaos, his golden scales gleaming as he unleashed destruction from the skies. But even his immense power couldn't drown out the horrors below—soldiers falling beneath the weight of axes, arrows finding their marks, and bodies crumpling into the dirt, never to rise again.

Beside me, Iris's sharp eyes flickered across the battlefield, her blade steady in her hand as if she thrived in this chaos. "Don't freeze up," she said, her voice low but commanding. "Focus. Stay sharp."

My pulse thundered in my ears, and my fingers tightened on the reins of my horse. "How do you do this?" I asked, my voice barely audible over the cacophony.

She didn't look at me right away. When she did, her expression was unreadable. "You don't think about it. Just move. Fight. Survive."

I swallowed hard, the weight of her words anchoring me as the battle surged around us. This wasn't just war. This was survival—messy, brutal, and unforgiving.

And if we didn't move soon, it would devour us whole.

I hesitated, and Iris must have sensed it because, for the first time, her voice softened. "Thea."

I turned toward her, and for a moment, she looked like she was about to say something. Something important.

"Promise me everyone we love will get through this," I pleaded.

She went still.

I saw the battle reflected in her eyes—the blood, the bodies, the fire raining from above. I saw the weight of everything she had lost. Everything she had suffered.

And I saw the moment she realized she couldn't lie to me.

Her silence was heavier than any reassurance could have been.

At last, she spoke, her voice quieter than before. "I can't do that."

A lump formed in my throat.

Before I could respond, she straightened and nudged me toward my horse. "Come on. Get ready."

In front of us, a path was forming, a narrow space traveling from our position to the palace.

I swung myself into the saddle, the leather cold beneath my fingers. Iris followed, pulling herself atop her mount with practiced ease. Around us, the other members of the Order formed a sharp V formation, their movements precise. Iris and I remained at the center.

She turned to me one last time.

"Follow me," she instructed, her voice steady and authoritative. "No magic, unless your life depends on it. Stay alert. And try to stay alive."

It was the closest thing to I still care about you I was going to get.

With that, she spurred her horse forward, and we surged down the hill into the chaos of war.

CHAPTER THIRTY FIVE

There was so. Much. Blood.

It coated the ground, squishing under the hooves of my horse. It splattered through the air, warm and sticky as it struck my face. It dripped down my hands, staining my skin where my blade had sliced through enemies.

Everywhere I looked, the world was painted in red.

"Thea!" Iris' voice cut through the chaos, sharp and unyielding.

I whipped around, heart pounding. She was already off her horse, her blade flashing with deadly precision as she cut her way toward the castle entrance.

I fumbled as I slid off my horse, nearly falling as my boots hit the blood-slicked ground. My legs felt like lead, my body sluggish as I forced myself to move. My vision tunneled, narrowing on the crimson coating my boots. I was on the bridge. This fucking bridge would haunt me for the rest of my days.

I swayed, nausea clawing at my throat as I took in the carnage around me. The clash of steel. The roar of fire. The screams of the dying. It was too much—too fast.

A sudden shove from behind sent me sprawling forward.

"Move!" Rankor bellowed, his voice cutting through my haze.

I hit the ground hard, knees slamming into the stone. My palms scraped against the rough surface as I scrambled to push myself up, but my limbs felt weak, disconnected.

Above me, Rankor's sword swung in a deadly arc.

A soldier fell, his blade clattering to the ground. His head hit the bridge with a sickening thud, rolling to a stop at my feet.

I couldn't look away.

The body collapsed a moment later, fresh blood spattering across my chest. I was drenched in it now, soaked to the bone.

Rankor grabbed me roughly by the arm, hauling me to my feet with a strength that seemed effortless. "Get in the castle!"

He shoved me toward Iris, his movements quick and deliberate, already stepping into the next strike.

My legs faltered beneath me, but somehow, I found the strength to run. Duck. Leap. Dodge. My breath came in shallow gasps, my chest heaving as fear clawed at me.

Ahead, Iris hurled a blade over my head, the rush of air sharp against my cheek as it embedded itself in a soldier. She didn't even pause to look back.

"Let's go!" she shouted, her voice steady and commanding, as though death did not surround us.

We sprinted across the bridge, leaping over bodies and dodging swinging swords. Every step felt like a struggle against an invisible force pulling me back.

By the time we reached the grand entryway of the castle, my legs were trembling. My chest burned as I gasped for air, each breath tasting of blood and ash.

Members of the Order flanked us, their faces grim and unreadable as they wiped blood from their blades. They moved with precision, their focus unshaken.

Inside, the blood was just as bad.

Streaks of it marred the white marble floor, smears turning the once pristine hall into a grotesque canvas. The metallic tang was so thick I could taste it, bitter and suffocating.

"Thea!" Iris' voice snapped me back to the present. She was calm, deliberate. "Where are they?"

I forced myself to close my eyes, to shut out the chaos around me. I reached deep into the untouched well of power inside me, sending it outward in waves. It stretched through the castle, searching, hunting, until—

"Grand ballroom," I rasped, the words heavy on my tongue.

Iris nodded, her gaze sharp as it flicked to the Order members around us. "Let's move."

They surged forward with practiced ease, their movements a stark contrast to my faltering steps.

Enemies emerged from the shadows, their blades glinting in the dim light. The warriors around me dispatched each one swiftly, the clash of steel ringing through the air.

To my left, a soldier lunged, driving his sword into the belly of an Order member.

A scream tore through the air, high and raw.

I gasped, instinct taking over as I lunged forward, my blade finding his neck. The spray of blood was hot against my face as he fell, his weapon clattering to the ground.

There wasn't time to check on the fallen ally. No time to grieve.

No one else even seemed to notice.

We kept moving, each step feeling heavier than the last as the weight of the battle pressed down on me.

Finally, we stopped outside the sweeping double doors of the grand ballroom.

My lungs burned, my chest heaving with every ragged breath. My fingers tightened around the hilt of my blade, the metal slick with blood.

"You're up," Iris said, her voice calm but firm. She adjusted her grip on her blade, poised to burst through the doors.

Right.

My turn.

We burst into the grand ballroom, weapons raised and ready, prepared to face a onslaught of the kingdom's most elite swordsmen. The heavy doors groaned on their hinges as they swung open, and we braced ourselves for the clash of steel.

But there was only silence.

I exchanged a wary glance with Iris as the stillness pressed down on us, thick and suffocating. Slowly, I stepped forward, every nerve taut, every muscle coiled to strike. The Grand Ballroom had always been a marvel—ornate crystal chandeliers, vivid banners cascading from the high ceiling, and flowers that seemed to bloom perpetually in defiance of the seasons.

But today, it was nothing more than a hollow shell. Overturned chairs and shattered tables lay strewn across the floor, their splintered remains darkened with smears of blood. The space felt cavernous, every footstep echoing as though the room itself were holding its breath.

At the far end of the room, slumped on the great throne of the castle, sat the Dragon.

My breath caught, my stomach knotting with dread. He was barely recognizable. His dark hair hung in matted, tangled waves, as though he'd been tearing at it. Dried blood caked his hands, streaking down his forearms and staining the open collar of his shirt. But it was his eyes—his *eyes*—that stopped me cold. Their golden glow, once fierce and commanding, now burned wild and unhinged, more beast than man.

"There!" he screamed when he saw me, his voice shattering the stillness. He lurched forward on his seat, pointing a trembling, bloodstained finger directly at me. "You've come!"

His words were a ragged snarl, laced with frenzied triumph. My throat tightened as he leapt to his feet, his movements jerky and erratic.

"Where's Pasnia?" I demanded, forcing my voice to stay steady. The Dragon only laughed—a deep, guttural sound that sent chills racing down my spine. I wasn't sure he even understood what I was saying. I glanced to Iris but she only shrugged, just as confused as I was.

"Vyncent," I said his name tentatively, holding my hands up in mock surrender, not wanting to upset him further. "Is anyone else here with you?

He only tilted his head at me, chest heaving as he panted. "*You* ruined everything. You poisoned my son against me. This is all your fault."

He snarled, the sound a violent roar that echoed around us.

Then he launched himself into the air.

Oily black wings erupted from his back, tearing through the fabric of his shirt with a sickening rip. They were grotesque, uneven, dripping with some foul substance that might have been his blood as they flapped erratically, propelling him forward in spasmodic bursts. The rest of his body refused the shift, leaving him a twisted, mangled figure as he careened toward us.

"Move!" Iris shouted, her blade already drawn.

He was too fast for that.

The Dragon's weight slammed into me, driving me to the ground with bone-crushing force. Pain exploded in my skull as my head struck the marble, the impact reverberating through my entire body. The world swam, my vision darkening at the edges as I gasped for breath.

"Thea!" Iris' voice rang out, sharp and panicked.

The Dragon roared, his wings flaring as he scrambled to his feet, his movements animalistic and uncontrolled. "Guards!" he bellowed, his voice raw and savage. "Arrest them! Kill them! Kill them all!"

The doors to the ballroom burst open, and a flood of guards poured in. Their eyes glinted with unnatural madness, their movements jagged and fevered. Pasnia's influence twisted them, bending their wills into something barely human.

The Dragon only stared down at me with rage and disgust as I struggled to steady my vision. "I'll take care of you once and for all."

Iris and her Order moved like lightning, their blades flashing as they met the onslaught of guards. I watched wide eyes as their blades met in thunderous crashes, but I couldn't move. I was still sprawled on the floor, my lungs fighting for air, my vision blurred.

The Dragon moved towards me.

Get up, I told myself, planting my hands against the cold marble. *Get up*.

His fingers finally extended into talons, too long and crooked to be correct, but sharp enough to slice me in half.

No. This man was not going to kill me.

He was not going to force Clay through another heartbreak.

Power surged within me, sharp and relentless. Golden threads of magic lashed out, snapping through the air like a whip. The guards fell to their knees, their bodies trembling as my power wrapped around them, holding them in place. I knocked the Dragon from his feet, sending him careening across the room before forming my connection with him. Their life forces quivered beneath my grasp, delicate and fragile.

If I wanted to, I could send them all to the Underworld in an instant. For a moment, the thought was tempting. It would be so easy to seize control and end them.

But I wouldn't.

The Veil had been raised because a God had been too reckless with the lives of Mortals. I would not make the same mistake.

"Where is Pasnia?" I demanded, my voice ringing out like steel.

The Dragon rolled on the floor, looking up absently at the ceiling as a twisted grin split his bloodied face. His laughter was low and jagged, spilling from his lips like broken glass.

"I'm right here, darling," he whispered, the words not his own.

The room stilled, an icy chill settling over us.

Click.

Click.

Click.

The sound of heels echoed across the marble, sharp and deliberate.

Pasnia.

I turned to the throne slowly, my lungs frozen, unable to breathe as I laid eyes on her.

The Goddess of Madness strolled into view casually, her movements unhurried, exuding an air of absolute control. Her crimson hair spilled down her back in flawless waves, a stark contrast to her alabaster skin. She wore a sleek black silk gown that clung to her figure, the neckline plunging daringly low, and a small pouch hung from a belt at her hips. She grinned, her eyes pinning me in place—cold, calculating, and brimming with malicious glee.

"That's impressive," she purred, nodding towards the guards still held motionless under my power. Her voice was as smooth and sweet as poisoned honey. Slowly, she lowered herself elegantly to the throne, crossing one leg over the other. Then, with a languid motion, she reached behind the shattered throne and withdrew a massive tome.

The *Book of the Gods.*

It's power rolled through the room in oppressive waves, nearly driving me to my knees.

"I'm more impressive," Pasnia whispered with a sly smile.

Then everything went to hell.

The guards turned their weapons on themselves, their screams piercing the air as they crumpled to the floor in pools of their own blood.

"No!" My voice cracked, raw with desperation, as the room descended into madness.

Pasnia didn't even glance at the carnage. Her focus was solely on me. And suddenly I was aware of her magic rushing toward me. Pointlessly, I threw up my arms as if that would do anything to stop it. Her power pressed against my mind, dark and insidious, threatening to overwhelm me. I struggled against it, the feeling of it so much more invasive than the interrogation of a Truthseeker. It was faster, harder, deeper than anything I'd ever felt before. Even as I pushed her away with all my might, with all my magic, she kept sliding closer and closer.

It took only a touch of her magic against my mind to know that while I may be a Goddess, I wasn't strong enough to fight her.

I wasn't even close to matching her power.

Which meant we weren't going to win this fight.

"Run," I whispered to Iris.

Her eyes flashed in horror, as she realized what I already had.

I was going to die in this room.

I just hoped I could give her enough time to escape. As I turned back to Pasnia, golden light suddenly flaring in my palms, warm and glowing. I had only a second to marvel at this new manifestation of my magic before I hurled it at the throne, shattering it into a thousand glimmering fragments.

But she was already gone.

"I think your friend should stay," her voice rang out, dripping with mockery.

I spun, my heart lurching. Pasnia stood behind Iris, a blade pressed to her throat. The Book of the Gods dangled carelessly under her arm, as though it were only there as an afterthought.

Iris struggled, but Pasnia didn't flinch.

"In fact," Pasnia mused, her tone light and cruel, "I think all your friends should join us."

The ballroom doors groaned open again and a swarm of guards dragged in the battered, bloodied forms of my friends.

Clay stumbled forward, blood dripping from a gash on his forehead. Rankor's eye was swollen shut. Kent—

Kent wasn't moving.

Two arrows protruded from his stomach.

"Kent!" I screamed, my magic catching his body as the guards threw him mercilessly to the ground. I scrambled to his side, my hands shaking as I pressed them against his wounds.

Blood coated my fingertips, flowing out of him too rapidly.

I wasn't a healer. I couldn't fix this.

He was going to bleed out right in front of me and there was nothing I could do.

A sharp yank on my hair tore me backward, and I cried out as Pasnia's laugh echoed through the room.

"Lower the Veil!" she whispered into my ear.

Her hand twisted cruelly in my hair, pulling me further back. I clawed at her wrist, desperation tightening my throat.

"No," I insisted through a locked jaw.

She snarled and threw me backward. My shoulders slammed into the ground, but I barely had time to breathe before she grabbed a sword from a guard and swung it sharply toward Kent.

"Lower it, or he dies," she hissed.

I didn't dare meet the eyes of my friends. I couldn't. Tears blurred my vision as I pushed myself to my feet. My whole body trembled, caught in the impossible choice before me, but the word came out firm, steady, even as my heart broke.

The fate of the Mortal Realm was at stake. Kent would understand.

"No."

Pasnia stared at me, incredulous, before a cold smile spread across her face.

"Fine. Her, then."

She spun, pointing the blade toward Iris. the tip of it pressing into her belly.

"Thea, don't," Iris growled, struggling against the guard who held her in place.

"*Thea, dont,*" Pasnia mocked in a high-pitched voice. "Lower it!"

I swallowed hard, my mind spiraling, and salty tears flowing easily now.

It was an impossible choice, one I'd never wanted to make. I'd already watched one friend die because of me. I couldn't bear to watch them all die before me.

But it wasn't just my heart at stake.

"No," I said again, louder this time.

Pasnia tilted her head, her crimson waves catching the dim light. She sighed as if bored. "Stubborn little thing, aren't you? I suppose you get that from your father."

I braced myself for the bloodshed, for the loss, for the screams. For the briefest moment, I closed my eyes.

But there was no scream.

There were footsteps.

Pasnia's steps were slow, deliberate, as she moved toward Clay.

Panic surged through me as she gripped his hair, pulling his head back to expose his throat. The blade pressed tight against his skin. I moved to rush forward but my feet were rooted to the ground, held there by a magic like my own, but so much stronger.

Unbreakable.

"I did all this for Hyrax," Pasnia said with a wistful smile. "What would you do for the man you love?"

Ice fell over me in steady waves. Clay met my gaze, his expression filled with love, respect, and... resignation.

No.

"Don't watch," he commanded.

No.

I couldn't do this.

I wasn't strong enough to watch this.

Pasnia laughed. "You're taking too long to decide."

She pushed the blade into his throat and as Clay hissed in pain, as a bead of scarlet blood began trailing down his chest, as I threw everything I had against the magic holding me to no avail...something in me *shattered*.

"Stop it!" I screamed, my voice cracking as my hands lit up in golden light. The ground began to tremble under my feet. Iris' eyes widened.

Pasnia narrowed her eyes, lips quirking slightly. She knew she'd won.

"No, I don't think I will," she said, moving behind Clay to better position the blade.

To move it into the killing position.

And when all my thoughts centered around *him,* she finally broke through my defenses and her power poured into me.

Her magic slithered into my thoughts, rapid and invasive until the world around me vanished.

I spun, searching in the dark.

I couldn't see them. I couldn't hear Clay anymore.

If she had hurt him...

"You can't stop me," I heard her whisper behind me and I spun, jerking my elbow towards her nose, but there was nothing.

"Let me go!" I demanded.

Then I heard their screams.

I felt their blood pour across my skin.

Their pain reverberated through my very soul.

Time was meaningless. Their deaths came again and again. I heard it over and over. I felt that blood splash over me until I felt like I was drowning it.

I felt the pain of their deaths a thousand times over.

And I broke.

"I'll do it!" I screamed, the words spilling from me in a torrent of tears. My legs gave out beneath me. "I'll do it."

Her magic released me, leaving me gasping and hollow. Pasnia tossed Clay forward like a broken doll, and he collapsed heavily to the ground.

I scrambled toward him on my hands and knees, pulling his face into my hands.

"Don't do this," he pleaded, his voice raw.

Gently, I brushed my lips across his, pouring all of my love into that one soft touch.

"I can't lose you," I whispered, choking on the words. It was selfish, I knew that. I knew everyone would suffer because of this choice.

But Clay chose me over his kingdom.

And I would choose him over this realm if it came to that.

"Enough!" Pasnia snapped, her hand clamping around my arm. Her nails bit into my skin as she dragged me to the center of the room. Clay launched towards me, but a guard stepped forward in Pasnia's place, holding him back. "Lower the Veil. Now."

I fell forward, hands aching from where I had tore them on the stone outside. Everything ached.

And I was so fucking tired.

I raised my arms, my power trembling at my fingertips. The golden light of the portal shimmered before me, growing wider with each passing second. My friends screamed, begging me to stop. But I couldn't.

Not yet.

Not when I still had one last trick up my sleeve.

Pasnia stepped closer, her eyes gleaming with triumph. "Make it larger!"

"You're going to see Hyrax very soon, Pasnia," I promised her.

Her smile faltered, confusion flashing across her face.

Then I struck. My magic snapped out, coiling around her waist, and I yanked.

CHAPTER THIRTY SIX

Pasnia stumbled forward, her heels scraping against the marble as she strained against my magic. The grunts of frustration she let slip echoed through the desolate hall. For a fleeting moment, I thought I won.

Were she Mortal, I would have shoved her through the portal already, sealing it with ease. But she wasn't. Her strength was a force of nature, making my power feel like an ember flickering against a roaring inferno.

Blood trickled from my nose, dotting the marble floor in steady, rhythmic splatters. I poured everything I had into pulling her closer, my magic tethering her like a golden chain. Just a little further. Just one more step.

She stumbled again. Her crimson hair hung in disarray, and her burning gaze locked onto mine with a hatred that seared. I pulled harder, summoning strength from the deepest, most desperate parts of me.

But then she straightened.

And *laughed*.

The sound grated, sharp and mocking, as she tilted her head with infuriating ease. "Oh, that was fun," she said, brushing at her gown as though she'd merely tripped on a step. With a flick of her wrist, my magic snapped like brittle thread.

The recoil hit me like a blow, rippling through my body and forcing me back a step. I gasped, clawing for the remnants of my power, but the well had run dry. My legs trembled, barely holding me upright.

Pasnia's smirk widened as she smoothed imaginary dust from her shoulder. "You didn't really think it would be that easy, did you?"

The suffocating fog of her magic crept into my mind. I clawed at my temples, trying to fight the weight of it, but with my power so depleted, it slithered through easily, filling my thoughts with screams and death. The images seared into my mind like branding irons.

"I didn't need you to lower the Veil all the way," Pasnia continued, her voice maddeningly calm, as if this were all a game. "I just needed you to crack it."

My vision cleared just enough to see her pull a small vial from the pouch at her waist. The crimson liquid inside shimmered and the tiniest bit of magic left in me flared, recognizing it.

That was my blood.

"No." The word came out as a broken whisper, my head shaking as if I could will it out of existence.

She uncorked the bottle with a measured twist, dipping her finger inside to smear a streak of blood onto the open pages of the *Book of the Gods*. Her lips moved, a single whisper—a sentence so soft it was barely more than a breath.

And everything changed.

Pain erupted in a white-hot blaze, consuming every nerve in my body. My knees buckled, and I hit the floor hard, but the impact was a distant ache beneath the agony ripping me apart. My screams filled the air, raw and unrelenting, but they sounded far away, swallowed by the torrent of shock.

It wasn't just pain. It was theft. My very essence—the magic stitched into my soul—was being wrenched free against my will. The golden threads that defined me, that were *me*, tore away violently, spilling from my body in radiant, blinding waves. They scattered across the floor like molten light.

"You naïve little girl," Pasnia's voice cut through the haze, mocking and sharp. "You think you've matured into a goddess, but you're nothing more than a child wearing a crown that doesn't quite fit yet."

The portal shimmered, alive and writhing, expanding as if it had a mind of its own. My stolen magic fed it, the golden glow pulsating with each beat of my heart, and every breath it took drained me further, leaving me raw and hollow.

Cracks splintered through my power. The windows shattered, golden light exploding outward as more portals, wild and uncontrolled, tore the world open. The ballroom filled with chaos, glass shards raining down as the threads of my magic unraveled everything around me.

I clawed for control of my power, desperate to summon even a flicker of strength. But nothing remained. Everything I was Pasnia now controlled.

Through the haze, I saw it.

A pair of boots stepped through the portal, their heavy tread resonating across the marble. My gaze followed, past the dark trousers and simple tunic that revealed strong forearms to the figure's face.

A neatly combed beard, streaked with silver. Eyes as sharp and as bright blue as my own.

Hyrax.

The God of Death. My father.

I couldn't move. I couldn't speak. All I could do was watch as Pasnia, wielding my stolen power, widened the portal further.

Behind him, shadows twisted and writhed. The legions of the Underworld poured into the ballroom, their forms monstrous and endless.

M y magic ran out.

Only hollow emptiness remained.

The portals flickered, their golden light dimming, then vanished entirely. I felt Pasnia's hold fade with the last of my power. My knees buckled beneath me, my body crumpling to the cold marble floor. Across the room, Pasnia slumped as well, falling heavily to her knees before collapsing entirely. Her head lolled back, her eyes rolling into nothingness.

"Pasnia!" Hyrax's voice boomed, raw and thunderous, shaking the very air around us.

Gentle hands slipped beneath me, pulling my head into a lap. I blinked, struggling to focus, until Caldrius's sharp eyes came into view.

"You're here too," I whispered drunkenly, my words slurring. My lips barely moved, as though even speaking drained what little strength I had left.

"It's a surprise to me as well," he murmured, brushing strands of my damp, matted hair away from my face. His touch was achingly tender, but his eyes betrayed his worry.

"I can't feel my magic," I said weakly.

No tingles. No energy. No hidden well.

It wasn't like when Camilla had pushed it out of my reach, or when Mortal blood had dampened it. This was different. This was pure nothingness, a gaping void where my magic used to be.

"Shh," Caldrius soothed, though his jaw tightened. "It's going to be okay."

But I saw the lie in his eyes. He didn't know if it would be.

"Pasnia!"

Hyrax's voice tore through the air again, dragging our attention back to the center of the room. He knelt over her, his enormous hands cradling her limp body. Her head lolled against his chest, her once-glowing skin now pale and lifeless.

"What's happening?" I rasped, my voice barely audible.

"She exerted herself too much," Caldrius said tightly, his hand still brushing against my temple. "She was already weak. She's entering the Eternal Slumber."

Hyrax roared, the sound feral and heart-wrenching, as Pasnia's body faded. Her skin lost its luster, the glow of divinity draining away until all that remained was a gray, brittle husk of what she once was. Her fingers crumbled like ash as Hyrax tried to hold on to her, his grief palpable.

Pasnia had risked everything to bring Hyrax to the Mortal Realm—and hadn't even lived long enough to greet him.

"Who did this?" Hyrax bellowed, his head snapping up as he rose to his feet. His power surged through the room, oppressive and suffocating, pressing down on every soul present.

In the Underworld, he had seemed like any other man.

Among Mortals, he was larger, stronger, more terrifying.

He scanned the room, his obsidian eyes blazing as they swept over us. They locked onto the Dragon.

The Dragon was still on his hands and knees, his misshapen wings jutting from his back at painful, unnatural angles. He groaned, his muscles straining as he flexed his back, desperate to either complete the shift or return to his Mortal form.

"That bitch cursed me," the Dragon cried, his voice a pathetic whimper as he clawed at the floor. "I can't complete my shift!"

Hyrax's steps echoed ominously as he strode forward, his fury palpable. He loomed over the Dragon, reaching down with deliberate slowness. His massive hands clamped onto the base of each wing, and with one violent motion, he tore them from the Dragon's back.

The sound was sickening. Flesh and bone ripped apart with ease, the wings falling to the ground in a bloody heap. The Dragon's screams filled the air, sharp and agonized, making my stomach churn.

Hyrax sneered, his lip curling as he slammed a boot into the Dragon's ribs, sending him skidding across the floor.

"You're the bastard who beat my daughter," Hyrax growled, his voice low and venomous. His words vibrated with an otherworldly power, sending chills down my spine. "And now you call my wife a bitch?"

The Dragon whimpered, clutching his chest, but Hyrax was unrelenting.

"*This is how you speak of your Gods?*" Hyrax roared, his tone dripping with disdain. He brought his boot down on the Dragon's leg, the femur shattering beneath the force.

The Dragon screamed again, a hollow, broken sound.

Hyrax grabbed him by the jaw, hauling him upright as though he weighed nothing. His fingers dug into the Dragon's face, forcing him to meet his gaze. The room seemed to darken, the shadows lengthening as Hyrax's power surged.

"You are nothing to us," Hyrax snarled, his voice like a death knell.

Shadows descended, curling unnaturally around the Dragon's body. His screams were short-lived, swallowed by the black mist that writhed and consumed him. When the shadows dissipated, all that was left of the Dragon was muscle and bone—his skin stripped away like a cruelly discarded shell.

I pushed away from Caldrius' lap, choking on bile as my stomach heaved violently. I vomited onto the floor in front of me, trembling as Caldrius reached for my hair, gently pulling it back from my face.

Hyrax turned, his movements sharp and violent, his gaze sweeping over the Mortals still in the room. "I am your ruler now," he declared, his voice cold and unyielding. "Bow to me, or meet the same fate."

One by one, they fell to their knees.

The Athenian guards, who had served the Dragon loyally, were the first to bow, their weapons clattering to the floor in surrender. Then came the resistance fighters, their heads lowering in silence.

The room held its breath, heavy with submission, until the soft scrape of boots broke the stillness.

Clay stood.

"No," I croaked, my voice barely audible, too weak to carry across the vast ballroom. I reached for him, my fingers trembling, but Caldrius held me firmly in place.

If I had my powers, I would have forced him to his knees, forced him to do the thing he would never do on his own just to be sure that he would live through this night.

But I didn't have my powers, and Clay was born to lead.

To protect.

To stand when no one else would.

Hyrax's expression shifted, disdain curling his lips as he looked Clay over. "You must be the Dragon Prince I've been so hoping to meet," he said, his tone mocking.

To my horror, Iris stepped forward next, rising slowly to stand beside Clay.

And then Rankor joined them.

My friends. My stupidly brave family.

"Kill them all," Hyrax commanded, his voice as calm as if he were ordering wine.

A sob ripped through me, ravaging my body like a tempest. I shuddered in Caldrius' grip, my chest heaving as my eyes burned, too dry now to produce anymore tears. "No, please," I whimpered, the plea tearing from my throat.

"My liege!" Caldrius' voice rang out, sharp and commanding, cutting through the tension in the room.

Hyrax turned, his eyes narrowing as if only just now realizing we were still there.

Caldrius rose to his feet, cradling me in his arms. "Your daughter is unwell," he said, his voice steady but edged with urgency. "She needs rest. Perhaps we can delay this... punishment until after she recovers."

Hyrax's expression softened marginally as he rushed toward me, placing a hand against my clammy forehead. His touch burned like ice, and I flinched.

"She's burning up," Hyrax muttered, his voice low, but sharp with concern.

"She needs a healer," Caldrius replied, his tone firm.

The two exchanged a long, silent look, unspoken words filling the space between them. Finally, Hyrax gave a curt nod. "Very well. I'll deal with this myself. You see to it that she is cared for.

No.

I struggled weakly against Caldrius' hold, my limbs too heavy to fight properly. He tightened his grip, pulling me closer to his chest.

"Don't you think she would prefer to be present for the execution of those who stood against her father?" Caldrius reasoned, his voice smooth and calculated.

Hyrax paused, his gaze flicking to me. His obsidian eyes softened slightly, his lips pulling into something dangerously close to concern.

"Take them to the dungeons," he ordered over his shoulder. "She can witness their fate when she is well."

"No!" I cried, thrashing weakly as the guards moved to seize my friends.

"Get her a healer," Hyrax barked at Caldrius, ignoring my pleas. "Now."

Caldrius didn't hesitate. He turned sharply, carrying me out of the room as I screamed for my friends.

Clay's voice tore through the air, raw and desperate. "Thea!" he shouted, his voice echoing after us even as the heavy doors slammed shut.

I cried harder, my sobs breaking me apart as Caldrius carried me farther and farther away.

CHAPTER THIRTY SEVEN

I almost didn't recognize my suites in the castle when I finally blinked my eyes open. The soft orange glow of evening light slipped through the cracks in the drawn curtains, casting the room in muted shadows. The fire crackled softly in the hearth, but its warmth felt distant, meaningless. I was alone.

My throat ached, raw from screaming, and my stomach twisted painfully with hunger. When I tried to sit up, my body betrayed me—every muscle protested, a deep ache spreading through my bones. A terrible dryness burned my mouth, and my fingers trembled as they brushed over the silk nightgown someone had dressed me in.

The room felt suffocating, eerily quiet. My gaze darted across familiar furniture that now seemed foreign, as though it belonged to someone else. I couldn't shake the sense that I didn't belong here anymore.

Then, like a dam breaking, the memories surged back.

Pasnia was dead.

Hyrax was here.

And Clay...

My chest seized, a silent gasp choking me. The ache in my body evaporated, replaced by a desperate, clawing urgency. I threw off the blankets, stumbling to my feet. My legs wobbled, but I forced them to move, sprinting through the bedroom and parlor to fling open the door to my suite. My thoughts spiraled. I didn't know where my friends were—I just knew I had to find them. I had to save them.

"Whoa!" Caldrius stepped into my path, and I collided with his chest. His hands steadied me, but the contact made my skin crawl. "Slow down."

"Where are they?" My voice was a hoarse growl, laced with desperation. I shoved him away, needing answers, needing action.

"Why don't we go sit down and talk?" he suggested, his tone patient but strained. His gesture toward the parlor felt more like an order than a request.

That's when I saw them—the guards stationed at the end of the hallway. Their eyes locked on me, their stances casual but unyielding, hands resting on the hilts of their swords. Their armor was all wrong. Black plate glinted ominously, scarlet capes draped across their shoulders.

It hit me like a punch to the gut. Hyrax had already claimed the castle. His soldiers stood where the Athenian ones once had, their loyalty stripped away like everything else.

I swayed on my feet, disoriented. "How long have I been asleep?" I muttered, more to myself than to him.

Caldrius touched my elbow, guiding me back into the room. "Bring her bread and water," he barked to someone over his shoulder.

I ripped my arm free, spinning on him. "Don't touch me."

His jaw tightened, but he didn't push back. Instead, he followed me inside, shutting the door with a quiet click. "Still angry, then?"

I ignored him, my thoughts spiraling into chaos.

"Sit," he ordered, his tone clipped. "You've been asleep for a week."

My head snapped toward him. "A week?"

He nodded. "You woke occasionally—enough to eat and drink. You don't remember?"

I shook my head, frustration tightening in my chest. Everything felt hazy, like I was trying to grasp memories through a fog.

"Where are my friends?" I demanded, my voice trembling under the weight of the question.

His answer came quietly, but it hit me like a hammer. "In the dungeons. I've done what I can to delay their executions."

The word executions sent ice down my spine. My knees buckled, but I caught myself on the back of a chair.

"No." The word escaped in a whisper, barely audible.

I lunged toward the door, intent on doing something—anything—but Caldrius stepped in my way, his arm like a steel bar blocking my path.

"Those guards outside have orders to keep you here," he said evenly.

"Let them try." The defiance in my voice sounded hollow, even to me.

He didn't flinch. Instead, his expression softened, his blue eyes dark with something I couldn't place. Concern? Regret? It didn't matter.

"Thea," he said carefully, his words deliberate, "can you use your powers?"

The question stopped me cold. My hands twitched, instinctively reaching inward, searching for the familiar warmth of my magic. It was always there, just beneath the surface.

But now... nothing.

"My powers..." I trailed off, panic bubbling under the surface. "Why can't I feel my magic?"

Caldrius sighed, his shoulders sagging. "Pasnia's spell forced you far beyond your limits. You've drained yourself completely. Hyrax believes its normal for someone as young as you. Your powers haven't fully matured."

He hesitated, his voice softening as he added, "I didn't know if you were going to wake up."

His words were a slap. My legs gave out, and I sank onto the couch, my body heavy and numb.

"What does that mean?" I asked weakly, though dread was already coiling in my gut.

"It means we don't know if your magic will return." His voice was steady but edged with pity. "Maybe with time. Maybe not."

The finality of his words settled over me like a shroud. My magic—everything that made me more than just a frightened girl—was gone. I had nothing left.

Mortal. Weak.

Powerless.

And trapped in this room. Just as I'd been before. But this time, the stakes were so much higher.

My friends.

My enemies had won, and my friends would pay the price.

Caldrius let the silence stretch, giving me space to absorb the crushing weight of reality. I stared blankly at the floor, too overwhelmed to meet his gaze.

Finally, I forced myself to speak, though my voice was brittle. "Why are you here?"

"I'd like to help you get your friends out of here," he said simply.

I turned to him sharply, narrowing my eyes. "Why?"

He hesitated, rubbing his jaw. "Because I'm the only one who can, Thea. You act like I'm some monster."

"You *are* a monster," I spat, standing abruptly. The room felt too small, his presence too close. "You lied to me. My face—my entire body—it isn't even mine. It's hers."

Caldrius flinched, but his voice remained steady. "I may be a monster, Thea, but I've never been one to you. I've been nothing but kind."

"Kind?" I let out a bitter laugh. "You manipulated me into trusting you. Into thinking I mattered. You wanted me to love you because I look like her."

His expression flickered, a shadow of something raw crossing his face. "You're nothing like Isidore, love. You may resemble her, but you're far more difficult—and far more interesting."

"Glad to know I'm such a challenge for you," I sneered.

His eyes locked onto mine, unwavering. "Hardly."

The tension between us was suffocating. I didn't trust him—I couldn't. But what choice did I have?

Without magic, without allies, I was nothing.

"Look, you want to save your friends, and I want to help you." He sighed, rubbing his temple. "But we both know that won't happen unless we give Hyrax something to hold on to."

With a sigh, I sank back onto the couch. My voice was thick with resignation. "So, what do you propose?"

Caldrius leaned forward, elbows on his knees. The fire crackled in the silence as he studied me. Finally, he spoke.

"I want you to marry me."

The words destroyed what little remained inside me.

"What?" I whispered, the word barely audible.

"You heard me."

I rose to my feet again. I was either going to vomit or punch him. Maybe both.

"Are you insane?"

"You asked what I wanted," he reminded me, with an infuriating shrug. "That's the price."

"We just established that I'm. Not. Isidore. Did you forget already?"

He stood too, his presence overwhelming. "You're not Isidore. And this isn't about love. It's about survival - yours, mine, and your friends. You need my help. And I need yours."

"What does marrying me possibly accomplish for you?" I spat, hands clenched into fists to stop their shaking.

"Hyrax will not be content here forever. He's spent a millennium missing his family - his brother. Once you're strong enough, he'll ask you to open the door to the Upperworld and when that happens, this realm will need a leader. You may be his heir, but I was born to rule. Marrying you allows me to do that." He stepped closer, jaw tightening. "And marrying me keeps you *and* your friends safe. No one in this castle will question your loyalty if you're my wife."

My vision blurred with rage, my thoughts a whirlwind of helplessness and resistance. I wanted to scream, to lash out, to cry.

But... he was right.

What other choice did I have? I was powerless, trapped, and surrounded by my enemies. Caldrius *was* my only chance to save my friends.

"I'd rather die," I said, but even I heard how hollow the words sounded.

"Hyrax won't allow that, Thea. But he will kill your friends if you don't do something about it."

I exhaled shakily, my fingers twitching, instinctively reaching for magic that wasn't there anymore. The magic that might never flow through my veins again.

"I hate you," I whispered.

"You'll have the rest of our lives to get over that." His lips curved into a faint, bitter smile. His tone wasn't mocking nor cruel. It was quiet, resigned. "So, is that a yes?"

I forced myself to meet his gaze. My voice cracked as I breathed the words to life.

"Yes. I'll marry you."

The woman who stared back at me in the looking glass was unrecognizable. Her hair was twisted neatly away from her face, but no amount of effort could mask the dark, sleepless shadows framing her blue eyes. The bruises were gone, but the scars—oh, the very many scars—they lingered, silent witnesses to everything I'd lost in just a week.

Even the gown I wore felt wrong. The soft white fabric, cinched at the waist and draped off my shoulders, might have been beautiful on me at one time. Now it only clung to me like a shroud. It wasn't the gown I'd imagined wearing on my wedding day. Then again, nothing about this was what I'd imagined. Nothing about this was supposed to be.

The guards arrived without ceremony, their gazes fixed firmly ahead as they led me down the hall. Their silence was unbearable.

Someone had attempted to clean the halls while I'd slept. The bodies had been removed and most of the blood washed away, but the stains on the floor remained. This marble would never look as crisp and pristine as it once had. My throat tightened with each step as the memories clawed at me—Pasnia's suffocating grip, the agony, the devastation.

The ballroom doors loomed ahead, creaking open with an ominous groan. My breath hitched as Caldrius greeted me. Dressed in a black jacket embroidered with golden thread, he looked every inch a king already. The sight made my stomach churn a little.

He stepped forward, his gaze steady as he dismissed the guards with a sharp flick of his hand.

"Are you ready?" he asked, his voice low, unreadable.

"I'll never be ready for this," I said, forcing the words through the lump in my throat.

He sighed heavily, studying me. "Well, this is your last chance to back out."

I almost laughed, a sharp, bitter sound that never made it past my lips. Back out? We were so far past that point it was laughable.

"Let's go," I said, stepping past him.

His hand snapped out, fingers wrapping around my wrist. A soft click echoed through the air. I glanced down to see the silver chain gleaming against my skin, cold and final.

"I may be loyal to Hyrax," Caldrius said, his voice like velvet, "but there are still traditions of my house I will honor. This is one of them."

I stared at the chain, its meaning sinking into me like a stone. It wasn't just an accessory. It was a mark of permanence. A claim. This chain would stay on my wrist for the rest of my life, a physical reminder that I belonged to him now.

He tucked my hand into his arm and led me into the ballroom.

The room was still a disaster. Shards of glass littered the floor, and servants scrambled to drape flowers over the wreckage in a desperate attempt to make the space look worthy of a wedding. It didn't work to wash away the shroud of bleakness that lingered in the room. The destruction was too deep, too raw.

At the far end of the space, Hyrax sat on his shadowy throne, his expression unreadable. The obsidian crown atop his head gleamed in the torchlight, a stark reminder of the power he wielded.

And there they were—Clay, Rankor, and Iris.

My steps faltered as my gaze locked onto them, kneeling at the base of the throne with their hands bound. Bruised but alive. My chest tightened painfully, and my breath hitched. Clay's golden eyes burned into me, flicking briefly to the chain on my wrist before returning to mine. The disbelief in his gaze cut deeper than any blade ever could.

"What are they doing here?" I hissed, gripping Caldrius' arm with enough force to make my nails dig into his skin.

He cleared his throat softly, his expression carefully neutral. "Hyrax wanted them to watch."

The words hit me like a blow, cold and unrelenting. I dragged my gaze back to Clay, willing him to understand, to see through the charade.

Hyrax rose from his throne, his booming voice filling the room. "Look at you two. It brings me such joy to see my family together. Finally."

Family. The word tasted like ash on my tongue.

"Let's begin," he said, stepping forward.

Caldrius took my hand, raising it between us. Hyrax moved closer, binding our wrists together with a coiled rope that pulsed faintly with magic.

"With this rope, I bind you," Hyrax intoned, his voice heavy with power.

Caldrius' gaze met mine, steady and unyielding. "For eternity, I accept this bond."

All eyes turned to me. I could feel their stares—the hope, the anger, the heartbreak. They bore into me like a thousand knives.

I looked at Clay, my beautiful dragon prince. His golden eyes shimmered with devastation, mirroring the ache tearing through my soul.

"Don't," he whispered, his voice raw, pleading.

I had to.

"For eternity, I accept this bond," I said, the words slicing through me like a blade.

Magic surged. The rope disintegrated into sparks that seared my skin. Caldrius closed a second chain, the one marking our marriage bond, around my wrist, his touch unnervingly gentle. His lips parted slightly, as if he wanted to say something, but he didn't. Instead, his fingers lingered, his grip tightening just enough to make me wonder if he hated this as much as I did.

Hyrax grinned, turning to a servant, who rushed forward with a gilded chest. From within, Hyrax pulled a golden crown, its edges sharp, almost cruel.

"I, Hyrax, God of Death and Ruler of the Mortal Realm, crown you Theadora, Goddess of the Veil, Princess of the Light, heir to the Mortal Realm."

The crown settled onto my head, its weight unbearable, crushing.

Hyrax turned to Caldrius, lifting a second crown into the air. "And I crown you, Caldrius, Supreme Lieutenant of the Underworld, Prince of the Dark, consort to the Mortal Realm."

The titles settled over us like chains, heavy and suffocating.

"How could you do this?" Rankor's voice broke through the silence, filled with fury and betrayal. Iris' disgust was palpable. But it was Clay's shattered expression that struck me hardest, breaking what little resolve I had left.

I turned to him, desperately wishing for my magic, for some way to reach him, to explain. But I had nothing. No power, no freedom. Only the chains that now bound me to this life.

A life that I now had no choice but to accept.

"I love Caldrius," I said, forcing the lie through trembling lips. "Only him. It's only ever been him."

A breath of silence.

Clay's golden eyes flashed, his expression shattering—but not in the way I expected. His shoulders tensed, his fists curled in his bindings, his breath stilled.

I prayed he saw the truth buried beneath my words.

Because if this was my new reality, then I would use every ounce of strength I had to tear it all down from within.

CHAPTER THIRTY EIGHT

CLAYTON

I sat in the dungeons of my own palace, slumped against the cold stone wall, my head pounding from the mortal blood pumping through the air. The metallic tang of it clung to everything, a suffocating reminder of how far I'd fallen.

I hadn't spoken since the guards dumped me here after the wedding.

Thea's wedding.

From the moment I found that damned drawing of Caldrius, I'd known my ancestor wanted her. How could he not? She was beautiful, powerful, impossibly intelligent—a Goddess among Mortals.

Of course, he wanted her.

And now he had her.

Forever.

The untouched meal the guard had brought hours ago sat at my feet, its smell turning my stomach. I'd recognized the man who delivered it—a soldier who had once sworn loyalty to me, now serving under Hyrax like a coward.

How could we have been so deluded as to think we could win a war against Gods? We'd been reckless to believe this could end any other way.

"Kent's not doing well," Iris whispered. The quiet barely carried her soft voice, and I noticed she had wrapped her arms in makeshift bandages torn from her clothes.

I didn't respond. What could I say? Thea's words had already ripped my heart out and left it bleeding on the ballroom floor. There was no saving Kent now. No saving any of us. By morning, we'd all be dead.

Maybe that was a small mercy.

Death would be easier than knowing she was trapped here with him, that I had no way to save her.

I had failed her.

She was my Goddess, my heart, my very soul placed into another being—and I had absolutely failed her. I had left her alone in a den of vipers.

"Clay," Iris pressed, her voice trembling. "We have to do something."

"There's nothing to be done," I croaked, my voice raw and hollow.

The door at the end of the hall slammed open, the clash of swords and the sharp stomp of boots echoing through the dungeon. Iris and Rankor leapt to their feet, moving protectively in front of where Kent lay, his hands clutching the wound in his gut.

Then Caldrius stepped into view.

He still wore his wedding regalia, the black and gold gleaming mockingly in the torchlight. He looked comfortable in it. Like he'd been wearing a crown his whole life, just waiting to reclaim it.

His calculating gaze swept over me, lingering with the satisfaction of someone who had already won.

"Get up," he barked.

"Fuck off," I replied, arching an eyebrow.

The bastard didn't have any magic—I'd realized it during the ceremony. He'd relied on Hyrax's shadows to lock the clasps around Thea's wrists rather than using his own Dragonfire. Death had taken his power.

So if he wanted me to stand, he'd have to come in here and make me.

He laughed, low and full of superiority. "She'll be so disappointed when I return to our bed this evening and tell her how you behaved."

I was on my feet in an instant, rushing toward the glass panel separating us, venom surging through my veins. "Stay away from her."

He smirked, unbothered. "I couldn't possibly stay away from my wife."

The word twisted like a knife in my chest. My fingers curled into fists, fiery rage poisoning what little rationality I had left.

If these damned cells weren't so secure, I'd have thrown myself at him, hands wrapped around his throat.

"Why are you here?" Iris demanded, her voice sharp and unwavering.

Caldrius barely spared her a glance before turning back to me.

"I'm here to help you escape."

I stilled, every nerve in my body coiling.

"Why?" The question came out low and dangerous.

"A wedding present for my wife."

Each word was another blow to my battered soul, twisting deeper with every syllable.

From the look in his eyes, he knew exactly what it was doing to me to hear her referenced as his wife.

"You're aware of the tunnels?" he asked, ignoring my glare.

Of course, I knew about the tunnels. It was my castle. Ennoss, Caldrius' brother and the first King of Athenia, had designed those escape routes centuries ago in case Caldrius ever returned to attack.

Now Caldrius had finally returned, and I was the one fleeing him.

"You have five minutes to get into those tunnels and out of this castle," Caldrius said, his tone matter-of-fact. "My diversion won't last long, so I suggest you move quickly."

I narrowed my eyes. "And what's stopping me from killing you the second you open the door?"

His grin was infuriating, full of smug confidence. But then he tilted his head, considering me. And when he spoke, his voice was quieter. More precise.

"Because she's powerless now."

The floor dropped out beneath me.

My breath hitched, my hands clenching at my sides. Thea.

"She burned herself out completely," Caldrius continued, watching me. Studying me. "There's not a spark of magic in her. She's more powerless than she's ever been."

Powerless.

The word hit like a fist to the gut.

No.

Thea was never powerless.

I had told her that myself. Held her hands, guided her through her first true spark of magic.

That might have been the exact moment I fell in love with her. I had looked into those shining blue eyes and known without a shadow of a doubt the woman could bring me to my knees without any effort at all.

Even then, she had more power than she could have even fathomed.

I let my breath steady. "You don't know her," I said coldly. "If you did, you wouldn't think for a second that magic is the only power she has."

A flicker of something passed through Caldrius' expression. Something thoughtful.

Behind him, Iris and Rankor were already hauling Kent to his feet, his weight dragging them down.

"Four minutes," Caldrius warned. "Want to keep chatting, or are you ready to run?"

I hesitated, bile rising in my throat.

"Three."

"Clay, we have to go," Iris shouted, her voice sharp with desperation.

I met Caldrius' gaze, my voice shaking with rage. "If you hurt her, I will burn your soul so completely there'll be nothing left for the Underworld to reclaim."

His grin didn't falter. He stepped aside as the barrier lowered. "Two minutes."

Rankor and Iris hurried past him, Kent barely conscious between them.

Caldrius leaned closer to me, his voice a low whisper that barely reached my ears. "Better run, little prince."

I didn't respond, but my eyes burned into his. "I'm coming back for her," I vowed.

His smirk widened. "What makes you think she wants you to?"

My laughter was bitter. Without another word, I turned on my heel, jogging to catch up with my friends and help lower Kent into the tunnel.

As we disappeared into the dark, Caldrius stood unmoving, his smug satisfaction filling the air. He was so sure of himself, so certain he had won.

But he didn't know. He didn't realize her declaration of love—the lie she proclaimed to the room—were the same words she had said to me only days before.

"I love you. Only you. It's only ever been you."

My Goddess had left me a message.

A message that only I could understand.

Thea would never accept this life. Powerless or not, she would become his greatest enemy.

And as soon as I could, I was coming to get her.

THE STORY CONTINUES

Don't miss the rest of the House of Hyrax series!

The Rose in the Shadows
To the Edge of Athenia – A Prequel Novella
The Crown of the Dark Prince

And next: The Blade in the Ashes

If you enjoyed this book, please leave a review on Amazon, Goodreads, and anywhere else you leave reviews!

Want the latest updates? Subscribe to my newsletter (HERE)!

AUTHORS NOTE

Wow—what a journey, right?! Are we feeling okay after that?

Thank you so much for coming along for the ride. I hope this book brought you all the action, emotion, and excitement you were hoping for.

Sitting down to write this author's note is a challenge—so much so that I saved it for last. (Seriously, the second I finish typing this, the book is off to the printer.) It's taken me a while to find the right words to express how much this story means to me.

Writing sequels is HARD. There's so much pressure that comes with a second book, and when I first sat down to write *The Crown of the Dark Prince*, I struggled. I wasn't connecting with the characters. Thea was lost—doubting herself, unsure of who she was—and in many ways, I felt the same.

That was when inspiration struck for *To the Edge of Athenia*, and stepping away from Thea's story for a while was exactly what I needed. When I returned, I was ready to dive in and bring this next chapter to life.

And then... my life kind of imploded. Almost overnight, a lot about my daily life changed, and coping with that and moving forward wasn't easy. I won't lie—writing this book came during some of the hardest months of my life. But in many ways, Clay & Thea became my escape. When everything else felt uncertain, their journey made sense. This book became my anchor. No matter how chaotic life got, Clay & Thea's story gave me something to hold onto.

And when it all finally came together?

I couldn't be more proud. This book built upon *The Rose in the Shadows* exactly the way I wanted it to. The character arcs, the tension, the emotional depth—it all came together in a way that makes me *so* excited to share it with you.

This book means the world to me—both personally and professionally. It will always hold a *very* special place in my heart.

To my family and the friends who became family this past year (Diana, Aarti, Sarah, Kendall, Desna, Viki, Sterling, Jenny, Sierra, and Erica)—I can't thank you enough for supporting me, encouraging me, and holding me up through it all. I love you.

To my Beta Readers—thank you for taking a chance on the early draft and giving your honest feedback.

To my PA, Sarah—I would be absolutely lost without you. From the incredible content you create to our voice chats on IG, you've helped keep this series alive. I'm so excited to continue this journey together.

To my street team—your constant support means the world.

To the artists who have brought these characters to life—I love seeing Clay & Thea through your eyes. Your talent is unmatched.

And finally, to my readers—you guys are the best. Truly. I love you. I appreciate you. I can't wait to continue daydreaming with you.